Panther
Across the Stars

Lon Brett Coon

Edited by Jennifer Quinlan

A Fallen Leaf
Published by Fallen Leaf Books

Book layout by www.ebooklaunch.com

Table of Contents

Introduction

Freedom - the indomitable will and spirit of a living thing to breathe free from all yoke and collar. The wit and openness of mind to break away from the stampeding herd all about. It is the clarity of all senses to break through the shrouded mist of reality's entanglements and confines; the daring to detach from the machinery . . . and cut the cords that bind.

Freedom's struggle endures the ages and lights our dreams. It breaks the shackles of our world through a bond of like-minded spirits, forged of courage, honor, and sacrifice. Such a bond is unbreakable. It is stronger than steel, more unrelenting than time, and upon which mountains fall and seas break against. It is not finite and trapped within some physical form, but alive and breathes eternal, from one generation to the next. It passes from the consciousness of one to another and connects the souls of living beings . . . and the higher form of ourselves.

Breathe the free air and bask in its serenity, but always honor the deeds, will, and memory of those among us who make it so . . . for freedom carries great sacrifice. The flame of freedom burns eternal only so long as there are those that stoke the fire. Those that rise up from places unexpected at fate's call and give their last straining breath to feed that flame in their time of impossibility and utmost need. Let us raise our cups high and filled to the brim to honor those who carry that flame - to freedom.

Prologue
A Voice of Truth's Past

Makya smashed fury upon the mirror. An ice storm of glass pieces blew upon him. His fist throbbed. A cracked reflection stared back. There was the same familiar face of failure, and it scorned him. It was the face of all of his kind. All he had ever known. Yet now, it had come to him to find a way when no others could before. The greatest of burdens was now his. That cold and heartless shackle gripped him tight and he was so small . . . so defeated. Who was he to do such a thing? It did not matter that the year on the calendar was 2023. Whether it was 1813 or some two hundred years later, the same end was assured.

He looked down. Blood oozed from his still clenched fist. Small shards of mirrored glass were everywhere, some embedded deep in the flesh. As his fist turned in the room's dim light, the glass sparkled like jewels. But those were not glittering gems to behold, as if some found pirates' treasure. They shone only menace and taunted him. In glee, their light cried out. Over and over, he could hear only one thing in his mind - he was a far lesser man than those who came before . . . and he would fail too.

He snarled disgust and exhaled deep. Muscles tightened and twitched. His insides boiled like lava, and something else needed to be smashed into pieces. Maybe smashing something else would release the pain. But around the room, there was nothing worth breaking; nothing that would bring some measure of peace.

The room was sparse . . . and rundown. There were few things about: a scarred and pitted table of weathered scrap wood, a hand-hewn oak chair with a broken off arm, an old faded gray sofa with a missing seat cushion, and some used dishes strewn here and there. A few ragged carpet scraps, browned by years of trampled dust, covered the barren wood plank floors. The sheet-rocked walls were speckled with holes and gouges, which exposed wooden beams. Faded paint peeled upon the walls in many places, like overgrown and bent weeds. And perched in the corner was a tiny archaic television, whose glass picture had been smashed out.

It was all a sad piece of artwork; the kind painted by the brush of poverty. It reminded Makya of his place in the world. And then seethed rage washed away into pity and a gnawing fear. He pitied himself, his people, and a lost hope; and a fear devoured him that he would be the one to let them all down again.

Suddenly, the front door swung open and in walked his mother, Nengala. He looked to her as emptiness filled him. She softly smiled and said, "Too many minds, my Makya. Let things come as they will. You may bend, but you will not break."

Makya just stared back, more a young boy than a man. He needed his mother. He needed her words.

Nengala moved in close to Makya. "You cannot run from who you are. You cannot run from who you will become. You are a great grandson of the long line of Panther Across the Sky. His blood runs through you."

"I know who I am," muttered Makya in a tired voice. After some quiet, he said, "I know his story . . . the story of our people. I am not afraid for myself . . . I am afraid for you . . . for all the people. For how many times can a peoples' hope be torn from them, before it goes out forever? I do not know if I can bear that burden. It crushes my bones and chains my soul."

"Makya, discard these dark thoughts. No matter what comes, you would never be a disappointment to the people . . . or to me. For not only are you descended from Panther Across the Sky, but unlike all others, the blood of the stars also flows through you," said Nengala.

Makya nodded a pensive sigh. Resentment flared within. Shoulders sagged. Even his mother would add to the great weight, as once more he was reminded of his bloodlines to the stars. Always he was reminded of it . . . everywhere he was reminded of it. There was no escape, no air to breath. It crushed upon him. His mind spun in a darkened haze and the crisp night beckoned.

In haste, he fumbled about a closet for a jacket, but there was only one with a gaping hole in its side. He sighed again. He needed more than his tattered and worn t-shirt to fight off the night's cold. Turning away, he just grabbed a grayed wool blanket fallen behind the old sofa and hurriedly flung it about him. There was a fleeting glance to his mother. In silence, he headed out into the cold dark. He was a desperate soul, who drowned in a river of doubt and fear.

Makya wandered the darkness like a ghost. He was a moving shadow. Lost in thought, he went wherever his legs took him. Through a mindless fog, rolling waves like a soft drum called out. Unsure of his way, he found himself on a beach. And up ahead, a lit fire flamed in the distance. Voices carried on the wind; but he did not stop or turn away. He just continued on, because that was where his legs took him.

His squinting eyes caught a gathering ahead. Happy voices mingled round a fire pit that roared in the dark. The people sat upon makeshift chairs and coolers, encircled by mountainous dunes of sand that oozed about toes and stretched feet in a peaceful bliss. Orange and yellow light gently flickered upon their tanned faces, while the embers within the fire's logs glowed and crackled.

Makya approached nearer, as the waves of cold gray water lapped upon the sandy shore. The flowing waters revealed itself to Makya now in the dim firelight. It was where the Neosho and Spring Rivers emptied out into the Grand Lake, which flowed farther south. He had been there before. The gathering was at first oblivious to him, until they turned and looked his way, as the bonfire's straining light had now caught his silhouette.

They called out, "Would you care to join us stranger? Would you care to at least warm your limbs by the fire?"

Makya said nothing and moved into the firelight's reach. Though there were no gasps, eyes widened and postures stiffened a bit as they looked upon him up close. They had not expected one of his kind. Though it was not so unordinary, for Makya knew there were remnants of many tribes that called Oklahoma home, whether on a reservation or not.

Makya politely accepted and sat among them, near to the crackling fire. His wiry frame flexed of muscles beneath his cloaked blanket as he moved. And someone saw his one hand that dripped of some blood and sparkled in the firelight.

"What happened?" they asked.

"It is nothing. I had slipped and fell . . . I am fine," said Makya.

They politely nodded and inquired no further. Though someone else leaned in and asked, "Do you have a name?"

"Yes, forgive me. I am Makya," he said.

"Well, welcome Makya. We are all friends here," someone else piped. Makya nodded his thanks in return.

Right away, Makya put all at ease with his warm demeanor and conversation. Though he saw the curious looks still upon their faces. Makya knew an air of mystery floated about him.

And despite the fire's warmth, he still clung tight to the blanket that enshrouded him. A bottle of wine was passed about, which brought on an easy-going drowsiness. Peaceful smiles and laughter carried on the night's air, and tales were shared.

After a while, one among them spoke up. "You know friend, a stranger roaming the dark, cloaked wholly in a blanket . . . some would be afraid. But you carry no air of menace . . . you glow only of mystery. Might you share something of your life's story?"

A faraway look painted Makya's face and he obliged. "Here is a tale . . . of freedom. Of what was, what is, and what may yet be. A story of a peoples' long struggle to survive the drowning darkness of the great white fathers."

All sat in stoned silence at such an unexpected tale so heavy and brooding. Nervous shoulders tensed and backs stiffened a bit. Makya knew why. They were all white. And cringing wonder sat upon their faces at what accusations might soon be coming their way.

Makya stared off into the flames that danced in silence. "From bones to dust, we are a dying river deep in the desert . . . a trickle of water across a cracked bed of mud, all but dried up. Just a shadow of what we should be, almost lost to the sands of time. There is nowhere to turn . . . nowhere to flee. Abandoned by hope, we stand alone and peer into the abyss. Fleeting pleas fall away unanswered in the cold dark.

"But from the depths of time come those to make things as they should be. Amidst our despair, they grasp our hand tight as if a father to a child and do not let go. Their gathering strength pulls us back from the canyon ledge. Their comforting warmth, like the midday sun in winter's cold, lights the embers of hope aglow deep within. Will the darkness flee before their light? Shall we endure and overcome? What does freedom whisper across the winds of time?"

Chapter One
A Father's Lesson

Tecumseh bubbled excitement. At long last, the dawn's light began to peel back the black shroud. To a six-year-old boy, the night was an eternity and he had hardly slept. He jumped up, bounded to his father's bedside, and gently nudged him.

"Father... father... it is time. The sun is up," he squealed.

Puckshinwa rolled over, smiled, and patted him gently upon his young head of hair. "Yes my young warrior... it is time."

Both father and son then gathered up their bows, knives, and tomahawks in the still morning. Tecumseh did not look to his mother to see them off, because he no longer had a mother. She had died from a fever before his first year. But that did not bother Tecumseh or hold back his excitement. He had no memories of her. And fate's hand served to make the love for his father only that much stronger.

The village still slept as they headed out, alone. Many moons back, Puckshinwa had promised Tecumseh to take him on his first hunt, and that day had finally arrived.

Tecumseh beamed with pride. He was at last on a hunt with the greatest man he ever knew. Though not a chief, Tecumseh knew his father was held in high regard by the people, for both his grace and how he wielded a tomahawk. His father was of ordinary stature, but sturdy and thick; and like an oak tree, could not be broken in mind or body. Tecumseh heard the stories of his father's great skill in battle. Hard Striker they called him, for one swing of his tomahawk could shatter bone. He was the fiercest of warriors, and Tecumseh wanted nothing more than to be like him.

Yet Puckshinwa always reminded Tecumseh that the true measure of a man was not just being feared with a tomahawk, but having the strength to save a life and show kindness where it was due. Tecumseh always appeased his father and nodded he understood, but then would dash off with his tomahawk to fight off one hundred warriors from somewhere in his mind.

The morning dew upon the grass soaked their elk-skin moccasins as they moved through the woods of the waking forest. Father and son were silent and unnoticed as they came upon a meadow. At once, a flock of crows burst from the forest canopy on the meadow's far end. And soon after in terror, a young mother deer and her two younglings ran from the dense woods and out into the open. The baby deer were small and had not yet seen their first winter. Their scraggly legs shook and buckled beneath their mother, who panted and quivered. They stared back into the forest's foreboding dark. And within moments, bushes bent aside and out came a pack of wolves one by one . . . and they growled death.

The possessed beasts encircled the lonely family of deer one long step at a time. Tecumseh was afraid. He was afraid for the deer . . . he was afraid for himself. Frozen, he clenched his tomahawk so tight the wooden handle nearly broke in two. The vicious wolves were now nearly upon the mother deer and her babies. Tecumseh turned away. He could not bear the sight of the young deer being torn to shreds.

But then something unexpected happened. As the wolves reared their fangs of lustful death, out from the forest thundered a young buck. He leapt upon the meadow, straight into the wolf pack. The startled wolves jumped back. It was unnatural for something to come at them. The young buck snorted and slammed his front hoof into the ground boldly. There was no fear in that animal. In a curious fear, the wolves backed up a bit more.

The buck then turned to the mother deer, nodded to her, and called out. Love carried in that sound. The eyes of the buck and the mother locked for a brief moment more, and then at once she exploded from the field with her two younglings. She escaped with her brood away into the forest. The wolves did not give chase, for there was a crazed buck that stood in their way.

Seeing its meal disappear, the largest wolf snapped into anger. His wild and ragged fur flexed and fangs were bared. Saliva drooled from its mouth that growled. The big wolf focused wholly upon the young buck, and moved in for the kill. The other wolves followed after. But the young buck would not waver. Unbowed he snorted, lowered his head, and charged headlong into the big wolf like a stampeding buffalo. He drove his antlers in deep. And they were sharp like an arrowhead, which spiked the wolf's eye and gouged its shoulder badly. The large wolf whimpered and backed away, but the other wolves lunged upon the buck. They sank their fangs on all sides and ripped flesh.

Though bleeding badly and gravely wounded, the buck fought on still. He swung his antlers around and gored two other wolves to death with wild thrashes. That gentle deer had the heart of the great brown bear that stood taller than a tree. The wolves all backed away for a moment, and the young buck faced back in defiance still. And while he did, the wolves would not come any closer. But after some time, the young buck's blood drained away and he buckled to his side. The light went out from his eyes . . . he was dead.

The wolf pack finally had their meal. But two wolves lay dead in the meadow and the large wolf, the pack's chief, limped off to die alone somewhere in the bowels of the forest. Tecumseh had never seen or heard of such a thing. What spirit had driven that young buck so? A deer was an animal that was ever quiet and gentle, which always ran from the hunter. Sometimes an old or sick one was a life-giving family meal. It made him angry at the wolves. They brought vicious death to that young buck. They were so brutal. He was a six-year-old boy and he did not understand.

Puckshinwa looked to Tecumseh, who festered in anger. "Do not hate the wolf. The wolf is only being a wolf and it does not know anything else. And the deer is only being a deer, it cannot be anything else. But Tecumseh, that young buck was something else, for it was touched by the Great Spirit. You could search all your days for the Great Spirit and never find it, and it would not be a life wasted. Yet today, it leapt before you.

"Through the Great Spirit, the young buck stood up strong to do right, even though it meant giving its life to do so. Tecumseh, you remember that young buck, for the measure of a man is having the strength to do what is right, even if it means your own suffering . . . or death." That was a lesson Tecumseh would try to never forget.

Later that same day, father and son explored the wilderness and Tecumseh was shown more of the lands of his people. And out of nowhere appeared the most strange-looking creatures Tecumseh had ever seen. They were some white frontier folk his father said. Like living ghosts from his dreams they were; though so pale, like the underbelly of a frog. Perhaps they suffered some sickness? They carried an ill look. On that sun-filled day, a pitted black cloud of dread filled his heart. Was a violent storm about to break and tear his world apart? Even six-year-old boys could smell something was not right. Something was brewing.

The white folk should not be there, as those lands were granted to the Shawnee by the great white fathers earlier that same year. Puckshinwa knew well of that and told Tecumseh so, as he had fought at the great battle in which those lands were exchanged for peace. Old gray beards had come to talk of peace, and drew lines upon parchment. Of course, his father said no matter how hard the Shawnee looked, they could not find those lines upon Mother Earth.

Puckshinwa could speak some English and called out to the palefaces as they moved closer. But they made no response. Brooding stares stabbed back at father and son. Storm clouds grew in the dark of their paleface eyes. One with a scarred cheek turned and spit upon the ground. They fingered their pistols and knife hilts tight, and yet his father did not reach for his tomahawk. His father called out once more, and again they received only iced stares. Maybe a father's teachings were not done that day. Perhaps there was one more lesson for young Tecumseh, one he would never forget . . . even if he wanted to.

Tecumseh glimpsed something in the bushes nearby. But it was just shadows and blowing leaves in the wind. The white folk now sauntered over to them, their brown stained teeth glowed yellow like a dim moon. Tecumseh drowned in an aroma of sweat and grime that floated on air, like someone had not bathed for days on end. The pungent stench burned the nose, and he turned away. And as he did, three other palefaces, unseen in the bushes, exploded upon them.

Young Tecumseh trembled and shook. His insides pounded, as if beaten upon like a drum, over and over. He screamed; but no sound came out. He could not breathe. He wanted to run and flee that place, but his legs, like heavy tree trunks, would not move. In that moment, his first hunt and the very best day of his young life was shattered.

Those pale men jumped upon his father and stabbed him, over and over. Blow after blow, the knife's blade fell into him.

Tecumseh tried to scream again, but he could make no sound. One of the white men grabbed Tecumseh, and his mean grasp was like a cold shackle of jagged ice. He was scared, afraid beyond words. The glint of glee sparkled in their eyes as each blow of the glistening blades drove down deep, which opened wounds that could not be mended. His father's blood splattered upon him and the grassy meadow.

A choking fear swelled inside as if Tecumseh would burst apart. "Father! Father!" he screamed at last.

But his father did not answer. Puckshinwa could not speak. He struggled for breath as blood gushed all about. He staggered a bit, stumbled, and fell back on his side. The whites just looked on and laughed. Tecumseh rushed to his father, though still in his captor's loose grip, and sobs of tears ran down his small cheeks. Puckshinwa looked up into young Tecumseh's eyes, his words cracked and heavy. "I am sorry this falls to our people in your time . . . for the burden you must carry. Search always for the Great Spirit, and one day you may find it. And if you do, follow its strength and wisdom to show our people the way home, where our forests and valleys remain green and free . . ."

Puckshinwa reached out and pointed to Tecumseh's chest. "Though my body will be no more, I will always be in your heart. Look for me there and I will smile upon you."

Puckshinwa then gasped his last few breaths. He swallowed hard. Deep red streamed down his mouth and onto his neck and chest. He leaned in close and whispered, "Tecumseh . . . never forget . . . the wolf is just being a wolf, do not hate him for it . . . for if you do . . ." But Puckshinwa could not finish his words, and he choked again. He was drowning in more flowing blood. Tecumseh's captor laughed some more and jerked Tecumseh back from his father, like some dog on a rope leash. Puckshinwa gasped, but no air came in. He looked upon his young son for the last time, and whispered, "Tecumseh . . . run from this place." Love's light then faded from his father's eyes. Death took him.

Tecumseh stared in breathless silence. His broken heart ached to awaken from that haunted place . . . but it never would. His father's dying words drifted away like an echo across a distant shore, as more budding tears crested upon his eyes and then were set free to roll down his cheeks.

Then his heart turned. It burned rage. He wanted to kill those murderers. He wanted to kill all the whites of the world he ever saw. His six-year-old heart beat now only of revenge. With a fierce thrust, he jerked partially free, grabbed a hunting blade from his side and jammed it deep within his captor's thigh. The man howled out in pain, let loose his grip, and Tecumseh ran before the others could grab him. They laughed as Tecumseh was but six years old, and they did not expect such fierceness. But they soon gave chase. Though six-year-old boys lost in the wild die alone, those whites wanted to make sure. Maybe they didn't want Tecumseh warning any other Indians, telling them of the grisly deed just done.

Tecumseh ran long into the night, deep into the dark heart of the woods. After endless strides, he found a hidden spot in the base of an overgrown maple tree trunk. It looked like a good place to disappear; he was safe at last. He listened hard. The rushed footsteps were gone. There were only leaves that fluttered in the breeze. But one of the men was relentless and had almost been upon him earlier. It was his captor, and he seethed of revenge; but now, there was only a heavy quiet. Nothing moved for many long minutes. Tecumseh sighed. He had outsmarted those strange men. And he needed a short rest, for his little legs could go no more.

And as he sat there, alone in the dark, he thought of his father and angry tears flowed again. He closed his eyes and his father hugged him tight like he never would again. But then love gave way, and his heart iced cold. He thought of the whites. He also thought of his father's words . . . what did he mean do not hate the wolf? How could his father not hate the wolf? His father was wrong. The wolf was a killer who took life cold and cruel. And the whites, like the wolf, did the same. How could he not hate the palefaces? That night, hatred was born in his young heart. He closed his eyes and heard nothing but his short shallow breaths. They were rhythmic, and he began to drift off to a drained sleep. And then a broken limb on the forest floor snapped. He was being stared at.

A hungry shadow stared death at him. It stank of a foul odor. Tecumseh's insides roiled at once, as if slammed upon the hard hull of an old wooden canoe, pummeled by a stormy river of rage . . . and fear. He could not catch his breath, as if a fish out of water that flopped about and gulped a slow tortured death. He fumbled for the knife at his side. His fingers clasped the desperate blade's handle at last and thrust it wildly into the air. The ghostly thing then lunged at him. Outstretched in its hand glistened the cold edge of a familiar steel blade. It breathed with life and called to him in a menaced hiss, "Tecumseh . . . Tecumseh . . . I have tasted the flesh of your father . . . and now I shall taste you." Clenched in nightmare's grasp, young Tecumseh screamed . . . but there was only silence in the dark.

Chapter Two
Tecumseh's Vision

Though a grown man, Tecumseh twitched of nerves. An ache filled his gut. Cold skin crawled of tightness. He breathed in deep, the heavy air pressed upon his chest. It pounded like a soft drum. The great flames stared at him, and like the blade before it is placed in the fire, he stared back. He stood before the hot fire of judgment. Would he melt away, or be forged into something stronger? A sea of piercing eyes was upon him like a flock of starved birds that eyed a feast to come. The warriors with him all backed away. They gulped and fidgeted. The glared looks of suspicion were too much for even their strong frames. But there Tecumseh stood, alone.

The feathered chiefs with the long draped headdresses looked down upon Tecumseh. He saw their smug eyes. Tecumseh knew they thought him to be just a plainly dressed warrior with black hair hung to the shoulders, wrapped in a red cloth headband, and just four eagle feathers that dangled loose . . . not some wise chief. Quiet stares called out to him. Could that truly be Tecumseh, the great chief they had heard so much about? No, he was not tall enough. Where was his headdress? No matter, they would show their people in whose hands the power was held. They knew why he was here. He needed them. The chiefs signaled for the drums to stop and then called out in triumph, "The great forest and mountains will protect our people as they have always done."

Tecumseh soaked in their words for a long silence. "The white man comes in growing numbers by the day, carried in never-ending ships across the great sea to the east. They will cut through the mountains and fell the trees of the forest to build their towns and square homes of shaved wood, like a village of hungry ants that burrows through the dirt."

The chiefs responded only with muttered silence and vacant stares. Tecumseh bathed in their quiet disdain. For them, he was just a four-feathered Indian who did not know his place.

Tecumseh shared more of his words. "The great white fathers are like a pack of wolves that run down each tribe one by one. We must not be a lone deer in the forest, for our death is assured.

"We must join together as a great pack of our own to face down the wolves' chief. We will stare fierce into its soul. And then the wolf will know fear. It will see our glaring teeth, sharp hooves, and the look of death in our eyes . . . it will not know what to do. The wolf cannot chase that which does not run."

At such words, the chiefs stared at one another with clueless looks, shaken heads, and frowns. Who was the young chief from the north to tell them what to do? Tecumseh knew the arrogant gazes of disapproval well, for he had seen it before among his kin. In that way, many of the white and red races were cut from the same cloth. Those chiefs whispered in hushed tones to one another, as if some peddlers of gossip. They possessed the strength only to do what was right . . . for themselves.

They then shouted out their steadfast opposition. "Our people should not fight the great white fathers, for their blood will run deep with anger. We should follow the ways of the whites and live as they do, and in that way we will have peace."

Tecumseh smiled with indignation, like someone who cannot be defeated. "You would have us live like them? The palefaces poison the rivers and lakes . . . raze the forests . . . and rape the land, leaving it barren and lifeless. When all the animals of the world have passed and the crops wilted, what will you feed your crying child whose belly burns with a hunger? Will you then eat the silver of the white man's coin and green paper dollar for life?"

Some of the chiefs looked blankly to the ground. They did not know what to say, which did not go unnoticed by the people.

And Tecumseh would not relent. He pressed on, for he saw the twinkle of thought in the many-eyed sea before him. "There is a wickedness of their mind. It gives the will to bend Mother Earth to their wants of this day, with no care of the future. And in this way, all will starve in the unending winter to come as the fruitful bosom of this world is burnt to ash. I have seen a growing dark in my mind, a putrid smoke that chokes all life. The great white fathers will bring nothing but ruin . . . we must not live like the whites."

At those words, one chief rose up and said, "We should bargain with the white man for Mother Earth cannot be diminished by one race of people. There are endless trees, game in the forest, and fish in the rivers for all to live on their own lands. In this way, only the forests and rivers of the whites shall be rotted with their poison."

Tecumseh smiled once more and shook his head. "I know what you would say, and it would seem wise.... But have you not seen how the white man shares this land with others? Ask the Narrangansett . . . ask the Chippewa and the Huron . . . ask the mighty Mohawk and Seneca? Where are their warriors and people? Ask where they have gone? Where are their fires that once burned so warm and bright, and in numbers so many as if to be a reflection of the night's endless stars? For these once proud peoples are no more, like leaves scattered before the howling wind."

The sound of silence echoed everywhere. There was only the crackle of the fire. Tecumseh quietly went on, "The light of the great tribes of this land is fading . . . the coming dark of night is upon us, until we are no more. Do you not see this? Will you not raise up your tomahawks together for freedom? Will you do nothing?"

The chiefs sat silent, stooped over, as if a great weight pressed upon them. Yet still they refused Tecumseh's wisdom. They would not become a pawn of the Shawnee and their grab for power to treat with the great white fathers on behalf of all. Tecumseh pleaded for the chiefs to open their hearts to his words . . . but they would not.

His insides sank away. The heavy air choked all hope and wrapped Tecumseh in a cold embrace. In a swirling fear of lost power, those chiefs would bow low before the paleface nation. Eager to take their table scraps of a safe plot of land. They had no vision of the past . . . or the future.

Tecumseh knew. In the end, you cannot save people from themselves. You cannot pull them to safety if they do not reach out their hand. And if those chiefs had not opened their eyes to the history of the tribes that came before them, then they would soon learn firsthand. The great white fathers were coming. First with cannon and musket, and then with pen and parchment to treaty, and it would not be a bargain in good faith. And only when it was too late, would they realize that truth. They would take their tribes over the cliff, to crash upon the hard jagged rocks below into death and oblivion.

Tecumseh jerked up. Eyes flashed open. His knife was clenched, ready to strike out. A blood-curdling yell pierced the night . . . but there was no one there. It was only his voice. He exhaled deep. Soaked in sweat, he had bathed again in the most painful of memories. A six-year-old son should never see his father murdered before his eyes. Even now, at forty-three years, it was a haunting memory. His warriors nodded back. They understood his burden. But after that short rest, it was time to move on. They had much farther to go.

The band of Shawnee trekked through the forest dark along a moonlit path. They crossed the border of Kentucky into Ohio, and headed toward somewhere near Chillicothe. The band numbered forty-five persons, all heavily armed. Moist air, thick and heavy, beaded sweat upon their brows as they moved and shifted through the dark hills and shadows. And those forests were ancient and filled with memory, for they were part of the vast Ohio Valley. The great white fathers called it the Old Northwest Territory of North America, but Tecumseh and his people just called it home.

Tecumseh was at the lead. And as the warrior party went, he moved with the wind. There was a purpose to his step. They all followed after him, yet he spoke not a word.

Tecumseh knew why. He heard their words. Though he looked like anyone else among them . . . he was different. He shined great warmth, they said. Like the sun. It would bathe others and draw them close. And his tongue could enchant even many of the stoned hearts among them. His words could move mountains. He was a boy become a man, and now a great chief of the people. Though like everyone else, he battled the same demons, for fear and doubt hunted him all his days.

It had been over four months since last they had seen their home, having left the warm fires of their village in the early part of winter's cold. And the winter of 1811 was colder than anyone could remember. They had gone to sit in councils with tribes south of the Appalachian Mountains. Tecumseh had met with chiefs of many villages from the Cherokee, Creek, Choctaw, Ojibwa, and Blackfoot tribes. He had desperately sought their joining to his great confederacy. And now in the moist heat and the stretched days of summer, they returned. They ran tirelessly on until nightfall and a camp was set up. They settled in for some sleep and an early rise the next morning. Their village was not far now.

A crackling fire was raised to roast some cattail roots and maple tree seeds gathered up from the nearby woods. It was not much. There had not been a good meal with meat for days, and their stomachs gurgled in protest. But at least they had something to chew on, while they recalled the day's events. The journey that day was longer than had been planned. Warriors sat about and rested their heavy bones. One warrior lamented, "My feet pound like a drum. They want to know why we did not bring our horses on this long journey. Why do we punish ourselves so?"

Tecumseh smiled and offered his regret, though lighthearted it was. "I would think throbbing feet to be a far less thing than the long knives' blade across your throat. Would you disagree?"

And the warrior did not. No one did. They all just sighed, for the long knives were many and would have been happy to do so. And they were aptly named, for the reach of the blade upon their musket barrel was long indeed and could reach far.

For that long wilderness journey, there was grave danger to travel by horseback. They must not be spotted. The journey's need was too great, if ever the confederacy was to roar with life. Stealth offered Tecumseh's warrior party a chance to remain hidden from the prying eyes of scouts sent out into the wild by the great white fathers. And though so useful a beast, stealth a horse did not possess. So back in the grazing fields that surround the village the horses remained.

But that truth did not change the aching fatigue carried upon their bodies. There was nothing for it but some rest. One by one, the warriors fell off to sleep . . . save for Tecumseh. He slowly tended the campfire's embers and dying flames. Racing thoughts spun about. He looked up to the starry night sky and spoke to the Great Spirit, "The journey is lost. The confederacy will fail. Only nineteen villages gave their blood . . . thirty-one did not. There are not enough warriors. There is not the strength to fight back the great white fathers. What are the people to do? What am I to do?" He stared into the night sky. He waited. The stars shone back upon him . . . but the Great Spirit did not answer.

His thoughts rambled some more, like a wild horse on the plains. Each tribe was a single arrow, possessed by a frailty that allows it to be snapped in two. But a bundle of arrows possesses the strength of an oak tree. It would bend, but it will not break; though the confederacy was many tribes short of a bundle. Tecumseh's heart sank deeper.

Despair grew darker still. Hopelessness spun about him. Shoulders sagged. He was a blind man in the dark. There was nothingness before him . . . nothing but utter defeat without the peoples' confederacy. He yearned to the stars . . . pleaded for a sign.

At that moment, a branch cracked. Tecumseh stared into the forest dark. An anxious moment stretched with no breath. Eyes strained. A shadow stirred in the darkness. It moved closer to the forest edge and peered into the clearing where he sat.

The chattering sounds of the nighttime forest stopped. The blowing wind fell away and time stood still. Two large yellow-green eyes glowed back at Tecumseh. A nervous chill passed over him. Fingers twitched for his tomahawk. Then a low and slow guttural growl came forth from the dark . . . and a large beast emerged. It leapt down from a rock ledge, out into the open - it was a panther. A mountain lion the palefaces called it. But to his people, it was a panther. Tecumseh knew it well. It was the Shawnee clan he was born into, passed down through the bloodlines of his father. Those great beasts were usually brown-furred like that of a darkened deerskin, though from time to time, one might cross paths with one that was bathed in black.

And that panther was as dark as night. It was the largest panther Tecumseh had ever laid eyes upon . . . and as big as a grown horse. It stood about twenty paces from Tecumseh, and lingered for a moment. The great beast stared through him. Tecumseh's hands throbbed for his tomahawk and pistol. To ready them for the swift panther lunge sure to come . . . but something stayed his hand.

That panther was bold. It answered to no other living thing, for it was the master of all in its world. It snarled and began to walk toward Tecumseh, one slow pace after another. Sinewed muscles flexed in the moonlight. The dying fire's flickering flames danced upon the panther's eyes as it came nearer.

The large cat possessed a noble air, as if the greatest of all chiefs among all the tribes. It reminded Tecumseh of something he had read in those books of history years ago at John Sackett's home. A vision of some ancient pharaoh king adorned in gold and brought forth from the dead to walk among its descendants. Whatever that great panther was, whatever drove it forward . . . it could not be of this world. It was something more than a dream.

Perhaps the Great Spirit had heard his call. It had come to show him the way. But did he have the wisdom to walk with the Great Spirit? Tecumseh's heartbeat slowed. He floated outside of himself, and took it all in. Despite its great size, the panther moved in silence. All the while, the black beast never broke its gaze upon Tecumseh. Those ghostly yellow-green eyes smoldered.

Closer it moved . . . and closer still . . . and yet Tecumseh just stood there. He did not call out for help to the others, who lay unawares in their fast sleep. The big cat neared even closer.

Tecumseh calmly reached out his upturned hands in peace. Surely the great cat brought death . . . but not that night. That night was different.

The panther was now upon him. It then lowered its head and rubbed against Tecumseh's outstretched hands. Tecumseh just smiled in wonder to himself. The panther then stopped and looked up at Tecumseh once more. Its soft eyes spoke that somehow all would be well.

The panther lingered for a short while more and then made a low guttural growl. Another fierce snarl escaped, as the inner wild boiled just beneath the surface. The great panther then turned away, and headed back from where it had come. As it neared the forest edge, it stopped and looked back once more. It gazed upon Tecumseh, and then disappeared into the forest dark, like a ghost in the shadows.

No one would believe, unless they had seen it with their own eyes. What was that great panther? Was it the Great Spirit? Though a chief of the people, he was still just a man . . . and it was all beyond him. Tecumseh was reminded of just how small he was, as he sat by the fading fire. He was alone.

Chapter Three
Arrival

Tecumseh's eyes clenched shut. Like a child, he called out to the stars to shine down their ancient wisdom . . . but they would not answer. Defeated, he looked up once more. And now there was a star that streaked through the night.

It shone brighter than the rest. And its size grew with each moment. It began to hang lower in the sky . . . and it headed straight to him. It was some kind of comet. He had learned of those years ago from the books of astronomy at John Sackett's home. And as the star came nearer, it grew ever bigger. So low in the sky it hung. Then it flashed bright, and glowed orange and blue. Thunder roared in the night.

The roar startled the others awake. They scrambled from their slumber and gazed skyward too. It grew bigger still and thundered louder. The burning star was falling. It hurtled toward Tecumseh, and screamed overhead as it shot by. The ground shook. It lit up the forest dark and parted a wide path through the treetops of the old evergreens. Flames lit the highest tree limbs like torches. And then it crashed into the valley below.

There was a screeching roar and booming thunder, like a great paleface cannon as big as a mountain had exploded. Then silence washed over all the forest and valley. Tecumseh looked to the fallen star, and then to his warriors. In the lonely quiet, wonder painted each face. Then Tecumseh said, "Let us see what has fallen from the night stars . . . what gift the Great Spirit has sent us."

With Tecumseh at the lead, the warriors began the walk down into the lower valley. Though not spoken aloud, fear and wonder gnawed at them all. Tecumseh saw it upon their faces.

They neared the forest edge and the valley was aglow. Flames lit up the night and chased the shadows. Tecumseh looked in silence upon each warrior, and back at what stood before them. He then began a quiet descent, and each Shawnee warrior fell in line behind him. Whatever that gift was . . . they would receive it together.

As they moved closer, it was something from a dream. A strange bird-like thing it was, as big as ten longhouses. It had a pointed beak, a protruded chest, a raised tail, and two frontward faced wings. The wings were curved, as if they reached to grab something. The bird's skin shined a luminous glow like a full moon upon winter snow. Debris was strewn all about. Black and gray smoke billowed upward into the night. Scattered flames shot out about the wreckage. And to the rear just below its left wing, a gaping hole stared back at them.

They stepped closer. Nerves stretched tight, like the string of a bow. The warriors readied their tomahawks and clubs for some unknown enemy; but Tecumseh said, "Stay your tomahawks. The Great Spirit would not send us death." All the warriors nodded and moved closer.

There was no life. Through the rising smoke, Tecumseh walked to the opening and stared into its black mystery. He inhaled deep and vanished into the smoky mist. A few warriors followed after, but many stayed behind, still filled with fear.

Disarray and destruction was everywhere. It reminded Tecumseh of some great sea going ship that brings the palefaces to these lands, though such ships do not fly among the stars. But as he looked about some more, it was unlike any he had seen before. There were many strange looking windows, like from the palefaces' square homes, which lit up and flashed like the stars. There were strange markings all about. And dangling from the ceiling, and jutting from the floor, were bent forms like stretched cannon barrels that shined. Smoke and mist was everywhere.

Tecumseh stepped further into the ship's cabin. Through the misty smoke, he saw the shapes of seven bodies strewn about. They were much larger than any Indian or white man, and still as a rock. And many leaked blood, though more a dark purple than red. It crept about their bodies from various wounds. But through the dark mist, he could not see their faces.

Tecumseh then moved forward and to his side. And he stood upon three more lifeless bodies in the foggy mist. It seemed he stood at the front of a ship's cabin; a place where a captain would be. Suddenly, one of the bodies flinched. Eyelids fluttered, which a dead thing would do. The warriors jumped to fend off any attack if that strange creature rose up with life. Tecumseh alone moved toward the being.

He said aloud for all to hear, "These beings mean no harm to the Shawnee." He tried to reassure his warrior brothers, and gulped his own fear. Then without warning, its eyes flashed open wide. The creature glanced up to Tecumseh. Its eyes stared a friendly peace. Tecumseh just gazed back, for up close the creature was a wonder to behold.

Its face had two eyes, two ears, and a sunken nose. The slender ears were raised and protruded from the back of its head. It had teeth, like a man in color and look, except for two biting fangs that jutted slightly from the upper jaw. A stretched and narrow face it had, with short silvery whiskers that hung from its mouth. Its hair was thickly layered, with wavy and shiny black braided ropes, like a nest of snakes that slithered here and there. And upon its chin was a short black scruff that evoked an aged wisdom. But what stood out the most were its eyes. They glowed yellow-green, like a great cat. And it hit him like a morning plunge into winter's iced waters. That creature carried the look of the great black panther. Wonder sparkled in him like sunlight upon rippled water.

Tecumseh then gazed about its full form. Stretched and long it was. It would look upon a great brown bear eye to eye that stood upon its hind legs. The palefaces called the great wild bear a grizzly, with its claws and fangs of death. But the creature before Tecumseh had man-like hands, though with several claws stuck out down its upper forearm. They curved away from the body, and were blackened with a shine, as if sprinkled with gunpowder dust. Its lower limbs were also stretched, as if the hind legs of a great cat, with several claws that protruded from the ankles and lower legs. And its toes were thick and padded with much smaller claws that stuck out, like arched spear tips.

The creature was midnight black, brushed with a soft dark gray and green, and faded markings upon its limbs and face. Like those of the tiger animal described in John Sackett's books, from the lands far to the east across the great sea, beyond even the lands of the British grandfathers. Those tigered streaks were lit aglow as the light caught its shapes upon the skin. They burned a ghostly green like a lightning bug in the forest dark. It was a vision breathed in by some shaman's smoked weed.

Its body was wrapped in a smooth skin, but aged like a well-worn animal hide. A blackened leathery covering was worn about its waist, with a crossed harness about its chest of the same dark covering. Within its center sat a strange jewel.

Tecumseh kneeled slowly. Their eyes locked, and dove deeper into the other. As they did, the being lightly grasped Tecumseh's forearm. He did not flinch or back away, and the being began to softly speak. Such strange sounds Tecumseh had never before heard. It then sat in silence, and its gaze beat upon him like the hot sun. A flood of distant memories and mumbled words wrapped up Tecumseh, like a thick-clouded mist. He was lost in a dream, yet awake at the same time.

But then, his mind's chaos was swept away. And in the Shawnee tongue, it said, "Tecumseh . . . peace."

The creature then slipped back into sleep, its eyes closed shut; though it still took breath. Thunder then erupted in the large cabin they had just left. It shook all of the ship with a great burst, and knocked several warriors to the ground. Tecumseh quickly glanced at the other two bodies nearby. And like the first, though their eyes were closed shut, they too were very much alive. Tecumseh called for the three bodies to be gathered up. That ship was dying . . . and they needed to leave; or else be consumed by the fire and flame to come.

The warriors hurried about and did so. It took all of their strength due to the beings' size. They were careful to dodge searing sparks and darting flames, making their way back out. Another cannon shot explosion erupted from where they had just left. The sheer force again knocked several warriors over. But they rose up quick and staggered on through the growing mist and smoke that suffocated and blinded. Choking air burned the throat and eyes, as if scraped with sand. But they followed the yells of their brothers who had stayed back. Fear carried in the calling voices. They stood upon a seething storm cloud, which yearned to unleash angry thunder and lightning upon them. But with quickness and some luck, they made it out.

They breathed in the valley's crisp nighttime air for a moment, but did not linger. They then rushed to the far clearing, as fast as their legs would carry them. As they did, a low rumble bellowed forth that rose up to fill the valley. The ground began to buckle, as if it would rip apart and swallow them whole. Many warriors were again knocked from their feet. The ship was then bathed in a great blue and white light that throbbed. It then exploded. The dark of night was chased away by the bright noonday sun. Such a burst of storm winds blew with a roar and all were flung about, like leaves before winter's howl. And then, it was over.

Quiet and dark returned. Tecumseh looked back in disbelief, for the great ship was no more. There was little sign that it had existed at all, other than some streaked and blackened markings that only keen eyes would notice. And of course the tinged and burnt treetops that still smoldered.

Whatever the great ship had been, it was not of the world. But Tecumseh had faith in the Great Spirit's message and followed his heart. Though they looked nothing like his kin, he would have the Shawnee show kindness in whatever way they could. Carriers were made of wood limbs, padded with soft evergreen brush, and large enough to hold the beings. Once loaded up, they began the walk back to the village. The moonlit path of the summer night sky showed the way, but Tecumseh wondered on what journey the gift from the stars would take them....

Chapter Four
Council Debate

Tecumseh's thoughts rambled. He saw the same haze upon the faces of his warriors. What are those creatures? Where did they come from? The night's wonder cascaded like a brisk waterfall, wild and free over a rocky ledge. The flowing thoughts quickened their pace and soon the sunlit dawn greeted them.

Through forests, hills, and valleys they walked, and came at last upon the crest of a small mountain. Down below was their village. Soon, the party entered its outskirts. Young children twirled about in chase of each other with a wooden stick and leather ball. Echoes of delight squealed out, and one boy with a welt started to cry. A young mother scolded the children to not hit each other as they ran by. Women stretched raccoon and beaver pelts upon wooden spikes to be dried for clothing. Other women carried corn and squash from the fields, held in heavy elk-hide sacks.

Some older boys sat about and carved thin pieces of ash wood, with a mound of arrow shafts near to them. A few young girls waved to Tecumseh, while they sat and ground corn into meal with stone. And about the village grounds were fire pits that roasted squirrel and rabbit. The burnt smell called out as they passed by. Lips moistened at the thought of fresh cooked meat. And it would be a fine meal; well-earned for their far travels and heavy guests they bore.

At first, there was little fuss of Tecumseh and what he carried. The people must have thought it to be some dead elk from a hunt. But as the party drew closer, the people stopped what they were doing. And they gawked at the strange creatures. With each bark-sheathed longhouse Tecumseh passed, curiosity and gossip bubbled. And there were many gawkers, for the village was quite large by Shawnee standards. There were about two-hundred longhouses, which was four times that of most villages. Soon a throng gathered, and murmurs grew into some shouts. But Tecumseh was unmoved. He and his warriors walked on in silence.

They snaked their way through the village, and neared its center at Tecumseh's longhouse. And several other warriors boldly approached. They stood before Tecumseh, and blocked his way. They stared at the beings laid before them. With scowls, they shouted doubting questions on that which he carried.

Tecumseh looked coolly upon his questioners. "These beings are a people sent forth by the Great Spirit . . . in a great ship fallen from the night sky in a bundled flame. We will nurture them back to good health as we can. They come in a good way."

Tecumseh's words brought puzzled frowns and gasps from the people. Ships only sail the great sea, not among the clouds and stars of the sky, they said. What story was this? Did Tecumseh bend the truth? Suspicion began to hold sway upon their faces. A great tension built as many more village folk flocked to the questioners. They cast their judging looks upon Tecumseh. And he knew why.

In times of struggle with the palefaces, why would Tecumseh endanger the people? Why would he bring strange creatures to their village? Perhaps those beasts served the great white fathers, like a dog on a leash. Maybe it was a ploy to find the village. And now, they would know the way. Anger festered and seethed upon their faces. If it were anyone else, Tecumseh knew the growing mob would have unleashed its venom in fists and blows upon the gift bearers. But he was Tecumseh, and so the angered held their tongue and stewed in silence . . . for the moment.

Tecumseh and his warriors parted a clearing through the throng. But as they did, an elder warrior stepped forward and asked, "How is this known to you? Surely they do not speak Algonquian, tongue of the Shawnee?"

Tecumseh again stopped, and faced the warrior.

The people gathered in close to the elder warrior. Their bodies tensed, with judging and fearful looks.

He gazed out among the crowd, and then to the warrior. "They have spoken to me through a vision. I will share it tonight at the council house with all who will come to listen." For the Shawnee, a vision was a thing not lightly set aside. At that, the elder warrior backed away. He was satisfied enough . . . at least for now. The gathering then dispersed at last with the same muted satisfaction. Once again, Tecumseh had swayed the people.

Although he was not an elder, there were few held in higher regard than he. But it had not always been so. As Tecumseh continued on to his longhouse, he remembered those days when the Great Spirit did not speak to him. There were none who followed him back then. Old memories washed upon him.

**

Tecumseh wanted to yell out like the others. But no sound came. He was shaking too much. He thought for sure someone else would notice; but no one did. All eyes were on the unseen enemy. One of the other young warriors cried out, "Today we kill our enemy. Today we become men." He howled like the wolf. But Tecumseh did not howl; he was no wolf.

Cold sweat streamed down his back. Lungs filled with iced fear, and he wanted to shrink away. But he could not. He was supposed to be a warrior. He was supposed to be a great warrior like his father, Puckshinwa. But he was only a fifteen-year-old boy and that was his very first battle. The tomahawk hung so heavy in his clenched fingers.

He had never killed a man before. He still hated whites, but in that moment, he hated being shot more. All he wanted to do was run from that place. He remembered the first time in his young life, so many years ago now, when he had that feeling . . . that same familiar feeling . . . the day his father died.

Indian calls shrieked out again, and that time they were met by the rolling roar of soldiers and militia. It thundered back. The air was heavy, hard to breathe. Heartbeats throbbed, throats tightened. All sat on a blade's edge. Warriors on both sides stared out from their forest hiding into the open plain. The waist high grass swayed like a wave at sea. And then muskets erupted. They flashed orange and yellow, and barrels smoked. Crazed warriors and soldiers alike rushed into hell. They charged with abandon, filled with a lust to deal death.

But Tecumseh was not among them. He remained silent and still. His legs would not move. Carnage and spilled blood ravaged the field. The many blades of grass painted a dark red. How were they not afraid? He saw the bully of his youth, Sakdayga, rush into the mayhem. Of course he would. Tecumseh remembered the times he had suffered a beating at the bully's hands growing up, when there were no elders around. And he heard the stories.

Sakdayga's mother died giving birth to him and he screamed rage into the world with his first mean breath . . . and he had been that way ever since. He should never have been born, they said. And for all his days he would set about to remind people of that. He had shot his father while on a hunt at a very young age. Some say it was by accident, but others

33

knew better. He liked to watch things die. Though fifteen-years-old himself, Sakdayga was built like a buffalo bull. And he stampeded horned death upon the soldiers. He was a natural born killer.

Still Tecumseh could not move. The ebb of the battle swayed, like a slithering snake, until it turned in favor of the Indian warriors. And then across the way, he glimpsed a most regal sight. A young paleface leapt through the musket smoke on a muscled battle steed. He wore the uniform of a captain, and oozed bravery. And that American wielded his war saber mightily.

The youthful lines of his face and wiry frame belied a fiery strength and spirit. He cut down one warrior and then another, like the palefaces' ship that carved through the pounding waves of the sea. And he inspired the soldiers more than ten years his elder into a rage. At his command, they could do nothing but follow. Tecumseh heard the chants and yells of the same name. They rang out proud and clear, over and over; Harrison . . . Harrison! The soldiers had found their leader. They would always remember that battle. And Tecumseh would always remember that name.

The dance of death spun about in a mad fever. And Tecumseh could not take it in. He could look into its grisly eyes no more. His shaking legs could move now at last; but he was not his father. Hands went cold and limp, and his gun and tomahawk fell weakly to the ground. Panic flooded his heart. And he ran from the battle, with all his might. He wanted to get far from that place. He did not look back, and ran and ran, until he keeled over at last, alone. His muscles burned and lungs stung. And then a great shame flooded over him. He shriveled up and crouched into a ball, desperate to hide from the stars in the night sky that shined down their judgment. He was so small and wanted to shrink away into nothing.

Tecumseh took many days to find his way back to the village. And when he did, he tried to hide from everyone. Judging looks and whispers greeted him. Words of the battle had already found its way home: they heard about Puckshinwa's son. Sakdayga was there and he smiled meanness. He mocked Tecumseh with a wave and a laugh. Though the battle had not been a victory for either side, they spoke of the young Captain Harrison that had taken the field to secure a draw. Some joked that Harrison must have had the blood of Puckshinwa in his veins.

Sakdayga called out, "There goes coward in the sky."

Tecumseh now hated Sakdayga like he hated the whites. But all the eyes of the village were on him, so he kept walking, burying his head into his chest. He knew some would call him a coward for what had happened. But most did not. When the musket lead flies, what young boy would not flee in terror? Most boys were not filled with an iron heart of jagged hate like young Sakdayga. But he could not escape the secret glances and whispers that echoed in his mind. Sakdayga's words stabbed Tecumseh. He was no fierce warrior . . . he was not his father. The pain tore at his heart, as if a steel blade's edge peeled it apart.

That shame grew in him. He was dirty and used up. He had lessened the line of his father. He did not have the strength to do what was right that day, and his father's words haunted him. In his shaking fear, he did not think of anything but himself . . . a shrinking fear for his own life. Thoughts of those with him, and the people, never entered his mind. He had let himself down. He had let everyone down. Puckshinwa would have told him so. Tecumseh did not carry the Great Spirit that day. It did not speak to him.

He crawled into his longhouse, alone in the dark. Some tears streamed down his cheeks as he consoled himself. But as he cried out all the cutting hurt and pain, some well of light, hidden down deep, shone upon his spirit. A fresh wind blew upon him. Strength imbued his limbs and heart, like a stream that flooded and washed over a dried out river basin. Self-pity did not fill his heart. Instead, he thought of the spirit of the young buck those many years ago. He was ashamed, because it was something he had long forgotten. But now it came to him. He remembered the look in its eyes . . . and it gave him strength. His father's hand was upon his shoulder and showing him the way.

The light of defiance was now lit. And he vowed it would never go out. Alone and holed up in the dark shadows of his family's longhouse, he made a promise to himself. He would never run from battle again, no matter the terror before him. It was a promise between him and the Great Spirit, and no other. He would never let the people down again. Tecumseh was a fifteen-year-old boy no more . . . he was becoming a man.

**

At last, Tecumseh and his three sleeping guests made their way to his longhouse. The first to greet them was Kykuitheh, the love of his life. Tecumseh's insides fluttered at her sight and warm touch. No words needed to be spoken, even after so many long months apart.

They embraced each other long and hard. And then, without a word, Kykuitheh glanced at those beings, and did not react at all to their strangeness. She set about gathering up supplies of medicine and comfort for the new guests. The creatures were placed upon makeshift bedding, enlarged to house their great size. Tecumseh called out for the village's healer to tend to his guests.

And his niece Nateelah abruptly entered to greet the newly arrived guests, for that longhouse she also called home. She was at first taken aback by those beings that carried the look of nothing she had ever seen before.

She snapped from her gaze, "My uncle, you are a great Shawnee chief, and so I will abide by your wisdom in bringing our shaman to heal these beings; but as this is also my home, you will respect my will to also provide healing for our guests." She stared firm at him.

Tecumseh looked back at her with eyebrows raised.

An awkward quiet spread among all those present, for it was rare that one would say such a thing to a tribal chief, especially if that chief was Tecumseh . . . and especially within his own longhouse. Of course, save for Kykuitheh, who smiled low. Tecumseh paused some more. Tension carried thick in the air.

Then Nateelah broke into a small smile, and walked over to Tecumseh. And before he could utter a word, she stretched up and kissed him on the cheek. "Thank you my most favorite uncle," and with that she left the longhouse as quick as she had entered.

Tecumseh looked around, as most everyone stared back anxiously. Would he erupt in anger, and chase after her for talking in such a way to a chief? Of course, Kykuitheh giggled to herself. She already knew the answer. And the others did not wonder long, as Tecumseh's face broke into the broadest of smiles. He laughed heartily. "Well, as I am her only uncle, it is a good thing to also be her most favorite."

At once, all the longhouse bubbled laughter. Of course, no one was truly surprised, for Nateelah was held tight to the most loving part of his heart. They knew why. Her young life had shown her great pain and hurt. It would have broken most people, but yet her spirit was bright like the dawn's glowing sun upon the valley. She would fly free from all shackle and dominion, like a soaring eagle in the clouds.

Amid the day's excitement, the guests remained in a peaceful sleep, attended to by the healer, though of course ever under the watchful eye of Nateelah. And all the while, rumors of the strange creatures' spread throughout the village as a wildfire spark to dry timbered brush. The council could not come soon enough.

Dusk came and darkness fell. Fires were lit about. Beating drums and chants rose up, and echoed out into the valley. The council house was much larger than ordinary, to hold a large gathering. But it was not nearly big enough, as it burst at all ends. All the village sought a firsthand account of Tecumseh's journey. They wanted to hear about those strange beings. Wonder and anticipation frothed, and sent a chill of shivers upon the spine.

Tecumseh readied himself, pulled back the elk-hide door covering, and stepped inside. At once, a hush floated over the crowd. All eyes fell upon him, as the council fire's flames leapt about his silhouette. The rhythmic drumbeats floated on the night. The people stretched and strained to bear witness. Tecumseh sat at the center with the other chiefs and elders, to first smoke the pipe of peace. They hoped for no bad blood to arise among the people.

As the pipe reached Tecumseh, he inhaled deep, much longer than the others. He then let out a great plume of gray smoke. The smoky wisps floated upwards and encircled the other chiefs and elders, as if it would bend their hearts and ears to hear his coming words.

Tecumseh looked around and took measure of it all. He then began his tale. It was just a whisper, which evoked a still quiet. All strained to hear his every word, down to the last before they could pass judgment. Eyes widened at the mention of the great black panther. It had been many moons since one had last visited the people. It surely was a sign. But as he went on, looks of fear gathered as he spoke of the strange beasts. The fear grew, until it rose up to choke all life from the council house.

And before Tecumseh could finish, another chief stood and spoke out. "My ears hurt. I have heard enough. These creatures are a poison. They will awaken and do bad things to us. They carry an ill look, and are sure to have something to do with the palefaces. They must be put to death." Many warriors joined in, and shouted fierce yells of approval. Many faces nodded their same belief.

Amid the cries, Sakdayga arose. He glowered at Tecumseh in the shadows. Hatred burned in his eyes. A hate born of fear those many years ago, for Tecumseh was the one who put him under the cold edge of a tomahawk. His voice cut like a sharp blade. "This is not the way. Would the Great Spirit have you bring those creatures of death among the people? Who are you to do such a thing?"

Tecumseh smiled, "Sakdayga, you are the great bull among us and yet you are always washed of fear. Always you would kill first and never would you wonder of another way. Though these beings are much bigger than you and look different, it does not mean they bring death."

Sakdayga scoffed. His face scowled and his dark eyes went black, like some ancient demon come to torture the living. "They say you are the one who walks like a panther in the sky. I say no. You are a lost soul, desperate to defeat the palefaces. You are desperate to show strength. This is not the way." Sakdayga then stepped back into the shadows and was gone. Some other warriors also arose, and followed after. In those trying times, all sought to follow their hearts. And what if Tecumseh was wrong?

But Tecumseh was unmoved by Sakdayga's stinging words and the cries against him. He rose up slow. Random sparks of fire embers crackled and wafted through the air, released through the roof openings and up into the night sky.

Tecumseh looked out to all, and like a father to a child he began to speak. "Look to the gifts from the Great Spirit before you. See the flowing rivers, the deep watered lakes, the soaring mountains, and the green valleys. Feel the warm wind in the flowering trees and the firm land that provides the people's sustenance."

He stood in silence. A sea of anxious eyes washed back over him. "The Shawnee did not make them . . . we do not have that power. And it is not for us to destroy these wonders. Only the Great Spirit can bring forth such things, and only it should take them away."

Some of those shouting in anger sat down, listening with all of their ears. But many fierce faces still stood against him.

He went on, "Though strange to our eyes, the Great Spirit brings forth this race of people . . . from a faraway star in the night sky. The Shawnee should not cower in fear. Yes, they do not look like us. But do not cut them down in fear.

"We are Shawnee, and see through our fear to reach out to a people in need. And then we reach out to the Great Spirit."

Many more of those standing in opposition began to sit as well, as something in Tecumseh's words was speaking to them. The wind of wisdom was blowing.

Tecumseh said, "Look deep within the dark and hidden places of your soul so that your heart may be opened with the light of trust and your eyes can rightly see what is before you. Does this truth not stare back at you?

A great silence fell over all the longhouse. From the youngest child to the oldest elder, they were all looking into their souls. There was only the crackling fire, the faint breathing of the many.

Tecumseh went on some more. "We are all but one leaf on the tree of life. So any good that we can do to nurture that tree, let us do it now. Look to your friends, family, and all the people. Let us have the strength to do what is right this day."

40

All of those standing against Tecumseh had now taken a seat. The heavy silence grew loud after Tecumseh's words like a beating drum. His strong voice blew upon the people, and even the hardest hearts felt its breeze. Their spirits were grasping for the truth.

Tecumseh then sat in quiet. Not once did he say exactly how the beings had spoken to him, only that he had received a vision from the Great Spirit and that they came in a good way. Heavy silence now gripped the council house. Each person hearing his message . . . weighing his words.

Then the eldest of all chiefs rose up slow, and all the people leaned forward. They strained to hear the whispered words to come. Tanogatay raised his hand and spoke in a hushed tone. "At first I did not want to hear Tecumseh's words. My heart was closed. I thought Sakdayga spoke the truth. But a great wisdom has been spoken upon my ears. The Great Spirit speaks through him now.

"At his birth, when I was a young warrior, the elder chief named him for a powerful vision he had received. A flying star shot through the black of night as he took his first breath, crying with life. The star streaked through the sky, and burned a yellow-green flame like the eye of a black panther. And when he looked upon you, it was the great panther that stared back.

"The same look as when the panther turns its gaze upon one who crosses its path in the wild. It is seen among the night stars in which the Great Spirit prowls to look down upon the world, leaping like a panther from one star to the next. Tecumseh is connected to the stars painted into the sky. And in the Shawnee tongue, his name means Panther Across the Sky. His vision now unfolds before us.

"These beings have the look of the great black panther that runs free in the forests. And they have flown in a great ship across the sky, fallen from the stars. Tecumseh was meant to find the shooting star that night. It was sent for him to share with the Shawnee, to help us open our hearts.

"I hear his message, and my heart is open wide to cradle the truth he speaks. I take these beings into our village. These are my words."

Tecumseh nodded his thanks to the old chief. The other elder chiefs arose slow, and nodded too. Then what started as but a drip of water, turned into a raging flood. All about, there was now a sea of smiles and happily shaking heads. Tecumseh glanced over at Kykuitheh, and she smiled back.

Serenity now washed over all the people, as they basked in the warm glow of peace and brotherhood. It reminded Tecumseh of what John Sackett had told him about the white man's religion and the peace of the week's seventh day, the day of rest. He had spoken of the feeling when a Sunday morning mass let out, releasing the churchgoers in a drunken friendship and peace on a sunny and warm mid-autumn day. The council was closed. Though in the back of his mind, Tecumseh wondered what would become of Sakdayga and his followers. A great bull does not just go away easy in the night....

Chapter Five
Awakening

Tecumseh's eyes pierced the deep shadows. They brooded. Yet the shapes of the three guests on the far wall remained still. No signs of life, other than the faintest of breaths. It was the same sight as greeted him those past several days. Would he ever again speak to the mysterious being that had uttered those two words within his mind's eye? The sunlight rays of the morning poked through slits of the bark that sheathed the longhouse's outer wall.

Tecumseh just sighed, and stared deeper still into the empty shadows. Then something moved in the dark. Eyes began to flutter, like a young caterpillar given birth to its wings and taking its first flight. They flickered open wide and then gazed straight upon him. In the stilled quiet, breathless eyes locked upon Tecumseh. He rose up slow, and sat beside that star traveler.

Words then began to come out of the strange being. "I come in a good way. Gahnoque I am called."

Tecumseh's eyes widened and his head shook. "How is it that you can speak the tongue of my people . . . how can you speak Shawnee?"

"It is by touch . . . when you risked life to save me from the crash," said Gahnoque.

Tecumseh nodded wonder.

"I looked into your life's memories and learned much of your words," Gahnoque said.

Tecumseh did not know what to say or think. It was beyond all he had ever known.

"This was learned by some of my kind long ago. With but a single touch, I can see into the mind of a living thing, be it being or beast," smiled Gahnoque.

"Where are you from? Why do you visit this valley of my world?" Tecumseh asked.

Gahnoque's face broke into a low smile. "When you gaze up into your night sky, there are stars beyond count. And there are countless other night skies beyond your own.

"My people come from another of these many night skies. My home is Celadon."

Gahnoque sipped some cold water that had sat by him for days. "We had begun our return to our own night sky from another world. We were in flight through a star-gate, a pathway through the black and stars of a night sky that connects to other night skies. Through it we fly at great speed, like the sun that flashes upon your face at dawn's first light."

Tecumseh breathed wonder. "The night sky is connected to other night skies of other worlds by unseen paths of dark and light?"

Gahnoque nodded. "It was within this pathway through the stars that we were hit by mountains of rock. It shook our ship like a great storm wind that would uproot the trees of your world. We would have perished. So for a chance at life, we left where there was no door, and were spit out into your night sky. And fate's winds steered us to your valley."

A blank stare sat upon Tecumseh's face. A chief among his people, yet he knew not what to say to such words. Gahnoque's words opened up a new world for him. To think the Great Spirit had touched other worlds untold and unseen was a thing beyond all belief.

Gahnoque again sipped a bit more water. "It would be as if you took but one blade of grass within the fields of your valley, among all the other valleys and rolling hills of this world . . . and even then, that would not be so vast as the villages of night skies connected to the one you gaze upon. There are no words to capture this vastness . . . even for my people, the Jhagir."

Tecumseh's head shook of more wonder. A low smile broke upon his face. "In all the many moons of my life, I have never dreamed of worlds beyond the night sky. With the troubles of this world, it is a thing so strange to think of how small we are in the vision painted by the Great Spirit . . . it is much to take in."

Gahnoque smiled low. "We too believe in your Great Spirit that flows through all things. My people call it the Ahyir. In my many long years, your kind would not be the first to believe there is but one night sky."

"And how long have you traveled the stars?" asked Tecumseh.

"In the years of your world, I am three-hundred fifty-three. But I am no elder, as some of my kind live a thousand years or more," said Gahnoque.

Tecumseh just smiled some more and sighed. He then turned and asked about the two others who lay asleep.

Gahnoque gently raised his hand and spoke proud, "To the end is Ithikkah, a fierce friend the last two-hundred years. He is three-hundred and seven and a great warrior among our people. And near to me is Taughannock, who is but a youngling in our world, only one-hundred and sixty-seven. He is the youngest, and now the last of Ithikkah's line, for his eldest son perished in the crash."

"Will they live?" asked Tecumseh.

Gahnoque turned silent. An unspoken burden seemed to weigh upon him. "I cannot say . . . we shall see what your Great Spirit decides." Gahnoque just brooded.

Pity filled Tecumseh's heart. Surely Gahnoque wondered if fate would have him walk alone, lost to his people in a strange and unknown world.

Gahnoque then smiled and turned back to Tecumseh. "But my Shawnee friend, I owe you thanks beyond words. If not for your deeds that night, we three would have perished with our ship."

Soft smiles then broke upon the faces of both, and Tecumseh stood up. He reached out his hand, "It is I who gives thanks for your coming to my valley. Let us feed our morning hunger and walk in the forest. You are a wise chief with much to share, the most elder among us, even beyond that of Tanogatay."

Unnoticed by them both, the others in the longhouse had also arisen, save for Ithikkah and Taughannock. In wide-eyed silence, they each offered Gahnoque their friendship. All then sat down to a hearty morning meal of smoked rabbit and corn cakes, though Gahnoque would have no meat. He said that for untold years now, his people no longer ate meat; just greens, seeds, and things birthed from the dirt. By sunlight alone, their bodies make their own food if need be, like a plant of this world. To that, Tecumseh just shrugged and smiled. Those beings were strange indeed.

Throughout that day and those that followed after, crowds followed Tecumseh and Gahnoque wherever they went. The people pointed and stared. Children squealed at his sight and at the sound of their Shawnee tongue that fell from his lips. They were certain the Great Spirit itself had come down among the Shawnee, housed within the body of Gahnoque so strange. He of course told all who asked that he was not. He was just a living thing like them. Seeking only the same happy pleasures that life could bring, just like them.

Many of the people did not believe those words. Lost in excitement they remained. Though toward the evenings, the crowds died down so that both Tecumseh and Gahnoque could take a stroll at dusk, alone.

But always before they set out, they would check on his Jhagir brothers who slept. Their bodies lay still, though still taking breath. And always, Tecumseh found Nateelah sitting by their side.

It warmed Tecumseh's heart to see Nateelah carry on in such a way, as it gave her purpose. It would do her soul good to help others and forget her haunted past. It was a tale of sadness, something he could never forget.

Just a nine-year-old girl, she was beaten like a dog, and made to watch her parent's brutal death. The palefaces emptied her father's insides and tortured her mother, Tecumseh's sister, at the end of a blade until her screams went quiet. Then they stripped young Nateelah naked and meant to rape her until she cried out for death.

But her young cousin had burst into the longhouse. He tackled the brutes, and screamed for her to get up and run. And she did. But her young cousin paid for the brave deed with his life, which was a guilt she carried still.

She made her way, and wandered days through the wild to Tecumseh's village. Bruised and bloodied, Tecumseh took her in. And she has lived with him ever since, rebuilding her spirit among the people, though never quite becoming whole. Yet somehow, Nateelah clung still to a ferocity for life that could not be stamped out. Tecumseh had always marveled at that. And he loved her for it.

Tecumseh looked to Nateelah, and asked how their guests were doing.

"My uncle, they still sleep. But I will wait here in the chance they arise. I would welcome them to our world," she said.

Gahnoque walked to her, and reached out his hand. "Nateelah, you are a kind soul. I thank you."

She nodded back.

"I have been told by a favorite uncle of your great will to bring life to my brothers day and night, despite his command for some rest. What do you say to this?" Gahnoque asked.

A wry grin broke across Nateelah's face. Her eyes sparkled, a soft giggle escaped.

"And what do you know of this?" Gahnoque asked, as he turned to Tecumseh.

Tecumseh smiled low. "My friend, that favorite uncle would expect nothing less from one he holds highest among the Shawnee." Tecumseh turned, and stooped down to Nateelah. He planted a soft kiss upon her forehead, as a doting father would to his young daughter.

Kykuitheh then stepped forth from the longhouse's shadows.

The others turned to her and bowed.

Gahnoque moved near to her and said, "Thank you for opening your home to the Jhagir. It is no small thing."

Kykuitheh smiled back at Gahnoque. "You are most welcome, for all the days that you walk among us, until you should ever return to your home," to which Gahnoque smiled back in thanks. And with that, Tecumseh and Gahnoque set out again for another of their evening walks and wherever its path would lead them.

Chapter Six
Two Worlds Become One

"Tell me of this paleface nation . . . America. What is the darkness that grows in your heart?" asked Gahnoque.

Tecumseh's chest heaved a bit. The choked air settled heavy upon his throat. Haunted memories of long ago flooded his mind. "I have seen many things in my forty-three years of life . . . things that tear the heart apart. The white man entered into the world of the Shawnee . . . and so came a growing shadow that suffocates my people like thick black smoke. And I learned what it means to hate. As a six-year-old boy, I first met the palefaces . . . and they drove a steel blade into my father. Is that not all you need to know?"

A grieved pain settled upon Gahnoque's face. And Tecumseh shared all of his soul in that most painful of stories.

After some moments of silence, Tecumseh went on, "I somehow found my way home. And a war party was sent out to deal death upon those whites, and to retrieve his body. Warriors fell upon them with swift vengeance.

"There was great sorrow as the village mourned the loss of my father. We returned him to the Great Spirit, as is our way. But I still remember the village elders talking of the white race. No matter how many we kill, more just replace them. And they seek all the Great Spirit's land with an insatiable thirst, which could not be quenched with all the water in the great sea."

Gahnoque's vacant eyes looked upon Tecumseh. "My heart breaks to know of such sadness. It is a thing more than any six-year-old boy should bear."

Those words lingered in silence, before Gahnoque asked, "Does the white race not see it is a part of this world?"

Tecumseh smiled regret. "The Great Spirit's white children see themselves only at the center of all things. And they will yield to neither the Great Spirit, nor their own God, until they have taken all that they want. The great white fathers push us back ever more, like a great waterfall that pounds away upon the rock below until we are no more than a pebble."

Gahnoque's face stretched of ache, a small frown hung upon his face. "But I saw also kindness between you and the whites, sharing a happy fire with paleface soldiers, letting them go in peace . . . that is not hatred?"

Tecumseh sighed. "It is the way of this world that the defeated be tortured at the hands of the victor, by both palefaces and the many tribes. But to mutilate and burn the flesh of another alive . . . this is not the Great Spirit's way. And I will not do such a thing. After the battle is won, I will not take the life of another. I will fight them again another day."

Tecumseh then dwelled in some more memories. "Hatred's flame burns in my heart for the palefaces; though there are some good among them. They wish only to be left alone in their small piece of the world. But that is not the many of their kind....

"My tomahawk will taste the flesh of the long knives again . . . for I have read their books of history. We are a rut of stubborn muck in their road to empire. We are the stones beneath their wagon wheels, ground into dust, as they roll the future upon us. They call it their manifest destiny."

Gahnoque nodded grimly. He then glanced upon Tecumseh, and asked, "But what of this John Sackett? How came you to know this paleface so well, though he is of the race that burned hatred in your heart?"

Tecumseh stared down. His mind raced to somewhere else. He murmured, though more to himself than to Gahnoque. "John Sackett . . . is no paleface. He is a good man . . . and my friend." And the past leapt into Tecumseh's mind.

**

They thirsted for white flesh. Like a pack of wolves on the hunt, the young nineteen-year-old warriors prowled the wild. Anger's hunger needed to be fed. They would teach the great white fathers a lesson. Sakdayga was at the lead, the sharp tip of the blade. And soon, some poor souls wandered into their world.

The warriors spotted a small wagon train of palefaces that moved across the far meadow. With a kick of his horse and a yell, Sakdayga shot out across the meadow. The others took off behind him. Some of the whites screamed out at the horde that came, and franticly scrambled for their muskets. They got off a few shots, but the Indians were too many.

Tecumseh rode wildly within the horde pack, but he pulled up as they came upon the terrified whites. He could not partake. He could only watch as his brother warriors did. He watched them become men. They howled like wolves. But they did not hunt the great buffalo or elk . . . they hunted only women, children, and old men. There were only a few strong whites among them. Tecumseh's insides convulsed at that bloodlust. That was not the way. It was not the deeds of warriors. And then shame flooded his soul. How could he just watch? How could he do nothing?

Young children cried out in terror . . . but the Indians showed no mercy. Mothers' pleaded for kindness . . . they begged for the lives of the children, as they quaked on their knees in the mud. But the Indian warriors granted only death of the tomahawk and war club. A glee sparkled in Sakdayga's eyes with each mighty swing. It was a slaughter. All were slain, with not a warrior lost. And hatred coursed again through Tecumseh. He hated the wolf. He hated its needless killing. But now the wolf looked just like him. And he hated himself.

Tecumseh stared vacantly as some bloody scalps were taken. Sakdayga took notice, and scowled at him. "You are still a boy, not yet ready to be a warrior among the people!" The others looked on, and said nothing.

Tecumseh just turned away from the ghastly sight. He headed his horse away from the butchery and the howling wolves. Thoughts rambled. What had his warrior brothers done? If that was the deed of a man . . . then he would be no man. Over and over in his mind, the Great Spirit scolded him . . . that was not the way . . . that was not the way.

They had no quarrel with those palefaces. Those were not the evil long knives that raped and killed. Those whites were different. They were not beholden to the great white fathers. Those poor souls were trying to hack out a life, free in the wild. And his warrior brothers had killed them just because they were white.

Tecumseh's insides smoldered in anger. Though he did not raise his tomahawk, he was just as guilty . . . because he did nothing. He did not have the strength to do what was right. Sakdayga was right, for Tecumseh was not yet a man. For a man would have done something . . . anything.

It was not enough to not flee from battle's terror. A man must have the strength also to show kindness where it was due . . . and save a life when he could. Tecumseh could hear his father's whispered words in his ear once more. Tecumseh boiled anger upon himself. And as his horse carried him on a slow gait, he made another promise to the Great Spirit. He would never again stand idly by, while others are struck down unjustly, be they his kin or the whites, or any other. It would be better to die trying to do what is right than to live many long years behind shame and a heavy heart. Once again, the hand of his father was upon his shoulder. His father would have nodded in pride, for his son was indeed becoming a man.

The warriors' horses rode on at a relaxed pace as they headed home. The bloodied scalps swung back and forth, draped over the horses' necks. On through forest, hill, meadow, and valley they went. Until in the early evening they came upon a lone square house of shaved wood, the home of a white family. The warriors all heeled their horses. There were but three men and two women that moved about. Sakdayga's eyes widened, excited for some more butchery that day. He again kicked his horse, and yelled out. His horse galloped out toward the white family, and the other warriors followed after. The white men yelled and grabbed their muskets. The women cried out and circled behind the men. A feathered horde descended.

But at once, Tecumseh's horse exploded after Sakdayga. And Tecumseh's horse was faster. Tecumseh collided into Sakdayga. He leapt upon him, and tackled Sakdayga off his horse. The other warriors pulled up, stunned with wonder. The white family too seemed shocked with curious fear, as those Indians fought among themselves. They must truly be savages.

Sakdayga was enraged, his eyes strained of red bloodshot. He had never been knocked down before in his life. He flipped up and swung his fierce fist. But Tecumseh ducked under. Sakdayga's fist found nothing but air, and his momentum toppled him over again like a drunken man.

Tecumseh leapt upon him again and screamed, "You will stop! You will not harm these people!"

But Sakdayga was strong. And made even more so in his erupting anger. Tecumseh rode upon a bucking bull. And the angry beast kicked, reared, and pummeled Tecumseh with several staggering blows to the head. Stars flashed about

Tecumseh as he was thrown off. Sakdayga grabbed his tomahawk. He meant to end this.

The warriors screamed out in horror and disbelief. They were to kill the palefaces . . . not each other. That white family was not worth the life of one good warrior.

Sakdayga's eyes sparkled with that same glee of death. He loved to kill things. And he never liked Tecumseh anyway.

But Tecumseh did not cower. He crouched like a panther, his tomahawk drawn. He smiled back at Sakdayga. And Sakdayga snorted and rushed upon him, as a charging buffalo bull would do. Tecumseh spun quick as a cat, and kicked out Sakdayga's legs. He smashed Sakdayga's face with the wood handle of his tomahawk. There was a loud crack, as if a branch limb had been snapped in two. His nose would now be forever bent a bit.

Sakdayga fell; his clenched grip let loose his tomahawk from the one mighty blow. Tecumseh leapt upon him once more. He slammed Sakdayga's head upon the hard ground, and held the sharp edge of his tomahawk tight to the great bull's throat. It pressed the skin, as thin lines of blood streamed down his neck. "Your bullying days are at an end. You will never touch another good soul, or my tomahawk will taste your bones!" Tecumseh said.

Sakdayga gasped, his eyes widened. The other warriors all gasped too. No one had beaten Sakdayga in battle in his young life . . . ever. Even the older warriors would not challenge him. And yet now before them, Tecumseh could kill the mighty bull with one flick of the wrist. Tecumseh's eyes growled upon the big bull like a great panther.

And Tecumseh saw something he had never seen before . . . Sakdayga was filled with fear. Though Tecumseh was of flesh and bone, he did walk with the spirits. The panther moved in him. He was Panther Across the Sky. Tecumseh felt it. Tecumseh saw the faces of the other warriors . . . and they saw it too.

And Sakdayga chose not to die that day. He yielded before the spirit atop him. His eyes lowered, his head sank in defeat. He nodded to Tecumseh, who relented and removed his tomahawk. Sakdayga stood up again slow. And though he was still the biggest among them, he was not as the bull had been. There was no raging nastiness that lashed out. He did not fight back. He looked somehow shorter now, not as menacing. He walked in the shadow of Panther Across the Sky that day. And there he stewed. Though Tecumseh wondered for how long? Would it be for all his days? He did not know, as only time would reveal that wisdom.

Tecumseh turned to the white family that looked upon him. He knew the whites wondered if now the Indians would fly upon them. But they did not. Tecumseh's eyes smoldered still, but now they burned of kindness . . . and the strength of doing what was right. Tecumseh waved back to them and nodded. The white family did not know what to do. They just stood there and waved back. And a great relief seemed to pass over their faces.

Then the oldest man, the head of the family, stepped forward and yelled out, "I am John Sackett. Thank you."

Tecumseh eyed that white man in wonder. He had learned some English in his young life, and that white man spoke words of kindness. The name 'John Sackett' settled in his mind. And it was a name he would never forget. He hopped upon his painted horse and galloped over to that John Sackett. He gazed upon him up close. He remembered the last time he was that close to a paleface . . . that was a day a six-year-old boy never forgets.

But there was something about that white man, and it was more than his snow-white teeth that gleamed in the sun. Tecumseh's deep brown eyes searched for something, but what, he did not know. He hated the palefaces . . . yet he did not hate that white man before him. Tecumseh then smiled, nodded his head again, and rode off back to the warriors.

Tecumseh saw the lines of confusion upon their faces. The warriors did not know what to think, for Tecumseh's hatred of the whites was well known; yet, in that moment, he had saved that white family and they did not know why. Tecumseh then called out and all the warriors jumped upon their horses and rode off, even the big bull . . . though now he took up the rear.

Back in the village, the tale was shared, and like a fire-roasted ear of corn, everyone wanted a piece. They had thought Sakdayga was a wild buffalo bull that would never be tamed. And yet, Tecumseh had now done the unthinkable. His father would have been proud. They had all wondered . . . and waited for a sign . . . did young Tecumseh walk with the Panther in the Sky? They now had their answer.

Over the next several days, Tecumseh thought about that white family. The face of the oldest white man was familiar. Where had he seen it before? Then it came to him. It was the lines of his father's face. He wanted to go see that man again. The next morning, Tecumseh headed out of his village alone and told no one. He was following his spirit, and the people would not understand. And though he had hated palefaces all of his young life, and still did, his heart now called him to go to that white family. His heart was searching for something . . . but what it was, he did not know. But his heart told him it was the right thing to do. His father's hand was upon his shoulder again, but where was it leading him?

**

Tecumseh's mind snapped back to the here and now. He looked back to Gahnoque, and whispered, "I have long feared the ending of my people is at hand. There is nothing so painful as to see your way of life and the Great Spirit's gift of Mother Earth taken from you. It is beyond words.

"We are the last leaves upon the tree of life that is the tribes of this land . . . all that is left . . . and once we fall, the tree will be barren and the tribes no more. The autumn of our people is at hand. Once the last leaf falls, there will be only the dark desolation of our winter. A winter from which there will be no spring, and the flower of our race shall never bloom again."

Gahnoque's shoulders sagged, his chest heaved slow. Emptiness painted his face.

He then moved close to Tecumseh. He took up Tecumseh's blade and made a small cut within his palm. "I have not come all this way through many night skies to stand idly by, while you struggle under this great burden. You risked life and limb to save the Jhagir, and now I pledge a blood oath. Whether by my life or death . . . I will help the Shawnee."

Tecumseh's eyes raised, brows furled. Then a low smile crept across his face. Tecumseh took back his blade and did the same. They clasped each other's hands tight in warm friendship, and Tecumseh shook his head. "Thank you, but not as my friend . . . you are now my brother and one of us - the blood of the Shawnee runs through you."

Gahnoque smiled kindly in return. "And the blood of the Jhagir runs through you."

Although of different races and worlds, they were now one with each other and the Great Spirit. And to whatever end, be it a triumph of happiness and peace, or desolation, they went together.

Lit fires warmly greeted them as they returned to the village. Subdued drumbeats and musical chants floated upon the night air. The shadows cast by the flickering flames and the shimmering moonlight upon Gahnoque's flesh painted a picture of some unearthly dream.

Finally, they came upon Tecumseh's longhouse and went inside. And many people were gathered about something. It was Ithikkah. He was upright, and trying to speak. In the midst of the talking sounds, gestures, and smiles, the group looked up.

Ithikkah's and Gahnoque's eyes met at once, and Gahnoque rushed to him. The Shawnee shouted out to Tecumseh. Excitement bubbled. The Jhagir spoke in their tongue at first, so strange sounding it was. Unlike anything the Shawnee had heard spoken before. Hushed, stretched, and a deep rhythmic sound it carried, as if the distant echo of some shaman's chant.

The Jhagir then both turned in silence to Taughannock who lay nearby. Ithikkah exhaled slowly, and his shoulders drooped. They both then gripped each other's forearm, and bowed. Their heads then lifted slowly.

Ithikkah stepped to Tecumseh, and his voice rumbled low. "I know much of your people, for Gahnoque has shown me. I have seen your quality. I too will walk Gahnoque's path."

As Ithikkah spoke, Tecumseh took in his full vision. Though of similar size and general appearance as Gahnoque, there was an air of forebode about him. It was unmistakable. There was a bubbling fury waiting to be let loose. Perhaps it was the jagged scar upon his face, which was a small mountain range of healed flesh that marked some ancient battle. Or perhaps it was the raised winter fur that was wild and overgrown like an unkempt bush. It was striking, and tapered down the neck and onto his backside, like a draping wolf skin. It gave off an air of might, and of one who lusted for battle. At his sight, any person of reason would head in the other direction.

Tecumseh looked at Ithikkah first, then over to Gahnoque. A low smile painted his face.

The Jhagir smiled and nodded in return.

Tecumseh called out for food to be brought in for his guests, though of course no meat. That night, the world's troubles melted away as kindred spirits enjoyed the warm glow of friendship. Though together but a few days or hours, an ancient bond hidden within the soul for all the years of their lifetimes was now being set free.

Of course, amid the good will that filled Tecumseh's longhouse, Taughannock remained lost still in deep sleep. If ever he were to awaken, it may require the Great Spirit's very touch. And ever Nateelah watched over him. The village and the Jhagir could do nothing but wait. And they all waited for the Great Spirit's answer....

Chapter Seven
Bond of Brotherhood Grows

Tecumseh stopped and looked down. He knew those markings in the dried mud. It was the lines of a paleface boot.

Gahnoque said, "There is a smell carried on the air."

The others raised their noses to the wind. The peace of the early morning stroll was no more. There was only a tightness upon the throat.

Tecumseh stepped forward a few paces. "It is the smell of roasted meat. We are not alone in these woods." Tecumseh gripped his tomahawk, and the Jhagir followed closely behind.

They traveled maybe one hundred steps, the path wound to the side. And around the bend, they came upon a small clearing, nestled in the forest's edge. They looked about, and there was no life. They moved in warily. A fire's flames flickered and meat sizzled in a pan with a hot hiss.

Gahnoque looked closer upon the fire. "There is a black water too that cooks by the flames."

"The palefaces call it coffee," said Tecumseh. "Someone has left their hot meal in a hurry." They all glanced about the camp and woods for peering eyes, but there were none.

Gahnoque asked, "Is this a camp of the long knives?"

"This is no soldier camp. It is too small and unguarded," said Tecumseh. "There, see the beaver and fox pelts. And also the small bags of the shiny yellow rock, the palefaces call it gold. These palefaces must be trappers . . . or thieves. By the markings upon the ground and the mild stench, someone must have taken up here for a few days at least."

Gahnoque pointed deeper into the woods, "Look there."

Tecumseh moved in close, and there before him were two white women. Their hands were bound by thick rope to a tree. They were bruised and bloodied, their ragged clothes removed from the waist down. And they were lifeless. Tecumseh kneeled down. "There was more than trapping and thieving going on here. Someone had their way with these poor souls . . . and left them to die."

At that moment, Tecumseh heard the cocking of guns behind him.

"Now Injun, ya put yer tomahawk down real slow like, raise yer hands, and turn round. And tell yer animals, or whatever they is, to do the same," said a low gravelly voice.

Tecumseh looked to Gahnoque and Ithikkah, and then they all did as they were told.

And staring back at them were seven filthy palefaces. Their heads of hair were like overgrown scraggly bushes, caked with dried blood and dirt. It had been a while since their last bath. They indeed were trappers or some wild mountain men, and they greedily eyed Tecumseh and the Jhagir with their muskets and pistols. Beads of sweat marked their faces as they called out.

"Looky here. Wonder what price the pelt of these beasts il bring?" one of them squealed.

Another one shouted gruffly, "What yer waitin' for? Let's be done wit it. Kill the injun and let's git to skinnin' these beasts. They'll fetch a pretty penny."

Tecumseh's mind raced. Something must be done, and quick. He glanced over to Gahnoque and Ithikkah, who nodded back.

As the palefaces argued back and forth, the Jhagir began to glow. A soft blue lit about their bodies. And the small jewels upon their chests glowed. The air about them began to bend in waves, as if a tossed stone that sends ripples along the water's surface. They were engulfed by a smoky black mist . . . and then they were gone.

The palefaces shouted, "Wat da hell?" And three of them fired their muskets where the Jhagir had stood. Tecumseh dove behind a tree. Lead whistled by and with several cracks, shattered tree bark sprayed all about. Tecumseh looked up and was dumbstruck. Gahnoque and Ithikkah now stood behind the palefaces. His eyes widened, his mouth fell agape, and he whispered, "They are but ghosts that move here and there . . . yet they are flesh and blood?"

Then in swift silence, both Jhagir grabbed hold of a handle from the harnesses about their chests. Their chest jewels breathed life with streaks of white light, wrapped about a light blue glow at its center. Another burst of soft blue light surrounded their bodies and their yellowish eyes glowed of blue flames. Then from the air, a stretched and curved light appeared, which protruded from the handle. They were like paleface swords, but much bigger. They were slender, though slightly wider at the tip than the bottom, and curved slightly outward. The blades glowed of the same white and light blue color as the small jewels.

And the Jhagir swung down those blades in a blur. There was a low humming sound that echoed here and there as the blades danced through the air. They rumbled air upon the chest as they came close. Each of the palefaces turned and looked up, and the hot blades met their flesh. As the blades struck, they lit further aglow, and echoed a distant lightning strike.

A pit settled in Tecumseh's gut at the sound. Those weapons would strike fear in the hearts of even the bravest souls. And Tecumseh saw the terror on the faces of each paleface. With but a few strokes, the Jhagir cleaved all seven of the palefaces into pieces, their limbs now like chopped wood for a fire. Just like that, the ambush was over.

Tecumseh arose and walked over to the Jhagir. His face was drawn, his eyes did not believe. He whispered in wonder, "There is no such weapon of this world . . . how many of these weapons do you carry?"

"The large blade, a thick and broad weapon like your tomahawk, and two smaller blades for close battle," said Gahnoque.

His thoughts still raced in wonder, Tecumseh went on, "And how do you move with the wind, like some spirit?"

Gahnoque smiled, "My people at one time were also awed at the gift to bend air and travel like the wind. It is to apparate."

"To apparate?" asked Tecumseh. More confusion clouded his face, as there was no such word in the Shawnee tongue. "Truly, your people are a fierce foe in battle. I am glad to call you a friend. But how is such a thing possible?"

Gahnoque smiled, as he pointed down at the harness that crossed his chest. "It is powered by the star of Ithreal, remnants of our night sky's greatest star. Ages ago, beyond the count of years, through massive flares like shooting stars, it bombarded our planet and embedded itself, becoming part of Celadon.

"The star of Ithreal is the brightest known to us through-out all our history and travels. It is our sun, though much larger than this world's sun, like a towering oak to a seed; yet even that does not capture its power. From even the smallest shard, it can turn the darkest black of night bright like day.

"We harnessed its power, giving us the gift of travel through the night's stars. And life was found upon other worlds once only thought of in our dreams."

Tecumseh gazed at the jewel that sat upon Gahnoque's chest. It was so small, no more than a walnut; yet it shimmered in magnificence as the sunlight fell upon it. Tecumseh asked, "How can a thing so small contain such great power?"

Gahnoque said, "Now you too understand the wonder of Ithreal's star. Its secret is hidden still, even to the Jhagir."

Tecumseh said no more. He just stared in silence.

A whisper then called out. It was Gahnoque's Ithreal jewel and it beckoned. Tecumseh reached out to it, like a hungry man that stretched for a chunk of meat. It was cool to the touch.

Gahnoque went on, "These harnesses were made by our early ancestor, Isstah. He was the high chief king, wisest of his time. They allow one to unleash the power of an Ithreal jewel that sits within it. The wearer can focus that power through your mind's eye, to perform great feats of the body and forge starlit weapons of war."

Tecumseh just stared some more in wonder.

"Of course, it takes many years to become master of one's Isstah and Ithreal, and your mind," said Gahnoque.

Ithikkah smiled low and said. "But there are few of our race who possess a mastery as he.

"You do not know that among our people, he is marked to one day be the high chief king of all. But he will not tell you this . . . and that is why his brothers follow him wherever he may go."

Gahnoque raised his hand at Ithikkah. "There are those among our people who would say this is not so . . . and I am not sure who is ever worthy of such a thing."

Tecumseh just sighed some more. Thoughts of the many hidden night skies spun again in his head, and the strange wonders of the Jhagir. His own world was so small.

They buried deep the two dead women out of respect, as was the paleface way. The filthy palefaces were placed in shallow graves, hidden while they rotted to bones. And then they headed the long way back to the village.

And Tecumseh asked the Jhagir to make no mention of those palefaces, for though it was rare for one to be seen within a day's walk of the village, tales of the ambush would only stir fear. On the walk home, Tecumseh basked in the glow of his newfound friendship with the Jhagir, and then his thoughts turned to his old friend John Sackett once more.

**

Tecumseh stared out from the thick forest, cloaked in dark, hidden from the glaring midday sun. A lump sat heavy in the throat. Curious fear pricked the senses. What was he doing? He was alone, both in body and in spirit. He was Shawnee, and the Shawnee do not speak with the palefaces by choice. The people would not understand. He was not sure he understood himself. A burning hate still flamed for the whites. He still hated the wolf . . . and he always would. Yet here he was, upon his painted horse on the forest edge, looking upon the square home of that white family. What would his father have done? He savored one last deep breath, stretched with a lifetime of thoughts. And then he gave his horse a gentle kick.

It took one slow step after another toward the home of the white family, quiet and in plain view. The family stopped their chores at once. There was a lone Indian walking upon them. The younger whites yelled out, "Pa, should we grab the muskets?"

Tecumseh saw the looks upon their faces. He knew the thoughts that raced in their minds. Wild Indians were dangerous. Fear throbbed upon them, for if there was one Indian, there was always more laying in the brush somewhere nearby. But Tecumseh moved so slow and calm. Peace filled his heart. And then he came nearer.

Lines of worry and wonder sat still upon the face of the oldest white man. And so Tecumseh slowly slid off his horse, tied it to a tree, and then laid down all of his weapons for them to see. He came in a good way. He turned, smiled, and walked slowly to them. A warmth flooded Tecumseh's insides.

Then a smile crept upon the face of the oldest man, the father of the family. Tecumseh thought the father recognized him. The father yelled, "Boys, leave the muskets. A good man comes to visit this day, the Indian from the other day; the one who saved our lives."

The sons were not filled with the same confidence, but did what they were told. Though Tecumseh thought their twitching fingers would have felt better wrapped around the barrel and trigger of their guns.

"Boys, bring out some chairs. We are going to visit in the shade with our guest. Rebecca, bring some water," said the father. And the children all did as asked, though the boys still kept a wary eye on Tecumseh.

The father gestured for him to sit, and so Tecumseh did. A friendly silence fell upon the gathering at first, and stares were shared back and forth. Tecumseh wondered what he was doing here. And he guessed the white family wondered the same thing.

The father then spoke up, "I remember you. You saved my family. Thank you again."

Tecumseh nodded.

"I am John Sackett. That is my wife Mary, my two sons, Joshua and Henry, and my daughter Rebecca," said John Sackett. He pointed to each, and warm nods passed back and forth. John and Mary looked to have seen nearly fifty winters. Henry seemed to be a bit older than Tecumseh, while Joshua was younger. And Rebecca was but ten years old. John Sackett then asked, "Do you speak any English?"

"Speak some. Learn more . . ." said Tecumseh.

The boys and young Rebecca gasped out. It seemed they had never heard an Indian speak a word of English, though broken it was. Of course, Tecumseh thought they probably never talked with an Indian before in peace. But the smiles upon their face spoke for them. They seemed to like Tecumseh.

And he searched their faces. Only goodness stared back. But how could that be? Palefaces did not come in a good way. And yet there was nothing but kindness in their eyes. His father's hand was upon his shoulder, leading him to that family . . . but why? To his wonder and surprise . . . he liked that family too.

It was a good start with smiles all around. At first it took a while, but Tecumseh was a quick learner, and so were the Sacketts. And both were eager to share and learn. Before long, Tecumseh and that white family were going back and forth. Beneath their skin and garb, they were not that much different after all. They loved their family and yearned for peace. Personal liberty was precious beyond all things. And they would not take another's property and would earn what they got.

It all surprised Tecumseh. His mind spun in delight of such an unlooked-for thing. Tecumseh stayed that night, and a few more days, before he headed back to his village. And his time with the Sacketts brought him to search his soul, for the seed of friendship had been planted. How could that be? It struck him that perhaps not all palefaces were dark souls after all. He still hated the white race, yet the Sacketts were a kind people. They were his friends. In whatever was to come, he hoped that no harm would befall them. And that was something to ponder, for he always had worry of the people from the palefaces; yet, now he had worry of that white family from his own kind.

Upon his return to the village, Tecumseh's mind tussled and turned. The people would want to know where he had been. Should he speak of the Sacketts? He did not know. Were the people ready to hear such things of peace and friendship, for like the night and the day, the whites and the Shawnee had always been enemies . . . and perhaps they always would be.

After much thought, it was settled. His heart told him the way. It was the right thing to do.

As Tecumseh entered the grounds, a few children chased by, followed after by some dogs. Soon after, the people descended. Where had he been? And Tecumseh did not hold back. He opened his heart. And out came stories of the Sacketts. He spoke of their goodness. They were his friends. And at that moment, for all to hear, he passed the word that no warrior shall touch them, or they would taste his tomahawk.

Of course, a rolling wave of gossip ensued. How could that be, they said? Tecumseh's heart was full of hatred for the white race, and yet now he spoke of that white family as his friends. It was a thing quite strange to think of any palefaces as friends. What would his father think to know of such a thing they wondered? Many shook their head, as it was a bit much to take in. But they would all heed the young warrior's request, as they did not want to rouse the panther spirit upon them. They would heed his wisdom, though many did not see it, for he was becoming a man, and one day might become chief of all.

Tecumseh would return many times again to speak with John Sackett over the years. And sometimes, he would bring other warriors with him. He wanted them to see a kind paleface, to show them what the world could be. The glow of friendship in Tecumseh's heart grew and grew, and he came to treasure his time with the Sacketts. And his mind opened to new thoughts and ideas so strange to him. That John Sackett was no poor farmer, but a learned man. Over the years, Tecumseh learned English quite well, and became able to read the white man's papers and books. He learned new ideas of farming, to help feed the people. He learned some of the world's histories and astronomy. Tecumseh also read some of the Bible and the white man's religion, Christianity. There with John Sackett, Tecumseh had found another whose mind sparkled with a curiosity to learn, and his soul smiled wide at that.

And in John Sackett, he also found a man to talk about the heart's deep waters and the soul's yearnings. Something he had found hard to do with his own kin. He talked sometimes of his father with John Sackett. He shared the lingering mystery of his father's dying words. He asked John Sackett, how could you not hate the wolf? And if you did, what would become of you? John Sackett never had an answer. He just listened and smiled, and told Tecumseh that maybe someday that wisdom would find them both. And Tecumseh always smiled back at that, as it was exactly the kind of thing his father would have said. Tecumseh thought in wonder as to what his father would say on his great friend John Sackett. Tecumseh was sure his father would have liked that paleface very much.

Perhaps, it was his father's guiding hand upon his shoulder that brought those two most unlikely of friends together. How could it be that the soul of his father came alive in that John Sackett? That riddle tossed in his mind many nights as he wrestled with sleep. But the answer remained elusive. It was always almost there, at the edge of the firelight, yet ever in the shadows just out of reach. What was it about that John Sackett? What was his father trying to tell him?

Chapter Eight
Kindred Spirits Abound

"Tecumseh, Tecumseh . . . Taughannock has life!" A young boy's high-pitched yell jarred the morning.

At once, Ithikkah jumped up. He took off back to the village like a wolf that had marked its prey in the meadow; his bounding strides ate up the land in a blur. Gahnoque, Tecumseh, and the boy followed after, short on his heels.

As Ithikkah came into the village outskirts, he slowed to make his way through the excited crowd of village folk. Tecumseh and Gahnoque were right behind him. There were erupting cheers everywhere.

Ithikkah made the final turn around the bended path. He burst through the door to Tecumseh's longhouse. Gahnoque and Tecumseh followed, and panted to catch their breaths. Beyond all hope, there was Taughannock. He sat upright and full of life . . . and next to him, Nateelah.

Taughannock was of the same general build of Gahnoque and his father. Though he was mostly bald, with a tightly wound knot of thick and shiny braids of hair that hung from the back of his head. The clump of winding braids descended neatly down his neck. They then fanned out from a second knot to drape upon his upper back. It all gave the look of a well-trimmed ancient samurai warrior that Tecumseh had read about in one of John Sackett's history books.

Taughannock rose up and Ithikkah rushed forward. He grabbed hold of his son as if he may never do so again. No words were spoken, and none were needed. A warm tear trailed gently down Ithikkah's cheek. Tecumseh knew why. The last of his family . . . the last of his line - Taughannock was all that Ithikkah had left.

They then made their way out into the village. Awe marked Taughannock's face at the kindness shown him from a people so strange. They came to him with warm handshakes, hugs, and shouts of pride from the men, gentle kisses to his cheeks and forehead from the women, and squeals of laughter and giggles by the young children that circled him playfully. It all made Tecumseh proud to be Shawnee.

The joyous clamor finally gave way to hunger and thirst. A call then rose up for a great feast. The village elders and chiefs all glanced dartingly about of something so unexpected. But there was never any doubt. Tecumseh just smiled. They then all looked to the most elder of the village, Tanogatay, who slowly raised his hand. A hush filled the crowd, as if a silencing wave of water had washed upon them. Tanogatay looked back to the honored guests, nodded at them, and then back at the people. He lowered his hand a bit, "Let us give thanks this day."

Many voices of joy erupted. All the Jhagir looked to Tecumseh, and deep laughter bellowed out.

That day, the Shawnees' troubles were put aside. Only the goodness in their hearts would be shared with one another and the Great Spirit. They sat about to busily prepare for the great feast. People scurried this way and that. All manners of greens and meats were prepared for a feast so grand.

Within hours, they gathered all. There sat Tecumseh, Kykuitheh, and their newfound brothers Gahnoque and Ithikkah. Near to Ithikkah sat his son Taughannock, who of course was flanked by his healer, Nateelah. The entire village was emptied out, down to the last woman, man, and child, and a not an open seat could be found. Bellies were filled with food and spirits made merry by drink.

Tecumseh then rose up and held his cup high. "May the love here today make a sacred bond among us, so that wherever we may go and no matter what becomes of us . . . we know we are not alone. Be you abandoned to the highest mountain peak, surrounded only by enemies and tribulation . . . you remember this day.

"Hold tight to this moment with all your fierceness, for in the end that is all we have. And for the rest of your days, take hold of the memory, so that it is a part of you like flesh upon bone. And through this memory, we shall remain unconquered and free."

A rising wave of shouts rose up at those words. And as the bubbling happiness subsided, tears of joy welled up in many. They were moved. After a moment of silence, a chorus of laughter and cheers built again and rang out. The great feast consumed the day and into the night, until at last, when their bellies could be filled with no more food, their thirsts quenched with no more drink, and their bodies soaked with no more fatigue, they succumbed to the sleep that called. Some stubborn few though, moved to sit by a small number of lonely lit fires. Quiet songs and whispered talk lingered, but most fell into their dreams.

Taughannock and Nateelah were some of those stubborn few. Their silhouette hung over a dimly lit fire and caught Tecumseh's eye. They sat together in deep talks of the heart, until the fire embers all but burned out. The young Jhagir was a quick learner and had picked up much of the Shawnee tongue when he had grasped her arm at being startled awake. It was plain for Tecumseh to see that Taughannock very much enjoyed speaking with Nateelah in her own tongue.

And it was not solely to her being his caretaker those many days, although for that deed Taughannock bestowed upon her a deep gratitude. No, there was something deeper afoot . . . something in the air. It was beyond the body, and tugged at the soul. Between those two spirits, something had begun.

Tecumseh approached and asked if they had not yet had enough for one evening. Perhaps it was best for Taughannock to get a good night's rest for he was still weak.

Taughannock nodded. "Yes. I still need much healing before I am whole. But perhaps you will allow me just a bit more time to sit with Nateelah . . . least until the fire dies out?"

Tecumseh turned in silence with a raised brow to Nateelah. She glared back playfully. A smirking smile took hold and he chuckled, "My friend, a great wisdom tells me now that I do not have a choice in this matter."

All three broke into soft laughter. Tecumseh bowed and headed off to sleep. And then on again the two talked, trying to stretch a lifetime of memories into that one night.

Dawn had not yet arisen upon the peaceful slumber. The air was still drunk with a joyous fatigue. Tecumseh stirred in the darkened longhouse. All were at rest, except for two open spaces . . . Taughannock and Nateelah.

Curious, he arose to look about the village grounds. He did not travel far. There the pair sat, by the fire pit where he had left them the night before. He reached down and gently nudged them. Taughannock awakened first. He looked up half-asleep, a bit embarrassed under Tecumseh's glare.

"I am glad to see that the both of you enjoyed a most restful sleep in the longhouse last night," said Tecumseh.

Taughannock's eyes lowered. "I am sorry. Our talk ran on many hours, and Nateelah had sat by my side for warmth as the fire faded. We meant to go to the longhouse soon after, but we drifted off…."

Tecumseh smiled deep. "Do not apologize. With all the troubles of the world, ever we should stretch the happy moments as long as we may."

Nateelah then stirred awake. She yawned up to Tecumseh. "How is my favorite uncle this morning?"

Tecumseh stooped to her, his brows bent, "I am well, though surely not as well rested as you." There was an awkward breath. Tecumseh held his stare a bit longer, and then the deepest of smiles broke across their faces. And it warmed his soul.

As summer faded to fall, Nateelah and Taughannock were inseparable. And always she looked after him so that his body's strength began to return. In turn, Taughannock also provided her with nourishment, but that of the soul, so that the troubles of her past were eased from her mind. And those gifts did not go unnoticed by both Ithikkah and Tecumseh, one being a father by blood and the other being a father in every other way. It softened Tecumseh's heart to think of the best in each of us. The souls of that pair were bonded to one another, if ever souls could be. Different worlds, different races . . . it made no difference. There seemed now to be only possibilities.

Tecumseh and Ithikkah walked upon Taughannock late one evening by the winding river, as Ithikkah had fatherly wisdom to share with his son. "It is most wise to follow your heart and strengthen love's bond; for it is sacred beyond words. It is not something you make or force upon another - it is something that finds you and is given freely in return to whoever you will."

Tecumseh smiled low and nodded.

Taughannock nodded back to them both. He then leaned back and softly said, "I know we are of different races and worlds, but I am drawn to her, like the flooding river that seeks the sea. There is a drowning loss when she is not near, even when I had slept. It is something I cannot explain. It is beyond the world we see . . . and something deep within. I do not know why. I just know that it is."

Tecumseh's eyes smiled. Happiness danced within.

Ithikkah smiled some more upon his son. "Love is the rarest of things . . . a sparkling shard of Ithreal. And when one comes across such a gift, they must give everything to pull it close." Ithikkah sighed as he spoke. He then looked away into the distance and whispered, ". . . I once knew such a love. I swam in its happiness . . . and it is why you are here today."

After some silence, Ithikkah said, "And when others are caught in its glow, it kindles the fire of hope to change the world." And with that, both father and son embraced.

Tecumseh just smiled some more, and his eyes beamed hope.

The three then quietly returned to the village and entered the longhouse, as Nateelah slept. Taughannock gently tapped her shoulder and whispered to her. She looked at him in wonder as she arose to leave. Tecumseh followed after a few paces and looked on, as Nateelah and Taughannock walked away. They went to their favorite place, the great oak on the southern bend of the winding river. Hands clasped as their silhouettes bathed in the silvery light of the moon that hung in the starry sky. Tecumseh then turned back to fall off to sleep, and left them to the night.

And they did not return until the dawn's breaking. Some villagers had already arisen to greet the morning's first sunshine, including Tecumseh. As Taughannock and Nateelah passed by, hand in hand, the onlookers could not help but notice the strangeness of it all. Tecumseh just smiled. It brought laughter to his soul. Despite all the death and loss of their world, love still somehow found a way to spring forth, like the lone flower upon a mountain rock ledge, and even in the strangest of places where you would not care to look.

And Tecumseh wondered why should it not be? He whispered to himself, "Are we all not flesh and bone? Does the beating heart not give life and love to us all?" He then bowed in silence. Reality settled upon him. The seeds of hatred for others not like us had been sown and their roots grew deep. They gripped the soul of most among us . . . passed on to the newly sprouted limbs and generations that came after. The differences had always been too great. And they always would. That was why it could not be. He was no different and his broad frame slunk. Hatred knew him well. And he knew he would always hate the wolf.

Chapter Nine
Spirit of Hope and Hate

Tecumseh looked upon Taughannock. He saw the young Jhagir carried more than the pain upon his limbs. A faraway look painted Taughannock's eyes as he spoke. "A shadow is upon my heart. May I never again look upon the beauty of Celadon, my home? I long to see the ever flowing waterfall of Namune one more time in the far kingdom of Nenyearthe, to bathe in the ethereal mist that sparkles the many colored hues of the seven moons in night's fading light.

"And the sparkling towers of Ahgohlar, the greatest of our cities in the lands of the mid-northern kingdom of Longrila, with its lighted gates of Ithreal. Its gleaming towers so high, as if to touch the night stars. Atop its perch, one can look down upon on all the five kingdoms of our world above the misty clouds, save the mighty mountains on the far western border of the kingdom of Ghandir. Those mountains are imposing beyond compare, overlooking all the lands and seas of the world."

Tecumseh smiled upon Taughannock in wonder of such a place.

Taughannock nodded and smiled back. "And the beautiful caves of Erelythdor in the lands of the southern kingdom of Nahil, the place where the living light of Ithreal was born.

"And too, the mystical pool of memories and truth discovered so long ago, Mythrea, in the eastern kingdom of Nalathruil. Within its shimmering waters, one can see their soul staring back at them. And beneath its surface, visions of what was, what is, and some things that might be rise up. Just one drop of blood, a blood memory, is needed to let free this gift."

Tecumseh gasped, "Your world is one of beauty and wonder, like a distant dream."

Taughannock nodded solemnly. "The splendor of these wonders forever marks my soul. My heart sinks low to know I will never again walk again among them."

Ithikkah nodded sadness.

Gahnoque then wistfully said, "My heart too longs to look upon those wonders once more, but I would say do not abandon hope. Though that door would seem closed, there may yet be another way . . . another path we might take."

Ithikkah blurted out, "What do you speak of? There is no way! We are a people lost to the stars. The Jhagir can ever search and yet never find their way to us. We cannot return home."

Gahnoque raised his hand in peace. "My brother of all these many years, I hold Taughannock close to my heart. Do you think I would falsely raise his hopes? And now, when we are the last three of our kind, stranded upon an unknown world, would we not hold true to one another?"

Ithikkah's face straightened and he bowed back to Gahnoque. His eyes drooped in apology.

Gahnoque continued on, "There is a path we may follow, though it is not well lit . . . for it has not yet been done. There has been a grand idea. Talk of harnessing the power of three Ithreal stones by the night's moonlight, to make a doorway into the stars. I speak of travel of oneself through a star-portal.

"One needs only a great mastery of your own Ithreal stone to bind its power and control the others, to find the way back home. And then, a ship could return to this world."

Ithikkáh and Taughannock both stopped. Their eyes beamed doubting wonder at Gahnoque.

Taughannock asked in raised hope, "Can this be true?"

Ithikkah held up his hand angrily and growled, "You go too far! Only death has come upon such a traveler; or they be lost forever to some unknown fate. There is no such pathway . . . it cannot be done."

Ithikkah then cooled and sighed defeat. "Even if someone as mighty as you could harness the other Ithreal stones with your own as the master, we have only three jewels among us . . . there is no fourth stone."

Gahnoque looked at Ithikkah and said, "What you say is true. But we are of utmost need. And all known things were at one time impossible . . . that is, until the deed is done. To that, I say why not here? Why not now? We are only in need of a fourth stone. Do not yet give way to despair, for my heart tells me an Ithreal jewel survived the crash."

Both Taughannock and Ithikkah bowed to their friend, for though small, the first real light of possibility shined upon their faces.

Gahnoque turned to Tecumseh. "Worry not, if we find the path I speak of, we will not leave you abandoned to the encircling wolves of the paleface nation. The Shawnee will not stand alone."

Tecumseh nodded. They came together and clasped arms around each other's shoulders. They were brothers indeed. And they hoped in Gahnoque's words . . . and in a fourth stone of Ithreal.

Just then, a mother fox crossed the trail ahead. And two little pups wobbled in tow after her. They glanced back at Tecumseh and the Jhagir, and then scurried on their way. High above, two squirrels chased one another. They jumped from one treetop to another, and chattered all the while. They stopped for a brief moment to look down below. They scolded the two-legged visitors and then ran off again.

Tecumseh and the Jhagir turned, and glimpsed a wood owl far off in the forest, hidden in the thicket of branches and limbs. Its beautiful coo echoed about the woods and soothed the senses. Upon being seen, the owl took flight. Its wings made not a sound as it vanished deeper into the forest's hidden places.

And then about them, floated and twirled a large butterfly. It fluttered in a painted picture of orange, red, and yellow. It flew this way and that, back and forth about Tecumseh and the Jhagir for a moment, and then encircled only Taughannock. And at some unknown signal, the tiny winged thing descended. It landed upon his arm that he held open and outstretched so as to offer it a wider perch. Taughannock was still, as his winged guest gently clung to him. Its wings softly fluttered in place.

"My brother Taughannock, the Great Spirit comes and speaks to you now. What does it say?" said Tecumseh.

Taughannock smiled. He looked upon the fluttering guest, "It says that though I am not of this world, I am a part of it. It says the spirit of life flows through all things, no matter how small.

"The Great Spirit sees me . . . it sees us all. And it bears the simplest of truths: though we linger here a short time, we leave our mark upon the world's soul, and what we do matters. Even the smallest thing taken up among us may make a difference for all and make this world a better place."

Suddenly, a village of butterflies emerged from the forest and passed overhead. They weaved in and out of the tall ash and birch trees. It was a dancing vision of all the many colors of the wild, which fluttered and spun about. A rainbow the palefaces would call it, which breathed with life. At once, the large butterfly took flight again up into the air to join the others. But as the floating herd of delicate winged creatures ascended ever higher, the large butterfly swooped back down close to Taughannock's face. It looked straight upon him, as if it extended its thanks for the short rest. After a moment, it took off, up high into the forest, following the others. Then they were gone.

Sakdayga and his warrior pack rode briskly into the village. Many fresh scalps swayed in the breeze, and still dripped fresh blood. Enough scalps to fill a regiment, as the palefaces called it. He yelled out, "These long knives will hunt the Shawnee no more!" Some happy cries rose up; but many stared in silence. Tecumseh was one of those. The wolf was always to be watched. Beware wild fangs in the dark. And Sakdayga was a great warrior, who could kill many paleface soldiers. But as Tecumseh looked over the warriors' swinging prizes, something caught his eye.

And there it was. Before him were many scalps, long and braided, with small red bows tied neatly into the ends. They were not the scalps of a paleface soldier, for their hair was always short and scruff, and never tied in a bow.

It staggered him. Truth struck a heavy blow to the gut. Tecumseh's knuckles cracked in a strained grip and teeth clenched. Sakdayga had killed few soldiers, but many women . . . or maybe even young girls. Here it came. Hatred throbbed again in him.

Sakdayga eyed Tecumseh through the jostling crowd. His horse sauntered over to Tecumseh, and Sakdayga smiled eerily down at him. "Is it not a good thing to rid our lands of an army of paleface soldiers?"

A heavy hush fell. Tecumseh just glowered up to the wolf before him. "Tell me Sakdayga, does the Great Spirit tell you to murder the helpless?"

Sakdayga's eyes spit disgust. "I bring these scalps to honor our great chief Tanogatay. They will burn in his honor in this night's fire." He shook them for the crowd to behold. And then he turned and lowered his head. All his venom coursed straight upon Tecumseh. His eyes sparkled again in that glee. Tecumseh knew he loved to kill things. And now his eyes gleamed of a taunt. Let the panther ride the great bull right here and now, for all the people to see, they seemed to say. In his feverish lust to give death, the great bull had grown horns . . . and he wanted to buck again. But this time the bull was ready for the panther.

Tecumseh's fingers twitched. His short blade hung to his side and called out to him. Let him rid the world of the wolf in his peoples' skin right now. Anger waved up within, its white capped fury ready to explode. He did not want to do the right thing. He wanted to kill too. But before that rolling wave was unleashed, something happened.

Ithikkah had emerged from nowhere. His crazed winter fur blew in the soft breeze, as if a wild fire that spread upon the land. He walked slowly up to Sakdayga. Eight feet of scarred malice stared upon him, and Ithikkah's eyes smoldered of blue flame. A stoned silence just stared . . . and taunted Sakdayga.

And now, Gahnoque also emerged. He stared too from a distance. His snaked hair hissed venom on the breeze. And the gleam of death in Sakdayga's eyes began to fade. He hated those strange creatures . . . and feared them. He always said they should have been killed while they had slept that first day. And of course, he hated anything that made him feel small. He then sat up fully upon his horse and pulled back. Perhaps the great bull was not ready for a ride after all?

And at that moment, a weight fell upon Tecumseh's shoulder. It pleaded for him to stay his hand. And his heart listened. No, there would be no killing of his kin that day before the people. Even of Sakdayga. Tecumseh stepped forward. His words parted the tense silence like a sharp knife through soft flesh. "Sakdayga, yours is a heart twisted and black like the great white fathers. You would burn all before you in rage. Ever the Great Spirit has tried to speak with you . . . and always you turn away. You will ever be a tortured soul . . . and you will not know peace in your heart. I pity you."

Sakdayga snarled. "Pity? A great warrior does not know pity!" His horse stomped the ground, and turned about a bit. Dust rose up like smoke. Sakdayga's simmering anger grew, like water about to boil over a pot. His clenched jaw ground teeth to bone. Red streaked fury lined the whites of his eyes. His frame shot up erect and rigid. Those near were sure the crazed wolf would leap upon Tecumseh at any moment.

There was no more pretending. Quarreling boys had grown now to hard men, and Sakdayga hated Tecumseh now more than he ever had. Sakdayga's horse moved close to Tecumseh, and its hooves pounded more dirt into a cloud of dust. He glared down again at Tecumseh, a hand length from his face. A tense hush and gasp fell upon the people. Weapons were clenched in nervous hands. The Jhagir fingered the handle of their star lit blades too.

Sakdayga then yelled, "Take your pity, it is for the weak!" He then pulled out his tomahawk and pointed it down at Tecumseh.

Tecumseh stood silent and still, like a great oak tree. What would Sakdayga do? Would one at last cut down the other? Somehow, it always had to come to that.

And then Sakdayga's voice rang out, blazed in fury upon Tecumseh, "Of all the people of this world, no matter your tribe or race, there are two kinds . . . the hunter . . . and the hunted. And I am strong like the great wolf. Be afraid, for I am the hunter, and I come for you. One day . . . I will kill you!" His horse rose up strong and wild and he screamed out like an unseen wild beast from the darkest nightmare. Sakdayga then turned and thundered off. His horsed pack glared at Tecumseh and the crowd, and then followed after. Sakdayga's brooding path was theirs too. They would follow the black storm cloud wherever it went.

Tecumseh showed no emotion. He just sighed and turned to Gahnoque. "The great white fathers' fire of hate will burn ever brighter now. For we have killed not just their soldiers, but many of their women and children. And the good among their race will look upon my people as wicked . . . worthy only of their cold bayonet blades. How will peace ever be in their hearts now?"

Gahnoque just stared blankly. He had no wisdom to share. And they would have to search their souls for that answer. Because in the coming weeks, Tecumseh received word that a wild band of Shawnee raided white settlements up and down the frontier. The storm winds of Sakdayga howled blood and fury. Though somehow, the family of John Sackett was always left untouched.

And Tecumseh's scouts said the great paleface warrior Harrison would have no more of it. The young captain was now a full-grown man, and thick like mountain rock. And the trees and brush would not grow upon that rock. They could not take root. Like his steel war saber, he could not be bent or broken, and no wild things could take a foothold in his presence. Tecumseh knew he was a force to be reckoned with. Harrison's coming rolled upon the tribes like a wagon wheel upon the road.

Harrison had killed countless Indian warriors over the years, in battles Tecumseh knew well. But his pen was mightier still, as he had made many treaties with the tribes. And by the lines on those parchments, he had taken for America more land than a man could walk upon in a hundred lifetimes. Paleface or not, he stirred fear in the hearts of many a warrior. Even the red jackets across the great sea, the old grandfathers to their children in America, were wary of his sharp steel blade; though they eyed again the lands of its lost colonies.

Harrison was now the great general of the American army and Tecumseh's scouts said he had dispatched a vast host of men to put an end to Sakdayga's savagery. And it was said that he would have come himself, but he had to tend to old British white hairs, for they were brooding again to test the nerve and mettle of young America.

Tecumseh remembered the rising chant on the battlefield of that young brave captain years ago. The name echoed in Tecumseh's memories . . . Harrison . . . Harrison. Perhaps one day Tecumseh would hear the thunderous chant once more, louder than any memory could be. But who knew what lay ahead, for fate and chance were like the wind . . . who knew which way they would blow.

Chapter Ten
Reality Beckons

Since the Jhagir had arrived, Tecumseh's people had known only an unlooked-for peace. There had been no long knives, no war and death. Perhaps by some happy chance, the great white fathers had boarded upon their wooden ships to return back across the sea. But in the coming days an ill wind blew . . . with a mighty vengeance.

One late morning, there were cries and shouts about the village. The peace had given way to the reality that beckoned. A young boy ran to Tecumseh, bearing the cruel message - a Shawnee village had been ravaged by an army of long knives.

None were left alive, save a few women and children who alone escaped. Tecumseh looked upon the survivors. They were starving all, beyond exhaustion, and some badly injured. That they had made it alive and unfollowed was no small feat. Their hearts were broken, they smelled of death. A cold fear hung upon their eyes.

The eldest came forward. He recognized the old woman, the lines upon her face. It was Katayea. She had known Tecumseh since he was a young boy. In a daze, she said, "Tecumseh my child, the long knives came in the night . . . some thousand or more. With a cruelty I have never known. Into the fires of our longhouses they came, to destroy all Shawnee life, down to the last man, woman, and child.

"The soldiers flooded our village like a rushing river that drowns a field of corn. Women and children ran out to meet them in the hope of life. They fell to their knees, crying out for kindness. But there was only empty blackness in their eyes. The soldiers smiled and began their butchery. Children were maimed, their brains beaten out onto the ground. Their torches burned our world to ash.

"The few warriors there were, fought back for a time, but so outnumbered they were that each fell. Those last few died to keep us hidden, so we could escape. If not for their bravery, we would have been slain. Now that my village is dead, they will move on to another like a spreading wild fire, until there are no more left. What can the Shawnee do against such hatred?"

Tecumseh moved close to her, and gently clasped her hands. "My heart is grieved at your tale. Rest now your weary mind and limbs, as our village is well hidden."

Tecumseh turned to the people, "The great white fathers no longer seek to trade musket shot and arrow among soldier and warrior; they come to burn our people from the pages of history. We will hunt down the ones who did this. We will find them in the wild. The last thing they will see in this world will be the sharp edge of our tomahawks."

Though Tecumseh's words fell boldly, doubt cut his insides. He sank in its heavy sea, and it would swallow him up. The great white fathers meant to end things, for never before had a roaming army been so large. Fear filled him up. Beware the wolf's glaring fangs. And the glare of one thousand long knives glistened bright. It would take all his bravery and cunning to defeat such a large force. He had never done so before. No one had . . . save for the lone great battle and victory for the tribes thirteen years ago.

Little Turtle's war they called it. Tecumseh knew it well, for he killed many long knives that day on the banks of the Wabash River under the command of Chief Little Turtle. That great river flowed in a place the palefaces called Indiana. And that day, a coalition of a few tribes defeated fifteen hundred, and killed and wounded nearly a thousand long knives. They struck in the early morning dark, and ambushed the army as it slept. But there were over a thousand brave warriors that day. Tecumseh did not have a thousand warriors at his call, not even half of that.

He sighed. But he must be strong for the people. Fear and doubt were his demons and he would not share them. Let the people feel safe . . . at least for a little while longer. But there was no time to send word to other villages for aid. A thousand long knives of steel were coming. He and what warriors there were must go. There was no other way.

Katayea looked up weakly to Tecumseh, closed her eyes, and leaned faintly against him. Tecumseh wrapped her in a warm embrace, as if a cozy fire that shielded her from the biting cold of a winter storm.

The call then went out. All the warriors of the village were to gather. And soon, some hundreds assembled before Tecumseh, as his village was among the largest of all the Shawnee nation. Nearly four-hundred tomahawks strong they were. And he would need every warrior that could be spared.

Gahnoque and Ithikkah stepped forward, for they too would come. And Tecumseh was glad, for the Shawnee would need all the help they could get. The war clubs, tomahawks, and muskets of all rose into the air. Fierce shouts rang out. Little food provisions were packed, for they traveled swift and for one purpose - to hunt down those paleface soldiers. They would leave the horses behind and go on foot, for every bit of stealth and surprise would be needed.

Tecumseh asked a hundred warriors to stay behind while the war party was away, for what if the long knives came upon the village. The people would need some chance to escape if need be. He looked to Taughannock, and asked him to stay with the village, for he still was in need of healing. He would not be able to keep up the quick pace needed for the war party.

Taughannock nodded he would.

And Tecumseh then looked to all. He reminded them that one Shawnee warrior was worth at least two long knives in battle, and laughed, "Maybe even three of their kind!" Many shouts rose up. And then at once, the spirited throng of three-hundred departed, with Tecumseh, Gahnoque, and Ithikkah at the lead.

As they went by, both Taughannock and Nateelah bowed back, and wished them strength for the deed to be done. And also there was Kykuitheh who stood strong. She looked upon Tecumseh as he passed out of sight. But before he did, Tecumseh's eyes smoldered upon her, and hugged her tight.

And as the three hundred headed out into the distance, the on-looking villagers waived to them in goodwill for a hopeful return. But Tecumseh saw the fearful looks upon their fading faces . . . they knew many warriors they would never see again. And Tecumseh knew it too. Doubt cried out in his mind. Did he lead them only to slaughter? Cold desperation flooded him. His mind told him he did, but his heart clung to some hope beyond hope he would find a way. He had no choice. He must try to protect the people. Though how does three hundred defeat one thousand . . . he did not know. But unbowed and steadfast, he swallowed hard and led his warriors on their way.

Sweat bathed Tecumseh with each heavy step. The war party was relentless, and stopped for nothing. They moved at great speed, and came upon Katayea's village in but a few days. Black smoke rose and longhouses burned everywhere, many charred to the ground. They slowed to a walk upon the ruin. The elderly, women, and children were strewn about, with all forms of mutilation. Even the most rugged warrior turned away in heartbreak. They were shaken. Slaughter's gruesome grin smiled back at them. That was beyond war, beyond torn flesh and mangled limbs. They were images of the darkest nightmares that would never leave.

Burnt flesh and terror lingered still about the village. Faded screams of panic and horror echoed on the air. And a swelling anger writhed up within. Souls ready to burst apart.

No words were spoken. Tecumseh kneeled down and moved some rubble. A lifeless child stared back. He grasped the child's hand, which clutched a small doll. The child's empty eyes stared to the sky. He closed its eyelids and whispered, "Go now in peace . . . go with the Great Spirit in your freedom." A tear swelled in Tecumseh's eye and streamed slow down his cheek. And all kindness left him. His body clenched with hatred. He hated the wolf.

He stood and looked into the eyes of Gahnoque and Ithikkah. They were both taken aback, for that was the first they had witnessed the cruelty that Tecumseh had spoken of. And his words, though moving, could not prepare them to look upon such hatred wrought upon another so up close. What souls could bring such death upon a child? Their faces burned fury.

A warrior walked up to Tecumseh and pointed to many tracks that led out of the village. Tecumseh spoke to all, "Leave the souls as they lay, we will send them to the Great Spirit upon our return," to which all nodded. With no more words, the war party headed out, and followed the tracks of their prey. Swift and true, they meant to bring vengeance.

For the next several hours, the war party ran on and on, and crossed hill, creek, and valley. They stopped for nothing and did not know fatigue, though they hunted a ruthless foe that far outnumbered them. And as they trailed their prey, Tecumseh pondered its true size. Though Katayea spoke of a thousand soldiers, in the terror and dark of night, her guess must be far short of their true number. That would explain the village's utter devastation and the endless tracks they follow. Tecumseh placed their number at something far greater . . . maybe two thousand long knives or more.

Iced fear stung his insides and smiled death upon him. Three hundred against two thousand, that was not wisdom . . . it was anger and hate. There could be no victory. But he must have the strength to do what was right. He must protect the people . . . or die trying. His father would have told him so. He thought of that young buck so many moons ago. And he smiled back at his fear. He still hated the wolf. He would always hate the wolf. Death's icy chill called out to him . . . and he ran toward it with a quickened pace.

Chapter Eleven
Shawnee Vengeance

Late afternoon gave way to dusk, as the trail led into the thick forest. The pace slowed through a shrunken path of more tightly packed brush and tree limbs. Under the cloudless sky, the moon's light filtered through the wooded dark. Hundreds of tattooed and painted warriors shifted through the shadows. The tigered markings of the Jhagir glowed green in the moonlight.

They came around a bend, up over a sloping hill. Down below in the valley clearing, there were many lit fires, with hundreds of tents staked about. Tecumseh's hand rose, the party stopped. Tecumseh and several warriors, moved in for a closer view. They needed a look at the wolf. How to attack the great beast?

As they did, two long knife scouts were spotted that guarded the forest's edge. In quiet, Tecumseh waved for two warriors to creep ahead alone, to their left about thirty paces. Breaths tensed, muscles tightened; the wolf must not be roused if they were to have some desperate chance. Two silent arrows flew through the air . . . and found their mark. The scouts fell lifeless to the ground, unnoticed by the great wolf.

Still unseen, Tecumseh moved closer to the forest's edge. There sat the beast. His earlier thoughts were true, as indeed some two thousand soldiers camped out before them. Sprawled out and eating lazily many were, while others drank merrily, engaged in talk and song. Arrogance floated on the air, the soldiers smug in their great size. And amid the sea of flickering campfires below, it came to Tecumseh . . . how the great wolf might be slain.

At once, Tecumseh and his small group returned to the war party. They all gathered in close, for the time had come. Tecumseh asked one hundred warriors to cross around the forested woods, to the backside of the clearing opposite where they stood. Another hundred warriors were to gather to the far right of the clearing. The warriors that remained were to attack from the front, at his lead. He told them to unleash hell, at the whooping call of the nighthawk owl.

They all nodded, and dispersed, just a whisper on the wind. Tecumseh and his one hundred warriors waited for their brothers to move into place. Breaths were short, the night air crisp. Muscles flexed and tensed. A great spring of hate was tightened and coiled. It twitched in wait of the bowstring to let fly, to unleash hell. Tecumseh's cupped hands then covered his mouth and let loose the nighthawk owl's call. The encamped soldiers were oblivious, and paid the call no mind. It was just another of the wild forest's strange nighttime sounds. And it began.

The warrior's line at the clearing's backside let loose a war cry. Its shriek pierced the nighttime air. Soldiers startled awake from their lazy half-sleep and drunken stupor. Tents hurriedly emptied out. There was stumbling about. Officers screamed out orders. The soldiers gathered in hasty confusion to face the forest's unsettling roar. They stared out into the darkness, and gripped their weapons tight.

And then there were many clicking sounds carried upon the air. It was the sound of the hammer on a musket being cocked back . . . the sound of a hundred hammers being cocked back....

At that moment, Tecumseh's tight fist flew forward, and the one hundred warriors at his side released a volley of musket fire. Desperation guided their aim, and it needed to be true. Unlike the paleface army, each warrior had only a few musket balls at most. So they had to make each one count if they were to have a chance of victory. The forest exploded. Cascading flashes lit up the dark. Musket balls whisked through the air and tore leaves and brush. They flew straight into flesh and the heart of the long knives. And most found their mark, as about eighty soldiers fell to death. The army tried to reform its lines, and turned to face where the musket fire had come.

But then, the forest edge to the right exploded with musket flashes. Smoke popped. The second prong of warriors unleashed a volley of musket fire. About seventy soldiers fell. Frantic, many soldiers scrambled their lines to face that side of the forest. In that moment, the third prong let loose a volley of leaden balls. The forest's backside lit up with a hundred flashes. A sea of lead washed upon the long knives. Another eighty soldiers exploded with bursts of red, and fell limp. The army lines then spun around in panic. There still was only the forest dark everywhere . . . and it closed in.

At that, Tecumseh's line had time to reload their muskets once more. They again unleashed another hundred musket balls into the paleface army. Another eighty soldiers fell lifeless. The great beast was wounded. And it smelled of fear. Tecumseh then let loose a blood-curdling war cry. Three hundred warriors sprinted forth. Out of the dark forest they came. They raced into their staggered foe. If they were to defeat the great wolf, they must strike now.

In a daze, the long knives scrambled about. Crazed warriors smashed upon them, like a swarm of angry bees. There would be no taking of prisoners that night. Those were no women and children. And what was left of the soldiers' proud swagger faded away. Panic painted their faces, and fear devoured the souls of every blue jacket that stood in Tecumseh's midst. Tomahawks swung down brutally. They severed limbs and ripped chests apart, like squash being smashed and sliced. War clubs smashed upon the soldiers, and shattered skulls.

The palefaces drove their bayonets deep into the onrushing Shawnee, and spilled their life's blood; but like a broken dam, they could not hold back the flood. Musket fire now exploded randomly about the field. Pistols fired into the gut of the enemy on both sides. Musket smoke rose up about the valley clearing, as they danced in death under the pale moonlight. Death was intimate, drenched of grime and sweat.

Through the thick din and misty fog of battle, there was the army commander in his emblazoned military regalia. Tecumseh saw he was a colonel by rank, the one who had brought the evil upon the Shawnee village those few days past. Tecumseh launched toward him. The colonel spotted Tecumseh, and spun to face him, with two soldiers who rushed to his aid. One soldier's bayonet lunged at Tecumseh, who dropped and slid under its reach. Tecumseh jumped up and swung his tomahawk into the soldier's back. It chopped deep to the bone. The soldier fell forward in death.

Tecumseh at once turned and grabbed another smaller tomahawk at his side. He swung it down upon the other rushing soldier who extended in a full-on bayonet rush. Tecumseh drove the musket to the ground, and kicked the soldier back with a strong leg thrust. The soldier staggered a bit, and Tecumseh ferociously swung his small tomahawk into his chest, and buried it deep. In vigor, he withdrew it. There was a gaping wound from which blood poured. In shock, the soldier stared at Tecumseh, and then down at his wound. The soldier then slunk away. He was dead.

Tecumseh turned to face the colonel who now stood alone. In a panic, he pointed his shaking pistol at Tecumseh, and screamed, "Drop your tomahawk savage, or I will fill your belly with lead!"

Tecumseh just stared. Their gazes locked. A smile broke across Tecumseh's face, and before the colonel could fire his shot, Tecumseh dropped, and rolled to his side. The colonel fired wildly, which exploded into the ground where Tecumseh had stood. And with the stealth of a great cat, Tecumseh sprung up, and in that same rising motion threw his tomahawk. It hurdled through the air with a tight whooshing noise . . . and it found its target. The colonel fell to the ground and gasped for air.

Tecumseh reached down and grabbed his large tomahawk from the backside of the other dead soldier. He walked slow to the fallen colonel, and stood over him. "I am Tecumseh. Know this night that we rid the world of two thousand long knives, so they shall never again bring terror upon my people.

"You leave this world now in fear . . . fear of your own death. This is because you think only of yourself as you walk upon Mother Earth. You take from others their lands, and you kill women and children along the way....

"Pray now to your Christian God, and hold to hope in its kindness, for your life's deeds will fall far from your heaven's gates. I think you go only to a burning hell."

The colonel stared back and trembled. He whimpered fear.

Tecumseh kneeled down and took his prize. He slit the colonel's throat. There the colonel lay, alone and cold. A river of warm red poured out over his neck and chest. He struggled for breath among the carnage, and gasped out one last time . . . and a lonely death took him at last. Tecumseh then rose up and rejoined the battle.

Upon the battlefield, Tecumseh saw the Jhagir spring through the lingering musket smoke and over the mob of soldiers and warriors. They hurtled in midair, and landed among the long knives. The paleface soldiers gazed up aghast.

Their silhouettes glowed blue, and their chests lit up with blue and white light. Starlight blades were held in their hands, and a low humming noise they carried. It was a sound of forebode that stirred fear within.

The Jhagir stood together, backs to each other, and faced out against their enemy. Those long knives nearest to them stood in awe, and that was the last moment of their lives. For the Jhagir raised up their whitish blue blades, and struck them down. With the sound of a distant lightning strike, the blades of light ripped through soldier torsos. Body pieces slid apart onto the grassy field.

Other paleface soldiers turned and took aim. They fired in fear, but the Jhagir leapt up in the night's darkness. They landed some twenty paces away upon another line of soldiers. The musket fire instead ripped into the flesh of their comrades, who fell dead. And Gahnoque and Ithikkah brought the same swift death upon more soldiers. Frenzied fear now fell upon all the soldiers. The Jhagir were birthed from the belly of the forest's dark. And now, shrouded by the musket smoke, they were demons from hell that could not be felled. Tecumseh was glad to have the Jhagir at his side.

Now all the American lines began to break, and flee to the woods in a drowning terror. In the scattering, they were engulfed by Shawnee warriors on all sides. And each soldier was slain in a most violent manner. The soldiers begged for mercy. The Shawnee paused with their tomahawks raised up, as if the encircling hawk just before it swoops down upon its prey.

The Shawnee warriors looked into those soldier's souls. They measured their worth . . . and those long knives were found wanting. With vicious thrusts, the warriors drove deep the tomahawk of the people into body and flesh . . . and the paleface soldiers cried no more.

It was no battle - it was a massacre. For every Shawnee warrior that was killed, at least twenty paleface soldiers fell dead. And at its very end, a few stragglers escaped the valley clearing and made their way into the forest. But they found no reprieve from death. The final few were hunted down like dogs, scalped alive, and left to die a slow death for what they had done upon the women and children nights ago.

And each soldier was put to death, save one. Tecumseh wanted the deed of that night, in all its savagery, delivered to the great white fathers by one of their own. That one soldier trembled before the two hundred or so Shawnee warriors that still stood.

Tecumseh eyed the soldier, and stepped to him. "Good fortune is with you this night. Of all your army, you alone still breathe life."

The soldier gaped in shock. He must have never heard an Indian speak English as well as any white man.

Tecumseh asked, "What is it they call you?"

The soldier stammered, "Um . . . um, Thalom . . . Private Thalom."

Tecumseh said, "Thalom, you take breath, but not of your peoples' might . . . it is because we let it be so. You now serve the Shawnee and all the tribes, for you will look into your peoples' eyes. Then they will know you speak the truth.

"We ask America to leave our lands forever, to stay within its own borders so we may all live in peace. Let us live free from the great white father's yoke and collar. If they do this now, the trespasses done upon my people will be forgiven, burying our tomahawks forever in a great peace.

"But hear me now, if the great white fathers do not heed my words, we will bring down the tomahawk. Tell the great white fathers that a long knife army of two thousand was cut down by just three hundred.

"And this will be only the beginning. We will gather such a great host of warriors from all the many tribes of this land, to rise up together. We will come to your towns and cities, and bring death to your people. You tell the great white fathers these are the words of Tecumseh - I am Panther Across the Sky."

The soldier's eyes widened.

Tecumseh smiled and asked, "This is not the first you have heard my name?"

Thalom nodded. "No . . . no sir. There has been much talk. You are a wanted man. Though with all the gossip, I thought you to be seven feet tall and draped in a headdress of eagle feathers, dried scalps, and wrapped in a great buffalo robe."

Tecumseh smiled again. "Well, I am afraid the great white fathers will be gravely disappointed."

Thalom just looked away and sighed. And as he did that, his eyes also captured sight of the Jhagir. Breathless, he now shivered fear and looked wide-eyed back at Tecumseh.

It appeared to all that Tecumseh's message had been well received and would be delivered in good measure. Tecumseh turned, and asked five warriors to escort the soldier to the borders of their lands. He must arrive back to the great white fathers with that most important of messages.

The small group set off at once, and Tecumseh and the others turned their attention to gathering up their dead. They built a great fire upon which to place the dead and send the hundred souls to the Great Spirit. The flames shot high and a warm glow lit up the night, and flickering shadows danced upon the forest's trees.

The Shawnee gathered about, and sat or stood in silence. They bathed deep in gratitude for the sacrifice of the fallen. Someday, they would join them in that journey, but not that day. The living had more tales yet to be told.

A satisfaction settled upon them, like a hot meal that chased away hunger. In some small way, they had done what they could to right a great wrong done upon the people; though none could find sleep as the next day's dawn came quick. And upon its arrival, they began their way back to their own village. And of course, along the way they stopped again at Katayea's village. They performed the same ritual of passing for the dead strewn about. The flames wrapped up the dead and took them on their way to the Great Spirit. They were free.

And as the warriors looked on the dancing flames, Tecumseh saw their spirits were buoyed, for they had done the unthinkable. Never before had such a great army of the long knives been defeated in battle with so few warriors. They shouted that all things were now possible, for Tecumseh was the greatest of chiefs. And the Jhagir stood by his side. Surely, the great white fathers would tremble at word of this great defeat and now heed the message of peace. The warriors' chests heaved with pride and vigor, and hope for the future.

But for Tecumseh, fear and doubt still gnawed at him, despite his victory. And a resounding victory it was . . . it was stunning. They had even secured a large cache of musket shot, gunpowder, wad, and flint. It was the largest single supply of munitions they had ever seen, and it more than replenished their stores. Yet, the same hope of his warriors did not fill his heart. He hated the wolf still, but it was not dead . . . just wounded. Would more have to die before the wolf heeded his message? On that he wondered. He asked the Great Spirit . . . but it did not answer. What would his father Puckshinwa say on that? He could only wonder. Maybe his friend John Sackett would know? Well, no matter, he was alone now and would have to find that wisdom on his own.

Chapter Twelve
Thalom's Message

Thalom's throat was parched. Muscles ached. Sweat dripped and stung open cuts. He would fall over from exhaustion, but for the forceful tugs on the rope he was led by. Through the mountains and valleys the Indians mercilessly dragged him along. His hands were bound tight, the taut line wore away marks upon his flesh. It burned. He was a lonely beast . . . a stray head of cattle being returned to its pen. The warriors walked on in fast silence. They did not look his way. He did not exist.

After many hours, those savages finally stopped for some water and a bit of food, though it was hardly a meal. Just a piece of hardened corn cake, with some wild greens he had never eaten before. Though the sip of cold water down his throat was an oasis, and with something in his belly, his body now ached for rest. But the Indians would have none of it. His rope line tugged hard. They were off again, and blood oozed down his forearms. On and on he was jerked along, until at last in the dark of night, when his throbbing legs could go no more, they laid for sleep. Those Indians offered no kindness. They would prefer to just cut his throat, but they were obliged to the commands of that plain Indian . . . that Tecumseh.

That hell went on for days, until one early morning they walked into an unlooked-for surprise. It was a large army encampment, somewhere in southwestern Pennsylvania. Worry hung upon the Indians' faces. They tugged Thalom close and muzzled his mouth.

Thalom knew straight away what they looked upon. It was Lieutenant Colonel Dandridge and his men. They too were on the prowl for Indian villages. Though the warriors spoke no English, Thalom could see they understood the meaning of the many soldiers below. And many there were, as Thalom knew Dandridge commanded some three thousand muskets. His Indian captors looked nervous, with hushed barks back and forth in their own tongue.

At once, the warriors turned to Thalom. There was no emotion as they cut his binds. He was set loose to the mob of soldiers below. They gave him a push and pointed him in the army's direction. Thalom stumbled forward a bit and looked back. There was just iced stares. Thalom just turned away, and struggled on to the encampment below. His legs strained with each heavy step.

The many soldiers were carefree at leisure. The smell of hearty bacon, sausage, and eggs carried on the air with the early morning sun. Some were shaving. Some gave haircuts to one another, and still others washed clothes.

Thalom called out. He did not want to get shot. Many soldiers turned at once and grabbed their muskets.

As Thalom moved clear into view, one soldier shouted, "Private! What the hell you doin' wanderin the wild by ya self? Don't ya know ther are Injuns bout?"

Another soldier shouted, "Ya know the orders. No movin about lest you be in yer company fool!"

Another soldier shouted snidely, "Maybe he deserted . . . ran out of fear of those savages!"

A chorus of soldiers shouted, "Yeah! Ya some damn deserter? We should just shoot the coward now!"

"Hey. Ain't he wit Dankin's army? Desertin yer post under Colonel Dankins? Ya crazy? He must be the nastiest son of a bitch there is. Wait til he gits hold of ya!" another soldier shouted out.

All the while, Thalom was quiet. He just trudged ahead, until he stood face to face with the mob. Thalom looked about. "There is no longer a worry of Colonel Dankins ... he is dead."

There was just silence.

Thalom went on, "I am no deserter. I am Thalom, last of Dankin's regiment ... there are none left."

Many soldiers gasped, "Wat ya talkin' bout? Dankin had two thousand men, tough as leather. Ya don't mean to say they all perished, but you?"

Thalom just stared back and shook his head.

Some soldiers shouted out nervously, "Wat the hell happened out there? Ain't no Injun village done that."

Desolation filled Thalom, and he spoke in a hushed tone. "In the darkness ... hundreds of Shawnee warriors there were. Led by that Tecumseh and they killed us in the most brutal of ways, save for me."

Those heavy words settled upon the soldiers. Then a soldier asked, "Yer sayin some hundreds of Shawnee kilt yer entire army?"

Thalom nodded.

Another soldier cried out disbelief. "Three hundred ... destroyed two thousand? How could such a thing be?"

Thalom went on, "I have never seen such a crazed look. They said it was because of what we did to a village. Things were done ... to their old, women, and children."

A brooding silence screamed. It was deafening. Emptiness filled the soldiers' faces. One soldier blurted out in defeat, "Maybe that Tecumseh is a different sort of savage after all. Everythin' we heard bout."

Thalom just stared blankly and asked, "Where is Lieutenant Colonel Dandridge? I bring a message." Still silent, the soldiers pointed to his tent. Thalom turned, and headed that way. The soldiers stared disbelief as Thalom walked by.

Thalom heard the stories. Dandridge was a most capable commander, tougher than an iron spike. He was a military man, whose family had played a prominent role in the American Revolution years ago. And ever ambitious he was in seeking a higher military rank, with aspirations of political office someday. He dutifully served with a devotion of the highest regard.

Thalom came upon the tent and a sentry stepped forward. He barked, "State your name, rank, and your business!"

He said, barely above a whisper, "Private Thalom. I come bearing a message from a Shawnee chief."

The sentry was taken aback. He looked at Thalom as if he were a drunk . . . or some crazed fool. He asked Thalom to wait, and disappeared under the tent flap. It was then flung back, and the sentry peeked out. He commanded Thalom to enter.

Thalom stepped inside. Dandridge sat far back at a wooden table, partially hidden in the shadows.

"Private Thalom, are you thirsty after so long a walk through the wilderness?" asked Dandridge. His voice boomed like a cannon. He turned and showed a glass and a bottle of whiskey.

Thalom raised his hand politely. "No thank you sir."

Dandridge replied, "Well, whiskey is not the preferred beverage of the morning, but I should think it appropriate in light of the tale that you have come to tell." The lieutenant colonel poured a half glass of whiskey. He then took a hearty swig and gulped it down. Dandridge then looked back up to Thalom and offered him a seat. Thalom obliged and sat down.

"It is said that you are the lone survivor from the detachment so ably commanded by Colonel Dankins . . . is this true?" asked Dandridge.

Thalom nodded.

"How can this be . . . two thousand so stout, yet decimated to a man?" asked Dandridge in disbelief.

Thalom hesitated for a moment, and then spoke. But he did so with a faraway look in his eyes. "They flew out of the night . . . one so black you could not see your hand upon your face. Three hundred there were, and all the forest dark roared.

"Blood and carnage was everywhere. War cries shrieked. Exploding musket shot lit up the night. And then I saw him through the rising smoke. It was that Shawnee war chief we all hear about, Tecumseh. By his hand, the Shawnee cut us all down that night."

Dandridge drank in every word that Thalom muttered. "Ah yes, Tecumseh; the one who seeks to gather up all the tribes of this continent into a great confederacy. He is a bold one, though now he takes things too far."

Thalom spoke some more, "He let me live so I could bear his message . . . so you would know my words were true."

And Dandridge leaned in and growled, "And just what is Tecumseh's message?"

Like a haunted soul, Thalom replied in a blank whisper. He spoke of Tecumseh's words. The great white fathers must leave these lands. And he spoke of what Tecumseh would do if they did not.

Dandridge bristled. He gruffly blurted out, "Tecumseh is a brash one indeed. Let us see how defiant he is when he looks squarely down the barrel of my pistol."

He turned and faced Thalom. "To have defeated Colonel Dankin's regiment is a grand feat indeed, but it was under the mask of a late night ambush. Surely he does not think he could face down an army, some thousands strong, head-on in an open field of war. Let us test the mettle of these crazed Shawnee when they face a steeled and loaded thousand man line unleashing a storm of musket lead into their ranks!"

But Thalom interrupted. He spoke of the two eight foot tall Indians. The panther-like faces that possessed strange blades of starlight, and death they were upon the battlefield. "They cut us down like a broad scythe swung down upon a field of wheat, which can do nothing but fall before it."

Dandridge held up his halting hand. He turned back to Thalom, his voice filled of disdain. "Private, better you had perished that night than to speak such false tales. Perhaps you are unfit to be a soldier, ill prepared to handle war's terror." Dandridge paused in anger, and then calmly said, "Nonetheless, I would be derelict in my duty in not sending you and your message on to General Harrison."

Dandridge called out for his sentries. Twenty soldiers were to be gathered. They were to escort Thalom to General Harrison's camp at once. He coldly dismissed Thalom, he was done with him.

Before heading out, Thalom turned and asked Dandridge, "Sir, what will you do?"

Dandridge replied with a swagger, "My good Thalom, we will head out in short order. We will hunt Tecumseh down like the dog he is, and when we find him and his pack, we will cut them all down. The Indians have always fallen before our muskets . . . and they always will."

And with that, Thalom nodded a hopeful look toward Dandridge, wishing him well. But that belied his true thoughts. Dandridge had not been there that night, and he knew not what his men went to face. Thalom was thankful that Dandridge was sending him away. He was sure the three thousand before him would soon meet their maker in the days to come . . . at the hands of Panther Across the Sky.

Chapter Thirteen
Fate's Howling Winds

Tecumseh and the Jhagir moved through the throng of villagers, and basked in the warm greetings. Happy lines were upon their faces. The rumors that reached the villagers' ears were true. Word of Tecumseh's great victory had spread on the wings of birds. His legend rose to new heights. He was something more than a man, larger than life. Maybe there was indeed one among them . . . one who could stand up to the great white father's might.

All the villagers wanted to reach out and touch him. Tecumseh had done the unthinkable. Though there were brothers who had fallen, it had been for the most magnificent happening in their lifetimes. It was a great honor to have bled the ground for that victory. The elders could not recall such a great defeat dealt the great white fathers. Surely they would listen to the free peoples now.

Tecumseh and the Jhagir waded their way through to his longhouse. And there stood a most pleasing sight; Taughannock, Nateelah, and Kykuitheh. Nateelah leapt upon Tecumseh, and hugged him tight. Kykuitheh smiled, leaned in, and embraced him too. Taughannock happily grabbed hold of his father and Gahnoque. They then gathered together, alone in a feast of thanks to their good fortune in battle and safe return.

Such feasts were done in all the longhouses of the village that day.

Amid that fine meal, Gahnoque said aloud, "You have sent the great white fathers a strong message, but one that is fair also. Let us hope their hearts are not closed to what you say."

Tecumseh said, "I hold to that hope . . . though I cannot see that far. And the many tribes still stand alone and scattered. The great white fathers know that.

"It has always been the way of things. If only the free peoples would unite . . . then perhaps the great white fathers would kneel to peace at last.

"Do not listen to the happy talk that surrounds the village. The people see only today. They do not look beyond. It will take more than one defeat in battle before they listen to peace."

Nateelah spoke up, "Likely you are right uncle. The great white fathers will not yet be ready to hear the peoples' message. More blood will be spilled before they treat with us as equals. We must somehow break their fist of war . . . but their spirit is unbending like cold hard steel."

As Nateelah's words trailed off, there was a long silence. All settled into a brooding mood.

Tecumseh then replied with a stoned face and hushed tone, "Then there is nothing for it; though steel is unyielding when it is finally made, we have but to apply a great fire to America's very bones. Then we can reshape that steel."

At those words, a hopeful mood emerged. It chased away the darker thoughts. Goodwill was shared. Cups were raised. And they drank down all the warm contentment it offered.

A feeling of peace enveloped Tecumseh's village that day and the days that came after. The deep scars and cuts of war healed upon the body and mind. The village was filled with happy sounds. The people frolicked like songbirds. There was good food, lazy afternoons, and fine company. It buoyed the spirit and rekindled the soul. Even the spirits of Katayea and the survivors of her village were on the mend.

And Tecumseh marveled at that. He spoke of it. Despite the terrible suffering, the people retained a deep well of unforeseen strength. It would spring back, reborn anew, like the lone green-leafed plant taking firm hold and flowering within a sea of jagged hard rock. That thought warmed his heart.

Though his heart then turned colder day by day. His insides began to bluster like a winter storm. He had spoken tough as a warrior chief should, because that was what the people needed to hear. And the village was drunk in its happiness . . . lost in it. But he drowned only in his own fear and doubt. It suffocated him. And he withdrew to himself. How could he apply a great fire to America's bones? He did not know.

Tecumseh was quiet and kept alone for days. That was his way when life's troubles bubbled up and washed upon him. And that water was a raging flood. Even Gahnoque could not bring him peace. After some more days of solitude, Tecumseh told the villagers he must go deep into the forest's belly to seek the Great Spirit's wisdom. The people all nodded. They knew where he was going.

Tecumseh hopped upon his brown and white painted pony, and looked upon Gahnoque and Kykuitheh.

Gahnoque asked Tecumseh, "Why do you leave the village? Where is it that you go?"

Tecumseh just sighed and looked straight ahead in quiet as he sauntered away.

Then Kykuitheh said, "His father's hand is upon him. He goes to speak with John Sackett."

As Tecumseh's pony passed by, Gahnoque said to Kykui-theh, "It is a strange thing that he would find wisdom from one of the very race that burned hatred upon his heart; the very race that seeks to take everything from him . . . and destroy his world."

Kykuitheh nodded slow, "Yes, it is a strange thing. But he sees far. He sees things that others cannot see. And though just flesh and bone, he carries the heaviest of burdens . . . for he carries our future.

"If this white man is a friend to my husband, and brings him some wisdom and a measure of peace . . . then Tecumseh must go to him. And I would ask the Great Spirit to let him find what he searches for."

Gahnoque smiled and nodded. "I will ask the same, for fear and doubt would scar the soul of even the most strong willed ones."

Tecumseh rode slow upon the Sackett's home. It was an old place of comfort. Troubles kneeled to happiness for a moment, as he saw the household still brimmed with life. He called out, "John Sackett! How are you my friend?"

All the Sacketts scurried about. They were happy too. It had been many long months since Tecumseh had seen them last.

Rebecca called out, "Papa, Tecumseh is here!" Her voice was deeper now.

Tecumseh stopped his horse. He hopped down and roped it to a tree. He smiled. "Young Rebecca, you are changed. You are growing into a woman."

She just blushed.

Tecumseh kissed her on the forehead. Mary, Joshua, and Henry also came out to greet him. Smiles, handshakes, and hugs were passed back and forth. And then John Sackett emerged from the square house of shaved wood. He strode to Tecumseh with arms wide, a twinkle in his eyes. They greeted each other in a great bear-hug.

They all then sat for a while, and had warm food to fill the belly. Then Tecumseh and John Sackett sat to speak alone.

"It has been a long time my friend," said John Sackett.

"Too long," said Tecumseh. "How are things on the frontier?"

John Sackett said, "Well, these are dangerous times. There have been raids up and down these lands . . . many white people have died. And some were my friends. There are bands of Indians about . . . and they mean to do bad things.

"They talk of some Shawnee, your people, who are the cruelest of all. It has stirred up a hornet's nest of fear . . . and hate."

Tecumseh nodded stoically. His face and shoulders bent of disappointment and shame.

John Sackett went on, "It was a few days back even, when I had spotted a lone Shawnee warrior on the far hilltop. He just sat there on his pony and stared death upon us. And he was a big man . . . bigger than most. We all grabbed our guns, even Mary and Rebecca, but he never came closer . . . and there was no trouble."

Anger's flame smoldered. Tecumseh knew who John Sackett spoke of, but he would not say his name. Tecumseh hated the wolf . . . even if the wolf looked like him. "Well I am glad no trouble came of it. You are right to be wary. And all of you should not move about these lands without your muskets, or alone."

John Sackett sighed and nodded. "All these raids have the settlers worked up. And it has Congress worked up too. President Madison has had enough, and ordered General Harrison to do something about it. Word is he sent out a large army to ravage Indian villages . . . any villages . . . so they get the message. These raids have to stop."

Harrison. That name Tecumseh would never forget. The young captain, one of the bravest souls he had ever seen in battle, now the great general of the paleface army. Tecumseh wondered, how long before their paths crossed? At the way of things, it would seem to be sooner rather than later, but life had taught him fate was a tricky thing. Fate was never early, or late; it arrived only when it meant to.

Tecumseh nodded, "Yes. I have heard of this army. And this is why I come to speak to you now."

John Sackett smiled and laughed, "Tecumseh, I am no warrior. There is no strategy I could offer someone as you. You are already wiser than most. And I think wise enough to know when to pick your battles. Best thing to do is stay away...."

"Two thousand muskets is the rumor . . . and led by a most ornery fellow, a Colonel Dankins. Best thing you can do is get your people out of their path . . . leave your village if you must."

Tecumseh said, "John Sackett, I do not seek your military wisdom. Not because you are not a warrior. General or not, you are one of the wisest I have ever known. It is because a strategy is no longer needed."

John Sackett's face wrinkled lines of curiosity.

"That two thousand man army has been found . . . and is no more," said Tecumseh.

John Sackett gasped. His eyes blinked disbelief.

"I had three hundred warriors, and we cut them down to a man, save one," said Tecumseh.

"Three hundred defeated two thousand? How can this be?" muttered John Sackett.

"The Great Spirit showed the way. But it was no easy thing, as we lost one-hundred brothers. But it had to be, for the palefaces soldiers were murderers. Always the wolf must kill.

They had already destroyed a Shawnee village and killed many women and children . . . in all manner of cruelty," sighed Tecumseh.

Still in shock, John Sackett just sighed. "So much death, I am sorry to hear of it. These times are more dangerous than I thought."

Tecumseh's back stiffened; he looked deep into his friend's eyes. Tecumseh searched for something. He yearned for John Sackett's words, like a child would to a father. "John Sackett, I do not know where this path will lead. But I must have the strength to do what is right for every day that I walk upon it. I look for wisdom wherever I can so I might do so. And my steps have brought me to you now.

"I saved one soldier of the two thousand, sending him forth with a message for the great white fathers; a message of our deed and of peace.

"What say you? Will the great white fathers listen? Can the trespasses and wrongs of the past be forgiven, so that all may live in peace? Now having a fear of its own death, will the wolf at last give way to peace?"

John Sackett leaned back and sighed. Tecumseh knew he was somehow like a son to John Sackett, and a father never wants to disappoint a child. But there were no easy answers. "My heart tells me the Congress and President Madison will not listen to the words of your messenger, for his words will be beyond belief. So there will be more soldiers sent out before the end...."

Heavy silence sat upon those two kindred spirits. They both knew what that meant. Great disappointment filled Tecumseh's insides. His face shook slightly from side to side in defeat and forebode. "So many more long knives must die . . . and with them my people, before the great white fathers will listen to peace. My heart cries tears of blood.

"I guess my father was right. He said the wolf will always be a wolf. I was hoping he was wrong . . . but I guess a father never is...."

John Sackett smiled low and put his hand upon Tecumseh's shoulder.

And Tecumseh asked, "But if a father is never wrong, he told me to not hate the wolf. How can I not hate the wolf? And how can I not hate the great white fathers?"

John Sackett nodded and took a deep breath. "Tecumseh . . . if I had all the world's wisdom, I would surely share it with you now. But my heart tells me there are some things even a father's wisdom cannot see.

"I do not know what is to come, but I fear dark days are coming. And it will be more important than ever for a friend to help a friend, and to show kindness for the good-hearted among us.

"From all you have told me, your father was a very wise man. Perhaps together, we will find what you seek. Perhaps one day we will find your father was the wisest of us all...."

Tecumseh sighed and bowed to John Sackett. Soon after, Tecumseh gathered up his things and departed, until next time. And with everything going on, they both hoped there would be a next time. Tecumseh and his pony sauntered away into the horizon, and the bond of friendship had been woven ever tighter. It was now a tightly wound chord of rope that could never be severed.

John Sackett had become more than a friend. Over the years, Tecumseh had grown to love that man and his family. And always he wrestled with that. He hated the palefaces, yet he had come to love a white family. What a strange thing. His own people could never quite understand that truth. Yet, the truth it was.

Always, Tecumseh had felt his father's hand guiding him . . . pushing him. Whatever it was that Tecumseh was searching for, Puckshinwa seemed to think John Sackett had the answer. Tecumseh always wondered how a white man could hold the wisdom he sought? Over and over in his mind, Tecumseh fought angrily with his father's words to not hate the wolf. It was not possible. There was nothing to do, but hate it.

Why would his father push him to search for something that could not be found? Sometimes he cursed his father's dying words. He wished he had never heard them . . . to be free of the burden of finding their true meaning. So onward through the dark forest, back to the village he went. He was a lonely man on a lonely pony, taking one long step after another, seemingly on a journey with no end.

One early morning, Tecumseh and his pony emerged from the forest. He had returned. And the people were glad to see him. The happy spirits of the village still filled the air, as if he had never left. Later that afternoon, Gahnoque and Ithikkah approached Tecumseh as he sat alone along the riverbank.

Gahnoque smiled and asked, "May we sit with you? We seek your wisdom?"

Tecumseh turned and nodded softly. He gestured for them to sit. For a moment, they gazed upon their rippling reflection. It stared back as the slow moving water went by.

Gahnoque spoke, though he gazed still on the flowing water. "My brother, many days ago I talked of my grand idea . . . the shining light of possibility; about seeking a fourth Ithreal stone."

Tecumseh looked to his friend, and lightly nodded.

Gahnoque went on, "Ithikkah and I have talked on it. We now must make this journey, while you await word on Thalom's message. What would you speak on this?"

Tecumseh smiled, "Well, I am glad you find me filled with such wisdom . . . though these days, I am not so sure," to which all three sighed.

Tecumseh's face then hardened. "This is a journey that would be most unwise to not follow. For its hidden treasure may provide the Jhagir the most precious of gifts . . . the gift of your world and the return to your people.

"I bid you take this path, for we are all in wonder of where it may lead. My heart tells me you will find what you seek . . . and it will bear something great for you, and may even for us free peoples all."

Gahnoque and Ithikkah smiled at Tecumseh's happy words. They each clasped hands.

Tecumseh said, "You should go at once. Young Tataeka will show you the way, for he was there those many nights ago. Do not be deceived, for though the lines of age do not yet mark his face, he is a most able guide and swift of foot.

"But I think it best to depart the village in the dark. Your journey will stir worry in that you may not return."

The Jhagir nodded. And with that, the three enjoyed what was left of the summer afternoon.

As dusk descended, the three arose and returned to their longhouse. Gahnoque and Ithikkah gathered up what they would need for the journey. Taughannock, Nateelah, and Kykuitheh were told of it and they all heartily approved. Within moments, Tataeka had arrived. After some quiet words and quick embraces, the party of three slipped away in the darkness. The winds of fate were blowing again.

And the next day, fate's wind howled once more into the village. It was an ill wind. The five warriors had finally returned, and that Thalom was not among them. The villagers greeted them happily upon their arrival, but the returned warriors did not stop for any idle chat. Tecumseh had sent them forth to bear a great message for America . . . and they now returned with a great message of their own.

Commotion approached Tecumseh's longhouse, and then the faces of the five warriors appeared. They walked brisk. Tecumseh said, "Now we shall see what the great white fathers say."

Tecumseh offered them a seat. The warriors sat still and quiet.

Tecumseh asked, "Was the soldier given to the great white fathers?"

The warriors each nodded, and one spoke up, "He was left unspoiled, to a large army camp in southwestern Pennsylvania, some two week's journey by swift foot and hidden trails. They took him in."

At once, Tecumseh stiffened. Concern lined his face. "It pleases me to hear this. But a large camp you say . . . and only a two weeks journey?"

The warrior said, "The camp numbered some three thousand soldiers, and fully armed they were. It will be on the move . . . and soon will be in Ohio country. It could be upon other Shawnee villages and even this village in days." The warrior's head then bowed low. "It is why we traveled in great haste . . . America is coming."

As those words fell upon his ears, Tecumseh stood. Forebode stretched upon his face. Troubling looks of alarm stared back at him. He gazed about for a moment and spoke slow, "So the wolves of America come forth, growling with fangs bared. And they may soon be at our door. The great white fathers seek to raze the free peoples from these lands, for never before have they sent out two such large armies to roam the wild.

"Well let them fight not our women and children, but the peoples' warriors. A large war party must be gathered in all haste. Send word for all those that are able, for we will need many tomahawks."

Taughannock stood and declared, "Tecumseh, I am now mostly recovered. I will go with you to meet the palefaces in battle."

Tecumseh bowed to Taughannock. He accepted his offer, for he had seen what the Jhagir could do in battle. And they would need all the help they could muster. He said, "It is most unfortunate that Gahnoque and Ithikkah are away on their journey. But no matter . . ."

He motioned to the few warriors nearby. In quiet, he told them they must serve the people one more time. They must take into the wild and look to the place of the crash that dark night so many moons ago, for that was where Gahnoque and Ithikkah had gone.

The warriors each bowed to Tecumseh, and in silence departed.

As Tecumseh's call spread throughout the village, and those villages nearby, the people were anxious to bear witness to the gathering of warriors. By nightfall of the fifth day, the warriors must go forth into the wilderness, in whatever strength they had. The army of long knives must be found.

And as the warriors came, the villagers could see that of the Jhagir, only Taughannock stood before them. Gahnoque and Ithikkah were gone. Whispers of their departure spread about the village. Tecumseh saw the peoples' faces, and he heard their words. It raised fear and doubt, as they had heard tales of their exploits in battle. The people had come to feel that the arrival of the Jhagir had been a mighty gift indeed, a gift from the Great Spirit in their hour of descending darkness and America's wolves.

But now at that moment of utmost need, and their gift departed, their hearts began to tremble. Uneasy fear grew of their coming ruin. It ate away at their minds and devoured their good spirits. Though Tecumseh was a mighty warrior chief, it was a weight that he could not bear alone without his Jhagir brothers. The peoples' hope was fading.

At the coming nightfall of the fifth day, Tecumseh gazed at the gathered warrior throng. He counted some seven hundred, as all the village and those villages nearby were emptied out. And they all looked to him now. His heart fluttered. Palms were sweaty. The air was thick and hard to breath. The weight of the world was upon him. He breathed in deep and stepped forward alone, like a great ship that broke against the waves and rain of a driving storm at sea.

Tecumseh calmly spoke, his voice firm, "I see before me a mighty people . . . a people standing together, giving us the strength to meet our foe. Now the hour is dark, and I can see the dread that would take us all as America approaches our door."

Silence lingered for a moment. He savored the quiet before he went on, "I know the fear that grows within you, for it also swells my heart. We all wonder where our new brothers have gone. Where is Gahnoque? Where is Ithikkah? Have they deserted us for there can be no victory against America's coming?"

Tecumseh simmered some more in silence. He looked out at the people and then said in a raised voice, "I will tell you that it is not so. Our adopted brothers have not deserted us to the winds of fate. They have undertaken a most necessary journey.

"They search for something of great value. Something they brought with them from the stars . . . something that may change the fortunes of all. And once the journey is made, they will return; though they may not return before war is upon us."

Tecumseh paused again. His heavy words sank upon the peoples' hearts.

He continued, "But America comes for us. And we will not turn, we will not back down. We will stare back at this terror, striking it down with our love. The love we hold for each other and the Great Spirit of life that flows through all things."

Tecumseh lingered for a moment more. He looked again about the people, and he could see hope and defiance rising. "And together, we will rise up to face this evil . . . and we will defeat it!"

The people erupted in bursting cheers. Clenched fists rose up. Faith washed away the bleak doubt that had enshrouded them only moments ago. The people had needed Tecumseh's words. They needed to believe . . . even if he did not believe it himself.

Tecumseh asked two hundred warriors to stay behind. Scouts were posted in the wild to stand watch, to protect the village. If the long knives found the village while Tecumseh was away, the people must be ready to flee in a moment's notice.

Tecumseh said, "So large a host, at some three thousand soldiers . . . it should make such a rustle in their coming through the wild, like a herd of buffalo." At those words, another cheer rose up.

Tecumseh then leaned close to a few warriors, and bid them to head out at once. They were to warn those villages that had not come.

Early dusk approached. And Tecumseh, Taughannock, and some five hundred armed brothers departed the village on foot. Into the wild they went. The many warriors were drunk with hope and defiance. Tecumseh just sighed. Five hundred against three thousand . . . it did not fill his belly with fire. Unlike his warriors, he could not see the coming victory. Could he defeat another large paleface army? He sighed again. With each lonely breath, there was only fear and doubt.

As the warriors passed by and out of sight, Tecumseh saw Taughannock glance back to Nateelah. The young Jhagir's fierce eyes hugged her close. Each nodded to the other. Though the winds of fate were howling, and for what would come, Tecumseh knew even the wisest could not say.

Chapter Fourteen
Brothers in Need

Tecumseh prowled. He stalked that paleface army. Crisp air stung the lungs in shallow breaths, at a steady rhythm. Light footsteps floated across the forest floor. A wave of warriors went by. On and on they went, for almost a week. Until late one evening as dusk fell, the Shawnee came upon something ahead. They cleared the hill's crest and smoke rose. Thick and dark black it was, with wisps of gray billowy plumes blown up and about the trees by a soft wind that howled. They slowed and moved in.

And as they did, it was plain to see. It was no enemy, but only the destruction left in its wake; the bones of another Shawnee village, bereft of all life. Devastation and ruin again encircled them. Lifeless and charred bodies lay strewn about as they smoldered. Freshly spilled blood stained the ground a deep dark red. And it sank in . . . that village was laid waste in the early morning of that very day.

And at that vision, something else smoldered. Anger beyond words rose up again in Tecumseh. It burned red hot. And Tecumseh saw the emptiness upon Taughannock's face. He looked to Tecumseh and said, "You spoke of the palefaces' malice, but your words could not prepare my eyes for such a thing. Burned flesh and broken bones of those so young and old . . . it makes my soul cry."

A hushed quiet came across all the Shawnee warriors. In unison, they bowed heads. Tecumseh hoped the kindness of the spirit world found those departed souls swift and true.

He then called out, "Let us follow the long knives from this place."

The tracks of three thousand soldiers left a trampled map upon the ground, to which a child could follow. And the map pointed north. At Tecumseh's signal, the war party headed out.

The air breathed of vengeance. Their rage smoldered and drove them in great speed, faster than before. Under the cloak of dark, onward into the valleys and forests they ran. They were relentless. The glint of sharp-edged tomahawks and long musket barrels shined in the pale moonlight. In faded moonlit shadows, an endless mass of tattooed flesh moved by on paths darkened by the forest's towering trees. They stopped for nothing . . . and then that moment arrived.

The sunrise was not far off as they came upon hundreds of campfires in the distance. They had found their foe. The warriors halted and moved in slow for a closer view. Though unless Tecumseh's eyes were deceived, there were maybe only two thousand soldiers before him. He wondered aloud why his warriors had guessed there was some thousand more. For that army was no larger than the one the Shawnee had already destroyed. His chest heaved with hope. Tecumseh was eager to begin, as surprise was with them. They might somehow find victory yet.

The long knives rested, unaware at their impending doom. Tecumseh would do the same as he had done to Colonel Dankin's army. And this time, it would be easier, as he had not three but five hundred warriors. But the dawn would soon come, so there was no time to surround the camp from all sides, as they had done to Dankin's soldiers. No, if they were to attack that night, the Shawnee must strike now, while the fading dark remained. And those soldiers looked ripe for the taking, drunk with fatigue. They would be unprepared for a war rush. Though most curious, there was not a single scout watching the camp's rear.

The word was passed among the warriors. Muskets were cocked, muscles coiled tight. And in the waning darkness, it began. The Shawnee moved close and stood at the forest's edge, arrayed in two lines of two hundred fifty strong. One behind the other they were, to launch volleys of musket fire into the long knives. They would decimate their foe, before sweeping upon them with tomahawks of fury. The Shawnee would have their vengeance.

One last moment of quiet was breathed in. The last savored hush before the plunging storm. They exhaled . . . it was time. Tecumseh unleashed a raging yell, which was followed by a rising roar of all the warriors. Its thunder beat upon the chest and stirred the forest's night. Animals and beasts scurried for cover. The soldiers scrambled to alarm. But it was too late. The Shawnee let loose their musket fire that ripped into the soldier throng. Flesh and blood splattered in all directions. About one hundred fifty soldiers fell, their bodies riddled with gunshot. The Shawnees' aim was true that night.

The second Shawnee line moved to the front. They stepped through the musket smoke that hung in the air and took aim. Another volley of death let loose. The forest to the army's rear again exploded in a cascade of musket crack and fire, and smoke blew about the dark. A barrage of lead engulfed the soldiers and dropped another one hundred fifty or so in death. The warriors then rushed their dazed foe with abandon. They ran far out into the clearing and were within fifty paces, with tomahawks and war clubs raised. Blood curdling screams and shrieks pierced the night.

But at that moment an officer yelled out, his stern voice boomed in the dark. The left side of the forest came alive. It lit up with hundreds of flashes of musket shot. The hot musket balls screamed toward the Shawnee. The thick night air was shattered again by flesh that exploded and leaden balls that whizzed by everywhere.

And though he stood in mayhem's midst, fate's hand spared Tecumseh. The breeze of lead blew upon him, but he was untouched. Tecumseh turned and looked on in desperation, for warriors all about him fell. The plain truth smashed upon him, as if a mighty axe upon a decrepit old tree that shattered wood. They had rushed into a trap. He had failed his brothers. About two hundred warriors fell away to death. And just like that, Tecumseh's mighty force was cut almost in two.

He guessed it to be about five hundred shots from the left side of the forest. His warriors had indeed been correct when they spoke of some three thousand soldiers before. His grievous mistake had cost the lives of many Shawnee. It was a mighty blow. His confidence was shaken. A breathless doubt consumed Tecumseh, as he felt so small . . . something far from a legend.

His mind raced in a fever, and searched for some way out . . . some escape. His mind clawed to break free from that certain death. He then guessed the other five hundred soldiers to be hidden to the clearing's right, ready to unleash more lead into his warrior lines. He stopped and screamed, "Drop now, for another volley of death comes for us!"

And so they did. The message reached the ears of many, and not a moment too soon. The forest to the clearing's right erupted in musket fire. A storm of musket lead whizzed over their heads and shattered the air about them. They gripped tight to the grass beneath them, and mean hisses flew by. Most did not find Shawnee flesh, as only twenty warriors at most were cut down. Much of the musket fire flew straight across the clearing, into the long knives hidden across the way. Tecumseh had greatly reduced the second volley's bite. The panther was ever elusive in the wild, and perhaps they would somehow survive death's trap.

Tecumseh sprang to his feet. He cried out to the two hundred eighty warriors that still took breath, "To the long knives! We cannot now turn back!"

Tecumseh was sure that each side of the forest filled with five hundred soldiers would now close in behind. His warriors would be encircled, as the long knives tightened death's noose. Their only hope now of seeing the dawn was to break an opening through the paleface army before them. And that would be no small task, for there were some fifteen hundred paleface soldiers. It looked like a black sea. The soldiers' blue jackets were black in the night, and their bayonets glistened in the moonlight. Survival would now depend on fierce warrior hearts and ferocious tomahawks.

Waves of fear smashed upon Tecumseh. He trembled, even after all those years. But he would not turn away. He gritted his teeth, flexed his gut. His mind flashed back to the crazed young buck of his youth. He would drive his antlers in deep and thrash wildly about. And he still hated the wolf. Tecumseh screamed out and charged into the dark sea of long knives. His warriors yelled out too and rushed forward with him.

Bayonet steel met Shawnee flesh, and was driven deep to the bone. But many avoided the thrusting lunges of the long knives. The Shawnee reared up and swung down their tomahawks and war clubs viciously into the blue jackets. Death was up close and personal. It was filth and dirt. Tecumseh saw the whites of his enemy's eyes, the sweat upon their brow, and paleface blood was splattered upon him. Heads were lopped off, limbs severed, chests ripped apart, and faces split in two.

And across the advancing line, about one hundred paces to his right, Tecumseh glimpsed Taughannock. The Jhagir launched into their foe and unleashed rage. His chest harness blazed of light, and surrounded him in a blue glow of moonlight. He held a blade of light in one hand and a starlight tomahawk-like weapon in the other. The fearsome weapon protruded jagged teeth like a great bear claw. Taughannock's angry eyes blazed aglow with blue flames. He was the hand of death.

The night air blew icy cold with fear. It stole the long knives' breath, as they gasped at his sight. Four soldiers stood just a few paces away, and stared in shock at his full vision. And it was the last thing they would see, for he jumped into the air, spun, twisted, and landed just behind them. In one fell motion, he swung down his lit blade and sliced one soldier quickly in two. A bursting sound of a distant lightning strike echoed. He then spun to his side, and swung around. As he did, his lit blade shifted and now shined forth from the bottom of its hilt, and he drove it deep into the chest of another soldier.

The other two on-looking soldiers snapped from their awe, and pointed their pistols at Taughannock. He glanced up and left the stuck blade in his victim, its handle protruded from the chest; and he apparated into black mist. The desperate pistols fired and found flesh, but only of their fellow soldiers. A black cloud then appeared behind the soldiers. Taughannock stepped forth and swung his tomahawk-like weapon into the backside of one soldier. The Jhagir kicked him down, and swung the loose tomahawk upward in a mighty blow into the other. With a lightning strike, it severed clean the soldier's head. The blow sent it flying some twenty-five paces in the air.

A great terror now began to grip those soldiers that bore witness to that ghostly Indian. He was death . . . and he now came for them. The terror began to spread among the ranks. Many were felled before Taughannock's might. But the sheer number of soldiers was still so great that many warriors were also killed as the battle raged.

And slow and sure, it began to turn ill for Tecumseh and his cause. Those Shawnee that still fought became fewer and fewer still. They were encircled on all sides by a drowning sea of blue jackets. Bayonet steel smiled death upon the Shawnee.

And though they were ferocious, taking many of the palefaces with them, there were just too many. With enough arrows, even the great grizzly could be brought down. And at last, the great size of America's army began to bear down in all its might, like a great wheel of stone that ground down a husk of corn into a fine grain of meal.

After a few moments more, there were but one hundred Shawnee warriors that still stood, surrounded yet by a black sea of some eighteen hundred strong. Through the din and smoke, Tecumseh at last saw the army's commander, who could taste his sweet victory. It would be soon now. In excitement, he urged his men on for the final telling blow. "Forward men; bring death to these savages - one and all! For God and country - victory is ours this night!"

The Shawnee now fought with an utter despair against such overwhelming might, as if a cornered beast in the wild. But still more of the Shawnee found their death on that field. Their numbers fell even more, to about fifty warriors who still faced about fifteen hundred long knives. And those long knives were hell bent only for the final destruction of the Shawnee horde.

Time stood still, with the clamored din of war seeming to echo from some far off field. Tecumseh, now bleeding a bit and dazed, took in the full measure of death that rose before him. There was the commander now, who sat atop his mighty steed but fifty paces away, and yelled vicious orders to his troops. In return, the commander caught sight of Tecumseh at last.

He stared down in arrogance at Tecumseh. His great victory was imminent. Tecumseh knew the paleface officer could taste it, he could smell it on the air. In glee, the officer raised his war saber and pointed out Tecumseh to his men, "Take the life of that heathen Indian there, and bring me his cut-off head!"

Everything swirled slow like a sleepy dream. And Tecumseh took it all in. A barren gloom and sadness carried on the wind and closed in around him. Death called out and whispered his name. He did not see that coming this day. But it was here. He and those with him had come to their life's end at long last . . . their days in the sweet Ohio Valley would be no more.

A great anguish washed upon Tecumseh, for the peoples' freedom was dying on that field. He reeled in a cold empty despair, and turned to his father's dying words. He had let his father down mightily . . . he could not lead the people to their freedom.

And as those dark thoughts flooded his mind, all hope faded. He looked the last on the first flicker of the new day's sun that rose. The last darkness of night was chased away. Dawn had come. The sunlight shot through the thick forest trees, over the crest of the nearby sloped hill, and into the eyes of the onrushing soldiers. It blinded them and halted their rush for a moment. The commander's horse reared up too.

All the field now turned to face the rising sun. It had never seemed so bright. Forearms were raised to block the light, and eyes strained to see what stood before them. And there it was - two shadowy silhouettes cast down from the hill's crest through the hanging musket smoke and early morning mist. At once, what was hidden and unseen, stepped forth. In that moment, before the drowning flood of paleface might down upon Tecumseh, he saw a most beloved sight . . . it was Gahnoque and Ithikkah!

The most needed aid of his Jhagir brothers had come - and with that, hope's fiery flame was relit. And it burned bright within Tecumseh and all the Shawnee.

The Jhagir's arrival had the most opposite of effects upon the army of America; for now before them stood two more of those large and strange colored Indians. Tecumseh heard the paleface soldiers' gasps. They yelled out that those things favored some great beast that had come forth from the forest and sprouted limbs. And they were possessed of supernatural gifts, so mighty as bearers of ruin and the world's end. There was a surging panic among the soldiers, and despite their still overwhelming numbers, many began to flee.

In his fury, the commanding officer screamed out, "Cowards! No one retreats under my command!" He fired his pistol in disgust at a fleeing soldier who ran by him. The soldier tumbled over to death; but that did not have its desired effect. Upon seeing their commander shoot down one of their own in the back, two soldiers raised up their muskets. They took firm aim, but not at their enemy, instead it was straight upon their commanding officer.

The commander wheeled his horse about. His steely eyes stared arrogance upon them. And as he did, the muskets rang out. One musket ball hissed through the air, and pierced straight through the hat upon his head. It ripped a hole clear through the hat's peak. Had the shot been but a bit lower, his skull would have been torn apart. And the other musket ball screamed toward him, but missed his upper thigh. Instead, it tore into the shoulder flank of his steed. The horse reared up in pain and bucked the officer to the ground. It galloped off wildly.

He sat alone upon the battlefield, bruised and dazed. Many soldiers fled by him in terror. And Tecumseh's insides smiled at the sight. He knew fate was a fickle thing. Glory was slipping through America's outstretched fingers, like the falling of clutched sand. For in that moment, the Jhagir in the distance disappeared into a black mist and reappeared within the midst of the warring soldiers.

With their backs to one another, Gahnoque and Ithikkah stood alongside Tecumseh, Taughannock, and those Shawnee that still breathed life. They were like some haunted ghosts brought forth from the Shawnee spirit world, possessed of mighty weapons of light, and they rained death upon the long knives.

They moved like the wind, and apparated here and there, and slashed long knives with brutal ferocity. Torsos were cleaved in two, with the cracks of lightning and the low rhythmic hum to which those weapons danced. Soldiers buckled to the ground, gasped their final straining breaths, and painted the field red with their blood.

Blue-jacketed bodies were littered all about, and more fell in all manners of fatal injury and wounds. Try as the desperate soldiers might, they could not pierce those shifting, dodging, and ghostly beings, with either musket lead or blade. Tecumseh saw the utter dismay upon the soldiers' faces at fighting a foe so deadly.

And for those hundreds of fleeing soldiers, seeing their hoped-for escape from that terror so close in the nearby forest, they went instead to their doom. They headed for the woods opposite from where Tecumseh's warriors had charged forth. But out stepped some two hundred Shawnee warriors new to the battle, like some ghosts stepped out of time. And while they still took breath, Panther Across the Sky would not stand alone.

They were painted for war, with tomahawks drawn, and a savage fury. They saw what the great white fathers' army had done to their Shawnee brothers on that field. The forest now closed in on the fleeing soldiers. A Shawnee chief stepped forward, raised his tomahawk, and let loose a furious war cry. And a great roar of the warriors with him rose up to the valley peak like thunder upon the mountain.

It lifted the spirits of Tecumseh and his few standing warriors higher still; while desolation overtook the faces of the blue-jacketed army. Their chests heaved and shoulders sagged. Those two hundred Shawnee warriors rushed madly into the sea of fleeing soldiers, and the hard stone of their tomahawks was soon drenched in blood. Limbs were hewn about the field, as if chopped wood from a tree that would soon fuel a flaming fire. The soldiers were all cut down to the last.

Death had come for the paleface army. Tecumseh yelled to leave none alive, as the darkest part of his heart throbbed of vengeance. And then Tecumseh saw the commanding officer hidden among the slaughter, some fifty paces away. He looked back at Tecumseh. The officer struggled to his feet and eyed his escape to the forest.

At once, Tecumseh rushed to him. He jumped over dead bodies in a single bound and launched his tomahawk through the air. It whooshed in rhythm as it flew . . . and then with a loud thud, it found its mark. The tomahawk embedded itself deep within the officer's back and he fell to his side and writhed in agony.

Tecumseh strode slow up to the fallen officer, who crawled still for the forest. Tecumseh's voice dripped disgust, "Leaving so soon? For one who sits so mighty upon your steed in battle . . . are you not a great warrior chief of the paleface army?"

The officer made no reply.

Tecumseh shook his head and went on, "It is so easy to send others to their death, as you sit safely to the rear. Even now at your end, you think only of yourself, leaving your soldiers alone in their hour of utmost need.

"And this is why your heart is filled with fear . . . fear of your death."

Tecumseh glared and stood over the officer, and then leaned in with a low growl, "Know that the Shawnee take the life of every paleface on this field. Panther Across the Sky has hunted you down and now cuts your beating heart from this world."

Tecumseh took out his blade, severed deep into the officer's chest, and cut out his heart. He stepped one raised leg upon the officer's chest and held the still beating heart aloft. He glanced down at the officer once more, who gasped back in fear. Then the light slowly ebbed from his eyes. He was no more. Tecumseh stretched the heart high, so all could see, and screamed defiance. The Shawnee and Jhagir scattered about the field looked back to Tecumseh. They raised their arms in victory and shouted back with wild vigor.

But it was hard won, paid for with many lives. Of the five hundred that had come, only thirty still lived. The living spent the rest of that day gathering the dead and building a large fire so the fallen may be set free to the Great Spirit.

No such respect was given their enemy. The dead long knives were left to rot where they lay . . . except for the commanding officer. He was beheaded. His head was placed upon a wooden spear to mark the field in warning to all other palefaces that may come that way. For any that should pass - they should go back from where they came; or else they would know what fate awaited them.

As the great fire burned, Tecumseh made his way over to a face from the past. It was his old friend, Otsaga. As young boys, they sometimes played carefree in the meadows of those lands. It was Otsaga who was the chief from the Shawnee village of northern Ohio who had heeded Tecumseh's call for aid on notice so short. It was Otsaga and his warriors who had struck the decisive blow to America's escape, and ensured the final decimation of the paleface army.

The two Shawnee chiefs, now much older and wiser to the ways of the world, clasped hands. A warm embrace was shared in the happiness you would expect of two lifelong friends, whose paths would occasionally cross in the comings and goings of life.

And Otsaga's eyes fell upon the three strange beings standing near to Tecumseh. He asked, "From what clan do these blackened ones come? Is it from some tribe far to the north in Upper Canada, where the cold air grows them tall, shapes their looks, and colors their skin so?"

Tecumseh replied, "No, these ones here have traveled a great distance much farther than that. They are blood brothers of the Shawnee, and call my village home. They are not of this world and come from the stars, though not by their will, and are lost to their own people. They are the Jhagir, and this is Gahnoque, Ithikkah, and Taughannock," as Tecumseh pointed out each.

The three Jhagir bowed slow.

And Otsaga returned the gesture, with wonder in his eyes.

Tecumseh went on, "In their short time among the people, they have proven their honor and strength beyond words. The Shawnee could find no better friend than the Jhagir. I trust them with my life."

A reassuring smile crept along Otsaga's face as he looked into the faces of the three Jhagir. "If Tecumseh can say no less of you, then I need hear no more. You are forever marked as a friend to me and my clan."

And with that, nods of friendship were had among all.

Tecumseh then said, "Let us go now in peace and return to our villages to share word of this battle. Let us comfort those families in mourning and honor their loved ones lost."

Tecumseh turned to Otsaga, "Go now in peace my friend. Savor this victory for a day, but then send out word to all the people of the north. We must be at the ready to gather up as many warriors as can be had should we face a coming storm. I fear dark and blackened clouds brood to the east.

"And if need be, I will send out word for us to meet in a great gathering of all who can come. We shall meet in the valley of the falls by the ruins, home to the long since passed ancients of old."

And with that, the old friends departed and returned to their villages with warriors in tow.

As Tecumseh walked on, his thoughts turned solemn. The sadness of it all settled upon him. Though the battle's victors, the Shawnee people had paid a heavy price indeed, as some four hundred seventy warriors were lost. It was a bad dream. Tecumseh had never led so many warriors to their death before. And those lost warriors were not some faceless paid soldiers like the palefaces, but were known among all, be they fathers, brothers . . . and sons.

There was a deep grief. There was no comfort he could provide the loved ones of those lost upon returning to the village. Families would be waiting with open hearts, but the fallen would not return.

For the second time now, Tecumseh had defeated the largest army of long knives ever known . . . but at what cost? Perhaps the cost of freedom was too much to bear. It did not feel the way a victory was supposed to feel. And he wondered, would the great defeat mean anything to the paleface nation? Would they now listen to peace? The great wolf was now surely wounded . . . more so than it had ever been before. Or would the wolf always be a wolf? Tecumseh hoped with all his heart that his father was wrong. But he could only wait now to hear word from the great white fathers. Perhaps fate was ready . . . perhaps the time had come and Tecumseh would meet the great General Harrison at last.

Chapter Fifteen
Victory's Many Tales

Tecumseh sighed. Muscles burned and ached. Shoulders sagged. He had never known such fatigue. Each step was heavier than the last. But his heart was heavier still, as it was washed in the loss of his many brothers. He had led them to their death. And it was something he could not forgive . . . or forget. The surviving band of warriors were weary in body and spirit from battle's horrors, and headed home one slow step after another.

After some three and a half weeks, they came upon their village at last. Shouts rang out and announced their return. Tecumseh saw the shock upon the gathering people. His straggling band must have looked like they returned in defeat. But some of his warriors shouted out their victory. And many gasps cried out. So many there were that did not return. The people looked on in silence. Most all the warriors were dead and gone, never to return.

The warriors walked through the village slow, drowned in somber quiet. Loved ones came forward here and there to greet their sons, fathers, and brothers as the warriors passed by. Where were they? They called out . . . but there was no reply. Tears welled up, and some began to wail. The loss of life was too great; there was no jubilation for Tecumseh's grand victory.

The greatest ever recorded against the great white fathers. Those left behind could look now only to their memories.

As Tecumseh and the Jhagir arrived at their longhouse, Nateelah rushed out. She hugged Taughannock and bowled him over. No words were needed. And Taughannock returned the same ferocious affection to her. Tears of joy escaped and rolled down her cheeks.

Kykuitheh also came forward and hugged Tecumseh tight, stretched with all of herself. She looked around and said, "So few there are to return . . . so many that follow Tecumseh no more. So many of our people . . . we will never look upon them again.

"Yet, this is the way of things . . . for how else can we hold back the great white fathers' hatred." A faraway look painted Kykuitheh's face. She sighed and all nodded back to her.

Later that night, many fires were lit about the village, as they all sat together in a heavy quiet. Burning heat warmed their faces, as they stared deep into the dancing glow of yellow and orange. They searched for visions of the fallen that rode the rising flames ever higher into the night stars above, up into the open arms of the Great Spirit.

That night there was only the sound of silence and the beating of drums. Low and slow, the pounding rhythm echoed into the forest dark.

As the dawn broke, there remained a somber feeling still among many. But through the grief, the reality of the great victory began to slowly sink in for some, as they bathed in the truth that the Shawnee had defeated three thousand long knives. And that sparked a hope for some of the people. Could the tides of battle be turning for the Shawnee? Never before had the Shawnee known such a victory against the new nation of America so mighty. Surely now, the great white fathers would bargain for peace.

And though the words had been said many times before in defiance and fury, only now did it begin to take a foothold within their hearts. Maybe they could rise up and defeat the paleface invaders . . . maybe they could keep their homelands free.

But as the tales of battle were recounted, rumors began to float about the village. Some said that though Tecumseh led the warriors into battle, it was not he, but Gahnoque who led the Shawnee to victory. Perhaps those rumors were given breath from somewhere in the deep and dark places of the loved ones' hearts of the fallen. Tecumseh saw the many faces. Their hearts festered in envy and anger while they watched other families embrace in joy.

And so great the losses were, the pain ran deep for many. The ground beneath their feet was ripped apart into an impassable river gorge, dead of all life. And with each passing day, the dark chasm only grew. That feeling took full life and boiled over, as anger hardened to stone. It was Gahnoque who borne hopeless victory from certain defeat. Many said mighty Gahnoque should be made a great chief of the Shawnee, to lead the people.

But many surviving warriors were angered at such talk, for they were there. It was Tecumseh who led them bravely, who bought precious time until the arrival so late of Gahnoque and Ithikkah to battle. It was Tecumseh who, after granting the Jhagir's request to search for a lost stone of light, had sent a message most urgent for their aid. He had no choice but to march out at once to meet the marauding horde of death before it fell upon Shawnee village after village. And in ambush, it was Tecumseh's cunning that allowed the war party to survive the initial musket volley. It was Tecumseh who avoided annihilation at the battle outset from a trap most well laid.

Many warriors felt quite strong in that way, though there were some that did cling to the rumors. And the harmony of the village began to decay and tatter over the coming days. As the fervor grew, a storm brewed that threatened to tear the people apart.

Though efforts were made to remain civil, emotions stirred and divisions deepened, and word of those rumors reached Tecumseh's longhouse. And it angered Kykuitheh and Nateelah. How was it, they asked aloud, that the people of the village could think such things? How could they not grant Tecumseh respect for what had been done . . . for the lives he had saved?

Tecumseh calmly raised his hand and said, "You must heed these thoughts and the feelings that drive them . . . for so many warriors there are that fell at my lead. What if it was you standing silent and alone as the war party returned, looking upon the joyful reunion of those survivors? Would anger not rise up and consume your soul?"

Both Kykuitheh's and Nateelah's stern anger passed from their faces, as the words seeped into their hearts.

Tecumseh continued, "People in such a way must be given time to mourn their loss. And others would be wise to let this hot blood flow, so it may one day cool to reason and forgiveness. And only then, may we reunite together in peace. Only then may we honor the great sacrifice borne by some for the many."

All sat in silence, and a great peace settled upon them. Even mighty Gahnoque had no words to offer at hearing such wisdom.

But outside the peace of Tecumseh's longhouse, the village tensions rose. And so, Tanogatay, the eldest of all chiefs, spoke on that with the other elders, and in their wisdom called for a council. Something must be done. Somehow, they must again unite the people, unless the village be torn in two.

Once nightfall arrived, seemingly the entire village and more had squeezed into the council longhouse. Flesh pressed upon flesh. There was not a seat to be had, nor any space to breathe in such cramped quarters. As everyone settled in, there were some shouts from both sides of the divide. Each was steady and stout in their beliefs. Then, through the rising din, Tanogatay stood. A rolling hush washed upon the gathering. "We meet this night to settle this matter, so we may stop a great tearing of the village and the Shawnee nation."

At the meeting's onset, there was tightness upon Tecumseh's chest. Heavy tension hung on the air, thick with anger that waited to burst forth.

An unnamed voice shouted from the dark, somewhere in the rear of the longhouse. It dripped of hot pain. "Tecumseh should no longer lead the people! He is not the great chief we have waited for . . . the needless death of many hundreds of warriors is on his hands, for he led them to slaughter. A great chief would never have risked so many warriors in attacking a large paleface army in that way."

At hearing that, many calls shouted out in agreement. Some yelled, "Tecumseh should step aside! He is no longer fit to lead!" There were more jeers.

Then shouts erupted in support of Tecumseh, as some surviving warriors stood in anger. They pointed to the detractors and shouted, "If not for Tecumseh, we would not be here. You know nothing of war's madness! Who is this chief who would leave a field of battle unscathed and all warriors returned home unharmed? Anger and envy have twisted your mind and blinded your eyes so that you cannot see!"

Angry folk stood, seethed, and pointed back. They shouted insults. The hostile din rose up to a roar, so that even Tanogatay's calls for calm were unheard. In that great defeat, America had at last found a way to remove Tecumseh, divide the people, and destroy the Shawnee nation from within.

Amid the rising mayhem and unrest, Tecumseh stood to speak. He raised his hand in a calming gesture and quietly pleaded, "My brothers, let us not carry on this way. Let us open our hearts and ears to talk with one another in peace."

And at those words, the angered shouts fell away one by one, until at last a quiet hush again fell upon the gathering.

In the stilled silence, Tecumseh nodded, first to the elder chiefs, then the warriors, and then all the people. "To the great chiefs and all who are here, listen to one another not in anger, for we are all a part of something bigger than ourselves - the people.

"If we speak on different sides, we are not enemies. We are simply brothers who look upon something with a different point of view. Hold not any malice toward another with whom you do not see the same river flowing before you . . . rather, let us both canoe downstream and see if we may yet land on some riverbank together."

The people looked on in quiet and nodded.

Tecumseh breathed deep and said, "So it is . . . one lives . . . and one dies. Is this not the way of life and the true history that is told? This is always the way of war.

"But it is not solely at our hands by that which comes. It is driven also by fate and chance. Now, some will tell you that it is not so. They say we alone have carved out our lot in life. However, the reality is that but for one step this way or that, it ripples out atop the water's surface of life for all the many steps that follow after. And so, despite our best laid plans, we never quite know where we will end up in the wild of life."

Silence gripped the council house even tighter at those words. Truth was speaking to them all.

Tecumseh looked all about the faces that stared back, and said, "What is it that makes the dark storm cloud bypass one village, only to release its furious storm of rainwaters on another, to flood and destroy the valley next door? Is it because one village is so chosen and another is not according to its strength or wisdom . . . or some ritual and ceremony?

"My heart tells me that it is not so. Try as you might, the great flood cannot be held back if the storm comes upon your valley. You have but your wits and a quick nimbleness to move to higher ground. In the end, that is all that is left us.

"And for those that possess this fortitude and strength of will . . . we may yet survive. But for those who do not, clinging blind to some higher power, or their wisdom and strength alone to save them from the rising flood waters . . . they will perish from this world or suffer great misfortune.

"The Great Spirit alone cannot make all things of this world as they are. It may move things this way or that, and provide the wind upon our backs, but it is also we who must wield all of our strength and will to move our canoe across the raging river of life."

Tecumseh breathed in the quiet again, and stared deep through the souls of all. "If by my death, or by any sacrifice asked of me, I could secure the peoples' freedom, I would give it. If it be the peoples' will that I step aside, I would do so with a great happiness in my heart.

"And for every brave warrior that has fallen, I would gladly exchange my life . . . but I cannot. I can only say it was not yet my time. And now, more than ever, we need to look to each other for the great wolf is still at our door." And with that, Tecumseh bowed his head slow, stepped back, and sat down.

The sound of silence was deafening, like a tidal wave upon the shore. It laid heavy and thick upon the air. The people and chiefs stared back at one another, until finally Tanogatay stirred. He rose up to speak; but before he could, mighty Gahnoque rose up. He stood steady and drawn. In a low tone, barely above a whisper, he asked the people if they would hear his words.

There was confusion, as that was something unexpected. Though mighty in stature, and an adopted brother, Gahnoque was not a Shawnee chief. The elder chiefs again looked to one another, and out at the people, not sure what to do. And many approving nods stared back at them. Some quiet shouts of approval rang out. Tanogatay then raised his hand, and bid Gahnoque to speak, for the people would hear his words.

Gahnoque turned to all and began. "When I first awoke and walked among the Shawnee, I was told though Tecumseh is not the loudest voice, have but the sense to listen. He walks with the Great Spirit and Master of all Life, they said," as he pointed to Tecumseh, and went on, "Be he of flesh and blood of this world, he is one of us and we of him. A great warrior, yet so wise a chief as there can be. But even one so mighty suffers fear and doubt, from both within and by others who look upon him.

"Life's truth is that there is only one certainty once we take our first thirsting gasp of breath at being born into the world. And it is this: whether this day, the next, or some many countless days to follow after, we shall all one day breathe in our last. So that all that is left us is to ask what we will do and what will we become with the time given to us from the first to the passing last of life's breath?"

Gahnoque dwelled for a moment in the heavy quiet. He again looked out over the council gathering. "I am three-hundred and fifty-four years and come from a world countless night skies from yours; yet, I would follow Tecumseh until the ends of this world. He is that rare soul and indomitable spirit . . . no matter the race of people and world."

Gahnoque broke for a moment more in silence, and gazed deeper into the eyes of those around him. "What we do in life echoes unto time without end. We are not just shadows and dust. Our deeds pass from the spirit of one to another, and live on long after the body is no more. Strength, courage, and honor . . . these are the rocks that hold up the mountain of life. And one who walks this path is someone to which others are drawn, as a river to the sea.

"Panther Across the Sky walks the world in this way. He is that flame to which I am drawn. Tecumseh is the one I will follow this day . . . and for all that come after, until my end of days in this world. But we must all look to our own path that we would follow . . . and let it be done."

Gahnoque sat down. The many faces sat still and silent. Then there were many low nods of approval. They too could see that truth . . . they too would now follow Tecumseh to wherever he would lead them. And those who had held tight to envy and anger began at last to set those feelings free. They let go in forgiveness and understanding of what had to be done. It was not by Tecumseh's hand that almost five hundred warriors were lost some days ago; no, it was by his hand that thirty warriors had survived and the people still had hope for the future.

It now came home to the village that this was indeed the great cost to be borne by the people for their freedom; and a cost not yet fully paid. It was more than just empty words, like countless cuts upon the soul that would go deep and leave a brooding scar . . . a wound that would always stay with you.

After some moments more of quiet thoughts and murmured talk, Tanogatay rose up fully. He gazed out to the people. "Then it is done. While Panther Across the Sky breathes life, he will lead us. Go now in peace."

And with that, the great tension that threatened to erupt in a storm of fury upon the village was let go, like a caged bird set free to spread wide its wings and take flight up into the sky. A friendly peace and warmth embraced the village, and the throng dispersed into the night. They ambled and lingered here and there, and strolled slow back to their longhouses in handshakes, hugs, talks, and laughter.

Though many still spoke in hushed wonder on what word the great white fathers would bring now. Would they bargain for peace at last? And Tecumseh's troubled mind raced on that most trying question. But he knew the wolf, and he still hated it. The wolf would not listen. It never had before. Though the wolf had never been so wounded . . . perhaps now fear would enter its heart. Tecumseh wondered on that. But like everyone else, he could only look to the Great Spirit and wait for that answer.

Chapter Sixteen
Falling Message
upon the Great White Fathers

Thalom fidgeted nerves as he and his escort arrived to the great camp. A camp officer stepped forward and shouted, "Where are the rest of your men? Where is Lieutenant Colonel Dandridge?"

The traveling party stopped. One soldier stepped forward. "Our detachment remains in the wild of the Ohio Valley. We come bearing this private here with a message for General Harrison himself, by order of Lieutenant Colonel Dandridge. We must see the general at once."

The officer looked upon Thalom. He then waved them on, and pointed in the direction of the general's tent. The party nodded thanks and moved along. Rumor of their arrival spread like the wind. The gathering camp soldiers gawked and stared. What message did that private bring?

The party snaked its way through the immense camp. Thalom knew it was somewhere in the Northern Virginia foothills of the Blue Ridge Mountains, though he had never actually been there before. The Shenandoah Valley it was called. They passed by an endless sea of tents, and row upon row of soldiers who busied themselves with daily chores.

They came around a final bend into the camp's center and there was the largest tent of all. Heavily guarded it was. Upon arrival to the grand tent, an officer came forward to greet them. After a short exchange, the officer bid them to wait in a sitting area, and disappeared behind a tent flap. After a few moments, he returned and bid Thalom to enter, for General Harrison would see him now.

As Thalom entered, the general sat upright and stiff, his shoulders broad like a mountain range. The general's steeled eyes locked upon Thalom's slow striding form. He seemed eager to hear of Dandridge's message. He raised his hand, and directed Thalom to sit. The general offered him a drink, to which Thalom politely declined.

The air was thick and heavy upon Thalom. After some measured silence, Harrison turned to Thalom, and asked, "Private, you have traveled a great distance under the order of Lieutenant Colonel Dandridge to carry a message. Well, I look upon you with my full attention and bid you to speak it now."

Harrison gathered himself tight, and hunched forward a bit in his chair. His hand and forearm were stiff against his lower cheek. He was prepared for the words to come.

Private Thalom went on and his haunted words told the same tale as he had told Dandridge. He spoke of everything but those strange beasts.

At that, Harrison leaned back in his chair. He muttered aloud, "I know of Tecumseh . . . Panther Across the Sky. He is a warrior of few equals. He is one of the few chiefs among all the tribes of this land whose name is not marked to any treaty, for he will sign none. Though strangely, he is also one of compassion, as several times captured soldiers have been spared death by his hand alone.

"I have heard the tales. He alone secured the freedom for several hundred soldiers from a torturous death at the hands of native victors at the Battle of St. Claire's Shame some years ago.

LON BRETT COON

Little Turtle's War the Indians call it. One can only marvel at this Indian.

"And now he seeks to block America's empire upon this continent. His oratory eloquence precedes him, as he seeks to enjoin all the scattered tribes of these lands into a Great Indian Confederacy."

Harrison then paused, and looked sternly upon Thalom. His eyes drooped of disappointment. "But still, though his skill in battle is renowned, such a victory that you speak of is beyond possibility. Private, surely you have drank one whiskey too many, or suffer some malady of the mind, so that you can no longer tell the difference between bad dreams and reality."

Thalom replied, "Sir, as a good Christian, my lips have never tasted whiskey, and I am sane as any man in this army. Upon the lives of my wife and child, I swear to you I have seen these things."

General Harrison sat back. He measured the private's sincerity. Harrison poured a small glass of whiskey, and gulped it down. He leaned back in his chair.

Private Thalom then stammered, "Sir . . . there is some-thing else . . ." to which Harrison glared. The general gestured angrily for Thalom to speak, and he obliged.

Thalom spoke in a hushed tone. He talked of the two strange Indians. Eight feet tall they were, and blackened in color with tigered markings. The favored look of a mountain lion painted upon their faces. He spoke too about the blades of starlight that danced in their hands. And they were death.

General Harrison sprang to his feet and shouted, "Enough private! I have heard enough!" Harrison paced back and forth, while Thalom sat in stoned silence. Harrison poured himself yet again another glass of whiskey, though much bigger that time. He gulped it down feverishly.

Harrison frowned. His head shook in disbelief. "Have you gone mad private? What the hell do you speak of?"

Embarrassed, Thalom glanced at Harrison sheepishly. He struggled to make eye contact. He knew how his words sounded. But he held true. "I only speak of what I have seen with my own eyes . . . it is no rumor."

General Harrison held up his hand. He could take no more of Thalom's stinging words. He just looked off into the distance.

After a few moments, the general turned back to Thalom and asked, "Well private, did Dandridge send any word?"

Private Thalom glanced down at his boots and said, "He bid me to bear Tecumseh's message to you. Then he gathered his force and headed out into the wild. He said he would cut that Tecumseh's throat, and raze his war party to the ground."

Harrison smiled, and his voice dripped confidence. "So, my loyal Lieutenant Colonel Dandridge and his three thousand are on the move about the Ohio Valley. Their muskets raised and blades drawn, ready to annihilate the Shawnee war party . . . perhaps even, Tecumseh is dead as we speak."

But as the general's words trailed off, Private Thalom spoke up again. "Sir . . . I know war's terror, and I tell you now that Lieutenant Colonel Dandridge knows not what hell he heads into."

General Harrison laughed, "We shall see! We shall see who takes victory when Tecumseh and his warriors face the full might of three thousand strong on an open field of battle!"

Harrison's smiling smirk then disappeared. He turned to Thalom and mocked him, "Is there any more great fantasy you come to share?"

Thalom shook his head low before the general's stern defiance. Harrison then informed Thalom his country thanked him for his service, and dismissed him. He was to be sent on extended leave, to return to his farm and home. Though Thalom was sure Harrison did not do that out of kindness; no, it was done so his story was not spread anymore among the ranks. Thalom's words would serve only to stir up fear and doubt within the soldiers' hearts.

**

Harrison called out the order in haste. A vast regiment was to be assembled, far larger than any that had been sent out before. A great need was upon America. They must dispatch of Tecumseh and his marauding war party once and for all.

In two weeks' time there would be assembled ten thousand infantry and one thousand strong cavalry. And just to make sure, they would bring some large cannon. The new iron barreled ones, stronger and lighter than any made before. And they could be wheeled in good speed behind strong horses. They would bring the twelve pounders, for the native savages had no defense against such weapons of war. Even proud Tecumseh would bow down before such thunderous might. Harrison talked of meeting up with Dandridge's regiment. Together, their combined force would crush Tecumseh into a final surrender . . . or death.

At once, the officers were dismissed. They spread throughout the camp and relayed the orders. Preparations began and the entire camp scurried about. The next several weeks came fast and at sunrise of the next day, it was a military splendor.

Brass buttons sparkled. Bayonets glistened. The mass of soldiers was like a rolling blue sea. General Harrison was most pleased. Upon his well-muscled horse, he rode to the vast column's front. He raised his saber high, and thrust it forward. The blue-jacketed armada sprung to life. The march began; cavalry to the front, then endless rows of stepping soldiers with glistening bayonets, then ten iron-barreled twelve pounders in tow, and supply wagons to the rear. Camp bystanders saluted the soldiers that went by, and brimmed with confidence. There was a surety within their hearts of the triumphant return when they would see each other again.

For many weeks, that enormous regiment made its way. It left Virginia's borders and on through the wild of western Pennsylvania, into Ohio country. They headed to the last known whereabouts of Dandridge's army. They stepped in precision. The heavy guns did not slow the pace. Harrison pushed them on steady and resolute. And the soldiers did not complain. They were lucky to serve at the behest of the great general, Harrison. Though there was now a strong smell that carried on the air. The soldiers covered their noses. Late in the evening on another long day, they came at last upon Dandridge and his men.

An advance scout on horse returned from up ahead, his face drained of all color. He was shaken. Wide-eyed, he rode up to General Harrison and quietly said, "Lieutenant Colonel Dandridge is found . . . at least what is left of him."

Harrison's face went gaunt. No words were uttered. At once, he rode ahead with several hundred cavalry. The galloping pace quickened, which matched his heartbeat's anxious thumping. His mind swirled in dismay and disbelief. What had happened to Dandridge and his men? Harrison had to see with his own eyes. He rode up over the crest of a sloping hill and there it was. It was a scene beyond his darkest nightmare.

What great power destroyed Dandridge's army so complete? There were many rumors. It must be true. They said Tecumseh was seven feet tall and wielded a tomahawk so mighty he could fell a full-grown oak with one swing, and cut down a line of soldiers just the same. And that he brought forth a distant tribe from the great north of Upper Canada. A tribe so strange in size and color, who wielded sabers of light that could not be felled by musket lead.

That talk only served to fan the flames of Tecumseh's legend. Harrison rode up slow to the last remnant of Dandridge. He dismounted and walked up to a staked spear that guarded that place. The lieutenant colonel's head was piked atop, and it stared back. Harrison looked upon Dandridge's haunted face, and it was marked with fear. Harrison wondered aloud, to no one in particular, "How did it come to this?" He turned and gazed all about the grassy plain. There was nothing but the rotting bodies of thousands of dead soldiers. A putrid stench rose, while buzzards feasted upon the corpses, as if they were neglected carcasses of some felled wild beasts.

In all his days, Harrison had never seen such devastation at the hands of Indians, no matter their savagery. For the first time in his life, an iced fear bubbled within. A stinging doubt began to wash upon him. He gazed upward to the heavens and wondered . . . had God deserted America?

Well so be it. Harrison would just have to defeat that Tecumseh on his own. He gritted his teeth. He snarled. Fear and doubt would not be his master. He was the commander of all things in his world. He barked out orders to remove Dandridge's head and provide a proper burial for the dead. Though out of concern of disease, there would be no shovels and dirt. A large fire was lit for a mass cremation.

It took all night to send the vast number of dead to the heavens. The flickering flames' great heat burned upon Harrison's face, and lit embers floated up into the night sky. Harrison pondered the once certain future of empire for his nation. What now would become of it? He did not know. But whatever was to come, he would meet it like a leaden ball shot from a musket.

The next day, the general bade the men to tidy the battle-plain and clear death's stain. They would forever erase that place as a memorial of the great Shawnee victory. It would remain nothing more than Shawnee myth, only a wisp of gossip to remain ever hidden from the world.

The soldiers informed Harrison that many tracks of Indians had been found. One path led west and one southwest. Which path would that Tecumseh have taken? Harrison pondered on that. He was not sure. The westward trail was well worn and lead to Fort Detroit.

Perhaps Tecumseh was so bold as to seek capture of the great fort. But he would fail. Fort Detroit was the mightiest on the western frontier. Imposing walls were well fortified with earth and stone, and it had a gate of iron. Ten large cannon manned it that could rain thunder. And five hundred brave soldiers called it home. With no cannons, how could Tecumseh attack the fort in any real way, let alone capture it? With but musket, arrow, and tomahawk, such an assault was foolhardy.

But that Tecumseh had already somehow done the impossible on two occasions. After some more quiet thought, Harrison decided. Tecumseh must be on the move to Fort Detroit; driven on by the fumes of his victories, emboldened to destroy that fort. So that is where Harrison and his army must go.

At dawn's first light, Harrison awakened his force from their slumber, and gathered them to formation. He yelled out, "Let us go this way and seek out Tecumseh. Let us chase them through the wild to the walls of Fort Detroit so they may fall under its mighty guns. There will be nowhere to run, nowhere to hide. And then they will find death!"

The ten thousand and more soldiers saluted Harrison with vim and vigor, and shouted, "Hoo-rah!" They were eager to go. They were eager to serve Harrison, America's greatest general. And with that, the endless sea of blue jacketed soldiers was on the move.

Chapter Seventeen
Peaceful Spirit
of the Flowing River

Gahnoque slowly inhaled the early morning quiet. Eyelids fluttered to life, as sunlight rays poked into the longhouse. Dust floated on air like soft snowfall. Looking about, all were still asleep, save for Kykuitheh, whose bedding was empty. Gahnoque stepped out into the dawn. A few villagers were already engaged in morning chores. He greeted them with a smile and a nod. And Kykuitheh was nowhere to be found.

Gahnoque strolled to the nearby river, to take in the early morning light that shined upon the water's rippling surface. A thing most beautiful to behold, it reminded him of home. He wondered, might he breathe in its splendor once more?

As those thoughts ran in his mind, he saw a figure on the far riverbank. It sat upon a large oak tree that overlooked the winding river. His sharp eyes looked closer . . . Kykuitheh was found at last.

Gahnoque took up a canoe to paddle to her. He sliced through the water with no effort at all, and glided close to Kykuitheh. Their eyes glanced upon the other, and they bowed in greeting.

The canoe pulled close to the shore's bank, and slid slow upon its welcoming sands. He stepped out and walked to her, and took a careful seat beside her. She sat on an ancient oak whose trunk was grown large and wide, and could host a party of many more folk upon its frame.

Gahnoque spoke softly, "You come to enjoy the early morning's peace . . . we must be of one mind." At that, both Kykuitheh and Gahnoque broke into soft smiles.

They both stared out again upon the rippling water's reflection. The sunlight frolicked as it traveled down the winding waterway. Gahnoque turned to Kykuitheh and said, "That before us is not to be overlooked, but savored. It is the simplest of things that are most treasured in life's journey . . . but the many among us are too busy to take notice. They rush on through their days, doing this and that, ever wondering and searching for the serenity that cannot be found. And all along, it was sitting right there before them. They need only be still for a moment and open their eyes."

Kykuitheh looked to Gahnoque with a low smile upon her face. She sighed and said, "I do sit here to take in its calming beauty, as I am troubled over the way of the world. Things are not as they should be. The cost that must be borne by our people in this struggle may be more than we can bear . . . more than I can bear."

She looked down and stared some more into the moving water. "So much pain and loss I have known. How much will my heart, and the heart of the people, bend before it will break and be forever torn?"

Gahnoque spoke wistfully, "So say all who see such things, but I see a great strength among the Shawnee, an undying spirit. It will not be put out no matter the impossibility . . . I see the fire that burns within Tecumseh."

Gahnoque reflected a moment and went on, "I know of the past and the suffering. I have looked into Tecumseh's mind and seen your loss, though he has not spoken on it with me. It weights heavy upon your souls.

"I see the anger and emptiness that rises up to take hold. Try as you might to bear a child into the world, the Great Spirit will not let it be . . . and now too many moons have passed. I know there was a son . . . who lived but a short time. I know of Laykhyaloh."

Watery tears welled up in Kykuitheh's eyes. A teardrop broke and cascaded down her smooth cheek. She whispered, "In the Shawnee tongue, his name means peaceful flowing river. It was given to him so that his spirit will flow ever free and at peace until the day we join him again.

"This is why you will find me here. It is not only its beauty, but to be once more with my lost son . . . if but only for a moment." Kykuitheh stared deep into the water's reflection below. And as she did, another teardrop was let loose. It fell freely into the river's flowing water, and sailed downstream.

Gahnoque knelt beside her. He softly reached out his outturned hands, and lightly grasped her forearm. "The passing of a child is a great sadness . . . one that never leaves. But you are not alone. You have the people's love, and the love of the Jhagir. We shall help you bear this burden for all of the days that you carry it."

Kykuitheh clasped his hand in thanks. She bowed her head and smiled, as she wiped more tears from her face. "Thank you for the kind words . . . and friendship; though of different races and worlds, our spirits are one. I see you and you see me in return . . . and I am glad for that."

Gahnoque nodded, stood, and said, "I leave you now to your memories. Enjoy a bit more time with the peaceful spirit of the river . . . and your lost son." He bowed and returned to the village.

Later that afternoon, after all the longhouse had gathered for a late-day meal, Gahnoque turned to Tecumseh, and asked,

"In all that has happened in the days of our village return, it did not seem right to share with you the happenings of our journey those days ago," at which he pointed to Ithikkah.

"Ah, in light of the battle and its great cost, I had all but forgotten. It must have gone ill, for you have made no mention of it?" replied Tecumseh.

Gahnoque nodded, smiled slow at Ithikkah, and then back to Tecumseh. Tension rose, like a taut rope. Gahnoque reached down into a small pouch hidden in his harness. From it emerged a blue and white colored stone. It was most similar to that which sat upon Gahnoque's chest, though a bit smaller. Gahnoque set it down before them.

At once, the stone came to life. It pulsed and glowed blue and white with light, as did the stone that sat upon Gahnoque's chest. The two stones talked to the other in their own way. In hope beyond hope, they had found a fourth stone of Ithreal. And it was a most sparkling jewel indeed.

Taughannock blurted out, "Can it be?"

Gahnoque smiled, "My young Jhagir, we may yet again look upon our home once more. But let us now enjoy the miracle in its finding, before we look for the second to come."

Taughannock jumped up. He hugged his father and heaved him into the air. Ithikkah laughed as he was wrapped in a son's happiness. Taughannock then turned and hugged Nateelah high into the air. Feet dangled from the ground, and Nateelah giggled.

Taughannock said, "We now have hope. Nateelah, perhaps one day you will look upon my world, as you have shared with me yours. You could walk among my people." There were more warm hugs, smiles, and excited laughter.

Tecumseh turned. "Gahnoque, there is now nothing left, but to try your grand idea. Now we will know if you shall be the first to make that journey . . . a living being in body to travel through the night's stars."

Gahnoque leaned back. "Yes. Now we are left to make it our reality. And there has never been one with such need as we."

Hope hung thick in the air about the longhouse, and jubilant sounds carried out into the village. At the rising happiness, other villagers came close for a look. And it warmed the hearts of the Shawnee that the Jhagir might again walk among their own people. The Shawnee knew that was a thing to be cherished.

Over the following weeks, an easy feeling again fell upon the village. And the people embraced that peace, though they still awaited word of the great white fathers. Would the wolf now listen to peace?

And during that time, they talked more about the fourth stone of Ithreal. They spoke of when and how to open a door to other worlds? In what would you set the stones? They did not know. That question ran like a waterfall upon their minds.

Gahnoque believed it best to do so under a full moon, as an Ithreal stone's power grew under the light of the seven moons of Celadon. Might it not also be so with the pale light of this world's moon? They would need every bit of the Ithreal stone's power. And the moon hung lowest in midsummer, which had already passed. So, it was agreed to wait until next summer. That of course would give Gahnoque time to build his door to hold the stones, and prepare his mind for the journey sure to be difficult beyond measure.

The weeks flew by. Late summer passed to early fall, and there were many new warriors that arrived from other Shawnee villages far and wide. Other tribes had also come, as word of Tecumseh's great victories had begun to spread across all the lands. They had come to answer his call for the great confederacy. There were warriors from the Sauk, Cherokee,

Creek, Miami, and Wyandot tribes. Their numbers swelled to some two thousand and five hundred strong, and fully replenished those that had been lost and more.

It was a moving dance of varied dress, weaponry, and painted markings upon the flesh. Feathers and bones of all sorts of beasts, great and small, adorned many who came. And it was a strange sight indeed, in seeing one-time enemies burying past pains and blood hostilities in a tomahawk of peace. To Gahnoque, it was a remarkable thing. They all bowed to Tecumseh's message. They all came together now for one thing - freedom.

But Gahnoque knew that some were just curious. They came to look upon him and his Jhagir brothers that fought with Tecumseh. To look upon the ones who danced in the starlight of the nighttime sky. The many warriors and tribes had heard the stories. And the Jhagir did not disappoint.

Tecumseh's long dreamed of vision had begun to take form. It breathed with life and soon would roar like a great beast to all the world. The growing numbers overflowed into the village grounds, with the people all too happy to provide food and shelter. With all the extra mouths, many more hunters than normal worked tirelessly. There was fishing up and down the river at all hours. And the women and children worked double time upon the fields to bring in extra harvests, and scout the nearby forests for berries and greens. And all waited on the words of the great white fathers. Would America bow to peace . . . or would the free peoples' warriors have to reach out and take it?

And at long last, the great white fathers spoke. Some scouts had finally returned. Gahnoque saw the frowned lines upon their faces. Tecumseh sighed. Tecumseh told Gahnoque his father was right, the wolf would always be a wolf. And like a bad dream, the scouts spoke on what they saw, "A vast force, some ten thousand strong, is on the move. We have never seen so many marching muskets. They are on the trails west . . . it seems they head to Fort Detroit."

Those words stunned the people. Gahnoque saw the vacant looks upon their faces. The number of long knives to be faced in battle was beyond fathom, they said. It was the largest army of long knives ever told of in the tales of any tribes of the land. But there was more. The scouts went on, with grim looks. "And with them come one thousand cavalry and many large cannons they bring too. Led by General Harrison himself they are."

A heavy silence choked the air. Gahnoque saw the worry and fear that rose up in the people. It crested into a mighty wave that would crash down upon them and wash away all hope. America had indeed gathered all might to it and now wielded it for one purpose - the breaking of the people's spirit. There would be no grand bargain of peace. And they were led by the bravest paleface soldier Tecumseh had ever seen.

Maybe Gahnoque would hear that rising chant Tecumseh said he would never forget . . . Harrison. Harrison. Gahnoque knew it was coming now. Gahnoque wondered just how brave this paleface warrior might be.

At once, Tecumseh sent out word to his great friend, Otsaga. They were to meet in two weeks' time at the ancient ruins. Every able warrior would be needed to face such a vast foe. And so, the fleetest of foot were sent on their way with that most urgent message. Tecumseh said he had aroused a great grizzly bear from its den, with the enormous cavalry as it claws and its many large cannon as it fangs. Never before had America tasted defeat in battle when bolstered by both a thunderous wave of cavalry and the dreaded large cannons. Tecumseh told Gahnoque so.

Against such weapons . . . the free peoples had no answer, but to retreat and flee until the next battle. Time after time, tribes of all nations had wilted against such might. Though

Gahnoque saw that the people clung to a hope that perhaps that time was different . . . for it was Tecumseh who led them. He would find a way when no others could. He had already done so. He had already defeated the two largest armies the tribal nations had ever faced. And he had the Jhagir. So they believed in Tecumseh. They believed in hope.

There was no time to wait. Tecumseh and his warriors must go at once. Warm embraces were shared. Tears of sadness fell free upon the ground. Taughannock and Nateelah held their longing embrace tight, and stretched every moment. Yet she held back her sadness, and did not send him off raining tears. And Taughannock stood there like a sturdy mountain to reassure her.

Tecumseh and Gahnoque lead the great procession out of the village and into the wild. Tecumseh's large war party turned in the direction of the hidden valley. They went to meet Otsaga and his warriors, and any others who would come to answer the call.

Chapter Eighteen
Gathering at the Ruins

Tecumseh exhaled. Slow and steady he ran. Beads of sweat rolled down his back. Painted flesh bobbed and weaved all about, like a great red-skinned serpent that slithered through the forest. The soft pounding of thousands of moccasined feet upon the ground echoed out.

Within several weeks' time, the war party had arrived. It was somewhere in the bowels of Southeast Ohio. Its exact location was not marked on any paleface map. Through a downward sloping path they entered, hidden by thickets of brush and cover. It would be missed by those who did not know where to look, even if it was right before your nose.

The path at first was ordinary, like any other forest trail. Though it ever descended, and after a ways more, a clearing came into view. And the gifted beauty of the hidden valley opened up wide. Its vision swallowed them whole. Unearthly tall trees peered in on all sides to cradle the valley like a mountain range. The thick tree trunks were massive and grown bunched together, as they guarded the valley. Those trees surely grew from seedlings at Mother Earth's birth, for their sheer size was unnatural. The heavily green-leafed trees could blot out all light from above if one stood below at its base. The leaves were grown thick, like several layers of leather hides sewn together.

The Jhagir had not seen trees such as those in all the forests of that world. And neither had the Shawnee, which is why it was kept unspoiled for the people. Only on special occasions did they come to commune with the Great Spirit, to seek out a vision to share with the people. As they walked out into the valley clearing, there was a sea of rolling hills with soft fields of grass. And there were many more trees, though more spaced about and much smaller in size. A great flowing river there was also that cut through the valley. It shaped a winding gorge down below, and exposed shaved cliffs of jagged edge rocks that jutted forth.

As the warriors moved farther into the valley, a sound thundered and beat low upon the chest. White wispy smoke rose in the distance. But as they followed the river's winding path around the gorge and came nearer to the great sound, it was not smoke, but a watery mist that sprayed high into the sky. And driven it was by the might of rushing water. It was an immense waterfall. The valley then came to its end, and fell off into another wall of tree and jagged rock.

Gahnoque turned to Tecumseh and said, "A beautiful valley this is my friend and most hidden it is."

Tecumseh nodded back and whispered, "This is but the front door," and he smiled at Gahnoque's puzzled look.

Tecumseh walked to the fall's edge and seemed ready to tumble into the raging waters . . . but then he disappeared into the thunderous mist. The warriors began to fall in line and followed after. As the Jhagir got close to the edge, the mystery's riddle opened up before them. Off to the side, there was a small stairway that led down. Ancient stone steps beckoned, lined with markings that belied their great age.

Down the steps went Tecumseh and his warrior army, which followed under the waters of the great waterfall that flowed wild. It wrapped the visitors in a wall of water to one side and wet dripping rock to the other. For some one hundred fifty paces or so it led on, until a bright-lit opening loomed at the far end. Tecumseh, his warriors, and the Jhagir emerged into the dry air, blue sky, and lush greenery. It was like another world. Large twisted vines overhung the bordering forest growth on the valley's edges. All about there were oversized green trees with broad leaves and large overgrown wing-like bushes, not natural to that land.

And deeper within the open plain was a land altogether different. There was chest high wheat-like grass that blew in the valley breeze and a scattering of low hung thorny trees. Another winding river also ran through it, though much smaller than the first valley. That valley was also surrounded by chiseled rock cliffs, as if placed there by the Great Spirit to keep it hidden. But there were no living beasts or things about, not even a bird that flew in the sky. Gahnoque noticed such a thing so odd and asked, "How is it that there is no life within this valley . . . perhaps there is something unnatural at work here?"

Tecumseh said, "Well my friend, I know that you have wondered why the Shawnee have not moved their villages here to the protection of this hidden valley to live safe and free from the white race. Now you have guessed the answer. For despite the wonder and beauty of this place, there is no game or fish. And so, this is a place in which you could never live."

Though Tecumseh lingered at the sight and stopped to breathe deep its beauty. Every time he took that path, he was left without words, as if it were the first his eyes had ever looked upon it.

Taughannock marveled at its splendor and gasped aloud, "This valley is like a dream from my own world," as his head nodded disbelief.

Gahnoque said, "It is a jewel upon this world and stands tall in compares to the many wonders I have ever looked upon."

Ithikkah nodded in agreement.

Tecumseh gazed out and pointed to stone ruins in the distance, "Out there is our journey's end."

In unison, the warriors turned and began their way over to a small village of stone longhouses.

As they neared the stone houses, Gahnoque asked, "Whose ruins are these? Who is their maker . . . and where have they gone?"

Tecumseh spoke softly, "These ruins were here before time began. They are so ancient that the elders of our elders, and their elders before them, knew not their makers. And there are no tales, written parchments, or graves of these ancients . . . save for strange markings that adorn the stone faces. The markings are not known to man of any race or tribe, and so their meaning is lost."

As Tecumseh and his party moved close, a glad sight stared back. Otsaga and many warriors he had brought with him, at several thousand at least. From several other Shawnee villages they had come, and also with warriors from some Sauk, Wyandot, and Winnebago villages too.

Tecumseh greeted his lifelong friend with a firm hand-shake, a hand upon his shoulder, and a broad smile. Tecumseh said, "My friend, I am very glad to see you again. I see you have brought many strong warriors with you," as he looked about.

Otsaga replied, "It gladdens my heart as well. I come with two thousand close friends, all fierce of heart and hungry for the scalps of our enemy. And I see many you have brought too," as he looked around at Tecumseh's large force. He nodded to Gahnoque and the other two Jhagir.

Tecumseh replied with a smile, "Yes, many warriors I have brought, at two thousand five hundred tomahawks, so together my friend we are a great host. And if my scout's eyes are true, we will need all that we have gathered. In a force of great number the palefaces come. And more brutal they will be now, in retribution for our great victories in battle.

"Let us sit and talk of meeting the coming storm. I have already sent out scouts before we came to this place. They shall return by nightfall. Then we may know where we will travel out to meet it."

Otsaga nodded. And so they did.

Thousands of warriors gathered in friendship and reminisce. Some looked upon familiar faces and friends; while other tribal enemies of old raised the pipe of peace. Together, all marveled at the mystery of the ruins so ancient. But Tecumseh heard much of the talk was of the Shawnee's new friends, they of the panther-like appearance and immense size. There was talk of their great strength, skill in battle, and starlit weapons so wondrous to behold. And in whispered awe, there was talk of how they move in both the world of the living and the spirits.

Such talk imbued many with a steely confidence and a budding hope; for with Tecumseh at the lead and the Jhagir at his side, they believed their time had now come. A lasting freedom was not just a wished for dream. They believed with all of their heart that the great white fathers could at last be pushed back and defeated - and that thought warmed their hearts.

But Tecumseh's heart was still cold. It bathed in fear and doubt. He wondered what strength was in him. He was just a man after all. Could he defeat the greatest of wolves? And what would his warriors do against the terrible large cannons? There was only defeat before him. He searched his heart. It ached for an answer . . . some path to victory; but there was none. He could not see it. If only he could speak a few moments with his father . . . what wisdom would he share? He did not know. What of his great friend John Sackett? He longed to speak with him too . . . but he was far from there. Tecumseh's world spun down upon him. It was a windstorm of despair. The great weight of his people bowed his shoulders . . . and though surrounded by thousands of his kin, he was utterly alone.

Dusk gave way to night and hundreds of campfires burned bright upon the open plain. The light flickered against the shadowy backdrop of ancient stone ruins. The chiefs and Jhagir gathered at one of those fires and passed a smoke pipe about, for there were things to discuss.

Gahnoque spoke aloud to Tecumseh, "I have walked about the stone village and looked upon the markings that adorn the aged rock. I have seen those before. They are from a people countless night skies away. And yet they do not fly through the stars. So the ruin's mystery only deepens for me...."

Tecumseh replied, "These ruins harbor only riddles . . . riddles in the dark. Perhaps one day all will be revealed." And with that, both Tecumseh and Gahnoque looked upward into the stars of the night. Did they sit upon the ruins of a lost race from a distant star above, far off into the darkness? They did not know. Perhaps, they would never know. Perhaps, some mysteries were meant to linger.

After some time, as the chiefs talked through the night, deep into battle plans, a branch snapped. The brush came alive. Something stirred in the dark. Some warriors rose up at once . . . and shadows shifted near. Tomahawks were raised up tight in clenched fists, and shouts of warning called out to the forest dark. In return, they heard the welcomed sound of a Shawnee greeting of peace. Tecumseh's scouts had returned and emerged from the veiled cloak of darkness.

"It gladdens my heart to see you returned. What word do you have on the paleface horde?" asked Tecumseh.

The scout sighed, nodded to Tecumseh and the other chiefs, and then sat beside them. As the flickering firelight painted their faces, he began to speak. "It is as you have been told, led by General Harrison himself. There are some ten thousand blue jackets on foot, one thousand more on horse, and ten large cannon. They move swift and with purpose. I caught sight of their trail, as I followed in the forest shadows.

"They travel west upon the trail to Fort Detroit. They go that way in search of you, my chief," as he looked to Tecumseh. "They go this way for they believe you mean to raze that fort. They go to bring our final ruin, for I heard words of your coming death."

A gathered silence rested upon all as Tecumseh inhaled again on the peace pipe. He held its smoke in, as the stilled quiet settled, then released its wispy white plumes. The smoke floated about and danced with the flames of the fire, up into the starlit night sky above.

Tecumseh then spoke aloud, fierce like a war club. "So, the greatest of all paleface armies go west to Fort Detroit . . . led by General Harrison no less. Shall we go out now and meet them?" Tecumseh stared out in silence. He inhaled again on the peace pipe, and held its smoke. And then he released another cloud into the air. It swirled about and he went on, "We are four thousand and five hundred tomahawks strong and we do not fear America's army. It would be a great shame if this army of long knives does not find that which it seeks." Tecumseh broke a low smile, as his spoken words fell.

He went on, "Let us depart at the morning's first light and seek out the general's horde. If he believes us headed to Fort Detroit, then to Fort Detroit we go. But let us find him and cut down his force in the plain before its gates. Let the fort's commander and his men look on as we desolate the general's army, out of reach of the fort's great cannons. We will sever limbs and their spirit . . . until it is shattered."

At Tecumseh's words, all the chiefs smiled, and the warriors about the fire let loose with defiant yells and screams at the hoped-for victory to come. The warriors then broke into festive song and dance. Over the coming days, they would bring death to their enemy . . . and a lasting freedom for the free peoples of the land. Beating drums and rhythmic chants rose up all about the ruins and valley, in the warm reflection of a hundred fires.

There was just flickering flames that lit up tattooed faces and silhouettes of dancing warriors.

Tecumseh's words were proud and strong. He said what the warriors needed to hear. But his insides still roiled in fear and doubt. How could he defeat an endless sea of long knives, more than a warrior would fight in a lifetime of war? And those dreaded large cannon . . . the Shawnee had no match for those fearsome weapons. And how would he defeat America's greatest general, Harrison. He was a great warrior, and the bravest paleface he had ever seen in battle. Even with the Jhagir, it all seemed hopeless. The wolf was too strong. Despite the dying words of his father . . . he would fail the people. His shoulders sagged and he sank away into himself. But he had no choice. He and the warriors must go . . . they must try, or all would be lost and his people destroyed forever.

At dawn, the gathering of warriors arose to a quick meal of dried berries and corn cakes they had carried with them, and went on their way. They departed the ancient ruins and the valley, and left its wonder and beauty behind. Tecumseh and all the warriors wondered if it was the last their eyes would look upon it. And to Fort Detroit they went. There was a great wolf on the loose, and it needed to be hunted down.

Chapter Nineteen
Brooding Muster of War

Sweat dripped like summer rain. Muscles burned as if roasted in flame. Breaths were long. Chests heaved, in and out. On and on they ran, but there was no fatigue. Tecumseh could feel it in the air. Nerves tingled and stood on end. Fate was calling. Endless limbs of tattooed flesh moved in great haste. It was close now. They sought their prey, the greatest paleface army and its general, Harrison. They ran in great speed to cut off Harrison's arrival to Fort Detroit. They must arrive first. Trees, rocks, and shrubs whirred by as they sped over hill, slope, and valley.

And soon, they heard the rush of water. The strong flowing Detroit River sparkled in the sunlight and rumbled on the air. They followed its winding path, and up ahead they looked upon the great fort in the distance. Tecumseh's hand rose, and his many warriors stopped. They stuck to the edge of the thick forest, to stay safely out of view.

And that fort was like a mighty mountain. Its walls were stout and gate massive. Many large cannons protruded in defiance like fangs. They dared any would-be attackers. Only a fool would do so. But Tecumseh was no fool. Before the fort's main gate laid a great plain, open and wide. And Tecumseh believed it was upon that plain that he must waylay the countless long knives to come. He just did not know how. But any attack must be out of range of the fort's cannons, lest his warriors be torn apart by cannonball from both the front and behind.

Along the way, Tecumseh's warriors did not come upon the tracks of Harrison's army. He guessed they traveled by way of the main trails known by the white settlers, which was the longer roundabout way. And they would be slowed by the large cannons. If he was right, Harrison would arrive in a day or two. So, he must set about planning for the attack. But how to defeat ten thousand strong? What to do with the cannon barrage and cavalry charge sure to come? His mind still told him that it could not be done . . . not against such might. But his heart pushed him on.

He gathered with the other chiefs and the Jhagir. It was time. They must make final preparations for that battle of all battles, the greatest he had ever known. They must do whatever could be done . . . or die on that field trying. A chilled silence fell upon the chiefs. In a most grave tone, one chief asked, "What shall be done in the coming battle with the great paleface army that comes for us?"

Tecumseh sat in silence, unmoved at that most important of questions.

Then his long-time friend and fellow chief, Otsaga, rose up. He spoke aloud, "Tecumseh, I do not fear the great army of long knives. And ever I desire to slit the throat of the great white fathers for the death and misery they have brought upon the people. But in such great numbers they come, surely we cannot meet them in open battle upon this field?"

The other chiefs nodded in agreement. It would be foolhardy to do so.

Tecumseh gazed upon the chiefs. His eyes smoldered. He breathed in slow and deep, and said, "Wiser words have never been spoken. It would be a great detriment to our cause, if we simply lined up in a row on that field and traded musket shot, which the long knives are want to do. And they have many more muskets than we.

"But some might think it wise to lay bait, to draw them out in a thrusting attack. Perhaps some two thousand and five hundred warriors assembled on the grassy plain would deceive the long knives. At such a sight, surely they could not stay their hand. The vision of so many warriors is large by any count, and they may think that is all we have. And so they will be emboldened by their own vast size. Though they know not our true numbers, and that some several thousand more warriors lay in wait, cloaked in the forest to launch upon them.

"As Harrison's army approaches the fort, his cavalry will launch head first in their excitement to cut us down all. We will wait as they descend upon us . . . and when they cannot turn back, we will unleash waves of arrows to darken the noon sky and unhorse many riders."

But at Tecumseh's words, Otsaga spoke up. "My friend, they ride a thousand horses. In all my brave life, I have never faced such a host that would fill the horizon. Such a sea of stampeding beasts cannot be brought down with a barrage of arrows, even if the sun were blotted out. For at best, five hundred will still thunder down upon us. What then shall we do, for we will be trampled to death? To stand against that is not bravery . . . it is madness."

Tecumseh nodded to Otsaga and said, "I know what runs through your mind, for my thoughts are also dark with doubt. But we will not stand with arrows alone upon the grassy plain. Hidden within our ranks will be tree trunks of young saplings. Hundreds all shaved to a point. Then unseen to the last, they will be raised, thrust into the horsed charge . . . and we shall drive the beasts back. But our warriors must hold the line. Many will perish in the wave of a thousand blue-jacketed beasts . . . but they must hold until the last stretched moment."

Tecumseh saw a flicker of hope upon the faces of Otsaga and the warriors. Never before had the warriors used such wooden spikes in battle. But in hearing Tecumseh's words now, perhaps they could bring down the cavalry with such weapons . . . or at least greatly weaken it. And it would be unlooked-for by the palefaces.

But then solemn looks passed among the chiefs and warriors like a rolling wave at sea. Tecumseh saw it. He knew their thoughts. They knew the terror and fury those upon the plain were sure to face. How does a man stand and face such a charge? And the forests laid far back to the open plain . . . much farther than remembered. For those forests had been cut back over the years to provide needed wood for fort construction, upkeep, and fuel for winter fires. And likely to prevent any ambush of an enemy horde.

After a short pause, Tecumseh looked again out among his warrior brothers and went on, "And in that moment, when the soldiers have advanced fully onto the plain and engaged wholly in battle . . . when America is fat and lazy, poised to taste its victory. It is then that our hidden brothers will strike. We will let loose one flaming arrow into the sky. And at that signal, from the depths of the forest's dark on each side of the battle-plain, they will charge into the paleface sea in fury."

All the chiefs and warriors stared blankly in thought. After some pensive quiet, Otsaga then spoke up again. He asked the question that lingered yet upon the minds of all. "Some would deem the distance too great from which to launch an attack upon the plain . . . it is too much to risk my friend. At such a distance, a cavalry charge could be reformed to our second wave of attack, and set upon the forest before the plain is reached. Is there not another way?"

A tense silence gripped each warrior. They waited in anxious breaths for Tecumseh's reply.

Tecumseh nodded. "Yes, it is a far distance, with much more ground to cover than hoped for. But it is why General Harrison will expect no such attack. And that is precisely why it is the thing we ought to do. It will provide us with surprise. And we will need all of it, if ever we are to defeat such a sea of long knives. No . . . there is no other way."

Stilled quiet engulfed the multitude, though they knew Tecumseh was right. Tecumseh saw it upon their faces. They had come all this way and could not turn back. Such an army left free to roam the wild would raze and devour any single tribe or village it came across. No, they must make a stand now and protect the people. Deep in their hearts, they always knew it would not be a thing so easy; yet now at the doorstep of that great battle, it was all the more steep and rugged mountain to climb.

Tecumseh's strong voice then parted the heavy quiet, "The long knives will taste the stone of our tomahawks and the flint of our arrowheads from every direction. And in this way, we may incite a great fear and panic among their ranks, beheading their officers, and soaking the grass with their blood. We will turn the tide and chase them from the field of battle. Then America will know that freedom cannot be so easily defeated." But those words fell hollow in Tecumseh's mind. It was a difficult thing to speak the words he did not believe. But that was not the time for truth. As their warrior chief, he must swallow hard his fear and doubt and speak the words they needed to hear . . . right to the end.

At hearing those words, the chiefs rose up, including Otsaga, and nodded approval. There was a feeling that Tecumseh's plan might just work. But then the unspoken concern was raised by a Sauk chief at last, "But what of the large cannons they bring? For you have not talked on these? Surely, they will wheel those guns about, firing upon us at first upon the open plain to destroy us?"

Tecumseh pondered that most grave of concerns, as did all. That question had gnawed upon their minds each passing day, as they had traveled to that great battle. Each chief knew of the might and terror of those guns. And any soul who denied that terror had never faced those mighty weapons in battle, or was a dishonest fool. Worry and doubt rose again among them all. How could there be any victory if they were at first blown to dust by those cannons? Tecumseh did not know what to say, no wisdom to share. Yet all the warriors looked to him. Their eyes begged for some answer. But Tecumseh said nothing.

Finally, Gahnoque broke the silence. "Let the Jhagir deal with those cannon weapons. We shall give the people a chance for victory."

Tecumseh exhaled deep. Relief flooded his body.

All the chiefs nodded to Gahnoque in startled wonder. What would the Jhagir do in facing those terrible guns? Well, all would see soon enough, for Harrison was coming. And as they placed their faith in Tecumseh, so too would they with the Jhagir.

Tecumseh went on, "I would not ask any warrior to do something I would not do myself. And the greatest sacrifice will be borne by the two thousand and five hundred who will lure our enemy onto the field. So I will lead that party. It is a burden I will leave to no other."

Tecumseh looked around and measured any challenge . . . but there was only lowered heads and submissive nods. It was agreed.

Gahnoque turned to Tecumseh and said, "I will stand with you . . . I will help hold the line," to which Tecumseh smiled and nodded his thanks.

As they sat among themselves, a quiet confidence grew in Tecumseh's plan. Though Tecumseh brooded some more. He wondered what strength was still in him. He felt drained of all life. His limbs were dead with weight. Was he leading his brothers finally to slaughter? That was the greatest wolf he had ever faced . . . and he still hated the wolf. And he would at last meet the great general in battle, Harrison. The winds of fate were howling again.

Tecumseh then took some comfort, as all was as could be done. There was nothing for it now but to wait upon the brink of battle. But he knew that once the musket lead flew, all the best-laid plans could be waylaid. And it would be the warrior who best moved to the battle's changing sea, and its rolling waves, who would survive to another day.

Quietly and to himself, Tecumseh asked the Great Spirit for the strength to do what was right; to have the wit and quickness to lead his warriors to victory. Despite what reason and sense said, he would follow his heart. He would follow freedom.

And no fires were lit that night, as Tecumseh and his warrior throng were but creatures of the dark. In stealth and quiet, they felled hundreds of young trees. They were sharpened to spikes and they prepared as many arrows as could be had. They then awaited the morning light . . . and just before sunrise they moved into position.

At dawn's first light, Tecumseh heard a horn of alarm that sounded within the fort's ramparts. The night sentries had awoken from a late night nap only to see amassed in the plain some thousands of Indian warriors at a distance from the main gate, all dressed in full regalia and ready for battle. Tecumseh knew what they feared. Like a great field of corn, red-skinned Indians beyond count had sprouted overnight.

The guards called out and sent hurried word to the fort's commander. Tecumseh heard the random shouts of urgency and fear that cried throughout the fort's walls. "Send for Major General Hull! An imminent attack is upon us! The plain is filled wide with Indian savages!" The fort's soldiers scrambled about and gathered their muskets to full attention. The gunnery soldiers readied themselves at their cannons, which were pointed straight upon the fort plain; though they cried out in frustration that the savage horde was just out of range.

In moments, the fort's commander appeared. He needed a view of the Indian horde. And Tecumseh's warriors gazed back. The commander stood proud in his grand uniform, his saber hung to the side. The feathery plume of his hat swayed majestic in the soft breeze. But from a distance, he did not look at all pleased. And his face seemed more pale than normal, as he stared back. The sight of the battle-plain filled wide with red-skinned warriors made him shudder. Then in exasperation, he fumbled his eye scope close for a better view. He gasped out.

Tecumseh could only guess the major general recognized him, for they had met before. And surely the sight of two thousand and more hungry warriors stirred fear in the major general's heart. Though Tecumseh smiled low in wonder, for he could not imagine the major general's thoughts on seeing Gahnoque. The major general must think he looked upon some ancient demon from the darkest of dreams.

Major General Hull then yelled out angrily, "Load the cannonball and your muskets, with triggers cocked and ready for battle! If they advance into range, unleash the cannons! And any man not defending his post will be shot or hung in the stockade!" At those terse words, he stomped off.

Tecumseh's ruse had worked. The fort expected an attack at any moment.

A warrior then called out to Tecumseh, "Where is it that the paleface chief goes? Will he not lead his men into battle?"

Tecumseh sighed, "I have heard word of this paleface chief. And there has never been blood upon his blade. I am sure he has gone to his private quarters. He will not be out in the open, for we are savages. And in a surging attack, he would not risk being felled by musket shot or arrow. That man is no General Harrison."

The warriors just looked on in wonder. The long knives were fierce in battle, but they wondered aloud why they followed such a paleface chief who was not? Those palefaces were strange indeed.

**

General Harrison's large army had been on the move for days. Now close to its journey's end, it still had no sight or whisper of nary an Indian. Eager to arrive to Fort Detroit, he awoke his soldiers as the dark of night flickered to dawn to make the trip's last leg. He would have his force arrive at the fort's gate in the early morning of that day. The still sleepy soldiers stepped groggily into line.

And as they did, two scouts who had been sent ahead earlier by Harrison galloped back wildly. The soldiers stretched and peered. They tried to glimpse that which stirred up the noisy excitement. The scouts rode past the soldiers, straight to General Harrison. They shouted, "General! General! Where is the general?"

The soldiers pointed farther to the back of the long unending line of blue jackets, where he rode along.

They rode up to the general and yelled, "We have seen the large Indian force. They do go in attack of Fort Detroit, and some thousands strong they are. They sit upon the battle-plain at a distance from its main gate. They prepare an assault upon its very walls."

General Harrison wheeled his large horse about in excitement. "So, the great Indian army is gathered at the doorstep of Fort Detroit you say. Did they see you at all?"

"No sir," the scouts replied.

The general pondered that, and asked, "Did you see Tecumseh among them? Was he at the lead?"

The scouts shook their heads and one said, "We cannot say. We had to keep our distance and in hiding, so as to not be seen."

The general wondered that it must be Tecumseh, for who else would lead such an attack on Fort Detroit. Only a great chief, buoyed by his stunning victories would be so bold. But if the scout's eyes were true, the general was emboldened, as he commanded a force far greater in number to that of Tecumseh. Surely, he would put an end to that growing talk of Tecumseh's legend and his great confederacy. It warmed his heart and brought a smile to his face to think that he would be the one to do so.

As all other Indians had before, Tecumseh would have no choice. He would flee ... or he would die. Before the thundering cavalry and ten large cannon, there was no other end. Legend or not, that Tecumseh would fall before Harrison's mighty blade. The general wheeled his horse about and galloped ahead. Word of the Indian throng spread like wild fire throughout the ranks. They all marched on to grand visions of victory. And why would they not, General Harrison had never tasted defeat in battle. Harrison barked out, the soldiers picked up the pace.

And late midmorning, they at last came upon that which they sought. The warm sun glowed yellow and beat down under a deep blue sky. The thick leaved and dark green trees of the forest passed them by as they moved near. Birds took flight in the other direction, away from the fort, as if they knew of what was to come. Around the last winding bend and there it was. The trail opened up before them. There stood some two thousand and more Indian warriors in all their savage majesty.

General Harrison raised his hand. His sea of soldiers came to a stop. They stared out across the battle-plain. The walls of Fort Detroit towered to the side. But the Indian horde was not at the fort's doorstep. It was still a good distance away from its gates . . . and not in range of the fort's cannons. That was disheartening. Harrison had planned to face the Indian force on two fronts. He hoped to pen in the Indians like herded farm cattle. But now that could not be, unless the Indian force could be pushed within range of the fort's guns.

Although that disappointment was tempered, as an ambush was not possible upon that plain. The forest sat too far back to provide hiding of some nameless horde in wait to join the battle. And always it was the Indians way to attack in surprise from a cloaked terrain. No, there could be no such attack here.

The two armies captured full the attention of the other. Glaring eyes stared across the field and measured the worth of each. They prepared for what was to come. The general raised his eye scope and looked deeper into the massed flesh of Indians. His heart raced upon the sight, for there in the center must indeed be that Tecumseh, for the others looked to that plain Indian for their orders. And there was a strange looking beast, the one Private Thalom spoke of. And it looked back at him.

Assuredness sat upon its face. That gave Harrison pause. For surely, if he sat upon a field with only two thousand soldiers and faced down an Indian army over ten thousand strong, with the aid of cavalry and large cannon, he would not be filled with such an air of defiance. What wind set them a sail and drove them forth against such odds? No desperation marked its face. But no matter, Harrison smiled and clenched his jaw. He had brought an armada. The great Indian conflict and the growing legend of Tecumseh would end that day.

Chapter Twenty
Rise of the Shawnee

Tecumseh breathed deep. His insides tightened like a coiled snake in the meadow. He knew what was to come. General Harrison snarled. Muscles flexed on his broad frame. It was time. Harrison turned abruptly and shouted to his officers with great vigor, "Bring the twelve pounders forward! Move them to the front!"

The officers called out the order, gunnery soldiers scrambled. They strained to roll the great guns, the wheels creaked under the weight. The barrels shined bright.

Harrison barked, "Let us measure their fierceness once our large guns explode upon them. No doubt, they will tremble at the thunder, and flesh will be shred from bone! They will soon be fleeing this field!"

Tecumseh and his warriors looked on. Doom settled in their gut. Though fierce of heart, even they were shaken at the sight of those barrels that now stared them down. The boom and roar that splits the air and shakes the ground. Chests tightened, breaths were short. Doubt circled Tecumseh's mind like a hungry vulture once more. Had he led his warriors all that long way just for slaughter?

Tecumseh clenched his jaw and bit down hard upon his fear. He must be strong for the people. He then spoke aloud, "And so it is, General Harrison means to soften our spirit and bring a barrage of death and terror upon us at the battle's outset."

He turned to Gahnoque and said, "It is now that my people call upon the Jhagir. If we are to have a chance of victory this day, these cannons must be destroyed, or we shall flee this place in defeat."

Gahnoque nodded and said, "The Jhagir are glad to do what we may for the people." He then stepped forward alone and stared across the field. The black barrels were like the darkest of storm clouds that approached. He inhaled slow the crisp morning air, a last breath of peace. The sinewed muscles of his frame flexed.

A gasp rose up about the blue-jacketed sea. Tecumseh heard the soldiers yell and shout. Excitement shot about the unending lines of long knives at Gahnoque's sight. His snake-like hair hissed menace and flayed in the wind. Harrison screamed to his men, "Ready the cannons! Prepare to fire!" Then it began.

Gahnoque exploded. He shot across the field, a lone arrow, into a sea of long knives and glaring cannons. His large strides chewed up the distance between them in a blur.

Harrison yelled out angrily, "Take that creature out!"

The cannon wicks hissed flame and spark. Then the barrels boomed. Upon the plain, chunks of earthen mounds sprayed into the air about Gahnoque. The ground shook, but the furious cannon fire did not find its mark. It was an impossible task. Gahnoque was too fast, too agile. Officers yelled again to fire. The barrage was relentless. But it did not matter.

Gahnoque was nearly upon them. Tecumseh could see the lines of panic mark the faces of many long knives. And a blue glow encircled Gahnoque as he closed in. Then he was gone, vanished into a black fog. Startled cries and gasps went up from the soldiers.

Then Gahnoque appeared from nowhere, as he flew out of a black mist. He was upon them and towered over one cannon. The blue jackets' faces were awash in awe, but then turned to terror as he raised in his hands two weapons of light. In one hand was a large curved blade, and the other an axe-like weapon. And they spoke with a low ominous hum.

But the terror was short lived. One swift strike of the blade cut clean through the torsos of three soldiers. With a lightning crack, body pieces slid to the ground. And before a breath could be taken, Gahnoque flipped back into the air. He twisted and turned, and beheaded one soldier with the axe as he rose up into the air, and ripped apart the chest of another as he landed. He then struck down the three soldiers still by the gun with another swing of his blade, and a lightning crack rang out once more.

The sea of soldiers was aghast, while Tecumseh and his warriors stood agape at that dance of death. Every soldier that stood by the big gun was cut down.

Gahnoque then turned and glowered upon the cannon nearby. In a panic, several of the gun's soldiers fumbled to raise their pistols and fired. The musket lead flew toward him. At once, he glowed blue and vanished again into a black shroud. He then reappeared in the same manner, and stood at their backs. They watched their pistol-fire shoot dead five soldiers of another big gun nearby. And that was the last thing those soldiers saw in the world. Gahnoque drove his starlit blade through their bodies and brought quick death. He then spun around and cut down the last gunnery soldiers. Just like that, another cannon was unmanned.

Several cannons began to fire again upon Tecumseh and his warriors, desperate to destroy something. The cannon shot threw mounds of earth into the air, and sprayed some warriors in a rainfall of dirt. Tecumseh and his warriors remained just out of reach. Gahnoque then turned and leapt in a great bound toward those cannons. He hurtled through the air and brought swift death upon another big gun. Limbs were sliced. Skulls were smashed against cannon barrels. Ferocious and wild, he flung the lifeless bodies like discarded carcasses. And then he vanished into a black fog once more.

Only to reappear at the barrel end of one more cannon and grab hold of the barrel. He began to curl it upward. The gunnery soldiers feverishly lit the fuse. They meant to blow a hole through Gahnoque as he stood. The wick hissed and a small sparked flame raced to explode. But just before it fired, Gahnoque cried out and heaved the barrel upward. He looked into the soldiers' eyes, smiled, and vanished into a black mist again. A thunderous boom rang out! A great explosion tore the barrel apart into iron splinters. It shot debris of death everywhere, like arrows.

And then things turned worse for the long knives. They gasped aloud in dismay, as now Ithikkah and Taughannock joined the attack. They appeared to the cannons on each far end of the artillery line, and moved with an unnatural quickness. In a blink, both gunnery detachments were slain.

Ithikkah and Taughannock then did something unexpected. With the strength of an oxen pack, they grabbed hold of the cannon barrel near to them and strained to turn them inward. They meant to face them toward the cannons at the line's center. The large wheels groaned, as each cannon was flexed into place. They then reached down, grabbed the lighting rod, and set flame to wick.

The soldiers' at those cannons froze in dread. They faced death not only by Gahnoque's starlit blade, as he stood among them, but also the two lit cannons about to fly upon them from both sides. The cannons exploded. A ferocious boom bellowed across the field. Gahnoque glowed blue and vanished again amid the fire that erupted. The barrels were blown apart, and shot into the air among earthen soil and body limbs. And all who had stood in their midst were dead.

The three Jhagir then grabbed hold of the barrels of those unmanned cannons that remained. They twisted them like the mangled roots of a tree, to be forever destroyed, unless they were melted down and reborn anew. While one bent a barrel, the other two flew here and there like ghosts, and killed soldiers cold and swift. And every time, they dodged bayonet lunges and musket fire. In moments, every cannon was destroyed. All three Jhagir turned one last time and looked out defiantly to the army of blue jackets. They gave warning of the hell to come. Then they vanished into a black shroud, as if they had never been there at all.

Gahnoque reappeared on the battle plain and stood beside Tecumseh.

"I hope to never call the Jhagir my enemy," Tecumseh said. His head shook of wonder. Tecumseh whispered to himself, "With the great guns no more, maybe we shall make a stand this day."

And his fear and doubt whispered back, "But the palefaces number is still beyond count...."

Gahnoque nodded in return, and they both turned to face the endless sea of long knives and what would come next.

Tecumseh saw the long knives now looked to General Harrison, for what could be done against the Jhagir. And Harrison was a mountaintop rock still. He could not be shaken. His eyes darkened with anger, he shouted fury, "Bring forth the cavalry! Heed not the deeds of those strange beasts, for we shall thunder a thousand hooves down upon them!"

At once, the soldier lines parted and the horsed soldiers galloped forth. General Harrison's muscled horse rose up and he swung his war saber forward, "To the Indian horde!"

At his command, a thousand horsed cavalry exploded across the plain. The ground shuddered, as the hooves of one thousand warhorses galloped down upon Tecumseh and his warriors. It was a most booming sound that beat upon the chest like a violent drum. And the ground was hard and dry, as it had not rained in days. Clouds of thick dust rose up and swirled about the field.

Amid that blackened storm, fear seeped into their hearts. And Tecumseh knew it was the same for a young warrior new to battle, or one of old. Whether fierce of heart or not, fear of those stampeding beasts touched the soul.

In that quaking terror, Tecumseh yelled, "Be strong for the people! Hold the line!"

The crazed cavalry flew closer. The sharp blades of steel protruded forth and the glint shone bright in the daylight that shot through the darkened and wispy clouds of dust that swirled. The thunderous stampede now rode at but two hundred paces, and closed in fast.

At that moment, Tecumseh's fist flew high and he yelled out, "Raise your bows and let loose your arrows. Blacken the sky and rain death upon them!"

And for those many warriors who carried bows, arrows were let loose. A great multitude of whooshing sounds sliced the air about them, as some one thousand arrows shot up into the sky. And indeed, the midday sun was darkened a bit. The arrows reached the height of the wispy clouds, and then began a swift descent down to the grassy field below. With each breathless moment, they picked up speed for the violent thrust to come.

The horsed cavalry looked up and saw the mighty wave of arrowheads launched upon them. But they could not stop now, for so fast the beasts they rode upon thundered. They were nearly upon Tecumseh and his warriors; one hundred fifty paces ... one hundred paces ... and now but seventy paces across the battle-plain. The horsed riders let loose a wild scream of fury.

And with vicious stabs, the arrows plunged down upon the cavalry charge, like a swath of diving birds at sea that strike deep into the water to pierce the flesh of the fish below. And many found their mark. Soldiers were pierced in all limbs of the body, and many fell lifeless, as their horses galloped on into the fray alone. The volley struck a mighty blow to Harrison's cavalry, as some four hundred riders found death in that one furious strike.

But six hundred rode on in rage through the black storm of arrows. With each gallop, Tecumseh saw their faces seethed revenge for their fallen comrades. In madness they flew, their faces stretched of hate. They raised their swords for the kill at last, mere paces away. But as they did, the warrior lines parted. And two hundred wooden and pointed spikes stared back at horse and rider.

Clouds of thick dust thundered and crashed upon Tecumseh and his warriors, like a storm wave that rammed upon a sea wall of stone and rock. Its furious water foamed and overflowed in all directions. Many a horse and man screamed out agony, impaled upon those shaved and hard-tipped spikes. The weight of the hooved beasts drove the spikes clear through, and brought quick death to many. Almost two hundred riders fell, while four hundred or so rode on through the spiked line. And warriors of many a tribe were cut down by the war sabers of the horsed riders. Cold steel sliced through flesh and bone.

But as they rode deeper into the sea of painted flesh, their speed slowed. Arrows were shot into the horses at the lead, and they tumbled to the ground. The fallen beasts slowed those that followed behind, and tomahawks were hurled upon their riders. Blue jackets were then pulled from their horses, thrown upon the ground. Fierce clashes were everywhere. Grime and blood of friend and foe splattered about. It was like red rain. Screams of hate and pain cried out in both English and tribal tongues.

The brave upon both sides fell upon the grassy plain. But the sheer number of Tecumseh's warriors began to overwhelm the cavalry. Though about two hundred and fifty warriors lay dead upon the field, the four hundred horsed soldiers were killed to a man in moments. And now Tecumseh had his own cavalry, as his warriors sat astride the beasts free from the yoke of their previous masters. Those horsed warriors numbered about three hundred and fifty, as they let the wounded horses run free and away from the battle.

The warriors had opened up wide and swallowed whole the cavalry. And Tecumseh could no longer see the endless lines of blue jackets through the clouds of thick dust that smoked all about. He guessed that surely General Harrison wheeled his horse around, and strained for a view of how the cavalry charge went. Tecumseh was sure Harrison awaited some sign of the cavalry's return, so that he could then launch his ten thousand infantry upon Tecumseh's warrior brothers.

And now Tecumseh would give him one. Out of the smoky shroud, shrieks and yells pierced the air. Three hundred and fifty horsed riders shot forth at a great gallop, with Tecumseh at the lead. In wild abandon they rode. Harrison's cavalry now returned, but with riders unexpected upon their war saddles.

The army lines scrambled at the sight, and mustered into formation to let loose a barrage of musket fire. But it was no easy thing to load gunpowder and wad, and ram it down a musket barrel, as a stampede thundered and screamed down upon you. Tecumseh saw the fear that gripped the tattered nerves of many a soldier.

Tecumseh caught sight of General Harrison too. The general's horse wheeled about and braced for the furious wave of savage and beast. His face was filled with doubt and wonder at how that could be. Tecumseh knew the Indians had never before turned back a cavalry charge, and at one thousand strong no less. He knew Harrison would not believe such a thing, unless he had seen it with his own eyes.

And there were nineteen hundred or so warriors on foot, in a wild sprint behind the horsed riders. The riders then let loose a rainfall of arrows into the army lines. Some two hundred palefaces collapsed lifeless upon one another. They then let loose one more arcing volley into the sea of blue jackets, and another two hundred fell limp to the ground. With each volley, Tecumseh saw Harrison snarl back to the sky. The general dared an arrow to fly into him . . . but none did. The arrows knew better. Harrison was the bravest of all the palefaces, and so the arrows were afraid too and did not go near.

Though the battle had gone ill so far, Harrison would not have defeat. Tecumseh knew Harrison never had before. He was the great general. Harrison gritted his teeth, snarled anger, and screamed to his men. He would still have victory on the field that day. And Tecumseh saw the over nine and a half thousand long knives that still stood were shaken from their fear. And there was that familiar chant again that rose up across the grassy plain . . . Harrison . . . Harrison. The blue jackets found their courage again and rallied to the great general.

Harrison barked to his officers, "Unleash two musket volleys straight into the horde! And then a bayonet charge! We shall see who takes this field!" His officers shouted out the command to the sea of soldiers; but with the horse riders almost upon them, there was time for but one volley.

Musket flash and smoke erupted across the lines, and lead flew into the horsed riders. Several hundred warriors were shot dead from their horses. But Tecumseh was not among them, though musket balls whizzed by, and pierced his cloth shirt and buckskin pants. The soldiers then fired wildly upon the riders that rode on. They found their mark in another fifty warriors or so, whose bodies fell. Yet again, Tecumseh was one of the fortunate few who made it through that firestorm. Although a musket ball did graze his thigh, which drew blood.

The hundred or so horsed riders that rode on smashed into the army's lines. Tecumseh was at the lead still, and he swung down his angry tomahawk from atop his horse. Its force threw the bodies of dead paleface soldiers backwards onto the hard ground. Blue jackets spun around to take quick aim at Tecumseh; but they fired wildly and missed. At such close range, he moved by in a blur. But a brave long knife rushed into Tecumseh's path, and kneeled before the hooved beast. He dug the butt of his musket into the ground and drove the bayonet blade deep into the horse's chest. It ran over and trampled the soldier to death, as it tumbled upon the steel blade. The horse's weight served to rip its chest apart upon the stuck blade and it thudded dead to the ground.

Tecumseh was flung into the air. He landed upon a clearing before a group of stunned soldiers. He turned about and prowled about on his limbs. His eyes smoldered, for he brought death through the foggy shroud of musket smoke that rose about him. Tecumseh saw the doubt and fear upon their faces. And then Tecumseh leapt upon them with a roar. He was a magnificent beast upon its prey, with its fur that flowed in the wind and its sharp fangs drawn wide and that glared - he came for the kill swift and true.

He carried his trusted tomahawk of many years in one hand and a thick war knife in the other. And as he sprang forth, he swung them down one and then the other, and smashed apart the chest of one soldier and slit the throat of another. He spun around and knocked the bayonet blow to the side with his tomahawk, and slit the throat of another paleface soldier that rushed to him. He spun backwards, and slammed his tomahawk down and severed the arm of one long knife and gouged the neck apart of another. Tecumseh then turned to his back, and looked upon a musket barrel raised straight at him.

He exploded upon the blue jacket in a mighty leap. He swung his tomahawk upward and smashed the musket barrel to the sky as it exploded. Tecumseh then let loose his tomahawk at the height of its upward swing, flipped it, and grabbed hold of it again. He thrust it angrily down into the soldier's head. Like a melon, the skull split in two.

But as he cut down those long knives before him, twice as many appeared in their stead. And they thirsted for his death. A rush of warriors came toward Tecumseh. They would save their chief. Tecumseh glanced back and ten long knives gathered quickly in a line, and readied to fire upon him. As he stared down the ends of those musket barrels, all moved slow like a dream. He dropped to the ground before his next breath and clutched the soil tight. He yelled for his brothers to do the same, but in their mad rush, they did not hear him.

As he fell, musket shot exploded and rang out. It whizzed through the air, over his head, and a warm breeze blew down upon him. And that musket lead found its mark, for it cut down the onrushing warriors all. Their bodies fell loose and limp to the ground all about Tecumseh, and stared vacantly to the sky above. He gathered himself again, with muscles clenched. More warriors came to his aid. He readied to launch upon those soldiers once more. But many more paleface soldiers stepped forward and formed up lines at once. They fired again into the new lines of warriors that rushed in, and brought death to more of his kin.

And Tecumseh and his warriors began to falter, and were pushed back. A confidence surged among America's lines. Among all the long knives, a self-assuredness now painted their faces, muscles flexed with might. They were emboldened with vigor at the turning of the tide. Tecumseh and his warriors drowned in a sea of blue jackets. Though Tecumseh knew that was what had to be, if the great paleface army was to be lured deeper onto the battlefield and somehow defeated that day.

Tecumseh rose up, spun, and knocked one paleface soldier to the ground with a kick of his leg. He struck down two more blue jackets with his tomahawk with but one stroke, as if he chopped down small trees in the forest. And at last, he turned and yelled for the warriors to retreat. Enough had paid the price for freedom. The great army's appetite had been fully whetted and their bellies hungered for more. Now it was for the warriors that remained to fall back, to draw in deep Harrison's army. Tecumseh must wind the snare tight before it was sprung.

A roar went up from the soldiers' ranks at that sight. They charged after at a quickened pace. Tecumseh caught sight of General Harrison, who smiled smugly. The general was a sure sight, who would have victory that day. It always had to be that way. Though Tecumseh had landed the first mighty blows of the battle and destroyed the large cannons and cavalry, it made no matter. Harrison's chest swelled upon his war steed. He was a bursting swagger, like some ancient bronzed statue of old that Tecumseh read about in John Sackett's books.

"Onward men! Victory is ours! We have but to reach out and seize it! Chase them to the walls of Fort Detroit! Run them down one and all!" yelled Harrison. The general began his ride to the battlefront to claim his victory. Harrison barked, "I will have Tecumseh kneeling before me, or his head upon a pike . . . either will do." Tecumseh saw a wild look that burned in the general's eyes. Chants again rose up like a storm from the blue-jacketed army. "Harrison! Harrison!"

Smoke drifted and the clamor of war clashed all about. And Tecumseh wondered if now at last they would meet in battle . . . would he have the strength to defeat the bravest paleface soldier he had ever seen? He breathed deep. Much of Harrison's force had moved far onto the plain, and Tecumseh's warriors could retreat no more, less they be in range of Fort

Detroit's mighty guns. Tecumseh took it all in. Death surrounded him. Many warriors lay lifeless upon the field. They had given the greatest of gifts, their lives. They had held the line as he had asked them to do.

And with America's victory just moments away, Tecumseh exhaled slow. He reached low for a bow and the lone arrow of a fallen warrior near to him. He bathed it in the rivers of blood that flowed about, and set it aflame with the spark of his pistol shot. He rose up and stepped forward from the embattled warriors that still stood. There were so few, against a sea of long knives still. An onslaught of soldiers rushed to him. And there he stood, with bow and flaming arrow in hand, alone against the blowing wind. The flame burned slow and smoldered, and the arrow waited to be let loose.

Unyielding he was, like a chiseled mountain of rock upon which all things would break against. And though it was midday, the field was thick and heavy with the smoke of musket fire. The misty swirls of smoke largely blotted out the sun, save for faint and scattered rays that broke through down to the ground below. And the day was much darkened, like its last light at dusk.

Curiosity lined the faces of the long knives that charged, and they slowed for a moment. Harrison wheeled his horse about, and shouted, "Let us give him that which he seeks. My brave men, let him taste the cold steel of our bayonets!"

The paleface soldiers screamed and let loose a war yell, "Hoorah!" as they sprinted forward and picked up speed, like they ran downhill. Musket barrels were stretched, the sharp bayonets spiked forward. In the dim and dusk of battle, a thousand and more silvery glint reflections of those blades flew toward Tecumseh, as if the many sparkled stars of the night fell upon him.

Tecumseh raised the burning arrow toward the thousand filled faces of hate. He strained the bow tight, as if that one flaming arrow would strike them down all. And though his heart would joyfully let it fly, he knew better its purpose and need. He then raised it to the sky, and released it to fly forth. The arrow screamed into the air, and arced over the battlefield. Its light scorched the darkened sky, and radiated a piercing flame for all to see. Silence fell for a moment. The arrow's billowing flame danced as it flew, as if a shooting star.

The silence was then shattered. A thunderous roar split the thick air and charged forth from both sides of the forest. It enveloped the senses of all living things. Tecumseh saw the paleface soldiers turn and peer out into the forest's dark. Their eyes widened and mouths fell agape at the rumble. The forest was alive and erupted all about them. The ground shook and the trees heaved and cracked. And the warriors of the free peoples spewed forth.

Out of the shrouded shadows rushed one thousand warriors from both sides. Endless in numbers they were, a flood that raged of painted and tattooed flesh. War cries screamed out and rattled bones. They flew upon the flanks of America with the vengeance of a great wave at sea that crashed upon a lone ship, its fury and strength so mighty as to swallow it whole and sink it to a cold grave in the waters deep.

Terror lined the faces of many long knives. Those two new waves of Indian warriors were fresh and fleet of foot, and covered the far distance to the battle from the forest's edge in but a moment. They smashed into the army's lines and devastated its ranks, and cut down the soldiers before them. They drove the army's flanks in on itself, surrounded on all sides by enraged warriors. So many thousands of long knives were now trapped . . . and doomed.

From a distance, Tecumseh saw General Harrison recoil at the sight. He reeled in a stupor. The general did not foresee that second attack. Tecumseh wondered if he had, Harrison would have surely fired his cannons upon the forest's edge at the first, and razed it to the ground. And then there would have been no wave of unseen warriors to swoop in to steal the victory from Harrison's grasp.

And Tecumseh saw the three Jhagir destroy any that stood before them. They were ghostly demons whose green markings glowed and whirred about, as if some stroke of a paintbrush upon the air. And it was at that moment that Tecumseh saw Gahnoque emerge out of war's smoky mist. Gahnoque hung in midair like some winged creature. His braided rope-like hair flipped and turned through the air. Through the musket smoke, Gahnoque cut down two long knives in midair. He was launched from a high perch down upon his prey below. And Gahnoque pounced upon two more paleface soldiers. He swung the weapons held in each hand away from his body, as if a graceful dance. And with that, two severed heads rolled about the ground.

Gahnoque then turned and stared at the paleface soldiers near to him. His eyes flickered in flame. A blue glow smoldered and lit up his silhouetted form. His muscles twitched and ached for the slightest challenge, but none came. They knew death when they saw it and backed away slow. And with that, Gahnoque turned about and rejoined the deathly feast.

Tecumseh looked upon the great general, and Harrison's face was drawn. He sat in silence upon his horse. Beyond anger, Harrison just looked on the battle in a daze, drowned in his own thoughts. Tecumseh knew Harrison had never tasted defeat before. It did not fit him. And now Tecumseh had changed everything with so many thousands of warriors at his call, and with the Jhagir. Perhaps, the great paleface empire would not be after all. Tecumseh knew he had wounded Harrison like never before.

Many long knives cried out their deathly screams. Then Harrison snapped from his stupor. The general finally seemed to accept it all. There was nothing for it . . . there could be no victory that day. He called out the order and bugles blared. Tecumseh thought to himself that he would have done the same. Better to live on and fight another day than perish on that field. Harrison snarled disgust, spit upon the ground, and then smiled low. With that, he turned his horse and began to saunter from the field. And what remained of the mighty paleface army began a full retreat, and trailed after the great general.

Of course, safe behind Fort Detroit's sturdy walls, Major General Hull finally arose again to its towers. He peered down upon the carnage. And he was aghast; the Indian horde had somehow decimated General Harrison's great army. And the general who had never been defeated now trudged away in retreat. Hull yelled out to the entire fort to prepare for an imminent attack. And then he shrank away to some hidden place again. Tecumseh looked upon the fort's great paleface chief and smiled. He knew his warriors had no worry of Hull and his men.

At the battle's end, with victory secure, Taughannock and Tecumseh lowered their weapons, and looked upon the retreating long knives. It was a slow moving herd of blue buffalo. They noticed an officer who oversaw the rear of the retreat. And he laid into a large brute of a soldier who walked upon a dying Shawnee. That soldier was large, as he stood about six foot eight. He was a giant, as most men stood nearly a foot shorter. And that beast of a man was imbued with a meanness, like salt in a wound. They had caught sight of the brute earlier in the battle. He seemed to enjoy the carnage of war, regardless of who was cut down or on whose side he fought.

And then they bore a vision of cruelty unimagined, even by war's standards. The brute looked down upon the dying warrior, his paleface eyes throbbed hatred. That beastly man enjoyed very much the suffering he looked upon. The warrior crawled about the ground. Blinded, he drowned in his own blood, let loose from gunshot wounds to his eyes.

The officer made his way to the beastly soldier and screamed for him to fall in line. But the brute ignored him and turned all his attention to the wounded Shawnee.

The officer screamed out, "Beckett! Damn it Beckett! You insubordinate son of a bitch, you get in line and that is an order, lest I have you strung up in the stockade!"

Beckett looked up. He smiled ever so faint and eerily. It was a look of wickedness; a black evil in his eyes that haunted the soul.

It was clear that Beckett was not a soldier enlisted for some sense of duty, who sought pay or rank, or battlefield honor. No, he was a truly dark soul that fought just for the pleasure of killing, be it anything or anyone.

The officer shouted again at Beckett, who just half-smiled back with a vacant look in his eyes. It seemed that Beckett itched to blow a hole in his own officer's head. But then, his hatred of the dying Indian got the best of him. He could murder that officer sometime later in the day if need be, because there was an Indian that needed killing now.

The young Shawnee was no more than seventeen years. Beckett reached down and twisted his black mane of hair. He pulled him close, spit in his face, and slammed the warrior's head into the trampled ground. Beckett pulled out his saber and slashed it across the Shawnee's forearm, and sliced it clear through. The warrior cried out, as the stub of an arm spilled blood. Beckett smiled and laughed heartily. He enjoyed a torturous death. The warrior's screams faded and then were no more.

Beckett glanced up and saw Tecumseh and Taughannock from a distance. He smiled, spit disgust on the ground, and snarled back at them both.

Taughannock glowed blue. He would apparate to the brute as rage filled him. He would cut off that monster's head; but Tecumseh grabbed hold of his arm. Tecumseh spoke and his words washed of sadness. "It is too late, our young brother is gone. His spirit is free from the pain of this world. Let him go. Such is the cruelty that can be done unto another, driven by hate and war.

"Let the paleface army go in peace, for we have taken their heart on the field this day . . . let us not give them pause or anger by attacking their retreat.

"You and I have marked that cruel soldier, and we will not forget. But we are not like him. We must be better. We must have the strength to do what is right. My heart tells me that we will see him again."

Taughannock held back in respect for Tecumseh's words, but he said, "My insides burn at seeing a soul so dark and twisted as that Beckett."

Tecumseh just nodded back, his face stretched of sadness.

The officer then rode up to Beckett and leapt down from his steed. His patience was at an end. The officer firmly cocked back the hammer of his pistol and placed its barrel upon Beckett's forehead. He shouted, "So help me God you filth, you get in line now or I will shoot you dead!"

Beckett just looked at the officer and smiled. He just spat again on the ground, and sauntered away from the field with the last of the line that retreated. But he stopped once more to glare back at Taughannock and Tecumseh. He stared smugly into their eyes, so proud of his butchery. He seemed to call out for them to follow after . . . if they dared.

The warriors looked on as the decimated, though still massive, paleface army retreated. Until at last, the long lines of glum head-drooped men marched out of sight. A tired happiness filled the warriors for the great victory. It was a day for the ages of all the free peoples of those lands. The heights they had now ascended in the struggle with the great white fathers had never before been reached, save only in their hoped-for dreams. They could taste the sweet nectar of freedom that dripped upon their parched lips.

Though in great respect they gathered up the dead. They would send them all to the Great Spirit. A very large bed of brush and wood limbs was built upon which to lay the lifeless bodies. A great fire was then lit, which flickered and flamed slow at first. Then it rose up vast and towered, and devoured the flesh of all within its bosom.

Then they gathered up themselves all and began the return trip back to their villages. They left the long knives corpses to rot as they lay. And their multitude was beyond count, which called out to the beasts and scavengers of the wild. The sky became filled with vultures and crows that marked their endless meals below. They waited impatiently for Tecumseh and his warriors to leave that place, so they could gorge themselves upon the stinking flesh strewn about.

In happiness, the Shawnee and other tribes returned to their homes. And a delight spread among the free peoples of the lands. Good feelings burned bright for all the coming months of winter, keeping the bone of winter's chill at bay and ushering in spring's bloom. And during that time, the free people's troubles melted away with no sight or incursion by the great white fathers in any way. The pleasure of that peace soothed the body, spirit, and soul of all.

Some hoped they would never again look upon another paleface and that the great conflict was done at long last. The hearts of many clung to that notion with all of their might; but

Tecumseh knew better. He enjoyed each day of peace with all the fullness of vigor as could be had, as he knew those contented days would not last. He felt it in his bones. The great wolf was not yet dead. And he would always hate the wolf.

Chapter Twenty-One
America's Doubt

Harrison's muscled frame sagged of doubt. He brooded. He had never met that Tecumseh . . . and he hated that plain Indian. Though to his surprise, he also felt some admiration for him. He was a brave warrior indeed, and cunning beyond measure. Tecumseh had done the impossible, and Harrison could not help but respect that. Perhaps in a different time and place, or a different color of skin, they would be friends in peace. But now, they were just enemies.

His army that survived retreated with heads hung low. A sea of vacant stares trudged on in gloom to the safety of Fort Erie. That fort bordered lower eastern Canada and the far west of New York, where Lake Erie met the white capped and wild waters of the great Niagara River. Although not so mighty and stout as Fort Detroit, it was still large and heavily fortified. It would provide a place to recover and regroup.

As they drudged on, the brooding weather matched their hearts, for the winds howled of an early winter in the chilled air. The leaves of late October fell, and faded into early November. And a blanket of snowfall greeted them one particularly cold morning. Winter's early onset was upon them, and they arrived to Fort Erie at last. It was decided. Harrison's army would stay the winter in that place, until the weather cleared in early spring for the long return trip home.

And as they settled in, a storm raged in Harrison's mind. Over five thousand infantry and one thousand cavalry felled, beaten soundly by a lesser foe. Harrison's world was flipped to its dark side. The extraordinary had happened. Something must be done, and quick, for word of Tecumseh's most stunning victory in that great battle would spread to the entire continent like a plague. And his numbers would now swell and bring forth even more warriors from the many tribes. He would at last forge his great confederacy, full and complete into a most formidable foe.

A foe that could make a young nation bow down and make terms. Harrison shuddered. Dark thoughts closed in. He was a lonely man adrift at sea. And it made the winter longer, colder, and darker than any that had come before. He sent out dispatches to President Madison that he would come at the first sign of spring, when winter broke. There was much to discuss. The full force of their young nation must be raised. Everything must be brought to bear to defeat Tecumseh now, before he can build up his confederacy.

The dreary and cold winter days ran into one another, and Harrison's insides churned. But with each passing day, despair would not take him. Somewhere down deep inside, faith found him. He was still a mountain of rock. They would just have to find a way to defeat that plain Indian. He just did not know how.

Harrison drilled his men through the cold of winter, to keep their spirits up, and from going mad with boredom. They could only wait for spring to come. And to the surprise of all, the days of winter flew by. But before it ended, a great surprise arrived at their door. It was President Madison. He and a large detachment arrived in late March. And Madison wasted no time, and headed right away to General Harrison's quarters.

The president threw back the tent cover, and entered alone with a brisk step. There the general sat, alone at a table. Silence welcomed them both with slow nods that echoed the graveness of that meeting. The general poured a small glass of whiskey, and drank it down heartily. A fire burned in his belly.

President Madison looked to Harrison and asked, "I hope the long, dark, and dreary days of winter have not driven you mad with desperation whilst you awaited my counsel?"

Harrison nodded that it had not.

Madison went on, "Well then, let us get to the business at hand, as we have each had some months to think on the crisis before us. Our young nation is in the balance. Tell me, what shall we do with the one who inspires the tribes of this land? What shall we do with this Tecumseh?"

At that most pointed question, Harrison responded with a sigh. "Long has he been a worthy foe as we have moved into the western wilderness. He is a fierce warrior, though also one of great compassion. More than once, he cast his gaze upon native victors and his words dispel their anger and hatred, as if by magic, to save our captured soldiers from torture and death.

"If there be such a thing as noble blood, surely it flows within that Tecumseh. And unlike any Indian that I have before met or heard talk of, he is one of great learning . . . for he has studied the bible, world history, and learned English. Some say he has taken up a friendship with some white settlers to learn such things, though with whom, I do not know."

President Madison's eyes widened.

Harrison went on. "He is the only of his kind who looks to the world beyond his own front door; and if the many tribes would but heed his wisdom, then an empire America will not be. For he has brought together warring tribes of years on end, that speak not the same language.

"He is uncommon; someone who springs up on occasion in history to produce revolutions and overturn the established order of things. If not for America, he would be the founder of an empire to rival that of the Incas I should think. And if he achieves but another victory in battle against our army and given the time to gather up to him all the warriors of this land . . . it will be our end."

President Madison rose up stiff upon his seat's edge, his brow furled. "Well, if that is true, I would wish that he had been born a white man to serve our cause, for we would surely become the world's superpower.

"But since he is not, then it is imperative that we do not give him the opportunity or the inspiration to enjoin all the many tribes to his cause. We will do what must be done and we cannot fail . . . or our nation will be no more."

The general hesitated, and added, "There is something else . . . with him now travels three strange warriors that possess great powers. Word has come that they are from an unknown Shawnee clan from the far north in Upper Canada. But others say they are fallen from the night's sky and not of this world. Well, from wherever their origins, they are a great aid to his cause, and helped turn the tide of the battle."

Madison just brooded in quiet. After a while he spoke, barely above a mutter. "Well, all living things possess a weakness. These strange creatures are no different . . . be they of this world or some other. We must discover their weakness and exploit it. And then we must assemble a force so mighty as to crush this confederacy in its infancy."

Heavy silence fell. They each sipped a few swigs of whiskey, and minds raced. President Madison lit up a thick cigar that bulged. Swirls of smoke released into the air, and engulfed the two men.

Madison then said, "Ah ha! That is it then," as another smoke plume escaped.

The general turned, and asked, "Mr. President?"

Madison stared off to somewhere else. His brows furled in thought. The cigar that hung loose from his lips smoldered. "General, the tribes of this land are a great serpent that slithers about in the dark, striking at us from places of hidden defense. And so, we must draw this serpent out from its secret lairs and paths, as then we will find its head and cut it off.

"And as Tecumseh is the serpent's head, we must remove him. Once the serpent is beheaded, it will thrash wildly about, and can most easily be dispatched."

Harrison looked upon Madison in doubt, though curious to hear of such a grand plan.

President Madison went on, "My dear Harrison, here is what we shall do: we will send out a messenger, unarmed and alone, to carry the colors of full surrender to be delivered to Tecumseh himself. We will offer our goodwill, asking him to treat with us at a great council of peace.

"As an act of our faith, we will bring forth our standing army, asking that Tecumseh do the same. And you, General Harrison, shall treat with him, which will demonstrate America's full respect and commitment.

"Tecumseh's heart will be glad with excitement by the chance for freedom. It will be a treasured jewel dangling before him; one his heart cannot ignore, no matter the warnings flashing in his mind.

"But all will be done under the guise of peace, for in secret, we will send out a force some several thousand strong to lay waste to his village and kill all those he holds close . . . which will be something not so difficult in that all its warriors will be emptied out."

The general's posture sagged. He leaned back in his chair, and his mind whirled at such deception. Lines of frown cast upon his face, but he said nothing.

Madison's voice rose in vigor as more words flew from his tongue. "And when news of the village's sacking falls upon his ears, Tecumseh will rush back in earnest; but it will be too late, for it will be destroyed. Driven mad with rage and mourning, he will no longer lead the people as he has and a great chaos will follow. It is then that hope will fade and Tecumseh's confederacy shall fall into history's shadows. And in Tecumseh's weakness, we will strike with the most massive force we have ever assembled. We shall deal once and for all a deathly blow, with final victory being ours!"

He then added calmly, "And of course, in delivering this message unto him in this way, upon the messenger's return, we shall learn of the village's whereabouts, which is information most vital. For learning of the village's location is key, as home is where the heart is, even for the uncivilized. Let us see how commanding he can be when we cut out his heart and destroy those closest to him."

General Harrison sighed as President Madison recited his strategies and schemes. The general was a great warrior, and great warriors meet in battle to decide things. They do not skulk about in the dark to deceive an enemy. There was no honor in that. Harrison then quietly spoke, "Sir, there must be another way."

Madison's eyes gleamed daggers at Harrison. "General, I do not have the luxury of being a soldier in battle. I do not have the luxury of honor. I have to run a nation . . . save a nation. Now, you are the bravest and best soldier in this army. And you will do what a good soldier does. You will follow your orders. Am I clear?"

Harrison just sighed, and his chest exhaled deep. He was a soldier . . . and soldiers always followed orders. After a moment of pained quiet, Harrison said, "Tecumseh would not allow someone into his village alive in the knowledge of its paths and trails, and then be returned to us . . . surely they would be blindfolded so that though returned unharmed, they would have no knowledge of its whereabouts."

President Madison thought on that, as another cloud of smoke bellowed forth, and said, "Well, then we will avail ourselves of bribery of some kind. Surely, there must be some

Shawnee, or folk of some other tribe, who would give up the village location for some trinket or bauble. We must put our spies to work in finding such an Indian."

After a short pause, Madison spoke up, "General, word reached my ear some months back of a great Choctaw chief, Pushmataha, who refused Tecumseh's call to confederacy. For many ages, the Choctaw and Shawnee have been enemies . . . and even now, their dislike is strong. We should speak with this Choctaw chief."

Late into the night, they discussed the plans of treachery, though still Harrison smoldered in disgust. Harrison's thoughts churned. Some would say such deceitful deeds was how a soul was ripped apart, and how the higher form of ourselves was forever lost. But in the end, he was a soldier after all. The best damn soldier a young nation could put forth. And so he would speak no more against it. At some late hour, it was agreed. Scouts were sent out at once to find that Choctaw chief. And the next day, in a rising spirit and mood, President Madison, General Harrison, and over five thousand soldiers departed from Fort Erie.

Warm weather greeted them that spring, and the large force made good time in its return back. When at last they arrived to the main base in Virginia, there were scouts waiting breathlessly, having arrived back themselves that very morning. They had word from the Choctaw chief . . . he would not aid America. But the news did not upset President Madison. They would just have to find that village some other way. They would just have to find some other Indians to help them . . . whether they wanted to or not.

At once, a soldier was brought forth to receive his orders. Private Jonas was to be sent out into the wild alone, armed only with a small pistol, as the blooms of late spring faded and the early summer breezes began to blow. Harrison thought the private's impression was one of a peaceful camaraderie, with a thin wiry frame. He did not suffer from too many meals. Lines of friendliness sat upon his face. And it would do no good to send out a fierce looking soldier, as Indian scouts would kill anyone with a look of menace about them before the message could be delivered.

President Madison smiled. He turned to Harrison and said, "Jonas is young and without family. So there will be no uproar if he suffers torture or death at the hand of wild Indians. We will have no worry about such a deed playing out in the papers, or any political meddling by members of Congress. No one will care."

Harrison just nodded.

Private Jonas was to be sent out into the heart of the Ohio Valley, Indian country. And he would give a parchment to the Indian chief, sealed with the President's mark, to show he brought the truth with him. And it would bear the words and signature of Madison himself.

President Madison and Harrison watched Private Jonas ride out into the wild. The private disappeared into the dark forest that swallowed him up. And the president sighed. "General, be thankful that we do not ride out alone into the wild. For that private is sure to suffer some terror along the way. He is at the mercy of those savages."

Harrison just looked on, and snarled discontent. Now, they could only wait for Tecumseh's reply.

Chapter Twenty-Two
Savages Among Us

Jonas swallowed hard. Tightness choked his parched throat like a noose. But he pushed on and made his way through the forest wilderness. Dusk was fading, and the forest's green was turning black in the dim light. The gait of his horse was steady; its head hung low and nose to the trail. Jonas was so small. And his heartbeat pounded louder with each lonely step.

The wild sounds of summer echoed out too. Animal chatter followed close. He guessed it to be some pack of quarreling squirrels or raccoons, but they did not reveal themselves. There was also the screeching overhead of some strange birds in the trees. Nerves tingled like needles upon the skin. There was also the occasional guttural growl of some animal in the distance. Did some mountain lion stalk him? Perhaps a wolf followed in the forest shadows. Or maybe, it was just in his mind. And as his thoughts raced, he clenched the handle of his pistol tighter.

The forest's tall and thickly bunched trees closed in tight. And he jumped at the errant crack and snap of fallen wood limbs. His senses were alive, awash in cold fear. The wooded dark tightened its grip, with each breath shorter than the last. Yet, he did not waver. He kept to the trail . . . he would not let his country down.

When nightfall came, he kindled a small fire to cook a meal, but also to keep him company. He was a lonely soul, and the flames were only companion. The dark of night, so deep in the forest, was one of pitted blackness, like your lids were closed over your eyes as they strained for sight. The fire's flames swayed about, and he would peer out anxiously. His eyes stretched with every bit of the flame's light to see whatever it was that moved in the shadows. If it was anything at all, for in the dark, one could see and hear things that did not exist. He slept light and welcomed the dawn. That was the way of things for the next several days and nights.

But then one night was different. There were muffled steps and rustling leaves. His heart leapt in the tense quiet. Until, out from a distance, he saw a red-skinned warrior on a painted brown and black pony that stared back. Hate oozed from the black of his eyes. And he was huge. The biggest Indian he had ever seen. Jonas could not breathe, and choked on the still night air. That Indian could kill him in an instant . . . yet at a distance it stayed. It just stood in the moonlight, and then was gone. Jonas exhaled deep. Death had decided to pass him by. Jonas did not get any sleep the rest of that long night, and was glad when sunrise came.

And luckily, over the next few weeks, he did not encounter another living soul, even that bull of an Indian. It was only him, his pony, and his lonely fire. Jonas wondered if he might just die alone in those dark woods that never ended. Until one night, he heard strange shrieks; the sound of which he had not heard before. Something was out there. Encircled he was by shadows in the dark. And it came home to him, how was it that the Indians had mastered the wild, living at peace upon those lands. They were so eerie, and made a man feel so small. That night he wondered . . . might it not be best to let the Indians have that land? Whoever of sane mind would want to take up home and live in such a place? Might it not be better to live in the comfort and safety of towns and villages? Many proclaimed the westward expansion a wondrous thing for a young nation; but they never spent a night alone in the wild. It was not a place for civilized folk.

And at that thought, he glimpsed reddish eyes that glowed back at him from the dark's deep. They shined in the firelight. At first, there was only one pair, but then there were others. The eyes prowled. Ever closer to him they moved. They carried a haunted look. He rose up steady, pulled out his pistol, and pointed it into the dark. His stiff arm trembled. He also grasped a log from the fire. He wielded it as a torch against what came. In return, a low growl greeted him. He had heard it before those past weeks. Only now, it was filled with a mean thunder that moved the air and rumbled upon his chest.

Private Jonas was stilled with fear. Breathless, he tensed for the attack to come of those unseen beasts. His pony whinnied in terror. It began to stomp the ground, and bucked wildly to break free. It wanted to escape that place too. His mind raced. His gut spun in panic, for it must be a pack of wolves in the woods . . . and they had now come for dinner. He gulped . . . he was a dead man. Jonas breathed in deep a last gasp before death's lunge.

But suddenly, there were arrows whooshing in the dark, flying over and around him. A loud whimper cried out. A jarring thud fell to the ground, no more than fifteen feet from where he stood. Then other whimpers called out and several beasts stampeded away, back into the bowels of the forest. Then all was quiet.

Private Jonas called out to the dark, "Who is there? I am Jonas, a soldier of the United States Army. I have been sent by General Harrison to bear a message for Tecumseh."

Jonas waited for a reply. But he was met only by the still quiet of the forest's night. Someone was out there. Then something moved in the dark. A silhouette walked amongst the shadows. And then like a ghost, a painted Indian emerged. The flame's light flickered upon the warrior as he moved near. Was it was some Indian spirit of the forest come to speak with him? Perhaps Jonas was already dead . . . and now he walked in the spirit world. Though that spirit had a kind look and wielded no weapons.

It looked upon Jonas and spoke, "Jonas . . . we take you to Panther Across Sky."

Jonas was startled. It was no spirit, but flesh and bone. And that Indian spoke English. Jonas stuttered, "You . . . you speak English?"

The Indian smiled. "Speak some . . . have learned. Some my people speak paleface tongue."

Private Jonas just looked on in wonder.

With that, the Indian spoke to those with him, who gathered up Jonas and his belongings. They set loose his pony back down the trail from whence Jonas had come. Jonas protested, but the Indians would not hear of it. They slapped the pony's haunch and it took off. The Indian turned to Jonas and said, "Not know who follow . . . we walk quiet."

Jonas had no choice. He sadly watched his faithful pony follow the trail back into the dark.

As the small group moved through the nighttime of the forest, the Indian said he was called Ahanu.

In return, Jonas nodded and greeted them with a friendly smile.

Ahanu spoke a bit with Jonas as they moved along. "Wonder . . . why one paleface soldier move through wild? You and horse so loud . . . we heard for many long steps. We could follow with eyes shut.

"And you lucky. We not only ones track you. Wolves follow . . . and small war party of Shawnee. We not come . . . you be stuck with arrows and scalped . . . or chewed up in wolf belly."

Jonas bowed his head a bit. He thanked Ahanu and his warriors, for they had indeed saved his life . . . twice.

The small party moved in silence, save for the occasional crackle and rustle of leaves beneath their feet. They walked on through the night, and stopped only once to settle for sleep in a hidden cave somewhere before they moved on again. And that was the way of the next few weeks, with each day filled with some friendly talk between Private Jonas and his Indians. And as they went on, Jonas was utterly lost. The Indians had cut through brambles and taken shortcuts unseen. They passed through lands surely never walked upon before by any white man, and covered much ground in haste.

Late evening came and darkness fell. The Indians turned, bound his hands, and blindfolded him. They must be getting close to the journey's end. Jonas struggled to walk, and stumbled here and there. But he had no choice but to move ahead at the hand of his new masters.

It was one bumbled step after another, tugged along in the dark. And he heard more voices that talked near to him in an Indian tongue. It must be close now. And still more voices rose up and called out. Jonas could hear many Indians now that talked back and forth. It was just voices in the dark. Then Jonas's hands were pulled forward. There was a slicing sound about the rope upon his wrists. Soon, they were free, and his blindfold removed.

Ahanu stood before him and said, "Sorry . . . sorry for cover eyes . . . you know why."

Jonas gently nodded that he did.

Ahanu then spoke some more, "Stand at door of Chief Tecumseh. Welcome and speak on message." He stepped aside, pulled back the fur-skinned cover, and gestured for Jonas to go in.

Private Jonas stepped into a smoke filled place. The dim firelight flickered. There were several Indians gathered about.

And there were three large beasts. Midnight black in color, with striped markings upon them that glowed green. Huge and muscled they were. The look of a mountain lion sat about their faces, and their eyes gazed straight upon him. Then another Indian motioned for Jonas to come and sit by the fire.

As Jonas walked further into the longhouse, he eyed an open seat next to one plain Indian. But where was the great Tecumseh? Jonas did not see any grand robed red man, no headdress of eagle feathers to the floor.

But then, everyone else looked to that plain Indian. Jonas just stared wide-eyed like a fool, for that plain Indian was the one.

The Indian with the plain red-cloth headband gestured for him to sit. There was a kindness about that Indian's face. Jonas obliged, and shuffled to his seat. All sat in quiet for a moment. That plain Indian took hold of a smoke-pipe and inhaled its smoke deep. He held it for a moment, and released wispy gray clouds into the air. He turned and offered the pipe to Jonas, who accepted. Jonas took a puff. He coughed a bit, which brought chuckles of laughter.

That plain Indian waved his hand and said, "We must give him some time, for he is a paleface. He does not know the pipe of peace and its wisdom," to which more laughter bellowed out.

That plain Indian then turned to Jonas and said, "What do they call you?"

"Jonas . . . Private Jonas," Jonas whispered.

"Well Jonas, I am Tecumseh. Some also call me Panther Across the Sky. I welcome you to my home," to which Jonas nodded. But a look of wonder crossed his face too, for that Indian spoke English . . . and so well.

Tecumseh went on, "My warriors say they found you alone in the wild. And none too soon, or a meaty meal for some wolves you would have been. They say you come bearing a message of the great white fathers for the Shawnee . . . a message for me."

Jonas then spoke in a hushed tone. "I am to tell you that the great white fathers wish to suffer your wrath no more. They wish for a great council of peace. General Harrison will treat with you himself.

"In good faith, they will bring their army that remains, and bid you do the same. They say for you to come to the fork of the great rivers of the Ohio and the Guyandotte. They will wait for you there." Jonas then handed a folded parchment to Tecumseh, with President Madison's seal still unbroken upon it.

A hush fell upon the gathering. Only the flickering of the fire's flames could be heard. Jonas saw Indian eyes widen. Tecumseh carefully broke the seal and opened fully the parchment. He gazed upon its marked lines, and stared off in deep thought. After some silence, he turned back to the private and asked, "Do you believe the words of your great white fathers . . . do you believe in this peace?"

Jonas pondered on that, and then said, "Yes . . . I do."

Tecumseh searched deep into the kind eyes of Jonas. And Jonas did not waver, as he gazed right back. And Tecumseh said, "Jonas . . . you are an honest soul. Perhaps this great conflict between our peoples can at last be settled to the satisfaction of all."

Jonas saw Tecumseh turn to one of those strange beasts who stewed in quiet, with troubled eyes and hair that dangled like black snakes. Then it spoke, and Jonas leaned back in shock. It said, "After but a few defeats in battle, why would paleface hearts now beat with kindness? Would you have faith in their word?"

Tecumseh replied, "Jonas speaks the truth as it was told him. And always I will wonder what broods within the great white fathers' hearts. But we must go to this council, even if just for a chance of peace. It is all we have ever sought.

"If I do not, I will carry regret for all my days. We have done what we can to secure our freedom upon the battlefield. We should do so now with pen and parchment, and let the winds of fate blow."

Silence met Tecumseh's words. Misty smoke of the peace pipe floated about. The beast looked about to the others in the longhouse, and then back to Tecumseh. Then it just sighed and nodded a vacant stare, and said no more.

Tecumseh looked upon Jonas. "You are a brave one to have ventured so deep into the wild alone, armed only with a small pistol. Go now. Relax with a hearty meal and a restful sleep. You are safe here. In the morning, Ahanu will see your return to the borders of where you were found. And you may tell the great white fathers that we will come . . . we shall treat with General Harrison."

Jonas nodded to Tecumseh and quietly said, "Thank you."

Another Indian then signaled Jonas to follow. And Jonas withdrew to a warm meal and peaceful sleep of some cozy longhouse.

Jonas slept hard. And he awoke to the gentle nudges of Ahanu. Dawn would break soon. They must go. Jonas nodded and Ahanu applied the blindfold again. They escaped the village in the fading dark. The trip back seemed much faster to Jonas, like they went downhill. And he very much enjoyed the company. Ahanu struck him as a fine man. Beyond wonder he thought, if not for the color of their skin, they might be friends. That happy time flew by day after day. They moved fast. And one evening after several weeks, as dusk faded to night, they arrived to within a day's walk of the army base.

Ahanu turned to Jonas and extended his hand in peace. "Jonas . . . we leave you here. There a kindness on face. Whatever comes . . . hope no harm finds you."

Jonas reached out his hand and said, "I will not forget you . . . I will not forget Tecumseh." Jonas looked fondly upon Ahanu. They held a firm handshake for a moment. Jonas nodded to the others as well. And with that, he turned and began to walk away.

After fifteen paces or so, Jonas stopped and turned back to the forest. He looked to Ahanu and shouted, "Thank you again Ahanu . . . for killing the wolves . . . for saving my life that night."

Ahanu raised his hand, and gestured in welcome back to him. And in a happy peace, Jonas continued on his way. After another fifteen paces or so, Jonas looked back just once more to say goodbye. But where Ahanu and his warriors had stood, there was nothing but tree and brush . . . they were gone.

Jonas spent one more night in the wild, and made his way into the army base the next morning. The city of soldiers were relaxed and at rest. As Jonas moved forward, some soldiers rushed to full arms.

They yelled out, "Jonas, ya lucky son of a bitch! What the hell ya doin' alive? Can't be . . . over a month alone in the wild with nothin' but your damn pistol?"

Jonas walked up into their midst. He stood face to face, smiled, and said, "Just lucky I guess. The Indians found me and brought me to that chief . . . Tecumseh."

At those words, another soldier said, "We saw your damn pony return without its rider; and took you for dead sure as day. The general had us search the wild for some sign of ya, be it dead or alive. When none was found, you was given up as dead."

Before Jonas could say a word, another soldier shouted, "Ya sayin' you was found by some wild Indians out in them woods, and they din't so much as give you a nick or scrape with their bloody tomahawks? How could some kind-looking fool such as you be among those savages and left unspoiled?"

The soldiers all stopped their yelling and chatter for a moment. They gathered in close and surrounded Jonas with glaring looks. They awaited his reply. They needed to hear his words.

Jonas looked about at them all. He breathed in deep. "Think what you want. I followed my orders. I was captured by some Shawnee . . . and brought to Tecumseh's village. And I spoke with him on the general's message.

"Now let me through. I need to speak with General Harrison."

Then another brutish soldier drawled, in nastiness, "Well now, we don't want to hold you up Jonas. But we'll find you later . . . and if you don't give up the truth, then we'll beat it out of you."

Jonas smiled and shook his head. He turned to the brute, "I survived many nights alone in the dark wild. I faced down a pack of wolves. And I faced down an Indian war party. Do you think I care about you?"

The soldiers were stunned. Jonas knew why. He had ever been hidden and quiet in the crowd. He had always backed away from hostilities, which sometimes invited the bullies of the ranks to find him.

But Jonas felt different. There was an air of strength in his lungs. An awkward moment lingered. The soldiers remained in a stunned silence. And then Jonas just pushed his way on through the soldier pack that penned him in.

Jonas brushed by the soldiers and their cold stares. He felt like the enemy. As he came near the tent that housed Harrison, he glimpsed a small group of Indians that stood off to the side. And then out of the tent came the biggest Indian he had ever seen. As Jonas gazed on that beast of a man, his mind spun. He knew the lines of that face. The Indian brute looked on him.

Jonas had seen that Indian before . . . but where? And what was that Indian doing here . . . amongst all the soldiers, unharmed and untouched? Why did he walk from Harrison's tent? That red-skinned grizzly stared hate into Jonas. Jonas moved by him slowly, and that Indian just smiled a low cruel grin. Then that big Indian turned away and was gone.

Upon his arrival to Harrison's oversized tent, the sentry guards whisked him in right away. He entered and there the general sat alone. At once, Harrison arose. He approached Jonas and greeted him warmly. "Jonas, you are one hardy fellow. We had taken you for dead when your horse returned to the camp without you those days ago. But you look to be in good health . . . how are you?"

Jonas replied, "Fine sir. The Shawnee found me, and took me to Tecumseh's village. I spoke with him and delivered your message." Jonas's chest puffed pride. He knew he had accomplished a task that many could not.

The general took a seat and leaned back in disbelief. "Private, that is no small thing. You survived not only the perils of the wild, but also the clutches of those savages. And without a single scratch upon your body. It is either great skill . . . or great fortune. You have done your country proud!" The general leaned in close for a handshake and pat on the shoulder.

Harrison went on, "So you have spoken with Tecumseh. Will he come?"

Jonas nodded yes. "Sir, he is not what I expected. The Shawnee were not what I expected. What with all that we have seen and heard talk of over the years . . . I did not see it. He is just a plain looking Indian . . . but there is something about him. It floats on the air. He speaks better English than many white folk."

The general walked about the tent and nodded. He said coolly, "Yes private, I have heard tell of what you speak. And though I have never met the man, it seems there are few with so eloquent a tongue that inspires."

Jonas interrupted again, "Sir, he was quite kind . . . and friendly. And he said he desired only lasting peace. His people want only to be left alone. I believe with the offer you have made, this great conflict will at last be no more."

The general looked sternly at Jonas and said, "Were you shown the whereabouts of his village? Do you know the way?"

Jonas replied, "No sir, I am sorry. I was blindfolded, so it was kept hidden. But that matters not, for now a peace can be reached. Is this not so?"

General Harrison pondered on that in measured silence. He then replied in a solemn tone. "Private, be not concerned with the whereabouts of his village for it has been found."

Jonas's face crumpled in lines of confusion.

Harrison went on, "Now you may think Tecumseh to be a kind soul, but be not deceived by his words and manner. If given the chance, he would rip apart our nation and burn it to the ground. He can be brutal beyond words. Ever crafty are the Shawnee and the native tribes. Do not be fooled by their kindness."

Jonas shook his head. That was not the Indian he knew; not the people he had been among. Harrison was wrong.

Harrison then said, "Your country thanks you for your service. Through you, the message has been delivered and now he comes. And while we meet at the peace council, a large detachment will burn his village to the ground." Emptiness crept over the general's lined face.

Jonas looked on, confused. He asked, "You mean to treat with him for peace with one hand, while cutting him down with the other?"

The general sighed, "Private, war is nasty business. And to win a war, soldiers have to follow their orders. And so we will...." Harrison turned away. His face stretched of discontent, as if a putrid stench rose up to fill his nostrils.

Harrison went on, "This conflict is more brutal than most. And for the greater good of all, we must end it as soon as we may, by whatever means we can. We will save many lives and bring a civilized peace upon the land, making it fit for our nation's westward expansion."

Jonas stood speechless. He looked upon the general with a great disappointment. He did not understand. Why did it have to be that way? And he wondered . . . how did Harrison find Tecumseh's village after all? Finally, Jonas blurted out his curiosity.

And Harrison just brooded. He would not say.

Then Jonas asked, "Was it that Indian brute I passed by in camp? I saw him leaving your tent."

Harrison just stared vacantly to somewhere else, until at last he spoke, "Yes. One of his kin will show us the way."

Jonas paused in curious dismay.

Harrison went on, "There is a Shawnee who wants to kill Tecumseh more than we. And he is a red-skinned bull. Sakdayga they call him."

Though Jonas did not know that name, he knew of whom Harrison spoke. It all flooded back to Jonas. He remembered the cruel gaze of that very large Indian that pierced the moonlit shadows those nights ago. And a cruel one he must be indeed, to betray his own kind.

Then they both just simmered in silence, until the general looked over at Jonas, and asked, "Does this trouble you private?"

"No sir," Jonas said, as his voice broke.

General Harrison said coolly, "Good soldier! I would not want to think you are not a patriot of this nation . . . a true American. Dismissed!"

With that, Jonas saluted the general, turned, and departed the tent.

Word of Jonas's news spread throughout the base. And it brought tidings of giddy excitement, for Tecumseh was a vicious warrior feared by many. That America could finally bring destruction to his long looked-for home was a thought most comforting. Jonas heard the talk. And now the stones would tumble and the mighty Shawnee and his confederacy would be no more.

Of course, the jubilation of what was to come only served to lay Jonas's heart low. He could think of only the kindness the Shawnee had shown him. He thought of Ahanu, the Indian who had saved his life in the wild. That was not the deed of a savage. And that Tecumseh, he spoke with such wisdom and kindness. He thought Tecumseh may well be fierce in battle, but away from it, he was most civilized . . . a person of the highest quality. He was no savage.

And Jonas's mind swirled. Tecumseh sought only peace and freedom for his people. Just to be left alone in their ways and their lands unspoiled . . . is that such a strange thing? Jonas's insides twisted of guilt. He had been a tool, deceived by his nation. And now, he had deceived Tecumseh. Shame flooded upon him. And sadness lay heavy upon his spirit. His mind and body sagged under the great weight.

And he thought in dread of what was about to be un-leashed upon the Shawnee. His heart then burned and festered in anger . . . at himself . . . at his general. But he dared not reveal his feelings aloud to anyone, for no one would understand. As sure as the sun rose each day, they would have him strung up and hung as a traitor, no questions asked. And he pondered on that.

The founding fathers and those before him laid down their lives for his new country: a nation based upon the rights of freedom and liberty written upon a parchment. A constitution they called it. And yet here he sat, with its ink not fully dried, and knew if he spoke his mind that he would be marked a traitor. He would be muffled, slain in the still quiet of night, and with no trial by a jury of peers. And Jonas wondered . . . who truly was the savage?

Jonas was troubled beyond words. He could take no more. He must leave these lands and strike out on his own. He would hack out a solitary life in the wild and live off the land, free from the civilized world. He would find some lonely mountain upon which to build his fire and find some measure of peace. And the next night, he slipped away, alone in the dark.

Chapter Twenty-Three
Meeting of Peace

Tecumseh put out the call for a great gathering of tribes. Word spread throughout the land. They would head out in several weeks' time to treat with America.

The village bubbled excitement. Young and old alike smiled, and giggled hope. The people basked in the sun's warm glow. Afternoons lingered, stretched with peaceful happiness and good feelings from just a glimpse of freedom.

Tecumseh saw Nateelah spend days in warm embraces with Taughannock in quiet hope.

Kykuitheh and Tecumseh spent many a day by the riverbank, and reminisced of their son lost and dreamt of a hopeful future to come. But Kykuitheh told Tecumseh that though her heart would shout joy, her mind told her to be still; for never in her lifetime could the great white fathers be trusted.

"We must go . . . even for a chance of peace and freedom," said Tecumseh. He just smiled and hugged her tight.

And one evening, Gahnoque spoke again with Tecumseh, as troubled thoughts chased him. After nights of little sleep and ponderings in the dark, Gahnoque smelled it on the air he said. There was some unknown treachery to come.

Yet, Tecumseh was steadfast. He would treat with the general. Tecumseh said, "Harrison is the bravest paleface I have ever seen. A great warrior he is. And great warriors do not stab you in the back. They stand before you, watching the light in your eye go out at their blade's sharp tip. No, I do not believe that Harrison would sneak around in the dark." The time had come . . . and he would meet the great general at last. Gahnoque just sighed.

Several weeks came quick and some two thousand warriors gathered to Tecumseh's village. Chiefs shared a pipe and words were spoken. Preparations were made. For those that could, the trip would be made on horseback for such a grand meeting that it was. Tecumseh would ride his painted horse of the brown and white markings. Of course, the Jhagir would travel by foot, as there were no horses to carry their great size. Tecumseh would leave one hundred warriors behind to watch over the village, as he would whenever he departed for battle. Though he now went to a battle of a different sort. There would be no need of tomahawk and musket; they would bring their mind and tongue.

Tecumseh could not deceive himself. He sighed in hope and the wonder of it all. As the days counted, his heartbeat raced, anxious at the chance for peace. And his mind churned. What if Gahnoque and Kykuitheh were right, and they did go to some treachery? But he had no choice . . . he must go. Tecumseh, the Jhagir, and two thousand warriors headed out, some thousand on horse and the rest on foot.

They passed by Tanogatay, who looked on in great pride. The old lines on his face stretched into a smile. Even the chance that the struggle with the great white fathers may be coming to a happy end at last brought the old chief much joy. Nateelah's and Kykuitheh's eyes burned love like the hot sun upon Taughannock and Tecumseh; though Tecumseh saw the lines of worry upon Kykuitheh's face that lingered. He knew she was right to question it all. The great white fathers never could be trusted before. But maybe this time was different . . . it needed to be different.

They waved one last time to their loved ones and disappeared into the cloaked forest. Those on horse rode at a slow and steady gait, while those on foot walked at a quickened pace to keep up. The force moved east and met up with the rushing waters of the Ohio River, and followed it south until it emptied into the mighty Guyandotte. As they went, more warriors from villages along the way joined them too. And Tecumseh wondered who would not want to attend the great council of peace? In all, almost another two thousand there were that joined Tecumseh's band of warriors along the way, five hundred on horse and the rest on foot.

One early morning, they approached the great host of America at last. They came over the crest of a large sloping hill, which led to a great plain before the fork where the two flowing rivers met. And as they did, a vast paleface army was assembled down below. Tecumseh guessed their numbers at some twelve thousand, which was many more thousands than had left Fort Detroit in retreat.

The army noticed Tecumseh's arrival at once. Two horsed soldiers rode out alone to meet him. Tecumseh halted his warriors atop the hill, and rode down with three others at his side. All approached at a slow gait, with arms raised in peace. The horsed soldiers extended General Harrison's welcome. The general bid them to amass to the left side of the plain, as the army sat to the right. The forked rivers would sit at their backs, and they would meet before the armies, for all to see. Tecumseh agreed to treat on the plain, but he would leave his warriors atop the ridge. Now that he was there, it seemed unwise to bring his smaller force down upon the plain, fully exposed.

The two riders looked among themselves, eyebrows raised. They then nodded to Tecumseh and rode back to the general, while Tecumseh returned up the hill to his warriors. The general did not seem pleased upon the riders return. Even from a distance, Tecumseh heard the heated words. Harrison was much displeased that Tecumseh's force would not sit openly upon the plain. Then he turned and looked back to Tecumseh.

Silence sat upon the field, save only the occasional horse whinny and an easy breeze that blew. Two vast armies stared each other down. There was a brooding tension. Tecumseh could feel it. Trust was hard to come by between two peoples that had done nothing but quarrel and kill each other for years on end. And though no weapons were raised, they were kept close and at the ready, lest any hostilities began . . . for old habits were not so easily forgotten.

The tense quiet then gave way. General Harrison rode out with several officers in a grand display. His long feathered hat swayed mightily in the wind, the flag of his country flew proud and high on a horse behind him. He was a broad shouldered man, with a muscled frame. His gaze was piercing like a war saber's edge. In the blowing wind, Tecumseh could hear the old chant in his mind, back when he was but a boy . . . Harrison . . . Harrison. There was the bravest paleface soldier Tecumseh had ever seen. And now, he would meet the great man at last.

Tecumseh breathed tight and short. Then with a gentle kick to his horse's side, he rode down to meet the great white father. Some other chiefs rode too, including Otsaga. They slowed their relaxed gallops and halted at the field's center. They dismounted slow and walked toward each other, one careful step at a time. There were gazes all about. Minds swirled. Polite nods and greetings were shared. Weapons were laid on the ground and all took a seat. And then the great council of peace began.

An officer asked, "Are all parties present to begin this council?"

Tecumseh shook his head softly and held up his hand. A call went out. Within moments, Gahnoque bounded up. Gasps rose up from the soldiers' ranks. Many of the long knives had seen glimpses of him before in battle. But still, their faces bathed in awe.

An officer blurted out and lectured, "It was agreed we are to treat with only the chiefs for this council . . . is this not so?"

Tecumseh looked around, "Of course. It shall be no other way. He is Gahnoque, a great chief of a Shawnee tribe from the far north lands in Upper Canada."

The officers were startled. They shared clueless looks with one another, and turned to General Harrison.

Harrison just smiled and waved his hand flippantly; he would yield to Tecumseh. And Gahnoque took a seat beside Tecumseh, and stared coldly upon Harrison.

A tight tension hung on the air. After some moments more of pained quiet, Harrison cleared his throat. His low voice rumbled strength. "This is a strange sight indeed. Two large armies of warring peoples standing upon the other; yet gathered here today not to clash in battle, but to negotiate peace." Harrison then stared deeper into Tecumseh. "And you look far different from that rage and fury before the gate of Fort Detroit."

One officer smirked.

Harrison's eyes demanded a polite response in return.

Tecumseh smiled, but it was not of happiness. It was of simmering defiance like a burning ember. "Yes, it is strange, though I hope not unpleasant. Perhaps our two peoples can be friendly, even if only for a few hours.

"And I cannot speak on your difference now and that upon the battlefield, for only far off in the back and away from the fray were you. I saw only your backside, as you retreated from Fort Detroit."

The officers stared breathlessly, faces flushed red, all except Harrison. His face stretched of anger that boiled upon his frame. Brown eyes blackened like a storm cloud. Tecumseh would test Harrison's peace right at the outset.

Harrison breathed in deep and slow. He smoldered. Harrison's fingers seemed to twitch for his saber handle, but then calmness found him. "Chief Tecumseh, do you not have the sense to begin a council of peace by not hurling insults?"

Tecumseh just smiled low and stared deep into Harrison. "I do not sit here and insult you or any other; I only talk of our last battle as it was . . . a battle that you first raised to me."

Tecumseh's strong words met only stoned silence. None of the other officers would look up. They smelled of fear of what they might say, lest they incurred Harrison's vengeful wrath. Hatred oozed from Harrison's stare. Holding his tongue, he nearly bit his lip. It was the brink of war between Tecumseh and Harrison.

But Harrison gritted his teeth, and forced out some words. "Tecumseh, of course you are right. Forgive me. Let us do what we have come here to do." And Harrison smiled an empty smile, sauced in meanness.

After a deep breath, the parties bestowed some begrudging respect to the other at last. The council then took on a more amicable air. Tension rolled away. But progress was slow, as an accord acceptable to all was no easy thing. And it went on for hours, back and forth, with seemingly a settlement reached, only to be hung up on one point or another, by one party or the other. Many breaks were held throughout the day, as Tecumseh and General Harrison convened with their chiefs and officers.

During those breaks, Gahnoque again raised his concern with Tecumseh. He sensed Harrison engaged in delay. The general meant to drag out negotiations.

Tecumseh nodded to his friend. "Yes, we do not know their full aim, be it true or not, but we have no choice. Let us follow this path and see where it will lead."

But Gahnoque would not hear it. "Perhaps, the great white fathers move a hidden force to surround us, in numbers so great we cannot escape. Something is afoot."

Tecumseh replied, "We shall soon see into the darkness. But with all of my heart, I do not believe the great white fathers would risk such a thing. We are too many. And we have marked their hearts with fear. Three of their large armies have already been defeated at our hands, such as they have never known. No my friend, they would not engage us upon this field."

Gahnoque relented, but he did not agree.

The meeting ran on through the day before an agreement was at last reached. General Harrison agreed to withdraw from the Ohio Valley, and leave it forever to the Shawnee and the many tribes. And he would provide reparations for those lands already lost, but only if those tribes forever relinquished their claims.

Though painful it was to lose those lands, Tecumseh knew such an accord was far better than anyone could have hoped. The Shawnee could live free upon their homelands, as their elders' elders had done for ages before them. For the other tribes, the Ohio Valley was vast with land aplenty for all to come and build their fires in peace.

Tecumseh could hardly believe the spoken words upon his ears. He did not think he would ever hear the great white fathers utter them. In tired happiness, he watched Harrison mark the words upon the parchment. And as Harrison placed his signature upon it, Tecumseh reminisced on all the many losses and sufferings by the people at the hands of the long knives. And yet now before him, with a simple stroke of a pen, it was being washed away.

Harrison turned and offered the pen to Tecumseh. For the first time in his life, Tecumseh would sign a treaty, and he readily did so. Tecumseh stared upon that aged paper. It was like a dream. He then rose up. Tecumseh would seal the accord with a handshake of goodwill.

But as he did, Harrison leaned back and subtly snarled, "Now that we have reached a treaty for the benefit of all, it must be sent to Washington for ratification by Congress before it is the law of the land."

At that, the light smile within Tecumseh's heart fell away. He asked in desperate suspicion, "General, I was told to treat with you on this matter. You were bestowed with that authority by the great white fathers . . . is this not so?"

Harrison replied, "Why yes, that is true. But only this morning, I received word that upon reaching a signed accord, I am to have it sent to Congress. Only then, will it have the full power of the law given to it.

"I will send riders at once in great haste. We shall have word in three days' time."

But as those words flowed from Harrison, his look betrayed him. There was a nervous air of shame in his voice. Tecumseh did not fear an attack, as there was no ambush lain. But his heart sank still.

There was something foul in the air. There no longer was any doubt. Gahnoque had been right. Tecumseh's insides drifted in disappointment like the blowing snow. He expected more from the bravest paleface soldier he had ever seen. He thought Harrison a great warrior, a man of honor . . . and now, he was wrong. Tecumseh's mind raced.

Suddenly, Gahnoque rose up. In a blink, he grabbed hold of the general's forearm. Warriors and soldiers on both sides jumped up and scrambled to their feet. Weapons were brandished. The old familiar urge returned. They wanted to kill. That fire just needed a match.

Gahnoque softly spoke in his own tongue and gazed upon Harrison. The general hunched a bit, and looked to be lost in a dream. Mighty Harrison then began to shake a bit. A scared look crossed his strong face. And then Gahnoque released Harrison's arm, whose muscled frame slunk away. Harrison looked down and shuddered a moment, like he caught a chill.

In disgust, Gahnoque stepped back and spoke to Harrison. "Your thoughts betray you. Tecumseh is right about your kind. You possess the darkest of souls, seeking only to consume all before you, with a thirst that cannot be quenched.

"I would slay you now, but I have given my word of peace for this council. And the Jhagir honor their word. But know this, when next we meet in battle . . . I will seek you out and cut flesh from bone. I will then choke the life from your spirit, so that you may know death in both this world and the next."

Gahnoque's words faded to silence. His gaze burned right through Harrison.

Gahnoque then turned swiftly to Tecumseh. "We have all been deceived. This meeting is false. America sent two thousand long knives to strike down your village while it is emptied out of its warriors . . . they mean to destroy all they come upon. Sakdayga has shown them the way.

"With all their venom, they seek to cut out your heart, for if you should fall, the Shawnee and other tribes of the land will perish into oblivion, scattered to the blowing winds."

Tecumseh turned and stared at Harrison. Hatred burned in his darkened eyes. Muscles flexed and fists clenched. He called out, "General . . . I thought you a better man. Each lie falls heavy from the tongue and slices a scar upon the soul. And the hurt and pain of a lifetime of cuts go deep, until one day the soul is severed to the bone. And for the rest of your days, you will wander the forests, ever searching, but never finding, for your soul is lost to you. That is your cruel fate for the deed you have done."

Harrison stared in silence. He seemed embarrassed by truth's words spoken aloud.

Though strangely, Tecumseh also felt some sadness . . . some pity for the general. He had thought Harrison to be not only a great warrior, but a great man, the best of his paleface kin. And now, Harrison was just like the rest. Tecumseh wondered that surely there were parts of those white souls that were just not there. Somehow, the Great Spirit's love had died in those living things, or perhaps it was never there at all.

Tecumseh then looked upon Harrison and growled, "The next time we meet . . . there will be no council of peace. There will be only death." Then he turned and rushed off. It took all of his strength to leave that field. He hated the wolf now more than ever. He wanted to kill all the twelve thousand long knives before him, to slit Harrison's throat. But there was no time for that now. He must go and try to save his village. He must save Nateelah . . . and his Kykuitheh. Those on horseback galloped on in a mad dash to save Tecumseh's village. Those warriors on foot followed behind as fast as their legs would carry them . . . and all wondered if it was not already too late.

Chapter Twenty-Four
Love's Light in the Dark

Kykuitheh breathed in deep and slow. But the air did not want to come. She did not move, yet she felt winded. There was a brisk chill in the night air. And it was tight upon the throat, like the firm grip of strong hands. Despite the night's calm, a heavy tension hung upon the blowing wind. Nateelah sat with her, and she felt it too, laden with worry and dark thoughts. And a mother not by blood, but in every other way, would bring peace to a young child now grown. "Nateelah, let us calm the thoughts of forebode spinning about." At that, they rose and strolled along the winding river at the village's outskirts under the silvery moon.

The river crawled along. It soothed a sound of a songbird's melancholy. Kykuitheh and Nateelah gazed upon the river, and breathed in the quiet beauty of its shimmering waters. Kykuitheh said, "I know the fear that fills your heart, but we must have faith in the council's purpose. No harm will befall him, or the others. Tecumseh will not allow it. The war party is too great in number.

"Maybe the cold and dark of the palefaces' twisted hearts has been warmed at last by the hard edge of our tomahawks these last battles. Perhaps they do come to make a lasting peace."

Nateelah looked to Kykuitheh and smiled, "I think only the light of the Jhagir blades has warmed their hearts and made them now consider such a council of peace."

"You may be right. But as long as they are driven to peace," said Kykuitheh. "To achieve a thing so mighty, that they did not seek it from the goodness of their hearts will matter not."

Nateelah sighed. In silence, her eyes welled up. A few soft tears fell. "For too many days, I thought my heart to be alone in this world. But then, he came to me. And though of a different people and world, it is something I cannot explain; beyond what you can see and touch. It goes deeper to somewhere else. And now, to lose him . . . it is more than I can bear."

Kykuitheh smiled. She leaned in and hugged Nateelah tight. "My child, you have strength of spirit more than you know; equal to even mighty Tecumseh himself. Don't ever forget that." She tapped Nateelah's chest.

Nateelah smiled through her falling tears, which Kykuitheh wiped with great care. In a warm embrace, they turned to soak some more in the night's beauty. The slow flowing river foamed, bubbled, and sailed by before them.

But then, a shrieking yell pierced the still night air. The pair swung about. And where before was but the black of night, there was now a thousand and more lit torches. Those hand held flames burned at the forest edge, and glared upon the village. Somehow, the long knives had come. Never before had the palefaces found their village. Then cannons thundered and cannonballs screamed. They ripped apart longhouses, sprayed dirt, and splintered wood into the air.

Though, how the palefaces moved the cannons in the dark unseen was no easy thing. Kykuitheh wondered that the warrior scouts keeping watch over the village must have been slain to allow such cunning. The hundred warriors that there were gathered up their weapons, and launched out to meet the long knives in the dark.

A sick horror washed upon Kykuitheh. Her insides wanted to vomit. In that moment, it came home to her . . . the true purpose of the peace council. Its wickedness laid bare. The great white fathers had come to snuff life from the village with one outstretched hand, while its other was offered in a false peace. Kykuitheh and Nateelah glanced at one another aghast, and took off in desperation to the village. They would save the children and any others they could, and moved as fast as their legs would carry them.

As they ran to the village, more longhouses blew apart. Scraps of bark and wood shot into the air. Fires ignited everywhere. They jumped from one longhouse to another like a living thing. One cannonball landed near to them. Its thunder shook and knocked them to the ground. As they staggered upright, the forest erupted with yells. Filled with hatred those voices were as they screamed from the dark. A thousand lit torches flew into the village. The horror of battle was upon them . . . long knives were everywhere.

An empty malice hung upon the soldiers' faces. Unfeeling eyes were glazed over. But there were so few warriors. It was no battle . . . only a massacre. Those warriors left to protect the village were overrun in moments, drowned in a sea of muskets in the attack's first angry wave. Then there were only women, children, and the old left to face that hatred . . . and they had no chance.

Chaos and panic swallowed the people. Fires spread everywhere, as Kykuitheh ran to the longhouse of Tanogatay. She would take him away from that horror. As she ran off, Kykuitheh yelled to Nateelah, "Gather up the children as you can! Bring them to the hidden trails in the far woods!"

Nateelah wasted not a moment in doing so; there was no time to linger.

Kykuitheh dodged the burning debris and dead bodies that littered the village grounds. She turned a corner and there was Tanogatay. He stood alone, his war club in hand, in one last desperate act to save the people. She ran to him and pleaded for him to come with her now . . . while there was still a chance.

But the great chief, the many lines of age weathered upon his leathery face, would not leave. "Kykuitheh, you must go now. Save the children, for they are our future. I am old, my body weak. I go this night to meet the Great Spirit, but you have much life yet to live. Tecumseh will return . . . so go now. And you tell Tecumseh of what you have seen this night." The great chief then softly touched her forehead, as if she was a treasured grandchild. And then he gestured for her to go.

A tear fell from her eye. She looked upon the great elder chief she had known all her life. And before she left, Kykuitheh caressed the old chief's cheek. Not a single word was spoken, and her eyes said goodbye. She then turned away and ran for her life. Though after forty paces, she stopped and glanced back one last time. And she saw the great chief's end.

There Tanogatay stood in a grand display. His headdress of eagle feathers swayed proud in the breeze, his old war club held in a clenched fist. His mighty image slowed the long knives for a moment. And the people had just a bit more time, a chance of escape.

But then two blue jackets charged him, with bayonets extended. They screamed out and laughed, "Hey ole' fool, you gunna save the village in yer purty feathers?" Kykuitheh knew what those words meant. She knew the English tongue well, as Tecumseh had taught her. She had no choice, being his wife. And Tecumseh had taught many village folk to speak that strange English tongue, including even mighty Tanogatay.

"Go now and I will spare your life," Tanogatay shouted. His firm voice sounded thirty years younger. He held up his hard hand.

The soldiers stared disbelief. "Are ya kiddin' ole' man? You da warrior who will save yer people?" They looked at one another, and smirks painted their faces. "Let's share a lil' wisdom wit ya," as they leaned in close.

And with that, one long knife raised his musket and drove the bayonet deep into Tanogatay's gut. The soldier leaned in close, "How dat taste ole man?"

Tanogatay said nothing. His war club fell meekly to the ground. He staggered back a step, and then fell. Blood oozed into a pool about him. The two long knives hovered over him and laughed. One soldier blurted, "Wat Injun, no mor words of wisdom?"

The other soldier smiled in glee and raised his musket barrel to the fallen chief's chest. He muttered, "One less Injun in da world." And with that, he pulled the trigger and blew a gaping hole in Tanogatay's chest. The great chief gasped for breath, but none came . . . and then he was no more.

Kykuitheh reeled. She drowned in sadness. A great old man she loved had passed before her in such cruelty. But there was no time to weep; she must find Nateelah. She swallowed her tears, turned, and ran back through the village that crumbled and burned. It would take all of their fierce spirit, and more luck than could be spared, if they were to escape that hell.

Kykuitheh caught sight of her in the mayhem. Nateelah followed the screams of children nearby and entered their own longhouse . . . Tecumseh's home. Kykuitheh ran after her. Inside, three young children clung to their lifeless mother, who had gathered them to her and hid in the nearest longhouse she could find, but was slain by an errant musket shot.

Nateelah rushed to the children and hugged them close. She asked them to be strong. It was what their mother would have wanted. The two oldest children nodded and walked to Kykuitheh, but the youngest wailed on. Nateelah gathered up the youngling, and asked them all to wear their bravest faces. They must go now into the forest dark, to escape that place.

But then two soldiers burst in. And they were followed by a beast of man, who ducked low to enter. "Well, well, what we have here . . . two filthy Injun women and some lil' rats," said the beastly soldier.

The other soldiers chuckled. That oversized soldier had an ill look of nastiness about him.

"Yeah, let us cut the throats of these lil' ones so as they don't grow into big Injuns . . . and then we can show these squaws a real man," the large brute growled.

Kykuitheh screamed at them to leave the children be. But one soldier stepped forward and jammed his musket butt to her head. Her mind flashed stars and she fell to the ground in a black daze. The room spun about. The soldiers grabbed Nateelah by the arm, and slammed her to the ground. She was thrown with such strength that she burrowed deep in the dirt like a planted seed. Kykuitheh looked on helplessly, as if she drowned in a bad dream.

The two blue jackets turned and knifed the older children coldly, as their bellies leaked blood. Kykuitheh tried to scream, but no words came out. The two children keeled over in silence and fell dead to the floor. The youngest child struggled away from the soldiers' hard grip, and began to flee. But a long knife raised his pistol and took aim. Nateelah cried out and desperate tears filled her face. But it made no difference. The pistol shot exploded and its lead blasted into the child's back. It fell to the ground and cried no more. The long knives grinned in pride. Kykuitheh tried to move. She tried to get up . . . but the room still spun in a daze.

In a rage of fury, Nateelah launched upon the blue jackets and grabbed a small blade on their belts. She unsheathed it in one fell motion and jammed into the upper thigh of one soldier. He screamed out and buckled over in pain. And as that long knife fell, she withdrew the blade in her hand, spun about, and cut a large gash in the cheek of the other long knife. He reeled from the biting pain, and Nateelah struck the blade back down upon him, and sliced his forearm with a deep wound.

But then, she was sent flying through the air, the blade flung from her hand. She smashed against a longhouse wall. The mountainous soldier smacked her with a mighty blow of his forearm, which hurtled her some ten paces into the hard wall of wood like a child's doll. She gasped about.

The brute of a man yelled for the two soldiers to hold her down. And she did not struggle. Kykuitheh saw her body choke and reel from the strength with which she had been hit.

One of the blue jackets yelled, "When ya get dun wit her Beckett, I'm gunna cut her good for wat she dun me!"

That beastly Beckett glared at Nateelah. He growled in a low rumble, "You'll god damn wait till I'm done, or I'll finish the cut job she put on ya myself." His weapons fell to the ground, and he took his belt off slow. "Yer gunna enjoy this you pretty lil' savage. There ain't none stronger, and I like 'em feisty," said Beckett. A sick malice burned in his eyes.

Nateelah then caught her breath and began to struggle, but she could not break free. Beckett stood over her, his tree trunk legs stepped to each side, and she leaned up to him.

"Look it boys, this lil' beauty is eager for ole' Beckett," he laughed.

But before they could reply, Nateelah spit in his face and snarled at Beckett. The soldiers slammed her back onto the ground, and Beckett wiped the spit that hung from his face. Beckett began to drop his pants, to carry out the deed; but before he could, Kykuitheh leapt up and let loose a shrieking yell.

Somewhere down deep, through the daze and stars that spun, she had found the strength. It startled the soldiers, and even that big Beckett. The two long knives screamed out, "Look out Beckett, nother Injun whore comin' for ya!"

Kykuitheh slammed into Beckett with every bit of her slender frame. She knocked him off balance and toppled him clear over. In that moment, the soldiers' hold of Nateelah was loosened. And a moment was all Nateelah needed.

She smashed her freehanded fist into the groin of one long knife, who hunched forward. Quick as a cat, she reached for the knife at his side, flipped it in her hand, and jammed it down into his neck. His eyes fluttered and rolled to the back of his head, and the blue jacket keeled forward lifeless.

The other long knife looked on in shock. Nateelah broke loose from his grip and grabbed for a war club set against the wall. The blue jacket lunged for her, but he was too late. Nateelah swung the club around. The meat of the club smashed upon the side of his skull. It split its insides out, and the long knife tumbled forward dead.

Beckett jumped to his feet and pulled his trousers up quick. He lunged toward Nateelah, and punched her with a wild swing. His clenched fist smashed into her face like a cannonball. Nateelah was flung like a tiny gnat through the air. The war club flew from her hand. She laid there on the ground, battered and bruised. She spit blood and gasped hard for breath again.

Kykuitheh stooped for the fallen war club. She would kill the beast of a man before her. Filled with anger and hate, Kykuitheh swung the club with all her might, but Beckett grabbed his musket to block the blow. He then swung the heavy butt of the musket around and upside her head. It sent Kykuitheh hurtling against the wall. She was limp. Her eyes closed shut. But she was still alive, though again everything spun about in a daze of muffled sounds.

She heard Beckett walk to her. He meant to stick her with his bayonet . . . but Nateelah sprung to life once more. She flew madly into Beckett.

Kykuitheh eyes struggled to look up, but her dazed and battered body could not move to help Nateelah. And she saw what was coming.

Beckett was ready for Nateelah's lunging thrust. He back-handed her again into the hard wall of wood. Though that time, the force was so great that her body broke a wooden support post in two. She rolled onto her back, still as a rock. Her body was shattered and surely broken in several places as she inhaled jerkily.

Beckett gloated over her and kneeled low with his sharp blade. He leaned in close and hissed, "I see ya like the blade, as you cut up my friends here. Well, I'm gunna carve you up real good." Beckett then carved her cheek.

Ripped flesh dangled loose. Blood oozed across her face and dripped onto her neck and chest. Though in great pain, she did not cry out. Nateelah just looked upon the beastly man, broken and helpless. Then Beckett drove the blade into her belly slow. He thrust it upwards, into her heart. He looked on with an anxious grin and greedily waited for death to take her.

She gasped, but could take no air in as her lungs filled with blood. The flowing red spirted and spilled out about her. Kykuitheh saw the sparkle of life, which danced always in her eyes like a summer butterfly, fade away.

Kykuitheh insides screamed out, but her mouth could make no sound. She could not move, and suffered still from shock with the great force with which she had been hit. She could only watch as Nateelah gasped out once more. A vacant stare then overtook her face . . . she was gone. And a part of Kykuitheh died too. Insides twisted and throbbed. It was beyond sadness, as if her own daughter had perished before her eyes.

A low smile passed across Beckett's face at his handy work.

At that moment, a bugle blared. An order was screamed out. There was not a living soul left in the village. The long night of death was over and dawn beckoned. Kykuitheh saw that big Beckett eyed her for a moment, and she held her breath. She needed to be dead . . . or that brute would stick her with his blade for sure. He just snarled and then turned away, and left the longhouse.

Then from utter exhaustion and sheer devastation of the soul, Kykuitheh's eyes closed shut. Her head fell away. Everything went dark.

Chapter Twenty-Five
Shadows and Ashes

Tecumseh swallowed hard. Tattered nerves spun about. His gut twisted in knots like a coiled rope. It was hard to breath . . . to think. He rode his horse faster than he ever had before . . . and it was not fast enough. It was the longest ride of his life. Forest and brush blurred by him as he flew. Were they too late? Not knowing was too much to bear . . . better to be dead than suffer that fate any more. And with a swift kick to the haunches of his horse, the painted beast galloped faster.

Tecumseh and his thousand horsed warriors rode across the valleys and hills of the land. As they rode, the ground shook. That trampling was as if a great herd of bison that stampeded upon the plains. All bird, man, and beast fled before them. And they stopped for nothing. There was no need for food, water, or sleep . . . there was only the drowning desperation of what they might find upon their return.

The Jhagir also ran at Tecumseh's side. They bounded in stretched strides that kept pace with their horsed brothers, for such a far distance they could not apparate. And a seemingly unending endurance they possessed, as on and on they ran.

A frantic fear grabbed hold of Tecumseh's heart. For the love of his life was back at the village . . . and the thought of some harm, or even death, coming to her, brought an unspeakable fear and words he could not speak. He saw the same worried look upon Taughannock's face . . . for Tecumseh knew the young Jhagir loved Nateelah, more than life itself. They did nothing but ride and run, with heads down, lost in thought. They could only cling to hope. And after days on end, beyond fatigue, they came upon the village in the early morning at last.

Smoke rose in the distance. Hearts sank. They came around a bend and the village grounds opened up before them. It was a vision that birthed hell's worst nightmare. Everywhere there were longhouses charred and burnt black, or that still burned. Tecumseh and his riders slowed their horses. Dismay and disbelief flooded the mind. Horses whinnied and nearly keeled over, as their bodies throbbed fatigue. They could go no more. Though their masters now forgot the tiredness of their own limbs, lost in the swirling desolation.

They all walked about in a daze, just shadows in a bad dream. It was their home, but now there was just death. Never before had Tecumseh's village fallen under the blade and musket of the great white fathers. And now that it had, it shook them to the bone. Many warriors fell to their knees and began to weep, while others franticly searched for loved ones. And only the slain were found, for none were left alive. Broken hearts were shattered into countless pieces, as if a large glass pane of the palefaces' church window that was blown apart upon the ground below.

Death hung in the smoke filled air. The smell of burnt flesh, like meat, was everywhere. Tecumseh stepped through his village that burned, which had held only love and happiness in his heart and memories until that darkest of days. Murdered women and children were strewn all about. Each tortured corpse was evidence of deeds done unto them not by men, but by a wicked evil carried within the forms of men. His insides screamed out hurt and pain, and bled all the love from his soul.

Hatred stabbed his heart, his muscles clenched tight. He must hurt the ones that did this.

Tecumseh then came upon Tanogatay. Once mighty in his younger days, the great chief was now just cold and lifeless upon the ground. All could see he was slain cruelly. Tecumseh knelt beside his great chief and friend, the one who had guided him on his journey from a young boy to a man. A tear welled up from the deep of Tecumseh's soul, and streamed down his cheek. The lone tear fell to the ground, as if a flower's aged petal that fell freely there and back to its final resting place. Gahnoque and Ithikkah walked up beside him, and touched his shoulder with heads bowed.

As they did, Taughannock bounded off to Tecumseh's longhouse. He went to find Nateelah, and clung still to hope beyond hope. The young Jhagir pleaded with fate that she had found her way to the morning light and still took breath.

Tecumseh followed after, though he no longer clung to hope's veiled treasure, for its shine had gone dark. He knew there was no spirit that could withstand such brutal hate. Without strength in number, Kykuitheh, Nateelah, and all the people of the village had no chance to beat back such force. No, he went now to find the lifeless body of his other half, Kykuitheh, and that of beautiful Nateelah. And each step he took was heavy, laden with dread. Though a mighty warrior who had seen many horrors of battle, he trembled to now look upon a cruel death visited upon those held closest to his heart.

All was silent, save for the slow pounding of his heart. Breath left him as he came upon his longhouse, which was one of the few not set aflame. Perhaps that was a sign. Maybe in the madness, the soldiers somehow overlooked his longhouse . . . perhaps Kykuitheh and Nateelah had survived. His heartbeat throbbed louder in a bundle of nerves and angst.

But Taughannock then emerged. And he carried Nateelah. Tears fell freely from his face, as her lifeless body draped in his muscled arms. No words were spoken as he walked up to his father. Tecumseh knew there was nothing that a father could say to comfort that pain. And though from a different world and race, Tecumseh knew the Jhagir felt grief's bite too. It was a language understood by all living beings, no matter your birthplace or the look of your kin.

Taughannock then turned to Tecumseh, inconsolable in grief. Tecumseh's heart was laid low at the sight. He loved Nateelah as his own daughter . . . he loved her more than life itself. And there were no tears deep enough to carry such pain away. His soul cried out. He would move mountains to hear her joyous giggle and bathe in her twinkling eyes just once more. But such a thing would never again be, save only in the shadows and ashes of memory and reminisce.

In a vacant daze, he lightly caressed her cheek. Then he kissed her ever so softly upon her cold forehead. Tears cascaded down his cheek and fell upon her face, as the droplets splashed in sadness of a father's love lost forever. Tecumseh then looked up and bid Taughannock to go now and be alone with her, to which he obliged. And Tecumseh's insides shook, for he must now swim deeper into the same sea of hurt and pain.

Tecumseh stepped into the longhouse. At first, he could see nothing but the shapes of fallen bodies in the dimly lit shadows. There had been a great struggle here. Death and terror . . . and now just sad stillness. But then at once, there she was. He rushed to her and knelt beside her. A throbbing ache drowned his senses in the quiet, as he looked upon her. And all the beauty and color of the world was washed away. There was now only a stone pale gray.

To live just one day without her in the world now so cold, it would be like the world without its warm sun. In such a world, he may yet take breath, but what kind of happiness could be found in a life empty of all love. And his head bowed from the heaviness of it all. His tears fell upon her skin and he slowly caressed her arm.

But to his surprise, her skin was warm. In that moment, his spirit rose to the highest night star, for there is no living thing that remains warm in death. He leaned into her chest, and indeed, she slowly inhaled breath, ever so slight as it was - Kykuitheh lives! At once, he gathered her up. He brought her out into the woodland forest, away from the village, to let her weak lungs take in the unspoiled air as she slept.

And as she did, Tecumseh sat beside her and sent thanks to the Great Spirit. His body quaked in joy that it was not yet her time; that she lingered but a little while longer. And as he sat, more tears welled up and fell to the ground. Though they were not tears of sadness, but of thankful happiness.

As she rested, her eyelids began to twitch. Then they fluttered awake and opened wide. She was in a daze at first, and slowly reached for Tecumseh. There seemed to be much pain in doing that. But she still managed a faint smile. And then she sat up and struggled to lean against him.

And she hugged him with everything she had left. She smiled and kissed him upon the cheek. But then as her head rested against his sturdy chest, she began to weep. "I tried to save her . . . but I could not," she said softly, between sobs and tears.

Tecumseh placed his hand upon her head, and whispered, "Do not burden your heart with the blame of her death. Such evil is visited upon those in the midst of war. You did all that you could."

Kykuitheh shuddered a bit, and spoke faintly, "It was a long knife as large as a bear. Beckett he was called by the other soldiers, his soul blackened with malice. He sought only to bring death to us, but a clean death would not do. No, he would dirty our Nateelah first, before putting her under his blade.... "

At those words, Tecumseh reeled. He remembered that name . . . and it staggered him. His insides wanted to hurl. That was the beastly paleface who Taughannock was certain to kill at the last battle . . . until Tecumseh stayed the young Jhagir's hand. Now, Tecumseh felt her death upon his own hand. He cursed himself and his kindness that day . . . it would haunt him for all of time now. But he shared not those thoughts with Kykuitheh. He did not want to overburden her already heavy heart.

"Say no more Kykuitheh. Nateelah will never again suffer the pain and hurt of this world." They both just sat in silence, in a warm embrace. They sat alone in mourning and remembrance of Nateelah . . . and all those lost in the burnt destruction before them.

Kykuitheh was the lone shining star in the night sky. And her light shined in defiance, as somehow she had survived to bear witness to the peoples' massacre. After a time, Tecumseh and she rejoined the warriors and Jhagir among the village ruins. And the story she told, and relived with each telling . . . it broke the heart of the teller and all who heard it.

Tecumseh saw a barren desolation fall upon the warriors' faces at her words. But a furious rage welled up inside too. A fiery flame of hatred, brighter than any that had burned before, bubbled beneath their flesh. Tecumseh could feel it. It threatened to spew forth and consume them, unless they rushed out to kill all the palefaces of the world. Though that was a feeling already held by many before that day, it was now stronger than ever before.

And Tecumseh spoke alone with Taughannock, who took it hard. Taughannock looked to Tecumseh. "To hear that Beckett killed my Nateelah . . . it is the cruelest of things."

Tecumseh nodded, his face full of sadness. Tecumseh saw an ancient fury behind Taughannock's eyes that drowned in a sea of pain. Tecumseh tried to comfort him. "Do not think of it. It is by my hand that she died . . . I should not have stopped you."

But Taughannock would not listen. He just whispered grief, "No. I could have slain that beast . . . I should have slain him . . . but I did not.

"And if I had, Nateelah would still be alive . . . it is a thing unforgivable. My steps now will always be haunted, as I will remember with each breath that I failed her."

Tecumseh put his hand upon the young Jhagir. "Do not ever think that. It is I who will always be haunted . . . it is I who failed her. You remember that."

Taughannock just stared blankly to somewhere else, and whispered, "A part of me has died forever."

The rest of that long day was spent gathering the dead and preparing a grand fire. They would send them in a good way to the Great Spirit. Once nightfall came, the great fire was lit. The bodies of the fallen were placed upon it, and their flesh succumbed to the flickering flame's embrace. The burning sparks and embers of each soul floated upwards into the night. They flew ever higher until they at last joined the other stars and shined down upon the world.

Nateelah was the last to be placed upon the fire. But before it was done, Taughannock set her upon a specially made bed of flowers, bathed of yellow and white petals. And the vision of her at peace upon that flowery bed was most beautiful. A breathless sight. She seemed to be only in a restful sleep, sure to awaken at any moment to join Taughannock once more for a moonlit walk along the riverbank. Tecumseh gazed upon her and expected her to rise up and look upon him once more with that beautiful sparkle of life. His ears waited for some joke for her most favorite uncle. But there was only silence. Those things would never again be.

The beauty that she carried in life now was imbued with a silvery glow, set about by the moon's pale light upon her form. Taughannock stood upon her in silence, drowned in his thoughts. He reached down, and with great strength, lifted her up within the makeshift bed that filled his arms. He strode slow to the end of the great fire, which was not yet caught up in the flames that grieved.

Along the way, he passed by Tecumseh with head bowed and a face of stone. He softly set her down, grasped a lit torch, and set the kindling beneath her aflame. At once, soft flames shot out from underneath and began to wrap about her body. The flames leapt higher and higher still.

Taughannock stepped close to Nateelah's body that burned before him. He stretched the last moment of her image. He then lifted out his upturned hands to the night sky and let loose a guttural roar. Its grief peeled apart the thick air. Tecumseh had never heard such a sound. It was like one of those wondrous beasts he had read about in one of John Sackett's history books, those lions of Africa.

The roar carried like nighttime thunder from a mighty summer storm across the valley, with its dark and blackened clouds that heaved in the wild winds. It rattled bones and thumped upon the chest. It startled all the birds and beasts of the forest, which went deathly quiet at the sound.

When the great roar at last faded away, Taughannock looked upon Nateelah one last time. Tecumseh knew the young Jhagir soaked in her beauty, for that memory would have to last a lifetime. And then as the flames began to take her, he turned and in silence walked away. But as he came upon Tecumseh, he stopped.

His eyes pleaded to Tecumseh. They begged for an answer like a child . . . why did she have to die? Taughannock spoke no words, and just stared grief. More tears streamed down Tecumseh's face, and he just shook his head. He did not know . . . it was a wisdom he did not have. Taughannock then whispered, "I go now to the river bank, to be alone with the moonlight upon the river. I am with her still, but now no more than a memory."

Tecumseh just stared through his tears as Taughannock walked away and disappeared into the dark. And then Tecumseh's old friend returned . . . his hatred. He hated the wolf. And now it consumed him like a flood upon the land.

Chapter Twenty-Six
A Friend's Goodbye

Tecumseh's breaths were short and quick. Something chased him in the dark. Closer it came. Outstretched hands lunged for him. He reached for his tomahawk and screamed out. He leapt up . . . and awoke. It was just a dream . . . of dread and despair. It was the wolf again. Though that time, the wolf had arms and legs of one of his kin. It was red-skinned hands that reached for him. That had never happened before. What did it mean? He did not know. The vision scared him . . . and haunted his soul. He tried to shake the fear from his mind, but it lingered.

The next day rose, but the dawn could not dispel the heavy sadness that sat upon the hearts of the living among the village ruins. Tecumseh looked about the desolation and saw Gahnoque alone, off to the far edge of the village. Gahnoque moved with a desperate fever. He had set about to build his door to the stars at last. The time had come.

As Tecumseh walked toward him, he could see Gahnoque had gathered up fallen oak limbs from some far off place, and bound them tight with thin pieces of worn animal skins. The oaken limbs were held into the shape of a large arrowhead pointed to the sky, with one oversized limb placed to the rear for strength. The wooden thing stood twelve paces tall and seven paces from side to side. Gahnoque had cut grooved notches in the wooden limbs, to hold the Ithreal stones at the two bottom corners and the arrowhead's peak.

Tecumseh asked, "What is it that you will do?"

Gahnoque's voice rumbled slow, "There can be no more waiting. Amid the horror visited upon the village, we must all do what we can . . . for there may not be a tomorrow."

"Yes . . . you are right. There is no reason now to put this off, whether it be a success . . . or failure," said Tecumseh, tired with grief.

Gahnoque said, "There can now be nothing for it. The palefaces will not ever bow to peace. They will understand only my blade, slit across their throat."

Tecumseh nodded in quiet. "I had held out hope for a peace. I was a fool who should have known better."

"Do not cast such blame, for you did what you thought to be the way of peace for your people," Gahnoque said.

Tecumseh nodded again slow.

Gahnoque then sighed. His body drooped. "This paleface nation is mighty, with an unending supply of men and weapons. The Indians of these lands cannot defeat this enemy. You need more warriors. And so, we must open this star door now, if ever it is to be done. I will then return with countless Jhagir warriors.

"Then we shall measure the might of these great white fathers once and for all. And when their end comes and they cry out for peace, there will be no negotiations of lies. The last thing they will see in this world will be the living light of Ithreal." Gahnoque stewed in silence. His fists were clenched tight, his face glowered hatred.

After some quiet, Tecumseh turned to Gahnoque. "In all of my days, you are the mightiest of all living things. The Great Spirit flows strong through you, and so my heart tells me that you will find a way. I see the future. It is filled with your return and that of many Jhagir warriors . . . and then we shall have peace."

Preparations were made that day, for at night's coming, it would be done. And the winds of fortune blew upon them, as that night a full moon would shine. The summer moon would hang low in the sky. And Gahnoque spoke again of the hope that the moonlight would strengthen the Ithreal stones, as it does with the seven moons of Celadon.

Tecumseh looked on as evening faded to night. And then it began. Ithikkah and Taughannock removed the Ithreal stones from their chest harnesses and handed them to Gahnoque. Uneasiness painted their faces, for Tecumseh knew it was a thing most unnatural for the Jhagir to give freely their own Ithreal stone to another. He knew the Ithreal star given at birth, was one's alone. And it was to be treasured and kept safe while one took breath, for if ever the light be taken or lost, bad things would follow.

But Tecumseh knew that Ithikkah and Taughannock had no choice. And of the three Jhagir, Gahnoque was the most gifted with the star of Ithreal. If any of them were to do it, it would be him.

The Ithreal stones were bound within the star door's grooved notches, secured tight. All was set. They would wait now for the full coming of dark and the moon's light. It would not be long now.

They stewed nervously in the darkness of what was to come. Gahnoque turned to Tecumseh, "I have a request to make of you."

Tecumseh looked upon his friend and nodded, "Surely, I will grant it in any way that I can."

Gahnoque asked, "In the chance of this journey's success and I look again upon my own world, there is something else I should bring with me. My people will listen to what I have seen and to what I have to say; but still, some will harbor doubt to this unknown world of what I speak - of your world.

"And as your people are in grave need of many warriors and soon, I should bring your words with me. For if they hear the wisdom of your tongue, then they will know what must be done."

With a smile, Tecumseh said, "What, am I to don a harness and walk through this portal door with you? And who would lead the people? I cannot leave them alone to face their fate." He then looked up to the night stars and said, "Though to fly through the stars would be a thing beyond wonder."

Gahnoque laughed. "No my friend, in this world you are the captain of the ship, and it will sail only at your driving wind.

"No, I ask you to give something else of yourself," and with that, Gahnoque pulled out the tiniest of glass bottles from some hidden place within his chest harness. Gahnoque called it a vial. It was very small, no more than a small caterpillar in length and the width of a small acorn. "I ask to take but a few drops of your blood, for upon my return to Celadon, I will convene a great council at Mythrea. Its ancient waters of memories and truth will give you voice.

"With but a drop of your blood in those waters, your image will rise up and speak to the Jhagir. You shall stare deep into their souls; your tongue shall stir their hearts to reach back through the stars to help a dying people."

Tecumseh turned to Gahnoque, reached out his forearm, and said, "Let it be done."

They both nodded to the other, and Gahnoque pressed the vial upon Tecumseh's forearm. It pricked like an ant bite, and red blood flowed and filled the vial.

Tecumseh said, "Nateelah always said there was no voice I found sweeter than that of my own. And now you will give my tongue eternal life in your world. She would think you do the Jhagir a great disservice."

Gahnoque just smiled deep.

Tecumseh broke into a slow smile too. He knew that Nateelah would have had a thing or two to say about that . . . and that thought warmed his heart, if only for a moment.

Once the vial was filled, Gahnoque secured it safely back within his harness. He then gazed up into the night sky and breathed in deep the fresh air. He soaked in the bright light of the full moon that shined down upon them in all its ghostly glory. He turned to Tecumseh and said, "It is time."

Tecumseh nodded and many gathered around the portal, but at a safe distance. There was a nervous silence, for not a living soul knew what was to come. Questions spun all about Tecumseh's mind. Would Gahnoque enter the star door, only to become lost in some night sky, unbound from both this world and his own? Maybe the star portal would just explode into a fiery ball of flame and burn all within its path. Or nothing at all would happen.

Gahnoque turned to Tecumseh and those few near to him, and said, "You must wait until I have passed fully through the portal door, away into the stars. Then if I reach Celadon, there will be a starlit shadow like a ghostly path to follow . . . a trail back to this door. The connection cannot be broken . . . or the way back will be lost."

Tecumseh and the others nodded.

Gahnoque then turned and with eyes closed, seemed to put all his thoughts upon the portal door. At once, his silhouette was engulfed in a blue glow. The Ithreal stone upon his chest throbbed of a blue and white light. The three Ithreal stones upon the portal also began to dance and throb with a light that glowed. That went on for some time, but nothing happened. Tecumseh glimpsed frowns of worry that lined Ithikkah's and

Taughannock's faces. Perhaps something was wrong. Or perhaps, such a journey was just not possible.

But then suddenly, the light of all the Ithreal stones erupted and smashed upon each other and out into the darkness. Starlight exploded and lit up the forest. Forearms were raised to provide some relief. It was blinding.

Then strong gusts of air were unleashed from the portal. Its mighty winds blew warm as if a summer storm that scattered tree limbs and brush all about. Tecumseh raised his hands, to shield his face. Buckskin clothing and hair all about was blown raggedly back and forth, like a paleface bed sheet hung to dry in the flapping breeze. But no matter how hard the wind blew, the wiry limbs and wrapped bindings did not yield. The star door held tight to the Ithreal stones.

After a few moments, the portal's storm winds weakened a bit so Tecumseh could at least now look upon it. And then within the portal door, the night's stars appeared, so close they could be touched; ripped from the air itself, as if there was another night sky right there before them. Tecumseh's eyes widened.

Gahnoque then turned and looked to Tecumseh alone. He raised his hand in peace and said, "If this be the last we look upon one another, I will say there is no greater honor than to help a friend in need. One who did the same for me in my hour most dire, when he had never before looked upon me or my kin. And so, I go now to do the same. I will not say goodbye, for my heart will not let it be so. Whether in this world of flesh and bone or that which comes after, I will say until we meet again my friend."

Tecumseh nodded in return and said, "I shall keep a fire burning for you and we shall share the pipe of peace once more."

Gahnoque nodded back. He then turned and bowed to Kykuitheh, who nodded her same feelings of kinship back to him.

And last, Gahnoque turned to Ithikkah and Taughannock and said, "Jhagir, I see you. I will return. One day we shall all walk again together in the beauty of our home, of Celadon . . . and we will reminisce of this night's journey."

Ithikkah and Taughannock both smiled and nodded their wish for that pleasant day to come. Ithikkah said, "If any Jhagir is to make this journey, it would be you. Until next we meet my old friend."

And with that, Gahnoque turned and looked straight into the portal door. Its blackened and starlit mystery beckoned. Destiny whispered his name. He inhaled one last calm breath, and then walked bravely into the unknown. The Ithreal stones pulsed brighter again and winds swirled and wrapped about Gahnoque. The mighty Jhagir leaned in hard against the strong winds and pushed his way through the portal. He made his way further along, about thirty paces or so, deeper into the doorway to the stars.

And then thunder erupted everywhere. Cannonballs ripped through them in all directions - they were under attack! Bodies and limbs flew through the air. The large guns of America had been wheeled about in the dark of night, and were now upon them. Lost deep in their haze of grief, they were caught in complete unawares. All trembled at the thunderous booms of cannon fire that rained down upon them that shook the ground. Chaos was unleashed, warriors scrambled about in terror.

Tecumseh saw lines of panic upon Gahnoque's face, as he tried to turn back. And still more explosions thundered and hurtled chunks of earth and warriors into the air. It rattled the soul. Tecumseh saw Gahnoque struggle to fight his way back to the portal door.

LON BRETT COON

But the pull to the stars was strong. And it grew with each moment. Gahnoque's great muscles flexed and trembled. His body stretched to the limits of flesh and bone, ready to be torn apart. With each step he struggled and roared out defiance, as if a pain ripped through him. He was nearly there now and Tecumseh stood before him, back on the other side of the world.

With all of his might, Gahnoque reached out to Tecumseh. His body trembled in a blur, as the great pull of the stars would whisk him away. And Tecumseh grasped back in desperation. He would pull his friend through. But cannon shot exploded and the portal door's wooden limbs were blown apart. The Ithreal stones' light faded to dark.

Tecumseh looked upon Gahnoque in one last moment. Their eyes interlocked helplessly, as the portal door closed in on itself. And in a flash of light and a wave of air, the door slammed shut. Gahnoque vanished like a shadow in the dark. Tecumseh was blown back a few steps. He screamed out for his friend . . . but he was gone.

A loud roar erupted and waves of countless long knives flew into the village. Musket shots exploded everywhere in rage. In the madness, Ithikkah and Taughannock scrambled for their Ithreal stones. They found the smashed and shattered wooden limbs that had held the stones, but the bindings in which they sat were torn and empty. They franticly searched the scattered debris . . . but the stones were gone.

And as the blue jackets swarmed like bees to a hive, the Jhagir were left to fight for their very lives, but now with no starlit weapons or the ability to apparate. Still mighty in battle they were, and many soldiers they felled, but some bodily wounds and gashes they did suffer. And in a short time, they were soon overwhelmed, as if a mountain of dirt that succumbed to a great village of ants upon it. Tecumseh and his warriors were overrun, with many cut down. He screamed for

260

those that remained to flee to the forest. But many did not hear his call, and they fought and struggled on.

In the desperate escape, Tecumseh searched franticly for Kykuitheh; but he could not find her. Everything moved so slow. The final ruin of his village played out as if some far off dream. In the rage of long knives and flames, he saw not Kykuitheh, Ithikkah, or Taughannock. He stayed to the last possible moment and strained for their image . . . but they were gone.

There was nothing but an endless flood of blue jackets, and so at last, Tecumseh ran to the cloaked darkness of the forest. Some long knives followed after in a frenzy. They shouted wildly in their anger, but Tecumseh was soon lost to them in the dark. There was just the trees and the moon. His heart pounded like a beating drum. Tecumseh was so small and swallowed up by the wild. He was alone again. Just himself and the same old demons that never really leave . . . fear and doubt.

Chapter Twenty-Seven
Freedom's Gift

Tecumseh's breaths were still. The night was sleepless. The long knives' torches did not find him, but relief did not come. He was a six-year-old boy all over again. Always the palefaces hunted him in the dark. He hated the wolf. He would always hate the wolf. And it occurred to him that he would never solve his father's riddle. His insides were as darkened as the pitted black sky. His world was lost to him. It all spun about, beyond hope. Maybe only death could bring relief from the despair that washed upon him.

The morning sun chased away the night, but not the darkness that dwelled within. Some warriors had found Tecumseh in the forest's womb, and anguish carried upon their faces. Their hearts were numb, laid low by the night before. Otsaga had found his way there, but Kykuitheh was not among them. Neither were Ithikkah or Taughannock; and Tecumseh's heart reeled in that desolation. Yet, the survivors looked to Tecumseh now, at the very crossroads of the people. And more than ever, Tecumseh knew he must be that wall of rock upon which the water's stormy waves broke against. But what could be done with his warriors scattered to the wind? He did not know.

Over the next few days, more warriors found their way to Tecumseh, and their numbers began to grow. Though

Tecumseh's troubled mind only spun more. He felt so conquered . . . so less than a man. Anger and hate filled his heart. It was more venomous than he had ever known. And it consumed him. There were only tightened fists and the grinding of teeth. Insides would explode, like being shot from a musket.

His thoughts turned to his father. He needed him, needed his words. But his father was gone forever. Now, he just needed to be alone. Something deep inside called to him. He told the warriors he must go to speak with the Great Spirit deep in the woods, but that he would return. Tecumseh saw the desperate looks upon their faces as he left. They needed him to find his strength for what was to come.

Alone in the woods, he wandered. Like a child on all fours, just crawling in the dark. In a dazed fever of hate and anger, he stumbled about. He walked far, until he came across a bubbling stream. He followed its flowing waters that emptied into a large pond of glass, like a paleface window that shimmered in the sunlight. It was a beautiful place. One he had never seen before. And his legs were tired. They just wanted to sit. He sat upon a smooth oversized rock that guarded the shore. His fists clenched and muscles flexed as the anger of everything poured all over him again. He had never hated the wolf so much in his life. The wolf had taken everything from him.

His insides were black like a storm cloud. He picked up a jagged rock in anger that filled his hand and slammed it into the peaceful pond. He screamed out all the ferocious hate in his belly. Furious water splashed into the air. Tecumseh leaned in to look upon the violent ripples of water. He snarled meanness. And when the rippled water slowly faded away to stillness, Tecumseh gazed in shock at the image that stared back.

It was not his face, but that of Sakdayga that gazed upon him. It was like a dream, but he was not asleep. He was taken aback. It scared him. Who was he becoming? Was he so filled with hate that he was now no different than Sakdayga? What did it all mean? His insides trembled in fear of where he was headed. Thoughts rambled for an answer to it all. He was desperate for that wisdom.

Defeated and so small, he thought of someone whose wisdom he valued over most. His mind drifted again to his great friend, John Sackett. He missed John Sackett and had not seen him for so very long now. John Sackett would help him understand that vision. But maybe John Sackett was already dead? The frontier had become so dangerous . . . he hoped him and his family were still alive. He must go to them, but it was such a long way by foot. He would never make it.

But then, he looked up and saw another old friend that stood upon the pond's shore. By some happy chance, fate smiled upon him. It was his faithful white and brown speckled horse. He loved that painted pony, and somehow his old friend had escaped the paleface army's attack too and found him. He greeted the pony with a warm hug and they quenched their thirsts with the pond's blue waters. They then rode off together, for there was one more old friend they had to go see.

Tecumseh rode on at a fast step for several days. Until one night as darkness fell, he slowed his pace. Familiar forests and hills soon greeted him. He knew that place. He always felt its warmth. It was John Sackett's home. Candles burned and flickered through the small glass windows of the square wood shaven home. He whispered in the dark, "John Sackett. John Sackett. Will you speak with an old friend?"

At once, a squeal pierced the chilled air. Friendly yells rose up. And the entire family of John Sackett ran out excitedly to see their old friend.

Tecumseh jumped down from his pony. He smiled, for his good friend and his family was still alive, and they all seemed in good health too.

John Sackett walked up and smiled wide, as did all his family. "It has been a long time my old friend." Then his gaze turned somber, and he said, "I wondered if your death had come at last. We heard of the sacking of your village. Even on the frontier, such news travels fast. A passing trapper brought word. I am sorry to hear of it."

Tecumseh sighed. "Yes John Sackett. It is true. My home is in ruins. Many people died . . . or have been scattered and lost to me." At that, Tecumseh stared off, his mind somewhere far away.

John Sackett nodded slowly and asked, "What of Kykui-theh and Nateelah?"

A somber pain painted Tecumseh's face. "Nateelah is dead."

Aghast, Rebecca Sackett cried out in empty dread and sadness, "No! It can't be so!"

"The blade of the long knives took her," said Tecumseh vacantly. A pitted emptiness filled him.

All the Sacketts then sat in silence. They did not want to bring any more sadness to their old friend.

After a while, Tecumseh went on, "I know not the fate of Kykuitheh. She is lost to me."

Tears flowed from Rebecca. She lurched forward and gave a weeping hug to Tecumseh. "I am so sorry to hear such things," she cried softly.

He hugged her tight, but no words came to him.

Mary Sackett then said, "Let us put these troubles aside for a moment. Surely, after so long a ride alone, you are weary and hungry? Will you not eat with us for a time, and let us talk of happier times?"

Tecumseh nodded and said, "I thank you for your kindness."

A warm fire was set, and it blazed of friendship. They all then enjoyed a simple dinner of roasted corn and beef stew. It had been a long time since Tecumseh had eaten such a fine meal. It filled his belly whole. And for a few hours, all the troubles of the world melted away from Tecumseh's mind. It was like old times. They laughed. They smiled. Happy reminisces floated on the air. He loved that family.

After some time, Tecumseh told John Sackett he needed to speak with him alone. He needed his wisdom. All the Sacketts nodded, bowed their heads, and left John Sackett and Tecumseh alone by the fire.

They both stared deep into the flames. After some quiet, Tecumseh leaned in nearer to the fire and told John Sackett of his visions. He spoke of the red-handed wolf that came for him in the dark. He spoke of his reflection upon the pond's waters, how Sakdayga's face had replaced his own. What did it all mean?

And he spoke of the anger and hatred that consumed all his soul. It devoured him. And he had nothing left. He had never hated the wolf more than he did now. And he never felt farther from the answer to his father's mystery . . . the riddle in the dark. He would hate the wolf until the end of his days.

Tecumseh turned to John Sackett and asked, "You are a great friend to me. And I need your wisdom. I have never been so small . . . so alone." His eyes pleaded to John Sackett, like the smallest child who gazed up to his father who was stronger and wiser than the oldest mountain.

John Sackett looked upon Tecumseh and smiled softly. He patted him upon the shoulder and then turned and gazed into the flames that danced. John Sackett was searching for wisdom . . . for the words to speak. Desperate lines marked his face, of one who would help his friend in the greatest of need. Then he turned to Tecumseh and said, "I think it is your father. He speaks to you now through these visions . . . he has not given up on you.

"Perhaps with all that has happened in your world, all would walk with heavy hearts, filled with anger and hatred for vengeance. But maybe he is desperate for you to be stronger than that.

"Some might say having the strength to do what is right is being brave in battle and facing down your fear of death. But maybe for your father, it is something more. Maybe it is the strength to face down your anger . . . and your hate. Perhaps your father wants you to reach down deeper to some place inside of you . . . a place you did not know exists. And then, you would find that strength."

Tecumseh just stared, his face painted with all the emptiness of the world. Then he leaned back in wonder. His eyes sparkled with the marvel of one who would look upon the beauty of their first sunrise. A lifetime flashed before his eyes. He saw it all. A few words from his friend and it all flooded upon him. The great mystery of his life was undone and set free. He had found the desperate wisdom at last. A serene peace settled upon his face.

He looked back to John Sackett and smiled. "All the many years of my life have led me to here. And always I have wondered what it was that my father had tried to tell me so long ago as death came for him. Do not hate the wolf, he told me. But how could I not? And what would become of me if I did?

"And this day at last, my father's wisdom speaks to me. It is that if my people are ever to be truly free, if I am ever to be truly free . . . I cannot hold hate in my heart. For trapped in hate I will be.

"Even if I cleansed the world of all my enemies and was free out there," as he gestured about, "but still a hatred for past wrongs burned in my soul, I would be a prisoner to the hate and never be free in here," and Tecumseh pointed to his heart.

He then looked straight upon John Sackett. His eyes delved deeper. "And hatred is the mightiest master we shall ever know. We would die alone and broken in the dark, kneeled for all our days before its power and might. We would know nothing but iron bars of blind rage and peaceless nights on end. We would shrivel away as it slowly gnawed upon our soul . . . until there was nothing left.

"But it is not as the priest of your paleface church would say, for you do not forgive. You do it not for others . . . you do it only for yourself. And you never forget . . . but you must let its poison go," Tecumseh said.

"This is why we must not hate the wolf. This is why we must not hate the palefaces. This is the gift a dying father would give his son. What would you say to these words John Sackett?" Tecumseh said.

John Sackett sat back. Wrinkled lines marked his face in a warm and deep smile. It was filled with great pride, as he seemed to search for the words to say. John Sackett then leaned in and put his hand upon Tecumseh's shoulder. "I would say a man must find his way, and not let others tell him what to do . . . what to think. And I would say your father was a very great man, for wiser words were never spoken.

"Tecumseh, you are like a son to me. I hold you to the warmest place of my heart. And I think my red-skinned son has just been given the greatest of gifts . . . the gift of freedom."

And there by the heat of the flames that flickered, Tecumseh and John Sackett sat in the tightest bond of friendship that could ever be between two living souls.

Their talk lasted long into the night. After a while, Tecumseh looked upon his great friend, "John Sackett, a Shawnee could not have a better friend. The Great Spirit walks with you."

John Sackett nodded back warmly.

Tecumseh sighed deep. "With what comes, I fear this night we look the last upon the other."

Silence filled the air, as two friends just gazed back at each other.

Then Tecumseh went on, "But I am one of the lucky ones, for I am a free man . . . free of all my masters. I cast my hatred aside forever.

"I wish freedom upon you and your family until the end of your days. May you always have the strength to do what is right." Tecumseh lingered in the stilled moment. He then raised his hand to John Sackett's shoulder and said, "Do not wake your family, for they are long lost to a peaceful slumber. But when they arise, give them my love. Goodbye John Sackett."

John Sackett nodded. They walked out of the house and into the dark. A tear or two escaped from the eye of each man. No more words were spoken. There were just long looks and deep breaths. Saying goodbye to John Sackett was no easy thing to do. But that time had now come. And with that, Tecumseh hopped upon his painted horse and sauntered away.

Chapter Twenty-Eight
Call of Tecumseh's Confederacy

Tecumseh returned from his one-man journey of many days, as dusk settled. Many more warriors had found their way to the gathering. And the warriors yelled out their greeting to Tecumseh. There had been worry on his delayed return. Some feared he would not come back, yet here he was . . . a hoped-for vision. And as he approached, a glad vision appeared to Tecumseh - Ithikkah and Taughannock.

They had emerged from the forest too. Though battered and weary of limb, and several wounds they carried, yet alive they were. Many warriors thought they had traveled in Tecumseh's company, but that was the first Tecumseh had laid eyes upon them since the ambush days ago.

"My heart smiles deep at the sight of you both," said Tecumseh, as he shook his head slow in disbelief and smiled deep.

"The Great Spirit is not yet ready for us to leave this world. There is still a little more telling to be told in our tale," said Ithikkah. The Jhagir walked slow up to Tecumseh and sat beside him.

They sat for a moment in happy sight of the other. Tecumseh looked on and gestured to all those survivors gathered about, then back to Ithikkah and Taughannock, and said, "Indeed, the Great Spirit has found that it is not yet our time."

Nodding looks were passed about.

"How is it my friends that you survived that night, for I saw nothing before me but a sea of soldiers and bayonets?" Tecumseh asked in wonder.

"Without our stones of Ithreal, we were nearly done in by their endless numbers and surprise. But through our strength and a bit of luck, we threw down our slayers and escaped their wrath," Ithikkah said softly.

Taughannock added, "Once within the forest, we bounded to safety behind tree and rock, though still they came and searched by torchlight. Yet, the forest would not give us up. And we have since found our way to you here."

"Did you see any sign of Kykuitheh?" asked Tecumseh in earnest.

"Yes my friend . . . we did for a short time; but when last we saw her, she was dodging long knives and in a struggle with one, whom she did kill," Ithikkah said calmly.

Taughannock said, "But then in the chaos . . . she was gone."

At those words, Tecumseh looked on with a distant smile upon his face and said, "Perhaps she is making her way through the wild . . . and may find her way back to us yet." The others bowed their heads to Tecumseh and nodded their hopeful wish at that thought.

And though his words brimmed with confidence, desperation rose within. Despite her strong spirit, she surely would not stand a chance alone in the wild. But he could do nothing now save wait and wonder, for her fate was no longer in his hands. Otsaga came up to Tecumseh and looked upon him with soft eyes. He put his hand upon Tecumseh's shoulder; but spoke no words, for there were none that would bring peace to his old friend.

As nightfall came, most all sat in a despair of discontent, as still more warriors trickled into the gathering. And though

LON BRETT COON

many had made it, a fair number had not. They had either perished in the nighttime ambush or remained scattered to the wild; and so, their numbers were greatly diminished.

And Tecumseh thought upon the destruction of the star door and the loss of Gahnoque to some unknown fate. What if Gahnoque had found the way to his own world, but he could now no longer find his way back to this world? No, with the door shut and gone, there would be no army of Jhagir warriors to come. Gahnoque had told him so. No, with the star door destroyed and the Ithreal stones lost, even the stoutest of heart were bent to the depths of their brooding reality.

Tecumseh looked upon his Jhagir brothers, and his insides wept heavy for them. He thought of the great pain that would sit upon his heart if he never again looked upon the wonders of his homeland or his kin. And he thought of the loss of the Jhagir's loyal friend Gahnoque, who was gone to where they could not follow. Tecumseh just sighed, as he could offer them no comfort from that hurt. But he thought to himself that maybe they could find the Ithreal stones . . . or even one stone. He would help his friends to look long and hard for those stones when they returned to the village.

Days later, once they were sure the paleface army had gone, Tecumseh and the warriors ventured back to the village ruins. Tecumseh looked for some sign of Kykuitheh, and hoped he did not come upon her lifeless body. He was not ready to face that. He did not have that strength, not today . . . or any day that would come after. And after many breathless moments, he exhaled deep. She was nowhere to be found. Maybe she had made her way to the forest . . . maybe she was still somehow alive. A quiet hope flickered faintly within him like a far off wind.

All the dead were then gathered up, to be placed upon a fire for their journey to the Great Spirit. Once the fallen had made their way, Tecumseh and the Jhagir searched for long hours upon the grounds for any sign of the Ithreal stones, but hidden they remained. Maybe Mother Earth swallowed them up for all of time in the bloody chaos. Perhaps the long knives had gathered up the stones in the ambush and stole them away. But it did not matter . . . they were gone. Gloom painted the faces of the Jhagir, as the lingering hope they might somehow find their lost stones was now gone. And a deep sadness washed upon Tecumseh's heart at that sight. An emptiness that could not breathe swallowed him up.

The world rumbled upon him like the palefaces' new iron horse, which smoked black on its teethed trails of shaved wood that snaked about the land. The palefaces called it a railroad. He had seen one far to the east a year back. It had shaken the ground, pounded his chest. He heard the palefaces talk of it being just the beginning, and that they would build many more of those great horses. It was the coming of a new age, the industrial age they said. Though strange to Tecumseh's ears, those were not empty words. He knew what it meant. Someday, the iron horses and their teethed trails would find their way to his homelands too . . . they were coming. The world was changing. And now with his village destroyed, his people scattered, Kykuitheh lost to him, and the Ithreal stones lost to his Jhagir friends, Tecumseh was defeated at last. He was smaller than he had ever been. It all was a battle he could not win.

All hope was lost. And then it came to him, a thing un-thinkable. There was only one path left in Tecumseh's mind. Though at first, his lips could not say the words . . . even to himself. If the people would choose life and freedom, then they must leave these lands. It broke his heart to think such a thing . . . but he did not see any other way. All who were able must flee to the far north to Canada, beyond the borders of the paleface nation. There was nowhere left to go, but to the great grandfathers' land. The old white hairs and their red jackets and gleaming brass buttons might be the only thing to save them.

The paleface nation would surely raise its greatest army now to wipe out a people forever. And Harrison would come at the lead. But Tecumseh thought that maybe even Harrison would not risk war with the great grandfathers. Though so far away across the unending sea, the red jackets were still mighty, with more muskets, guns, and ships than even the great white fathers. Tecumseh was sure that Harrison would not follow his people into Canada, for fear of what the old white hairs might do. The people just needed to get to those lands.

But Tecumseh's warriors could only try to give them some time and hope of passage against the great wolf. He could no longer hold back the rage of America's anger and might . . . he could only hope to slow it for a while. He sent out messengers across all the lands to pass word of the people's passage over the coming months. Tecumseh called out for the greatest gathering of all the tribes who would come. It was time to honor the oaths and promises made by those who would stand up together . . . those who would fight for freedom. To the land in northern Ohio, near to the village of Otsaga they were too come. From there, the many people might make their way to Canada and freedom.

Tecumseh and the warriors then left the valley forest, and wished to hope still. They moved to Otsaga's home village far to the north. Along the way, people from many tribes, the old and the young all, joined the warrior escort. And as they went, Tecumseh's heart wondered to what fate Kykuitheh had gone. Day after day, his mind raced with thoughts of her. He walked the forests in search of her along the way at each resting stop they made. He whispered her name . . . but she was gone.

In time, they all made their way safely to Otsaga's village. And over the coming months and into early fall, many more came, both warriors and the people. Tecumseh saw that many villages heeded the call, including some from the Lakota, Ottawa, Wyandot, Delaware, Winnebago, and Fox tribes. There too were many warriors from the Miami, Ojibwa, and the Potawatomi . . . and some warriors of the Blackfoot, Cherokee, and Creek nations. Into and surrounding Otsaga's village they came, hundreds by the day . . . until all who were willing had come.

Tecumseh looked out upon the largest gathering of tribes that ever was, and ever would be. All the tribes had told him so. There were ten thousand strong. There were so many tomahawks and war clubs that many tribes were now emboldened. Strong was the feeling by many that with their great size, they could still find a way to defeat the great white fathers. Then they would not have to flee to Canada.

Even Tecumseh began to ponder if the great size of the war party might be enough to change things. Like many, as he gazed out upon the endless numbers of warriors, he thought that just maybe there was a way to defeat the great paleface nation. But then that fleeting vision was shattered like breaking ice upon a frozen river.

Some Shawnee and Sauk scouts had returned with word of the great white fathers. The words hit Tecumseh like a charging horse that trampled upon him. He exhaled in defeated wonder. They told Tecumseh the great General Harrison was coming once more. And this time, he brought more muskets than trees in the forests. The scouts spoke of some twenty thousand or more long knives on the move, with several thousand cavalry, and some thirty cannons.

It did not seem possible. It was something beyond reality. A moving paleface city of blue jackets and muskets came for them. And word too that the French had sent five thousand mercenaries. Tecumseh's insides shrank away. No, he knew he could not defeat the great white fathers. If the people wanted their freedom, they must leave their homelands forever . . . they must flee to Canada.

As word spread, Tecumseh saw a great fear upon many warriors and chiefs. It rolled like a wave upon the sea. They called out to Tecumseh, "We need aid! We should send our swiftest scouts with word for the old white hairs. The red jackets would send help, as they had long ago. Once they have heard of our great war party at your call, they would do so once more."

Tecumseh just smiled low and nodded, "Yes. If we allied with the great grandfathers, we could raise two fronts upon America . . . and maybe bring an unlooked-for victory.

"But there is not enough time for our message to be received. Harrison and a sea of long knives come for the people as we speak. No, we have no choice. We must face the great white fathers now. We need look only to ourselves; whether we rise or fall . . . it is on us to give the fleeing people a chance for freedom. We are alone."

The warriors and chiefs all bathed in silence. They heard Tecumseh's words. They knew he spoke the truth. All veil of doubt was pulled back. Tecumseh and the free peoples' were utterly alone. And the next morning, Tecumseh's confederacy suffered a great setback. During the night, word spread among the warriors of the loss of the great Jhagir Chief Gahnoque. Lost to a magic star door he was. And the truth spread that the two remaining Jhagir no longer possessed the starlit stones. They no longer walked as ghosts in the spirit world.

Tecumseh had kept that hidden for as long as he could, as he was sure some warriors would break at the learning of it. And once the word had finally spread, it was as he feared. Some war chiefs called it a bad omen. Tecumseh's medicine was no longer strong they said. And many openly questioned Tecumseh. Who was he to lead the warriors? After heated words late into the night, many chose to leave the confederacy.

They would return to their own homelands and not flee to Canada. Better to negotiate a peace for their own villages and lands that remained they said. Some began to depart in the dark, while others waited for dawn's light.

That was the scene Tecumseh awoke to, many thousands of warriors and people that left. Tecumseh stepped outside his longhouse in the early morning and looked about. There was a foggy mist, brought on by the first light of the warm sunrise upon the cold dew. Lines of departing warriors and their families stretched into the distance. They were ghostly images that trudged away. Heavy disappointment settled upon his heart. His spirit sank. In total, nearly four thousand warriors and their families passed by. Now, only six thousand warriors remained, four thousand on foot and two thousand on horse.

Although an Indian war party that size was still beyond the tales of any tribe, it would not nearly be enough. A flooding wave of American might came for them. But for those six thousand warriors that stood with him, there was no turning back. They must provide the peoples' safe passage to Canada. They must at least try.

Tecumseh gathered those that remained. He asked them to be not angry with their brothers who left, for they must follow their own freedom. It was the very reason they rose up together that day. "To my brothers from all the tribes of this land, from this world and beyond . . ." and at that, Tecumseh looked to Ithikkah and Taughannock.

Tecumseh went on, "It is true our great brother Gahnoque is lost to us, his fate unknown. Perhaps one day he will return to the people. My heart tells me it is so; but today, we have only one another.

"And we look now deep into our souls for our fate is at hand. Our people's future now stands on a blade's edge. We stare into an abyss of darkness. Shall our people live free from all yoke and collar? I say yes!

"So let us raise our tomahawks, loose our war cry, and bleed together, for the freedom of sacrifice must be carried. It has fallen upon us to stoke freedom's flame. And it is more precious than nature's bounty and the deep blue water that gives life, for though you may not suffer thirst or hunger, it is no life to lead without free will. Absent our liberty, we are no more a rock stuck in its spot, with no ability or desire to alter our stars of fortune . . . or that of any other."

Tecumseh dwelled in silence and then his voice rose, "I see into the heart of you and I behold the Great Spirit of life that stares back. The Great Spirit cannot be caged! And even if our flesh should fall away, its indomitable will cannot be defeated . . . it echoes on through the ends of time.

"And I say to you now, will you not walk with me, Panther Across the Sky, so that we may forever light the stars of the night with our great deeds. They will shine on to those that come after us . . . so that they may look up into the night sky and know we were here - for freedom!"

There was then a raging river of warrior yells and shouts. The heat of his words melted their souls and raised six thousand spirits to the sky. A rush of vigor flowed within like a great wind that rose up. They were with him.

Scouts said the great paleface army moved to the far north in Chatham, Ontario, so that was where Tecumseh must go. Harrison's great army would meet up with its newly arrived French force, to strike out from a place of strength, down through Upper Canada and into the Ohio Valley. Mighty Harrison would then be able to cut off the free peoples that fled to Canada, and wipe out any tribes and villages along the way like a wild fire that spread upon dry brush and tree that suffered from not enough rain. Tecumseh could not let that happen. So his great war party would make its stand at Chatham. And then the people could take the trails and passages away to the northeast, to escape into the lands of Canada.

After a quick morning meal, the large war party began its journey. The great flood of people followed close behind and moved on their desperate way. And Tecumseh pushed them all on, swiftly and tirelessly, as there was no time for delay. They would make the journey together for a ways, up into the lands near Fort Detroit. Then the people would head northeast alone, while Tecumseh and his warriors would move northwest, straight toward Chatham.

And as the warriors walked and rode on, they hoped the Great Spirit would smile upon them just one more time. They hoped the peoples' journey would escape mighty Harrison and his endless long knives. Maybe somehow they could make their way into the great grandfathers' land before Harrison came upon them, and somehow slip through unseen. The winds of fate were howling like a wolf once more . . . though Tecumseh smiled to himself, as he no longer hated the wolf. Hatred was his master no more . . . he was free.

Chapter Twenty-Nine
Going Home

Tecumseh exhaled deep. Cold sweat trailed down his back. Bones ached. The thick muscles of his faithful painted horse flexed upon his legs. Step after step, he sauntered along the way, lost in a sea of thought. The brisk air blew upon him that mid-autumn day, as the forest's leaves burned yellow, red, and orange like fire. And something was different that day. He felt it on the wind. He tasted it in the water. Had he cast his last gaze upon the night stars? And that morning, had he awoke to his last sunrise? Winter was coming. And like the still quiet before a dark clouded winter storm, was death finally coming to swallow him up? He wondered on that. Something was different that day.

Tecumseh's warriors made their way from the northern Ohio Valley and came upon Chatham, Ontario at last. They had split off from the peoples' journey days ago, as the people traveled further inland to Canada. Tecumseh sighed to himself. Were the people well into the great grandfathers' lands by now, away from the great white fathers' long reach? He could only hope, as they were beyond his aid.

Tecumseh's war party crossed up onto a hill-topped ridge and the valley sprawled out before them, bordered by the Thames River to the far side. They looked down below and gaped at the sight. Amassed before them was the greatest paleface army anyone had ever seen. It filled the whole valley. It seemed that there were indeed more long knives than trees in the forest.

Tecumseh gazed out in shock. All the warriors did. America had brought forth its armies from all its territories to end a people at last. Tecumseh swallowed hard. It was an impassable mountain. Now to see the valley of long knives, he did not think he and his warriors could do such a thing. How could they give the fleeing people some time against that? And if Harrison's great force was to come upon the people . . . not a single soul would survive.

Tecumseh then eyed mighty Harrison. His broad and muscled frame stood out even in that sea of blue jackets. The great general shouted commands to those about, and men scurried forth and back. An endless train of supply wagons skirted the valley back into the forest. And the winds of fate had blown ill, for Harrison's great army had been expecting Tecumseh and his warriors. They stood in formations about the valley plain. Endless corn rows of men. Bayonet blades glistened in the sun.

And the Shawnee would not have the surprise they had hoped for. They had been betrayed. But by whom, Tecumseh could not guess. Maybe the great bull Sakdayga had one final act of treachery . . . but now, it did not matter. Though there was one break of fortune, as the cavalry was still back to the rear, not prepared yet for battle.

Tecumseh sighed. He looked back to his warriors on each side, and then to Ithikkah and Taughannock. They all nodded back . . . they were with him. Tecumseh knew his force, though mighty and fierce at some six thousand strong, was no match for the vast foe below. How could they break Harrison's lines? He did not know. And now it did not matter. There could be no victory . . . only death. Yet, they would not turn back. They must give the people a chance of life and freedom in their passage to the far north in Canada. It was the last deep breath before the plunge into the sea of battle and the world's end.

And in that last fleeting moment, Tecumseh stepped out on his trusted white and brown painted horse and turned back to the amassed warriors. "I know the dread in the dark places of your mind, for it is also in my mind. I know that gathering fear would seize your beating heart . . . but let not despair flood your soul. Stand with me now, strong, like the great oak tree in the woods. Though we may bend to the coming storm, we will never let loose our roots and the clutched soil.

"My brothers, think of the feast of thanks not so long ago with those you hold close. Take up that memory, holding it tight. And then you are not alone. You are with the people. For them, go forth with your tomahawks raised to chase all the darkness from this land.

"And through this deed you shall remain forever free in both this world and the next. My brothers, the time is now. Ride with me . . . for death has come! And we will not turn or run. Let us look back at death with a smile for we are warriors of the people . . . and we go home now in freedom!"

The warriors cried out as one.

Tecumseh then reached down to a spear that was slung at his horse's side. He raised the long feathered shaft to the sky. He flexed it in defiant fury. Then with a violent thrust, he slammed it into the ground. And there it stood, and it quivered back and forth. The warriors all cried out again, as their spirits rose to the clouds. They were like a soaring eagle in the sky. Soon they would come screaming through the air, crashing down upon their enemy with sharpened talons drawn.

And Tecumseh kept a single thought to himself. He remembered that day so long ago on his first and only hunt with his father. That young buck returned to him. The same defiance that flowed through that creature now flowed in his veins. Though one was beast and one man, they were bound by the same spirit. He promised himself to be strong that day, and like the young buck, lay down his life so that the people may live. He would kill many wolves before his end. And he hoped beyond hope that Kykuitheh was among those making their way to Canada.

Tecumseh turned and raised his hand. At once, the warriors began their descent down the ridge. The horsed warriors led the way, with the thousands on foot that followed close behind. Slow at first, and then picking up speed, the riders unleashed themselves in a full gallop . . . down into hell. The last ride of Tecumseh began. He was the sharpest tip of the arrowhead that flew straight and true into the heart of America.

General Harrison yelled out orders and bugles blared. Formations tightened, cannon barrels were raised hurriedly into position, but the cavalry was not yet mounted for battle. Tecumseh's thundering stampede approached to within two hundred paces of the paleface army lines, and closed in fast. At Harrison's order, the cannons unloaded a volley. Cannonballs screamed through the air and burst all about. Warriors were cut down, both horsed and on foot. Limbs were blown off, and pain and death cried out.

But Tecumseh and his painted warriors did not scatter. Still onward into the forest of long knives they rode. The footed warriors broke out in a mad dash and loosed their war cries. The hooves of two thousand horsed warriors thundered fury. It was deafening. It moved the air and shook the ground. A crashing wave of horses, feathers, and tattooed flesh smashed upon the unending sea of blue jackets. The last battle of the free peoples began.

And General Harrison did not expect such a swift attack. The horsed warriors sliced through the army lines like an arrow through flesh. War clubs and tomahawks were swung down in hatred to sever blue-jacketed arms, chests, and heads. Tecumseh then heard a chorus of paleface horns call out again. Harrison's several thousand cavalry had mounted too, and they rushed out to meet the horsed warriors. But the lack of open plain and the close quarter of battle greatly slowed them.

The din and holler of war overtook all things. Musket fire exploded everywhere. The sound of leaden musket balls whizzed by . . . and some hit their mark. Horses for both the palefaces and warriors rose up and whinnied terror. Warrior riders were felled by mighty swings of steel blades and bayonet lunges, while blue-jacketed riders were cut down by fierce tomahawks and war clubs. A hail of arrows flew from the many warriors on the move, and rained down upon the long knives and French soldiers. The arrowheads cut through flesh, and war cries carried across the valley.

A smoky mist rose up about the battlefield. And the crashing sound of sword and steel against the stone of tomahawk echoed. The battle lines began to break, as Americans, French, Shawnee, and the many other tribal warriors clashed, man to man . . . face to face. Many fell to breathe no more. The field was awash in blood.

From a distance, Tecumseh caught sight of Ithikkah and Taughannock launching into the battle. Though still formidable, both were now more like a man. Without their Ithreal stones, they brought only their agile strength, tomahawks of stone, and steel blades. Through the clamor of battle, Tecumseh then caught sight of the army that had raided his village those months ago. The ones that murdered Nateelah . . . it was that Beckett!

And Tecumseh saw Taughannock explode in rage toward that Beckett. With a mighty leap, Taughannock sprang upon the paleface enemy. He bounded over three rows of soldiers, and moved in for the kill. No distant musket shot or arrow would do. Tecumseh knew that Taughannock wanted to see the light of Beckett's eyes go out by his hand.

And as Tecumseh killed paleface after endless paleface from atop his painted pony, he desperately looked upon Taughannock. Enraged, Taughannock slaughtered nearly ten long knives all about him, in all manners of death. Tecumseh heard Taughannock call out to Beckett, as he charged at him. Beckett snorted and snarled back, and rushed Taughannock like a wild bull. The Jhagir jumped and twisted through the air to avoid Beckett's bayonet lunge. He landed behind the beastly soldier and knocked the musket to the ground with a forearm blow. Beckett unsheathed his long sword, and spun back to face Taughannock, who had flipped again over him. With a violent downward swing of his forearm, he smashed loose the sword from Beckett's grip. Taughannock then madly swung his free arm back into Beckett's neck. Dazed, Beckett dropped the sword and staggered backwards.

Taughannock lunged forward and grabbed Beckett by the neck with one hand. He lifted that beast of a man into the air like a child. Beckett's feet dangled loose, as he struggled and strained to find the hard ground. The iron grip began to crush Beckett's throat. Taughannock stared into Beckett's eyes as he flailed. The paleface beast gasped out desperately. His face turned whiter than fresh snow. And Tecumseh took it all in between swings of his tomahawk upon soldier after onrushing soldier, and he kept moving closer to the young Jhagir. Tecumseh would help Taughannock do the deed.

Taughannock took his time. It would be slow and torturous, as had been done to Nateelah. But as death began to fall upon Beckett, he desperately fumbled for something. He reached down and grabbed hold of something in his pocket . . . it was a small pistol. Tecumseh could see that Taughannock, still consumed in a furious rage, did not notice. Tecumseh screamed out to Taughannock, to give warning to the young Jhagir. But the sound and din of battle was too great.

And Beckett fired a pistol shot into Taughannock . . . it struck clear into his gut. A flow of purple blood oozed. In shock, Taughannock's arm began to tremble. His strength wavered. And then Beckett dropped freely to the ground. Taughannock staggered back a few steps, and stared disbelief at his leaking wound.

Beckett writhed on the ground and gasped wildly.

Then with a struggle and wince upon his face, Taughannock reached down and picked up a nearby fallen blade. He rose over Beckett and glared. Taughannock then cried out "Your evil shall be no more." He then raised the blade high and readied a final thrust of steel fury into Beckett.

But at that moment, seven soldiers with loaded muskets rushed to Beckett's aid. Taughannock was surrounded. Tecumseh struggled to get to him, but he was lost still in his own sea of blue jackets that seemed to sprout out of the ground and replace those he had just killed. The soldiers took aim and let loose a barrage of musket lead upon the young Jhagir. And Taughannock could not apparate away . . . his harness of Isstah sat empty. The leaden balls flew to Taughannock, who tried to twist and turn away . . . but it was too late. Musket shot tore through his flesh. A flood of blood gushed about his body. He was hit in the belly, the upper thigh, and chest. Tecumseh cried out!

All strength left the young Jhagir. His blade fell harmless to the ground, and he stumbled backwards several steps and hunched over. Two long knives then rushed him. Sabers were driven deep in his gut. They glared over him, as Taughannock stooped over. The long knives then leaned in, placed their feet against his belly, and kicked him to the ground. Blood bathed sabers were withdrawn slow. Tecumseh screamed out again, and fought ferociously to get to him . . . but he could not part the blue-jacketed sea.

Taughannock was helpless. He rolled onto his back and just looked skyward. And as he lay still, Beckett regained his wind. He sprang to his feet and picked up Taughannock's fallen blade. He walked slow over to the fallen Jhagir and stood over him. Tecumseh screamed out wildly again.

A low smile broke along Beckett's face and he let loose some spit. He gloated with a gravelly voice, "I heard bout you . . . and your unnatural coupling with that Indian whore. I'm gunna cut your belly, the same as I did to that Shawnee wench."

Taughannock just stared back. He could not move, his body broken. And Beckett raised the blade up with glee in his eyes. Tecumseh just looked on helplessly . . . he could not get to him. He could do nothing but watch his Jhagir friend die.

Then the air moved. A whooshing noise parted the musket smoke, flying toward the paleface giant. A blade shot through the air and pierced Beckett's back. It protruded with great force, a half foot out of his belly. Beckett staggered back in shock, dropped his blade, and fell over. It was the blade of Ithikkah.

Tecumseh had not seen him, but through the carnage of war, Ithikkah had followed his son on the battlefield. He had found a way through the fog and clamor, and cut down soldier after soldier in his path. But Tecumseh was not surprised, as Ithikkah was a great warrior. And even without the power of his Ithreal stone, Ithikkah was a grizzly bear let loose among men.

And at that moment of greatest desperation, he had let loose a perfect throw to beat back his son's would be killer. The seven soldiers who had come to Beckett's aid, now swung about at the sight of the enraged Ithikkah. Tecumseh saw the fear upon their faces. Ithikkah furiously rushed them. With the blades he held in in each hand, Ithikkah gutted two soldiers with deep thrusts into their bellies. They fell limp to the ground. Blade handles protruded from their backsides, and their innards hung loosely about. Ithikkah stepped over those fallen soldiers, reached down, and grabbed two loaded pistols from their belts, one in each hand. He turned and fired into the faces of the two nearest two soldiers. Holes exploded in their heads where eyes had been.

Ithikkah then leapt clear, twisted in midair, and landed between two other soldiers. Ithikkah grabbed one soldier with both hands and spun its head with a violent twist, and ripped it away. The headless body keeled over to the side. He then turned and smashed the dangling head into another soldier's face, and indented his skull. The soldier's eyes spun upward, and showed only the whites of his eyes as he fell over. Ithikkah then reached down to the fallen soldier and grasped another pistol. He stepped over the lifeless body and took aim at the seventh soldier who took flight from the bloody scene. Ithikkah's sight was true and the screaming musket ball shot clear through the back of his head. Flesh exploded and the long knife fell.

Ithikkah turned and walked calmly over to Beckett. He reached down and took up his son's blade. Beckett's face now drowned in fear, its color turned paler than the moon. That great beast knew what was coming . . . and he was afraid. In silence, Ithikkah picked up Beckett with one hand and raised him to the sky.

He then set Beckett down slow to the ground. Another moment passed, as Ithikkah stared into him. He nodded disgust with no spoken words. He then slowly thrust Taughannock's blade into Beckett's jaw, straight through his head, as if stuck into an oversized piece of meat. The blade handle protruded from his lower jaw, the tip stuck out through his hairy head. Beckett took breath no more. Ithikkah flung the lifeless body away.

There he stood, unmoving among the bloody chaos. In what seemed an hour as time stood still, Ithikkah had slain the seven soldiers and Beckett in mere moments. As the battle raged all about, Ithikkah turned and kneeled down slowly beside his son. He lifted Taughannock up, whose head tilted back, and rested upon him. Ithikkah held him tight, in an embrace. Tecumseh fought hard to get to Ithikkah . . . to comfort his friend. He was almost there . . . just several long strides away. But long knife after long knife lunged at him. Tecumseh was fighting for his life.

Tecumseh saw Taughannock look upon his father and try to speak. He heard the young Jhagir cry out only one word, ". . . father . . . ," and then no more.

Ithikkah then placed Taughannock's arms on his chest, and laid him upon the ground. Tecumseh saw Ithikkah just stare upon his son. Lines of emptiness sat upon a father's face. The grief was beyond words. It was too much to bear for even his broad shoulders, and he could take no more.

Ithikkah rose up and turned to the battle that raged all about. He dropped all weapons and walked forward. His hands and arms were held upturned and aloft. Tecumseh screamed out to Ithikkah. He was frantic to help his friend. Tecumseh was almost there.

But the gathering long knives would not wait. The soldiers aimed and let loose a hail of musket fire. Ithikkah's body and limbs were torn apart. Musket lead ripped through flesh everywhere. His lifeless body fell. Tecumseh looked on in a vacant daze . . . his Jhagir brother had left the world . . . he was gone.

From atop his horse, Tecumseh looked on helplessly through the clouded smoke. He staggered in grief . . . then anger flooded upon him. He reared his painted horse about. He would ride over to Ithikkah's killers and slay them. But as his faithful horse turned and rose up, the musket fire of two long knives blew into the great beast's chest. The horse faltered and careened to the ground. Tecumseh tumbled down.

He turned and reached up to his horse. Its chest heaved as its heart struggled to beat. The horse gasped its final empty breaths and stared into Tecumseh. And Tecumseh gazed back in love. His eyes said goodbye to a loyal friend of so many years . . . and it was gone. Then a blue jacket leapt up and charged hard at Tecumseh. Quick as a panther, Tecumseh jumped to his feet and ducked under the lunging bayonet. He spun about and drove his tomahawk deep into the soldier's back.

Tecumseh rose up, turned, and saw three warriors at a short distance; but then two were cut down by mighty swings of a tomahawk. Tecumseh's insides cried out in horror. The third warrior had been stooped over, and now stood upright. His hulking form flexed through the drifting smoke of battle. That warrior then eyed Tecumseh down. Blackened and bloodshot eyes glared of hatred. The warrior's face now came full into view. Tecumseh knew its lines and features well . . . it was the bully of his youth.

Tecumseh breathed deep. He knew it always had to come to that. Somehow, among tens of thousands at war upon the battlefield, Sakdayga and Tecumseh had found their way to each other. Fate's wind howled, and at last, those two Shawnee brothers would settle things forever.

Sakdayga raised his tomahawk proud that dripped of blood and shook it with wild vigor, and screamed out hate from deep in his belly. He then exploded toward Tecumseh like a crazed bull. Such quickness startled Tecumseh. Sakdayga slammed his thick tomahawk up into him. And the blow was so strong that although Tecumseh did block it, it flung Tecumseh's tomahawk that spun away into the air.

Tecumseh jumped back a few steps and quickly pulled out a smaller tomahawk hung to his side. And an enraged Sakdayga did not relent, and leapt upon Tecumseh again. He swung his great tomahawk down upon Tecumseh, again and again, like a paleface hammer upon a nail. Each time it shook Tecumseh's bones. Those swings felt like Sakdayga would cut down an old oak tree with one blow, each swing stronger than the last.

With each blow, Tecumseh would take a step back, and Sakdayga would move even closer. The wooden handle of Tecumseh's smaller tomahawk creaked with each mighty blow, and the wood began to crack apart in places. Another blow or two, and it would be smashed to pieces.

Sakdayga screamed out again and swung his tomahawk down and pressed in, his body heavy upon Tecumseh, face to face. Tecumseh's arm shook and quivered as he desperately tried to hold back the weight of a mountain upon him. The handle of Tecumseh's small tomahawk held for a moment, but began to buckle. Tecumseh then reached low for a thick knife at his side. And just as he did, the small tomahawk handle burst into pieces, and the stone edge of Sakdayga's tomahawk slid down in great force and caught Tecumseh's upper arm a bit, which gashed open a wound.

But Tecumseh spun on the ground behind Sakdayga, and jammed the knife deep into Sakdayga's thigh. And with a great swing of his other arm, he smashed Sakdayga's forearm that held the tomahawk. It surprised the great red bull, who howled in pain, and his big tomahawk flew loose into the air.

Tecumseh leapt up and tried to gather himself. He glanced at the wound upon his arm. Flesh was torn away and dangled, and blood oozed. But he could not worry about that now.

Sakdayga turned about and stared upon Tecumseh, and looked down to the blade that protruded from his thigh. In silence, he glowered at Tecumseh, snarled, grabbed the knife's handle, and slowly removed it. He did not wince or make a single sound of pain. Then he exploded again and held the bloody knife high. He fell upon Tecumseh and knocked him to the ground, and sat atop him. And with both hands, he leaned in. He meant to drive the blade right through Tecumseh's chest. Both warriors heaved and shook with might. Faces stretched with desperate lines of anger and hate. Spit dripped from Sakdayga, as his mouth clenched tight.

Tecumseh could see the sharp steel-edge of the blade gleam as the sunlight caught it. It moved closer and closer. He could not hold it back much longer. The gashing wound in his arm throbbed now of pain, and his strength was fading.

And as the blade tip inched even closer, he saw warriors and blue jackets run by all about to cut each other down. There were fearful cries, shrieks of hate. Pistols and muskets exploded all around. Gray wisps of smoke drifted all about, and the smell of burnt gunpowder filled each breath. Death's sounds echoed everywhere, like some faded dream.

Tecumseh's arms now began to shake and shudder. He did not have much left to give. He looked deep into Sakdayga's black eyes and he saw only a hateful glee. It would not be long now. Tecumseh did not think death would be so cruel. He expected to die on the field that day, but at the hand of a paleface . . . not by a Shawnee.

But as his final moments circled in about him, he glimpsed a jagged stone in the ground nearby. It stuck out a bit, and the soil was loose. It was his only chance . . . and he took it. He inhaled one last desperate breath, and then with all the strength left him, he kicked his legs and grunted. And somehow, he was able to shift Sakdayga forward. And in one lunging move, he kneed Sakdayga forward just enough, to use his weight to drive the lunging blade to the side. The sheer force drove the blade deep into the dirt, all the way up to the handle.

And as Sakdayga drove the blade into the ground, Tecumseh reached out for the jagged rock. His fingers stretched, strained, and fumbled for that desperate rock, now his only friend . . . his only chance.

Sakdayga let loose a yelling growl, filled with more rage as the blade did not find Tecumseh's chest. He angrily ripped the knife from the dirt and sat up again fully upon Tecumseh. He snarled and his eyes flamed of hate. "I told you I would kill you. I am the hunter . . . I am the wolf. Now you will die!" He then raised the blade up high with both hands.

But as he did, Tecumseh screamed out and swung his jagged rock-filled hand about. Sakdayga never saw it coming. The rock smashed upon Sakdayga, his face exploded sideways. Blood splattered out, and the side of his head was indented like a valley gorge.

The clutched knife then fell free to the ground and Sakdayga toppled over. He was lost in a daze, and moaned. Tecumseh gasped for breath, and slowly stood upright. He looked down at Sakdayga, who writhed in agony. Tecumseh wiped some blood and sweat from his tired eyes. He reached slowly down for the fallen blade and stood over Sakdayga. And his heart filled with pity. "Sakdayga, in your hate for me you would betray your people . . . betray everything you know. Why would you help the palefaces destroy your own kind? . . ."

Sakdayga said nothing. He spit some blood to the side and looked up again to Tecumseh. In silence, his eyes still only bubbled hatred and anger.

Tecumseh then sighed. "You are right. You are the wolf. You always have been . . . and always will be. But I no longer hate the wolf. So let me bring peace to your heart and soul at last. Only death will set you free. Let us rid your hatred and anger forever." Tecumseh then kneeled down beside the great red bull and stuck the blade deep into his heart. Sakdayga gasped out, his eyes widened, and then he went limp. His eyes gazed up to the sky, and for the first time in his life, they were no longer filled with hate . . . there was only peace.

In a daze, Tecumseh rose slowly up and took in everything. His bones ached and upper arm throbbed louder. He breathed in deep the fog of war. Adrift in a sea of death he was. Throughout the valley plain, his proud Shawnee and the many warriors of the other tribes fought with ferocious desperation, like a cornered grizzly. But they were drowning in a rushing wave of long knives that flooded everywhere.

Tecumseh's long fear unfolded before him . . . the warriors of the free peoples were dying . . . Ithikkah and Taughannock had perished . . . and Gahnoque was lost to some unknown end. He knew not the fate of his lifelong friend Otsaga. All was lost. His heart ached beyond pain. He knew he would never again look upon Kykuitheh. Never feel the loving warmth of her touch. And he wondered, did she still take breath . . . or did she wait for him in the spirit world. His warriors' sacrifice had not been enough to defeat America's horde. Harrison would move on from that battlefield, and he would hunt down the fleeing people before they could make it far into Canada's lands. His soul hurt beyond tears.

From a distance of a hundred paces, General Harrison approached with a slew of men at his side. Tecumseh knew what they brought.

He breathed in slow and deep. His senses gathered tight. It had come . . . the end. And his fleeting thoughts drifted to his lost father Puckshinwa . . . and of Kykuitheh . . . and to the love of his baby son Laykhyaloh, who was taken from him too soon. Tecumseh whispered to himself, "What person might he have grown to be in this world, while I grew weak and aged?" He could only wonder.

Thoughts of thankfulness filled his head for the Shawnee people. All the many kindhearted women, children, and elders back in the villages that touched his soul while he had taken breath upon the land all those many days from the first, as but a young boy, until that day. He pondered the untold ancestors yet to come that now would never be born into the world. Tecumseh drowned in the end. The Shawnee people were taking their last breath. Everything he had fought for was lost.

He had failed to find a way through the peoples' darkness. It carved a hollowness within.

He muttered to himself, "Footprints in the sand . . . that is all we are. The hungry waves of the great white sea have beaten upon our shore, and at last they will now just wash us away...." A mountain peak of despair stood upon Tecumseh's heart. The drowning hopelessness of his people settled in tight like a noose around his throat. He was so alone. The world spun. It would be soon now.

Tecumseh stood for a moment more in silence as General Harrison and the long knives came upon him. Like a cornered beast in the wild, he was encircled by his hunters. They charged in from everywhere. Death burned in their eyes, and they would make Tecumseh pay for all his deeds. But Tecumseh would not simply bow to fate's hand. No, he would be fierce to the end. He sprang forth and struck down those soldiers nearest to him. He fought on. Relentless fury flamed in his eyes. His tomahawk was bathed with the blood of his would be hunters.

Senses reeled. All moved in a slow motion, as if he watched someone else in a great battle for their life against an overwhelming foe. But death was coming. It had found him at long last, after all those years. Yet many more he cut down in his wrath and desperation. But fatigue overcame his weary body. And a sharp pain bit through his upper thigh and lower leg. He glanced down and blood oozed. Musket fire had found him. He turned to face his enemy once more, and another pain shot through his side. A musket ball ripped through flesh. Then cold hard steel carved through his lower gut. A saber dug deep into him. His strength faded. Rivers of his blood flowed . . . and then he dropped to his knees, surrounded by long knives.

At that moment, the general's strong voice boomed like a cannon. The long knives stopped their attack at once. Harrison's muscled steed slowly sauntered to Tecumseh. Harrison glared down upon him. They shared a glance.

Harrison then pulled up near and jumped down from his horse. He walked slowly to Tecumseh, and measured each step of his utter victory.

Harrison gazed upon Tecumseh and asked, "Is this the freedom you seek? You will be no more, and your people will fade away . . . nothing more than a footnote in history. Does the mighty Tecumseh not fear his own death?"

Tecumseh looked stoically up to Harrison. He spoke softly, with a regal defiance still, "My body is broken and death has come . . . but I do not run and quake in its presence.

"To live swallowed up in fear is to already be dead. And death is feared by those that have not lived each day, stretching every smile and shedding every tear, embracing courage and honor in serving others to do what is right. Only self-serving folk fear death.

"We should all seek to live a life well-lived, for when death comes, smiling at us all, as it surely will, those that do may smile right back. And they may sing their death song like a warrior going home. I, Panther Across the Sky, go home now to be with my people where our fires burn forever bright. And there I shall remain, unconquered and free."

As Tecumseh's words fell from his tongue, the general was taken aback with a lost look upon his face. Harrison hesitated for a moment. He was listening to Tecumseh's words, bowing to his wisdom . . . and his hand was stayed.

They both just gazed upon the other. They peered deeper into the soul, and stretched to grasp life's purpose and meaning. The world of utter chaos, pain, and death crashed all about them. That dance from two very different worlds played on seemingly forever, though just a moment had passed.

But then, that spiritual bond was severed. Harrison's senses snapped back. A cold smugness returned. The general shook his head slowly, as if he had heard only the utterances of a drunken fool.

Tecumseh turned and looked up to the sky. He was met with wisps of clouds that twisted and swirled so beautiful. They moved with a strange grace. And then a silhouetted form appeared. It moved closer to him. It was Nateelah. She smiled deep and wide. Her proud and defiant spirit was as beautiful as ever. She nodded to him, as if telling him to be at peace. And then up from behind came Taughannock. He smiled at Tecumseh, as he lovingly embraced Nateelah. They were the picture of the highest love one living thing could feel for another. And it stirred Tecumseh's heart. Ithikkah too then appeared. He smiled and waved in peace. In happiness, he stood beside his son.

Then Nateelah, Taughannock, and Ithikkah turned and looked back for a moment. They stepped to the side and smiled even broader upon Tecumseh. Something else moved in the cloudy wisps. It was then that another silhouetted form emerged. Who or what at first, Tecumseh could not say. Closer now it moved. Then it gestured to him. The form kindly beckoned him to come forth.

It was his father Puckshinwa, and he was filled with good health and joy. And within his arms, he held a baby who giggled and cooed. It was his son Laykhyaloh who stared back. His little eyes sparkled of love. And then the child stretched out its hand to Tecumseh. A lost son called his father to come home.

That vision stilled Tecumseh's heart. Tears welled up and flowed slow down his cheeks. And they were not tears of sadness, but of utter happiness hard to come by in the world of the living. His father and son had come to welcome him that day with open arms to the spirit world. They had come to tell him it was okay to let go. It was time. But before he did, Tecumseh thought of Kykuitheh. He sent her all his strength that she make a happy life with the world and time left her. In his heart he now knew, Kykuitheh must live, or else she would have surely appeared now before him as the others. He would just have to wait for her until that day she made her own journey. And then he would be the one to welcome her home.

Tecumseh also wondered for a moment of what would become of his brother and friend Gahnoque. Would he ever see him again? He held tight to the thought that somehow and in some way he would. And he thought on his good friend, John Sackett. He hoped his friend would survive that great conflict, and enjoy many sunsets in peace before his end. Tecumseh then smiled, stretched out his hand skyward to his father and son, and began to hum a quiet song. Ease washed upon his worn face, etched in lines of wisdom gained through his forty-five years of life. His body was utterly spent from a lifetime of battle and strife. In serenity, he gazed into the clouds. He was ready to take his journey, ready to go home.

General Harrison slowly raised his pistol to Tecumseh's head . . . he hesitated for a moment more . . . and then pulled the trigger. The shot rang out with a striking crack. There was only silence in the dark.

Chapter Thirty
Hope's Flame

Word reached Kykuitheh's lonely ear, far to the great north of everything. A sparse few of her kin had somehow made their solitary way unfollowed. And they were the only ones. It was just trees, beasts, the wild . . . and them. But some white trappers and their Sauk scouts for hire had carried a message as they passed through one day. Those trapper parties were Kykuitheh's lone connection to the world of people for many long years, and in this way, she heard about the comings and goings of the great white fathers and the scattered tribes.

He had fallen. The great wind blew no more. Tecumseh was dead. It was all the palefaces would talk about, as Harrison trumpeted America's might. It was said chests burst in great pride. But it all sickened her. Her insides cried a river of tears. He had given his life so the people could escape to Canada for a chance at freedom.

She heard at sight of Tecumseh's death, the still standing warriors had stopped the fight and lost all will to go on. Weapons were let loose and fell lifeless to the ground. Forlorn and empty, the warriors withdrew and scattered from the valley plain. They went into hiding, deep into the wild. And in that chaos Kykuitheh wondered, had they taken Tecumseh's body with them, for it was never found.

In Tecumseh's death and the scattering of the great confederacy, Kykuitheh's spirit remained fierce as ever. And she needed all of it to somehow survive in the wild, despite all the wickedness the palefaces could show her. She fled with the remnants of her people, dispersed to the winds. She made it to somewhere in the lands of Canada . . . and kept her freedom.

Kykuitheh lived on, for in all that darkness, a hope burned still within. She had a secret, and held it tight. She kept it hidden and shared only with those she most trusted. And that was not a hard thing to do, for everyone she knew had since perished. Or they had fled in terror before the great white fathers' wrath. They were just trying to eke out a life in whatever way that could be had, just as she.

Kykuitheh did that for Tecumseh had burned a deep scar upon the palefaces, a wound that would never heal. Even now, the great white fathers would go to the world's end to erase his memory. She feared the great white fathers still. She feared what they would do were they to know she lived. In wrath, they would come and snuff her life.

And even more if they knew of her secret. If they knew she was not alone after all . . . if they knew of the child in her womb, Tecumseh's seed. They would bear any cost to stomp it out forever. All in fear of what the child may one day become. Kykuitheh knew that even in death, there was a dread of Tecumseh. It was a gnawing fear, an undying worry for the great white fathers. Somehow, Panther Across the Sky would rise up again to lead his free peoples' return to their homelands.

And that fate was not lost upon her. For in all the troubles of their joining, the Great Spirit would not bless them with child since the death of Laykyhaloh. And only now in Tecumseh's death, was the gift of life granted once more. It grieved her beyond words that Tecumseh would never look upon his child so filled with life, never to wrap the child in his embrace. That painful thought made her cry until there were no more tears. Bittersweet it was.

If she could have told Tecumseh just once. Maybe it would have stayed his hand. Would he have gone into battle's end still if he had known that the fire of their future, though so small, was lit? What if his eyes looked just once upon his child, and love's sparkling light had shone back upon him and gripped his soul tight?

Kykuitheh knew the love of a child did strange things to a man, no matter his fierceness and strength of will. Perhaps he would have remained with the people. Maybe he would have sought a different path in the great conflict with America. Everything might be different had he known Kykuitheh still took breath . . . and that she carried his daughter, Skahnatheh. But now she would never know. She just sighed. That question with no answer just burned inside her . . . and brought an unending heartache.

In the Shawnee tongue, her child's name means rebirth of the Great Spirit among the people. To the forsaken and scattered Shawnee, it is a most beautiful notion. A thought so treasured, even if only for a fleeting moment somewhere in their dreams. And that stirred Kykuitheh's soul. She knew reality's truth. It was not simply caged by the binds of the world before you. No, it rested deeper within the mind's eye. She knew how one views the world from within, as you swim about the waters of the mind and move to life's dance . . . that determines your place in it, who you truly are. And Kykuitheh would cling to that thought . . . and that dream.

Skahnatheh was a most beautiful child. A child to whom Kykuitheh held tight with all the love a mother and a lost father could give. Kykuitheh protected that child with the fierceness of a great mother bear that looked after her newborn cub. And when Kykuitheh gazed into the eyes of her child that stared deeply back at her, they peeled back the many layers of her soul. It was a vision of Tecumseh that looked upon her, for that child's eyes were the same hue and color of mighty Tecumseh. The panther looked upon her still. It filled her heart with a joyful sadness, if there could be such a thing. And Kykuitheh would cling tight to that love and the last bit of Tecumseh left in the world . . . until the very end of her days.

And many long years later, word of the great white fathers' world reached Kykuitheh's ear once again. In time, Harrison had ridden the rising wave of his great victory against Tecumseh all the way to the white house, they said. He had become the greatest of all the great white fathers, the President he was called. Kykuitheh hated that man. And more than ever, she wanted to choke the life from him with her bare hands. But she was so small and aged. And it was a paleface world now . . . she could never get near him.

But then something unexpected happened. Word soon after arrived and it brought old Kykuitheh a happy smile of vengeance. Harrison's reign as the great chief of the paleface nation did not last long. After only one month . . . he died. The palefaces said it was the common cold. But Kykuitheh wondered how was it that the bravest paleface warrior, their greatest chief, could be slain by a child's illness? No, Kykuitheh knew the truth.

For those that would look just beneath the surface, through the tangled webs and quiet lies, there was something else at work. Wrinkled lines smiled upon her face. Kykuitheh knew what caused Harrison's death, though no palefaces cared to ask. It was Gahnoque. Being robbed of his battlefield glory against the great white fathers, he had reached back through the stars and returned from the spirit world. And he brought death to Harrison, in both body and soul at last. The Shawnee people knew of Gahnoque's words at the great peace council, and now he had fulfilled his promise.

And as the many years came and went, Kykuitheh knew her end was coming. She had seen too many winters. Yet before Kykuitheh would pass from the world, she would leave her child something worth holding on to . . . the only possession she held dear - a lost stone of Ithreal. It had come to her in the disarray and scattering of the people upon her village's desolation long ago. When the wolves of America had descended in that one final and ruinous deed, the Ithreal stone had called out to her. Partially buried and hidden it was. And she reached down amid the clamor and terror and took up the stone in her grasp. Hidden and unnoticed, she fled to safety and escaped the great white fathers' reach.

And Kykuitheh held the otherworldly stone as the most sacred of family heirlooms, to be kept safe and in secret until the day came when its mystery could be unlocked. She had been there that day when the hidden door was opened. Kykuitheh saw mighty Gahnoque walk through a door of air into another night sky.

And a most gleaming jewel it was, that shone brighter than the sun. But those were younger days far in memories past, as its light had now gone dark. Though Kykuitheh still held that jewel stone tight to her and placed it within a handmade leather necklace. It hung round her neck and sat upon her breast all those years. Close to her heart, yet hidden always it was. Kykuitheh hoped that one day it would lead her to the other lost stones of Ithreal.

She knew the stone's mysteries were tied to the other two Ithreal stones . . . but they remained lost. So the one found Ithreal stone served as a memory to hope and two lost peoples, one from this world and that of another.

Kykuitheh had waited patiently for that day to come . . . the finding of the lost Ithreal stones. But it never did. And as the lines of many moons became etched upon her stretched face, she still never gave up hope. At her end, she placed the necklace upon Skahnatheh's neck and breast. Kykuitheh whispered the story of the Ithreal stones to her daughter, to keep it and hope alive.

They just needed to find the two lost Ithreal stones. Then they could build their own star door of wooden limbs. She believed with all her heart that the three stones united would awaken something. And then somehow, they would call out to the stars and open a path to another night sky. She just knew that Gahnoque would hear that call. She knew he would find his way back . . . somehow the mighty Jhagir would return to them then.

And on that day when the Ithreal starlight breaks through the darkness and reaches out, the people must be ready. They must reach back with all their might, to grasp the light's warmth tight. Patient and ever vigilant, with eyes open wide and ears stretched to the ground, they must never stop the search. And she bade Skahnatheh to never give up . . . to never stop looking for the slightest sign, faintest whisper, or rumor that lingered of the lost Ithreal stones come arisen again.

Epilogue
Words that Linger

Makya stared blankly ahead. His mind was somewhere else. In stoned silence, he glanced down at the streamed blood upon his ragged fist. Its vivid red had dried to a deep and aged burgundy, bereft of all life. The flames' shadows danced upon his vacant gaze. He brooded on that which had come before him, and its great weight pressed heavy to his soul. Though hours had passed and dawn was near, the strangers sat as statues, mesmerized by the tale of sacrifice and heartbreak. They then fidgeted and strained in wonder and curiosity. Makya saw the flood of questions that raged in their eyes . . . yet, where to begin.

But before a single question was uttered, Makya whispered, "With America's great victory at the Battle of the Thames and Tecumseh's death, his great confederacy of tribes faded away into the white man's history. In time, all the tribes of the continent fell, fulfilling Tecumseh's prophecy. And America took all dominion from the oceans of the Atlantic to the Pacific.

"A great genocide was then done upon my kin, to bend them to the palefaces' civil society. Those that resisted were exiled to small plots of poisoned lands upon which to live in squelch and squalor - the reservation."

The strangers squirmed a bit. Makya guessed they had witnessed with their own eyes such conditions and plight of another . . . at least as they had passed through on some road trip, or heard tell by another. Though Makya was sure they probably had never set foot in such a place.

Makya went on in a haunted whisper, "The reservation - a token gift to the savages that holds up America's humanity. General Harrison would be most pleased at the tremendous rank achieved by his descendants. For in time, America has become mighty indeed.

"Alone, it lords over the world. Yet its origins of liberty and freedom remain obscured to the deeds of its founding fathers and their ancestors . . . an inconvenient truth. They invaded my peoples' homeland and took it for their own, justified and blessed by their God at the end of a musket barrel."

The gathered strangers winced. Their twisted faces said it all. It was not something to attach to or take pride in . . . but of course, they had no part in it. It was a sad tale yes, but it was another time long ago and far away from these days. The strangers' eyes pleaded to just let history be.

Makya swam in the floating visions of the dying firelight's flames. "My ancestors live on these reservations still, with our own true story forgotten. The numbing pain those days so long ago has since been washed away with whiskey and other bad medicines.

"And for the Shawnee tribe from the far north, though you may look, you will find no mention of the Jhagir in any American history book. And that is the funny thing about those books, for what are we left as the one true accounting of things? For those among us were not there. There are only the written texts and stories passed down by the conquerors that came before us."

Makya inhaled a deep breath and went on, though more to himself than to the strangers. "The history that we have been told is no doubt a thing of marvel to some, while others may find it rings hollow of the truth. If you inquire sincerely in the places of the world untraveled, hidden amongst the shadows, perhaps you will find those who believe this to be so. What does your heart tell you?"

Around the fire pit, the gathered stared into the flames and their souls . . . and they awaited their heart's answer.

Anguish and regret passed upon the lines of Makya's face. "This was seemingly the story's end, our flame of freedom all but snuffed out. Yet a flicker of hope remained. For in the scattering of the three Ithreal stones, two were found by the Shawnee. And they ever searched for the missing third stone, in quiet and in secret. But it would not show itself.

"The third jewel of light was lost to time. It was sunken to the darkest depths of the deepest sea, beyond all reach. Abandoned by hope once more, the Ithreal stones and the Jhagir faded into Shawnee myth . . . and legend. Their memory forgotten by most all, like desert sands blown there and back that erase all trace of a once proud city, so as if to have never been.

"But a precious few among my people held tight to the memory in their private thoughts and secret talks. They would not let it perish from the world. It lingered long upon their minds and stirred deeply their souls. And through their undying spirit, from one generation to the next, hope was set sail and my peoples' fire of freedom rekindled . . . for the third stone was found at long last."

But Makya would speak no more. There was only silence. The gathered looked upon Makya in amazed and curious wonder, for such a grand tale that it was. And they waited for all to be revealed, but only silence sat upon Makya's lips. He would say no more. Makya arose at last, nodded, and offered thanks for their warmth, wine, and company. All nodded back, unsure of what to say. Makya saw the burning question upon their faces. He knew they wondered what part in the tale he played . . . if any at all.

And then, as Makya shifted the blanket that wrapped about him, the eyes of those gathered opened wide. Makya heard one of them mutter in a hushed tone, "There is a leathery harness upon his chest. And in its center sits a blue and white jewel."

Someone whispered back, "It is like from his story."

Makya saw their faces turn an even paler shade of white, as if they had just seen a ghost walk amongst them. The firelight flickered upon Makya's face.

One of them leaned in again and whispered low, "Do you see that . . . his eyes now favor the look of a great cat. And there are blue flames that smolder."

The others just gasped, with faces drawn and eyes widened even more.

Makya saw they were stilled with fear, but none of them mustered the courage to ask on that strange vision and the marvel it inspired. Until one among them blurted out in faded wonder, "Who are you . . . what are you?"

Makya just looked upon them kindly in silence.

Someone then quickly flipped out a phone. They were searching for something . . . for any secret to be had. Makya heard them whisper. The one with the phone leaned into the others and said, "All I can find is the meaning of his name in the Shawnee language . . . the one who hunts eagles." The gathering then slowly turned and gazed up at Makya. Their stretched and vacant faces, devoid of all color, drowned in a silent fear and wonder.

And something new had grown in Makya right before them. He was different. He felt it. In his eyes, defiance smoldered and stared out. Deep inside, the drowning anguish of earlier that evening had burned away; the Great Spirit had risen up. A strength and warmth radiated in him, like the glowing sun. He was changed. Somehow, sharing that tale with the strangers had changed him.

Makya had discovered something within himself. It had been there all along, just waiting for him to reach out and grab hold. He was found. He was ready for what was to come. Ready to put the boy aside and become who he was born to be. The man the people had always needed. The one they had waited for. In silence, Makya slipped away into the dark. It had begun.

www.ingramcontent.com/pod-product-compliance
Lightning Source LLC
Chambersburg PA
CBHW020924120726
47905CB00008B/2369